Enlightened Virginity in Eighteenth-Century Literature

ENLIGHTENED VIRGINITY IN
EIGHTEENTH-CENTURY LITERATURE

Corrinne Harol

First published in 2006 by
PALGRAVE MACMILLAN™
175 Fifth Avenue, New York, N.Y. 10010 and
Houndmills, Basingstoke, Hampshire, England RG21 6XS
Companies and representatives throughout the world.

PALGRAVE MACMILLAN is the global academic imprint of the Palgrave Macmillan division of St. Martin's Press, LLC and of Palgrave Macmillan Ltd. Macmillan® is a registered trademark in the United States, United Kingdom and other countries. Palgrave is a registered trademark in the European Union and other countries.

ISBN-13: 978–1–4039–7494–5
ISBN-10: 1–4039–7494–2

Library of Congress Cataloging-in-Publication Data

Harol, Corrinne.
    Enlightened virginity in eighteenth-century literature /
Corrinne Harol.
        p. cm.
    Originally published as the author's thesis (doctoral-Univ. of Calif., Los Angeles) under the title: Novel virgins.
    Includes bibliographical references and index.
    ISBN 1–4039–7494–2 (alk. paper)
      1. English literature—18th century—History and criticism.
    2. Virginity in literature. I. Title.

PR448.V55H37 2006
820.9′353—dc22   2005057926

A catalogue record for this book is available from the British Library.

Design by Newgen Imaging Systems (P) Ltd., Chennai, India.

First edition: September 2006

10 9 8 7 6 5 4 3 2 1

Transferred to Digital Printing 2009

CONTENTS

ACKNOWLEDGMENTS

This project would not have been possible without significant financial support from The University of California, Los Angeles (UCLA), the University of Utah, the Jean and Irving Stone Foundation, the Huntington Library, and most especially from the William Andrews Clark Memorial Library, which, besides money, provided me a room of my own at crucial times, with untold conferences and congenial repasts, and with a library staff so helpful and supportive that I came to think of the library as a second, more enticingly furnished, home. Thanks to Le Scott Jacobs, Jennifer Schaffner, Elaine Shiner, Carol Sommer, Suzanne Tatian, and Bruce Whiteman for favors too numerous to mention.

This book began its life as a dissertation at UCLA, whose graduate program was rigorous and convivial. The faculty members who supervised that dissertation have continued to be a source of invaluable support and inspiration. Felicity Nussbaum has untiringly provided the kind of sound and yet rare advice that can make all the difference in one's career. Helen Deutsch bantered with me through countless lunches and in the process has revolutionized my idea of what makes exciting scholarship. Jayne Lewis, the best and most generous dissertation supervisor imaginable, never failed in her unaccountable enthusiasm for the project. I owe an endless well of gratitude to her for being my first and best reader, for being an exemplar of intellectual independence and creative scholarly writing, and for her cherished friendship throughout this process.

At the universities of Utah and Alberta, many colleagues eased the transition from dissertation to book; thanks in particular to Charles Berger, Katherine Binhammer, Brooke Hopkins, Howard Horwitz, Tamara Ketabgian, Kim Lau, Brian Locke, Brenda Lyshaug, Susan Miller, Crystal Parikh, Barry Weller, and to Maeera Shrieber, who read every chapter and whose camaraderie during the process proved a most welcome respite from solitary writing. Gillian Brown, a dear and loyal friend, was a key interlocutor for the book's feminist arguments. She did not live to see the final book, and I cannot flatter myself to think that she would have been proud of it. But I tried, in her honor, to work with as much seriousness and joy as she did.

Many other people read all or part of the manuscript and offered invaluable suggestions. These include: Sarah Ellenzweig, Lowell Gallagher, Susan Lamb, and Leilani Riehle. Ava Arndt deserves special thanks for repeated readings and cheerleading. Susan Staves, the reader at Palgrave Press, offered a uniquely keen and comprehensive reading of the manuscript. Copyediting and research assistance were most competently provided by Suzanne Taylor and Lindsey Whitson.

Earlier versions of some of the book's main arguments were presented at conferences and lecture series. For helpful feedback, thanks to various audiences at The American Society for Eighteenth-Century Studies (ASECS), The Group for Early Modern Cultural Studies (GEMCS), the International Conference on Narrative, the University of Utah Humanities Center, and the Southern California Eighteenth-Century Studies Group. A version of chapter 4 appeared in *The Eighteenth Century: Theory and Interpretation* 45.1; parts of chapters 2 and 5 were published in *Eighteenth-Century Fiction* 16.2. I am grateful to these publications for permission to reprint from these essays.

For friendship, entertainment, good humor, and loving kindness throughout the process, I am exceptionally grateful to Kristine Barakat, Tom Barbar, Mark Quigley, Cindy Rosene, Kathi Tavares, Beth Wightman, and Lisa McGowan. My family has always entertained a deluded belief in my genius, for which I could never repay them adequately. For refusing to indulge my anxieties, for reminding me that if all else failed I might get by on laughter, and for crucial financial support, thanks to Kimberly, Kristen, and Michael Harol and especially to my mother Marcia Harol, whose generosity, enthusiasm, and perseverance have made her a muse and a mainstay of precious encouragement over the years. This book is for her, because she appreciates narrative originality.

Introduction: Virginity and Patrilinear Legitimacy

"Consider, of what importance to society the chastity of women is. Upon that all the property in the world depends."

Samuel Johnson, quoted in Boswell, V, 209

"Female Chastity is, in its own Nature, built upon a very ticklish Foundation"

Mandeville, 49

Samuel Johnson, writing in the mid-eighteenth century, articulates an attitude about female sexuality that might strike a twenty-first-century reader as both obvious and rather quaint. Female chastity, so the story goes, matters to men because it guarantees patrilinear legitimacy and therefore the legitimacy of patrimony: the virgin girl will seamlessly transition into the chaste wife and bear her husband's legitimate heirs. Virginity and chastity are crucial for women but not for men because, according to Johnson, "the man imposes no bastards on his wife."[1] Female chastity assures men that the children who bear their names and inherit their property are in truth their legitimate progeny, and thus that inheritance, or "worth," will follow biology, or "birth." In John Locke's famous formulation, the very purpose of human society is the protection of property: people gather together and submit to government so that government will protect their private property (1967, 285–302). If Locke is right, then Samuel Johnson endows female sexuality with tremendous authority in political affairs. Together, Locke and Johnson offer an explanation for why, in a post-Lockean political landscape where the function, at least imaginatively, of government is to protect private property, virginity and chastity would figure importantly. And indeed, mid-eighteenth-century England was uniquely obsessed with both female sexuality and the inheritance of property, as evidenced by the early novel's obsessions with virgins, foundlings, and inheritance. This literary obsession with virginity is generically pervasive: virgins figure prominently in mock-epic and lyric poetry; in ballads; in comedies; in seduced maiden dramas; and in the most popular novels of the period, Samuel Richardson's *Pamela* and *Clarissa* and their satiric antagonists, such as Henry Fielding's *Shamela*, Eliza Haywood's *Anti-Pamela*, and John Cleland's *Memoirs of a Woman of Pleasure*. This project began with questions about this literary phenomenon. Why is virginity such a central representational problem for the eighteenth century? Why does a new genre, the novel, develop alongside a new kind of obsession with virginity? Why would satiric, pornographic, and sentimental novels all take their themes and plots from virginity and defloration? Underlying these questions are the assumptions that there exist links not just between virginity and political theory, but also between virginity and the early novel and thus between virginity and a particular moment in the history of patriarchy.

But then again, everyone knows that patriarchy has always loved a virgin, for reasons that appear to be transparent and that Johnson has already articulated: virgins help patriarchy reproduce itself. When I would tell people that I was writing a book on virginity, their reaction was frequently one of incredulous bemusement: what is there to say, after all, about something so obvious? Despite what seems to be the obviousness of the question, there have been multiple and competing explanations for the endurance of the long-term, if tempestuous, relationship between the patriarch and the virgin, and their relationship has a complicated history. At least three explanatory models for the pervasive importance of virginity to patriarchy have been propounded. They are often conflated, but they are, in some ways, logically incompatible, so it seems crucial to start by delineating them. Under the incest prohibition model, articulated by Lévi-Strauss, virginity facilitates the expansion of political and economic ties because it guarantees compliance with the incest prohibition and therefore promotes exogamous marriage and expanding social allegiances. Conversely, under a theory of patrilinear legitimacy, the explanation that Samuel Johnson finds so manifestly obvious (and that Frederick Engels will theorize with respect to Marxist political economics), virginity contributes to the consolidation of property and the strengthening of nuclear family ties because it guarantees the legitimacy of male progeny and thereby promotes the linear descent of one man's genetic and real property. There are several contradictions between these two explanatory models. The former is a model of expanding social and economic networks, while the latter contributes to the consolidation of property and the contraction of social ties. Incest prohibition is routinely associated with extended kinship systems and more primitive cultures, while concerns over patrilinear inheritance belong to vertically hierarchical cultures organized around class, the nuclear family, and the autonomous state. Finally, these two models focus on different figures and different inheritance problems: the incest prohibition model impinges on the reputation and property of the virgin's father and brother, while under the patrilinear legitimacy model, it is the reputation of the virgin and the estate of her husband that are at stake. Already in conflict with each other, both of these models are discordant with a Catholic model of virginity, in which the sanctified virgin is directly subject to the will of the supreme patriarch. The passivity of the Catholic virgin makes her attractive as an abstract subject of patriarchy, but she forgoes involvement in the realms of procreation, property, and worldly sociability that matter to actual men. She can do this because her virginity engenders both sanctification and, at times, special epistemological powers (the divination of God's will), which allow her to circumvent those human activities—like sexuality, procreation, and even death—that are products of original sin. If concerns about legitimacy are fundamentally about historical linearity, a chronology that begins with the fall, the Catholic virgin is somehow outside that history.

Of these three explanations for the attractions of virginity, the patrilinear legitimacy model holds the most currency right now, especially in feminist studies. This is the model that we assume to be trans-historical but that I will argue assumes a particular historical form—and prominence—in eighteenth-century England. I began this book with the desire to debunk this model; that is, I wanted to disprove what seemed to be obvious: that the source of patriarchy's infatuation with virginity has to do with inheritance. Although I ultimately explain the historical construction of this model rather than discredit it completely, it seems crucial, nonetheless, to start by pointing out several inherent weaknesses in its logic. First of all, there is an unnecessary, perhaps even counterintuitive, relationship between virginity and procreation. A commitment to perpetual virginity, or even a fetishization of the value of virginity, conflicts with a procreative mandate. The Virgin Mary, who combines the inherently opposed values of virginity and maternity, stands as an exception to this rule, a fact that accounts, at least in part, for her iconic status. Chastity is another model that reconciles virginity and maternity, and the link between virginity and chastity became a commonplace in the eighteenth century. But there is no necessary relationship between virginity and chastity. What a woman does after her "first time" may, especially if one accepts the notion that virginity is important, differ from what she did before, and thus virginity is not necessarily a predictor of chastity. Virginity and chastity cannot be conflated without significant hedging, which no doubt occurs more frequently than logic would predict. It is, for example, a paradox of eighteenth-century femininity that chastity is what is valued, but that literary representations of the same period focus much more frequently on virginity—in particular, the career of the virgin and the signs of virginity. Perhaps the most important challenge to the logic of the patrilinear legitimacy model is that female virginity/chastity is a rather shaky ground, or in Mandeville's words a "ticklish foundation," upon which to rest masculine and national legitimacy. Several things argue against virginity's ability to act as a material foundation for patriarchal legitimacy and the legal transfer of property. First of all, the hymen, the entity that proves virginity, is, as I will argue in chapter 3, flimsy and notoriously difficult to employ as evidence. This is an especially salient problem during the scientific revolution that constitutes an important context for the book. Moreover, even if one can determine a woman's virginity, postvirginal sexual activity, or chastity, is even less epistemologically verifiable.[2] The notion that virginity matters because it promotes patrilinear legitimacy rests upon an assumed link between virginity and chastity, a myth that this book seeks to denaturalize as it tries to answer the question: why would patriarchal legitimacy, even mythologically, rest on such an insubstantial and counterintuitive foundation?[3]

It is perhaps possible to reverse the causal relationship between interest in virginity and interest in legitimacy by positing virginity, rather than inheritance, as the realm of primary interest. This is the narrative of causation that underlies feminist arguments—like those of Gerda Lerner, Sherry Ortner, and Carole Pateman—that patriarchy reproduces itself via control over female sexuality. Enforced standards of virginity and chastity are disciplinary devices used to motivate women into servicing patriarchal mandates. In this feminist account, investment in patrilinear legitimacy is merely a symptom of the desire to control female sexuality; it is the subordination of women, not the production of heirs, that motivates a requirement that brides be virgins, that wives be chaste, and that widows be celibate. But this line of reasoning makes two rather treacherous leaps of logic: that a virginity imperative is an effective way to control sexuality and that patrilinear legitimacy makes a good alibi for female subordination via sexual control. Both of these premises are difficult to maintain in the face of evidence about the difficulties that inhere in policing virginity and, until very recently, paternity. In short, given its notorious unreliability, virginity seems an unlikely foundation for the source of male authority over women. But of course, cultural myths do not have to be logical, and they persevere precisely because they screen complexity behind simple and essentialist explanations. This book traces the history of this myth in the eighteenth century.

I argue that a very specific chapter in the history of virginity and patriarchy manifests in the eighteenth century for complicated historical reasons. I locate the eighteenth-century English historical obsession with virginity, and its manifestation in literature, especially the novel, in two related cultural developments: the "long" English Reformation, and its accompanying series of monarchical crises, and the new science. Virginity assumes a new shape and takes on new importance at this time because of coincident pressures from religio-political conflict and from the new scientific methods. The dates 1685–1750 are the focus of this book for specific reasons. The study begins with the decline of the Stuart monarchy, in the thick of the transition to a new kind of legitimacy problem along with a new theory of government. It opens with the Exclusion Crisis, which was an unsuccessful attempt to interrupt the legal rules of succession by installing the illegitimate child of Charles II, instead of Charles's brother James, as monarch. Although the attempt to exclude James II was unsuccessful, the birth of a legitimate heir to James and his Catholic wife, Mary of Modena, only a few years into his rule incited the Protestant revolution, which interrupted succession by transferring kingship to James's Protestant son-in-law. As a condition of his ascension, William III had to accept a move toward parliamentary government. His status as monarch was thus neither absolute nor strictly "legitimate" according to divine right of succession as England had traditionally implemented it.[4] The final Jacobite uprising, in 1745, heralds the end of my project, as it precedes the publication of the first English pornographic novel, Cleland's *Memoirs of a Woman of Pleasure*, and its sentimental antithesis, *Clarissa*. During the period 1685–1750, the novel gains massive popularity while the theater struggles and popular forms like the ballad all but disappear. At the same time, a theory of government grounded in parliament, property, and individual rights, rather than divine right, gains ascendance, and a major revolution in scientific method challenges older models of epistemology. By focusing on the figure and fate of the virgin, I account for the links among these political, cultural, and generic changes in a new way. During this time, virginity becomes gradually disembodied, as it becomes a figure for virtue. It also gains such symbolic importance that it can serve as both tenor and vehicle in a number of symbolic systems. Not merely a popular theme, virginity, this book argues, is a heuristic and a site of contestation for the theological, political, and ethical controversies, and for the generic innovation, of the period 1688–1750. Throughout this period, the twin problems of legitimacy and epistemology figure prominently in shaping ideas about virginity as well as the emergent novel form.

Virginity assumes a new shape beginning in the late seventeenth century at least partially because legitimacy was a key problem facing early modern British political rule. The legitimacy crisis in England's monarchy coincides with its incipient Reformation and inheres in the fact that so many English monarchs, like Henry VIII, Elizabeth I, Charles II, and James II, had trouble producing legitimate heirs or produced ones of the "wrong" religion.[5] As a result, England was faced with a series of monarchs of questionable legitimacy. Henry VIII solved his succession problems by converting England to Protestantism, a religion that denigrates lifelong virginity but that, especially in its Church of England incarnation, idealizes marital chastity and the female virginity that forms its foundation. And Elizabeth, whose gender contributed to her illegitimacy, used her self-presentation as the virgin queen to authorize her Protestant rule. Virginity, it would seem, is a myth that can resolve crises of impotence, illegitimacy, and theology.[6]

The resolution to England's crises of monarchical legitimacy is commonly attributed to the philosophical attack on the divine right of kings and is credited with provoking political reforms that lead to modern democracy. Seventeenth-century political philosophy challenges the theory that monarchs and patriarchs inherit divine right, and it posits, instead, pragmatic arguments about how governments develop in response to human needs, desires, and natures. Since inherited monarchy is tied to the idea that divine inheritance is passed physically from father to son, a theory that is articulated most famously if rather belatedly at this time by Robert Filmer, one might expect concerns for legitimacy and inheritance to dissipate with a decline both in the theory of divine right and in the English monarchy's ability to claim that divine right. Anxiety over the biological legitimacy of monarchs makes sense only if the right and the capacity for rule is a biological inheritance. And if virginity is linked to legitimacy, then one would expect a decreasing emphasis on virginity at this time. But this is not what the epigraph from Samuel Johnson and the popular fascination with the novels of Samuel Richardson suggest. One of the ironies in the history of virginity that I am tracing is that virginity becomes most closely tied to "legitimacy" only when genealogical legitimacy can no longer, except by staunch Jacobites, be defended as a model for establishing political rights.[7] That is, the mythological link between virginity and chastity reaches an apotheosis at precisely the historical time when the physical inheritance of "legitimacy" is challenged. Under a model of divine right and inherited patriarchy, the significance of female chastity is relatively clear: if the right to rule is a genealogical inheritance passed through the male line, then it is crucial that a woman not sleep with anyone but her husband. The significance of female chastity to a liberal government is less clear, unless one accepts a "natural" desire to pass one's property to one's heirs, a theory that is disproved by many examples, in real life, in literature, and even in the Bible, in which a father desires to bypass primogeniture (Dryden's *Absalom and Achitophel* a story that spans real life, fiction, and the Bible, being only the most historically relevant example). It is also unclear how a virginity/chastity imperative solves one of the most common legitimacy problems: the illegitimate children of the father.[8] And yet the idea that virginity matters because it regulates "legitimacy" and the inheritance of property is perhaps stronger in the middle of the eighteenth century than at any other time in modern Western history.

Laws of primogeniture, founded in a theory that birth, or blood, and worth, or virtue, are inherently connected, traditionally combine the inheritance of property and the right to rule over others, passing both to the firstborn son. But there exists an important distinction between an inherited right to rule and the right to transmit real property to one's heirs. One is concerned with genetic or biological inheritance (though of course it would not have been called that it in early modern period) and the other with material property. These two "rights" become uncoupled in the long aftermath of England's monarchical crises, with a decline in the emphasis on genealogy and a renewed interest in property as the foundation of political rights. These two different models of inheritance thus belong to political systems that we usually claim as distinct. Genealogical inheritance is the foundation for inherited monarchy, while concern with property rights underpins a liberal theory of government, in which citizens legitimize a government in order to protect their property and their right to determine who inherits it. One model of political "legitimacy" privileges "birth," assuming that worth follows birth, while the other stresses "worth," in both its literal (wealth) and metaphorical (virtue) senses. In short, although primogeniture traditionally encompasses the heritability of both kinds of rights, seventeenth-century political theory, exemplified by Locke's *Two Treatises on Government*, challenges the inherited right to rule while maintaining that the right to control one's property, although not necessarily the mandate to pass it on to a firstborn son, is the fundamental purpose of government.

It thus seems counterintuitive, on one hand, to find a renewed obsession with virginity coincident with a decreased emphasis on genealogical legitimacy. In the absence of inherited nobility, why worry about legitimacy? If little is being transmitted in the genetic exchange, then why must the genetic child inherit the money? Yet, on the other hand, it is possible to predict that a decline in the "legitimacy" of genealogical inheritance might provoke a renewed interest in the links between virginity and legitimate inheritance. If nobility can be inherited, then it will be passed down irrespective of a legal sanction of legitimacy—this is of course the premise of the foundling tale that forms the basis of many tales of romance as well as the romance's gothic successors. But if all that one can pass to one's heirs is material property, then it might become even more crucial to determine the correct heir. Perhaps it is precisely because "birth" does not confer "worth" that property must follow a man's children—after all, his "nobility" will not. Indeed, in a most provocative and compelling study, Rachel Weil has shown that the emergence, in the seventeenth century, of the category "Whig" relied on the notion that female sexuality was linked to property. But the emergent anxiety, exemplified by Johnson, about female sexuality and about the biological legitimacy of progeny almost immediately casts itself as resting on tradition. From this perspective, eighteenth-century interest in virginity seems to reflect the anxiety that genealogical legitimacy does not carry any real value and to mitigate that anxiety by a renewed commitment to ensuring that real property is correctly transferred and by the insistence that this value is the traditional one.

But this is not the whole story, since "virginity" mutates quite a bit as it travels from one system to another. The shift from patriarchalism to modern patriarchy, in Michael McKeon's words, is accompanied, in the history of virginity that I am tracing, by a shift from thinking about virginity as primarily a physical entity to thinking about virginity as a sign of virtue (1995). Just as the inheritance of the right to rule is quite distinct from the "right" to bequeath one's property to heirs, virginity is something completely different from virtue. The first set of terms relies on the biological body whereas the second does not, necessarily. The particular manifestation of virginity obsession that develops in mid-eighteenth-century England, exemplified by Richardson and Johnson, promotes the notion that virginity's value inheres in its ability to predict not only chastity but virtue more broadly conceived.

In the eighteenth century, virginity is superseded, in moral and material importance, by a number of abstract qualities—purity, originality, moral virtue, constancy, and, most importantly, marriageability—for which it is a sign and a precondition. Virginity becomes less literal, or at least physical virginity has more metaphorical than literal value. Eighteenth-century virtue is thus a system of value that competes with, rather than complements, the value of genealogic inheritance and thus the traditional *raison d'etre* for virginity: it famously values "worth," not "birth" and is based on immaterial rather than material referents. This is why, ironically, the scientific revolution, with its emphasis on investigating the material reality of the body, is an important aspect of my story.[9]

It is no coincidence, this book argues, that virgins assume such importance in an era that is commonly recognized as deeply vexed by both the materiality of objects and the efficacy of signs. Questions about virginity are simultaneously epistemological (is she or isn't she a virgin? what constitutes proof?), semiotic (what signifies virginity and what does virginity signify?), and teleological (what is its proper narrative?). These are questions that were raised and worried about by religious, scientific, and fictional texts in a the eighteenth century. Epistemological problems have always plagued virginity. The hymen— a corporeal entity whose existence was long debated, which disappears as it reveals itself, and which is found only in a limited class of bodies, virgin women, and only in some nondeterminable subset of them— seems at once to promise evidence of a woman's sexual history and, perversely, to refuse to provide that evidence consistently. This characteristic of female anatomy turns out to be especially problematic during the scientific revolution. I have already discussed legitimacy problems caused by religio-political change as a source for the eighteenth-century obsession with virginity. But the epistemological issues raised by virginity are an important parallel causation, since reliance upon virginity as a source of legitimation suggests a need for epistemological credibility. If legitimacy is, at its heart, a mode of establishing rights via compelling both belief and action, one might say that empirical science becomes the arbiter of legitimacy with the demise of divinely ordained legitimacy. And if claims to legitimacy are claims to both epistemological and political authority, then it is not surprising that during the Enlightenment virginity, historically a way of transmitting legitimacy, develops into a key battleground for shifting ideas about epistemological, moral, and political authority.

It is a commonplace (to scholars of the period) that the scientific revolution, monitored by the Royal Society, contributed to the emergence of Anglican parliamentary government as well as to the advent of the English novel.[10] In its insistence on the importance of evidence, witnesses, repeatability, and materiality, the scientific revolution dealt the final blow to the mysticism and magic associated with both Catholicism and the radical sects. It also, so the story goes, provided the epistemological method for the novel.[11] I do not argue with the contention that these events are linked, but I find the relationships among politics, science, and the novel to be motivated by compensation rather than by causation or complementarity. The transition to Protestantism necessitated the evacuation, or colonization, of Catholic and monarchical models of female sexuality and ideal femininity. At first, early modern medicine supported this project by pathologizing virginity and promoting chaste, married feminine sexuality as natural. However, with the emergence of the new science of anatomy and the ascendance of male midwifery, female anatomy confronted medical practice with a number of epistemological, moral, and logistical problems and thus threatened the very "legitimacy" of the new science. Virginity, a supposed guarantor of legitimacy under the residual system of inheritance, could not be made to comply with the new epistemological methods for determining belief. As a result, I argue, the scientific/medical community abdicated responsibility over female virginity. Epistemological problems are thus a contributing factor in the emergence of a literary obsession with virginity. Viewed from this perspective, it is possible to see the early novel's obsession with the subjective qualities of virtue, not as an extension of scientific practices, but rather as compensation for their failures. One can also see the novel's interest in transferring virtue from the body to subjectivity as an adjunct to the de-emphasis of physical "legitimacy" as a foundation for political rule. The sentimental novel disembodies the concepts of virginity and legitimacy and deploys them for new political and epistemological mandates.

Because eighteenth-century virginity signifies not merely chastity but a number of intangible qualities that come to be associated with moral virtue, it is a characteristic that justifies making distinctions among people. As such, it must be seen as an agent in the reorganization of the class structure. The right of the monarchy to rule was always based on both "blood" and "virtue," because these qualities were seen to be inherently linked. In this older model, virginity is the conduit for both blood and virtue. But with the emergence of critiques of models of inherited virtue, virginity becomes not merely a chaste vessel through which virtue and rights can pass, but rather a sign of virtue and a mode of creating rights in itself. As mentioned earlier, under political models that rely upon the heritability of political rights, the virginity and chastity of women matter only—or mostly—to people who have rights to pass on. This is why the virginity of the queen, a mandate imposed as recently as Princess Diana, matters more than the virginity of the dairymaid. But eighteenth-century England's most famous virgin, Pamela, is closer to a dairymaid than a princess. She has neither property nor nobility to pass on to her heirs. What she has, in spades, is "virtue," and this virtue is the foundation for her promotion—and her husband's "demotion"—to the middle class. For in the eighteenth century, virginity and virtue become middle-class values: lower classes and the aristocracy are associated with sexual promiscuity while virtue comes to reside, at least potentially, in the middle-class woman who defends her virginity for its own sake, not primarily in order to transmit the property of her class. Her virtue, which requires her investment in her own virginity, becomes the inheritance that she will bequeath. Essentially, virginity becomes, in the eighteenth century, a way to transmit both moral and material "worth," and, as such, a form of heritable female property. Eighteenth-century virginity thereby both protects and denies a link between birth and worth, and between worth and "rights." For this reason, it is the perfect bridge between two different patriarchal systems and also a convenient vehicle for bourgeois ideology, which rests on the idea that immaterial merit produces material value.

I have been suggesting that the gradual de-emphasis of the significance of physical virginity parallels a decline in emphasis on the inherited right to rule. As rights increasingly become legitimated more by "virtue" than by "blood" (at least, e.g., in things like the increasing power of the House of Commons), so does virginity. Under a liberal theory of government, virtue becomes more important than virginity and concerns with material inheritance supersede concerns with genetic lineage. While we now take for granted the link between virginity and chastity and the notion that virgins make the best (most chaste) wives, I am suggesting that the historical ascendance of this obsession is more complicated than simply the desire to control female sexuality or to transmit property to legitimate heirs. The link between "chastity" and "property" that Samuel Johnson finds so obvious is in fact a careful, and historically motivated, response to twin crises in the realms of legitimacy and epistemology. The emergent idea of virginity—and the novel that is its advocate—resolves these crises by converting not just the virgin but the very terms associated with her. In the novel, virginity becomes more about virtue than material inheritance, and the legitimacy crisis is transferred from the patriarch to the virgin herself. This metaphorization and migration of virginity happens because virginity was an epistemologically unstable entity and because genealogical legitimacy as a foundation for political legitimacy became destabilized. It is these shifts that this book traces and endeavors to explain.

It is a story that, in its most elemental form, is a narrative of conversion. The Catholic virgin, as exemplar of femininity, gets converted into the paragon of Protestant virtue. As a result of the conversion of England into a Protestant state, two models of Catholic ideal femininity—the virgin martyr and the Virgin Mary—become less available to English women. In their place we find the virtuous, and highly marriageable, heroine of sentimental fiction, whose virginity is a temporary but exceedingly important stage in her narrative progress. There are two obvious ironies in this story of conversion. First of all, in Catholic dogma, virginity is a denial of the material world, including childbearing and the accumulation of property, and thus it is exactly opposite of a guarantee for legitimate children and the transmission of property. Moreover, Catholicism's most prominent exemplar of female virtue is the Virgin Mary, whose perpetual and yet fertile virginity is both a reward for her virtue and a sign of God's sanctification. But Mary, once one begins to think about her, is the supreme example of the unfaithful wife, and Jesus is, if you will excuse the profanity, a bastard child. How these overdetermined models of Catholic virginity become converted into the model of Protestant chastity provides the structure for my story. This story follows the virgin from her controversial appearance in religious texts, through her destabilizing influence on medical authority, and into her triumphant emergence in sentimental plots. Throughout the book, she and the men who care about her fate are dogged by satirists whose antagonism plays a crucial role in shaping her character and her narrative. This is because throughout the story, the twin problems of legitimacy and epistemology make the virgin and her admirers vulnerable to charges of hypocrisy. I argue that the epistemological instability and charges of hypocrisy that plague our heroine are ways of transferring the threats that are posed to male modes of authority (because of political and scientific change) from male to female realms of authority. Thus, at the end of the story we find a virgin heroine with an equal share of virtuous capital and tragic—or satiric—danger.

Since this is a story of conversion, the first chapter examines representations of nuns in the late seventeenth century. Nuns appear prominently in several very different arenas: in anti-Catholic propaganda that directly responds to the monarchical crisis; in pornography and amatory fiction; and in political philosophy. I begin the chapter by showing how the Catholic nun is "anglicanized" in a variety of discourses and through a myriad of methods: sex is naturalized, celibacy demonized, and Catholicism depicted as a religion that has both bastardized true Christianity and oppressed women, even as many of these texts belie their anxiety about the importance of England's Catholic past. The second half of the chapter analyzes the representations of the cloister by two very different women writers: Mary Astell and Aphra Behn. These more ambivalent representations of the nun's conversion foresee that the attempt to transfer her from one system to another cannot be accomplished in the absence of serious negative social consequences. Both writers focus on the problems around female will and female desire that emerge with the abdication of absolute and divinely ordained patriarchy, and they predict that the Catholic virgin will not be "converted" in the absence of a new ideology of female subjectivity and a new genre to accommodate it.

Moving from religion to science, the second chapter traces a history of medical texts on virginity from the early seventeenth century to the middle of the eighteenth century, a time of massive change in medicine and science. I argue that early modern medicine at first supported the Reformation agenda of devaluing spiritual virginity but that the new science, with its injunctions to produce stable evidence and objective witnesses, lost authority over female virginity. This chapter thus anticipates the metaphorization of virginity, and, in making a new case for why the early novel is so interested in virgin female characters, it argues for a re-evaluation of the relationship between the epistemologies of new science and the sentimental novel.

Chapter 3 analyzes a variety of texts of popular culture, mainly ballads, in order to demonstrate that the religious and medical crisis over virginity permeated popular culture. These texts provide evidence that emergent ideas about the relationship between virginity and property were satirized as middle-class pretensions and that the threat of satirization motivates a certain kind of interest in virginity: one that insists it is women, and not men, who stand to lose by mismanaging or misrepresenting virginity. It reiterates the claims, made in chapter 2, that female virginity at this time represents a threat to, rather than a foundation for, male authority and legitimacy, and it links concerns with legitimacy to monarchical politics, as sex and politics were the two most common topics of the ballads.

Chapter 4 focuses on the semiotic problems raised by theological debates over the Virgin Mary and idolatry, and it uses those debates as a context for analyzing Alexander Pope's mock-epic of virginity,

The Rape of the Lock. This chapter argues that the poem iconoclastically disrupts valued ideals of both Catholicism (perpetual virginity and material objects) and Protestantism (chastity and the "word") and that it deliberately does not fill the void created by its own iconoclasm. The first chapter shows how the virgin is the center of theological controversy, and the second chapter shows how virginity could not be accommodated to the new science, thereby creating an epistemological crisis. This is why, I argue in this chapter, virginity is the vehicle for critiques of both theological and secular modes of meaning and for a meditation on the meaningless of material objects, including the hymen.

Chapter 5 reads Samuel Richardson's first novel, *Pamela*, as a response to the crisis of virginity that this book has been describing. This chapter demonstrates that anxieties about the materiality of virginity account for many of the novel's formal features and for its obsession with the transcendence of virginity by that famously immaterial ideal of virtue, and it argues for a new way of seeing the relationship between early modern science and the novel. At least in terms of female "virtue," the novel does not extend the scientific project by mimicking its methods, but rather compensates for its failures. Instead of the novel absorbing the epistemological methods of science and applying them to human subjectivity, fictionalized representations of virtue are shaped by virginity's resistance to scientific methods and its threat to male systems of epistemology and authority.

Chapter 6 extends the analysis of the links between sentimental, satiric, and pornographic representations of female virginity via an analysis of John Cleland's infamous *Memoirs of a Woman of Pleasure*. This novel depicts defloration as having a narrative that moves from pleasure to pain, and it uses that narrative as the benchmark for evaluating all its representations of sex, as well as the marriage plot that the novel seems to satirize. This chapter shows how the aesthetic tensions in Cleland's pornographic novel, between satire and erotic pleasure and between originality and repetition, are worked out through the establishment of defloration as the paradigmatic narrative structure.

The conclusion shows why and how such an exceptional book as *Clarissa* emerges from the literary history that this book has been tracing. It analyzes the novel's length, its originality, and its narrative conflicts in order to account for *Clarissa's* status as both exceptional and exemplary, and to account for the novel's ability to be simultaneously conservative and prophetic when it comes to representing the tempestuous history of the virgin and the patriarch.

This is a book about the middle-class English fascination with virginity, a preoccupation that was mainly, although not exclusively, a masculine domain. While class as a category of analysis figures importantly in my argument of chapter 3, and while women writers and lower-class texts do provide occasional points of comparison, this book does not claim to be a comprehensive survey of eighteenth-century ideas about virginity. I am sensitive to the problem of treating some authors as "minor" while saving my extended interpretations for others. I chose to write on certain writers—like Aphra Behn and Mary Astell—because I felt that I could make substantive arguments about how their interest in virginity intervenes in the mainstream obsession that I am discussing. And I chose not to use many other women writers—like Jane Barker, Mary Davis, and Con Philips—merely as foils for male writers, when they clearly deserve extended consideration on their own. Finally, this is a work of literary history and analysis; as such, I am not making any claims about how real women and men experienced these ideas about virginity.

CHAPTER 1

Blessed Virgins: Anti-Catholic Propaganda and Convent Fantasies

Thou art a God, Almighty Love!

Behn, *The Town-Fopp* (IV.i)

When it was published in 1678, *The Portuguese Letters*, a fictionalized account of a Portuguese nun loved and abandoned by a French army officer, captured the imagination of the English reading public, at least partially, for nostalgic reasons.[1] The political and theological cynicism that we often attribute to Restoration England made way for the enthusiastic reception of the story of a nun seduced and abandoned who nonetheless seems, remarkably, to have maintained both religious and amorous devotion. The nun's Catholic spirituality produces a kind of rapture—or, epistemological certainty about the metaphysical combined with physical ecstasy—that may have seemed both naïve and attractive to readers in late seventeenth-century England, whose worldview had been subject to a dizzying array of ruptures: Thomas Hobbes's dissociation of action and conscience, the Protestant Reformation's division of religious and political authority, and what Michael McKeon describes as an emergent anxiety about the separation of epistemological and ethical authority.[2] *The Portuguese Letters* came out in multiple English editions, it produced a sequel—*Five Love-Letters Written by a Cavalier* (1694)—as well as at least one parody.[3] It is also credited with sparking the genre of amatory fiction, which is an extremely popular proto-novelistic form in the late seventeenth and early eighteenth centuries. The Catholic influences on amatory fiction are relatively obvious although usually overlooked: they frequently take place, like *The Portuguese Letters*, in Catholic countries, convents figure heavily, and much of the excitement and scandal of the sexually desirous and active heroines seems predicated on the contrast between ascetic expectations and quasi-libertine reality. In amatory fiction, as well as in pornography and later in gothic novels, convents are permeable sites of libertine intrigue: women are constantly entering and leaving them on all kinds of unholy pretexts. The late seventeenth-century fascination with nuns, moreover, extends well beyond amatory fiction, also appearing prominently in poetry, in philosophy, in drama, and in the anti-Catholic propaganda that saturated the streets of London every time a Catholic plot, real or imagined, threatened Protestant hegemony. The prevalence and remarkable variety of these representations suggests that feminized Catholic spirituality—and the spiritual community in which it takes place—are not merely popular themes but are rather heuristics and sites of contestation for the theological, political, and ethical controversies of the seventeenth century.

Even though nuns were not necessarily virgins, their symbolic power derives from the ancient tradition of mystical virginity. Early Christianity often idealized virginity by linking ascetic celibacy, for both sexes, with miraculous sanctification. The third-century celibate St. Methodius claims that the "science of virginity" allowed its practioners to "stand upon the very vault of heaven and gaze directly upon immortality itself" (44, 42). And Gregory of Nyssa thinks that those who practice the "pure mysteries of virginity" can thereby "become themselves partakers in the glory of God" (9). England's own legend of the Holy Grail highlights the importance of chastity, for only the chaste have access to the miracles associated with Christ. Susanna Elm explains that the purpose of asceticism is to "transform the practitioner into a pure vessel of divine will and so to create the possibility for a communication with the divine through some form of *unio mystica*" (14). The roots of ascetic virginity thus inhere in the dual problems of human moral and epistemological insufficiency. But ascetic virginity also reflects optimism about overcoming the insufficiencies that make humans inferior to the divine and unsure about divine will. Christian asceticism always rests upon the assumptions that humans are capable of salvation, that the soul (or the mind) and the body are inextricably connected, and thus that the body is necessarily implicated in salvation.

During the Reformation, celibacy and monasticism became important litmus tests for Catholic/Protestant conflict. The Catholic Church maintained a belief in the spiritual, even mystical, effects of virginity and elevated it over marriage. By removing herself from many of the physical cares of the world—sex, childrearing, and maintaining of a house—a Catholic nun has the opportunity to achieve a higher state of spirituality. Paul, the central Biblical source on this topic, says, "She that is married careth for the things of the world, how she may please her husband," whereas the "unmarried woman careth for the things of the Lord."[4] Protestant reformers attacked the Catholic emphasis on virginity and monasticism. Although female virginity was still accorded respect under Protestantism, reformers like Martin Luther and John Calvin argued that virginity was not better than marriage, and they even argued that enforced celibacy of the clergy was idolatrous. Luther argued that under religious seclusion "a new God is invented by Satan for men without their even being aware of it" (148).[5] Reformers countered Catholic views about the advantages of virginity with an increased emphasis on marriage and on the egalitarian doctrine of equality between clergy and laity. Celibacy implies a higher status for Catholic clergy than their flock, which is antithetical to Protestant emphasis on predestination (only God can separate the elect), on justification by faith alone, and on the laity's unmediated relationship with God. Under the mandate of Reformation, male clerical celibacy was decried both for its separatism and for its impracticality, and official ecclesiastical careers for women were eliminated. Anti-Catholic writers uncoupled celibacy and sanctification through several arguments: they argued that celibacy is unnatural and leads to perverse sexuality instead of the fulfillment of the mandate to procreate; that seclusion prevents one from accomplishing good in the world while achieving nothing toward the afterlife; and that ascetic celibacy blasphemously debases the body, a gift from God. One writer argued simply that celibacy, like many Catholic practices, imitates a sign of sanctification but does not bring it about; celibacy mimics the "state and privileges" of angels, but not their "knowledge or perfection of nature."[6] In other words, virginity is the shadow of sanctity, not the substance. In sum, belief in the supernatural powers of virginity falls victim to the larger Protestant critique of Catholic miracles, which Hobbes derides as "the turning of Consecration into Conjuration, or Enchantment."[7]

In general, Protestant critiques of celibacy were aimed at male clergy and were motivated by their abuses of power. Female virginity has always been perceived differently than male celibacy. Christian female saints, for example, are dominated, much more so than male saints, by virgins. Early Christian hagiography is replete with the escapades of virgin martyrs whose religious raptures, miracles, and stigmata testify to their sanctification and supernatural protection and also justify their resistance to pagan and tyrannical regimes. Moreover, the supreme exemplar of Catholic femininity is indeed the Virgin Mary, whose virginity enabled the virgin birth of Christ as well as her own sanctification and unprecedented assumption. This differential treatment of male and female asceticism persisted, or even became magnified, under the mandates of Reformation. In England, female monasteries were a particularly vexed arena of debate and representation because when Catholic monasteries were appropriated, Catholic priests could become Anglican priests and young men who might have entered a monastery could go to a university, many of which were built in the old monasteries. Catholic nuns, by contrast, found no place in the Church of England ecclesiastical system, and young Catholic women could not go to university. At the same time, ideals of femininity and female virtue remained tied to Catholic models of female sanctity and were rooted in the iconic power of the Catholic virgin. Early Protestantism linked premarital virginity to female virtue, so female virginity, unlike male celibacy, remained central to the ongoing Reformation. This project depended upon depicting Protestantism as the religion of true female chastity and reason, rather than of magic, sexual deviancy, and corruption.

In response to Protestant critique, the Catholic Church endeavored to modernize Catholicism. The Council of Trent de-emphasized miracles by establishing standards of proof for sanctification, but it also confirmed the superiority of virginity over marriage and the importance of religious seclusion for women.[8] And the Counter-Reformation had its own miraculous virgins. In Spain, St. Teresa's "Extasies, and Rapts and Flights of the Spirit upwards," for example, provided a counter model both to Protestant models of femininity and to emergent Enlightenment models of reason (1675, preface). This woman of "most inviolable chastity" founded a number of convents for women all over the continent (1642, preface). She was canonized in 1622 and immortalized by Bernini in 1647–1652. Many English translations of her writings were published in the seventeenth century, and at least one was dedicated to the notoriously Catholic Queen Henrietta Maria. St. Teresa is one example of the way that reinvigorated Catholicism, tied to ideals of virginity and the cloister, challenged Protestant models of femininity, rationality, and spirituality.

Virginity and monasticism were complicated theological and political problems throughout Reformation and Counter-Reformation Europe, but England's "long" process of Reformation encompassed an especially complex attitude toward monasticism because it was officially instigated by Henry VIII's problems with paternity and desire for divorce and because its most effective proponent, Queen Elizabeth, maintained that her reputed virginity authorized her rule. In making the seizure of the monasteries one of the first and most central aspects of his break with Catholicism while at the same time maintaining the importance of clerical celibacy, Henry VIII set in motion a particularly English relationship to questions of religious seclusion, sexual abstinence, and marriage that persisted throughout the early modern period in England.[9] Lawrence Stone and others, although not unopposed, argue that "holy matrimony" played a considerable role in the English transition from Catholicism to Protestantism.[10] And scholars such as Patrick Collinson and Linda Colley have shown that British national identity, and its imperialist project, was founded on Protestantism. Collinson calls anti-Catholicism the "lynchpin" of English identity. Yet Church of England Protestants constantly had to defend themselves from charges of Catholic sympathies. Sorting out a newly Protestant concept of virginity and marriage was a central component of the transition to a new English Protestant identity. This chapter argues that mainstream Anglican Protestantism both distanced itself from Catholicism and appropriated it via the conversion of the nun into the figure of the chaste wife.

Because of its historical association with magical and miraculous power and because of its complex relationship to the Protestantization of England, virginity was a constant site of contention in the early modern period. During the seventeenth century, there were many efforts to appropriate miraculous models of virginity. Dislocated from its spiritual purpose under the Protestant reform, the power of virginity was claimed for secular purposes, as Elizabeth's self-representation as the virgin queen makes clear. Theodora Jankowksi locates an early modern English concern with the subversive potential of what she terms "queer" virginity. And in an analysis of the vitalist movement, John Rogers (1994) argues that for a short time from 1640 to 1660, virginity—especially for men—was linked with the doctrine of passive resistance and thus was accorded the possibility of almost miraculous political efficacy.[11] Similarly, alchemy and some marginal religious movements, like Rosicrucianism, that thrived in late seventeenth-century England claimed special capabilities inhered in sexual abstinence.[12] Even the puritan John Milton toyed with the advantages of celibacy and explored the magical powers of the "sage and serious doctrine of virginity" through the Lady in *A Maske Presented at Ludlow Castle* (1634).[13] Religious views of virginity persisted, although usually in explicitly non-Catholic ways. Philip Massinger and Thomas Dekker's *The Virgin Martyr* (1621), for example, is set during the Roman persecution of early Christians, an identity claimed by Catholics and Protestants alike. In their play, the virginity and piety of the heroine Dorothea reward her with a protective supernatural spirit, allow her to withstand multiple rape attempts, and convince numerous pagans to convert to Christianity. *The Virgin Martyr*, like this chapter, thus implies that virginity can be crucial to resolving localized politico-religious conflict.

The English Reformation leading to a permanently Anglican monarchy was definitively completed during the eighteenth century but was threatened at the end of the seventeenth century. My interest in the history of virginity begins here, with the decline of the Stuart monarchy, when the future of Protestant hegemony was in question, and when that question was intimately connected to Catholic sexuality. The Catholic inclinations of the late Stuart monarchs, who were linked to France, via exile, and to Catholic spouses, threatened many times to bring the country once again to civil war. Even after the "bloodless" Protestant revolution of 1688–1689, Jacobite supporters haunted the Protestant succession until the middle of eighteenth century. And the Stuarts' sexual excesses—Charles II's libertine court and his illegitimate and insurrectionist son being the most prominent and controversial examples—meant that the links between virginity, sexuality, and religion were, at this time, particularly ripe for political exploitation and redefinition. In 1688, the supposititious heir scandal, motivated by Protestant fear of a Catholic heir, fueled anti-Catholic sentiment (especially, as I discuss in chapter 4, anti-marionism). The scandal depended upon impugning Catholic veneration of Mary, as well as the naïve belief in miracles like the virgin birth, and it instigated the revolution of 1688. Thus, while miraculous virginity had been entertained by such unlikely persons as Milton earlier in the seventeenth century, by the end of the century, miraculous virginity could only be associated with sexually and politically corrupt Catholicism.[14]

Along with anti-Catholicism, the other lynchpin of emergent Protestant society in England was reason. Mystical Catholicism, so often associated with virginity, employs a model of knowing that (like enthusiasm, which I discuss below) exceeds both rational and empirical models of human reason. In opposition to these models of supernatural epistemology, Anglican theology posited the logic of its middle way, endeavoring to explain even revelation (things we could not know with our human reason alone) and the limits of human knowledge (things we could never know) in reasonable ways. In the heated debates of 1685–1688, Protestant writers deliberately constructed the choice between Catholicism and Protestantism as one that could be made on reasonable grounds. William Sherlock, for instance, admonishes Anglicans:

> Here then let our Protestant fix his foot, and not stir an inch, till they disown Infallibility, and confess, that every man can and must judge for himself in matters of Religion, according to the proofs that are offered to him. (5)

This example shows that as the Church of England made its case against Catholics, it based its claims on the ground of individual reason and criticized Catholic belief in papal infallibility, personal revelation, and miracles such as virgin birth. Anti-Catholic propaganda of this time depicted monasticism, along with the worship of saints and transubstantiation, as among Catholicism's most irrational practices, and it relied upon the notion that Catholic doctrine and Catholic belief in supernatural phenomena are ripe for political exploitation by the depraved, at the expense of the ignorant or innocent.

In short, emergent Protestant political ascendancy required a derogation of Catholic models of sanctification and a conversion of the figure of the virgin from sanctified and ascetic nun into the chaste and fertile wife, the paragon of Protestant virtue. This conversion of the nun required her to turn her desire and faith from the next world to this one, or from God to a man. It thus depended upon active heterosexuality, either for licentious (in the cases of pornography and amorous ecstasy) or virtuous (i.e., chaste heterosexual) purposes. The figure of the nun inevitably evokes questions about desire and the will: the ascetic regimen of the monastic promotes control over (or annihilation of) the individual will so that God's will may be enacted. But the nun's privileged relationship with knowledge of God's will, via revelation, also means that she can offer political resistance to the will of mortal men—this is the foundation of the virgin martyr tradition. That is, the nun can represent both the most attractive subject of patriarchal will and its most intractable antagonist. This is why she becomes a figure of such interest during late seventeenth-century political conflict, why she must be "converted" to Protestantism, and also why she serves as a litmus test for theories of the will and of desire that were the focus of seventeenth-century philosophy and theology.

The first half of this chapter, "The Nun's Conversion," explores the ways that Protestant-influenced writing imagined that the nun's iconic power could serve Protestant ends. Some Protestant writers, both Anglican and puritan, rewrote England's Catholic past as a means of securing its Protestant future by arguing that the wealth and the procreative power represented by the convents should be put in the service of national English Protestantism. Writers like Andrew Marvell admitted, however indirectly, the libertine attractions of the convent but denied its mystical or political efficacy, and they imagined that political duty, whether freely chosen or by force, would prevail over ruthlessly rational and self-interested libertinism. Other convent stories, like *The Portuguese Letters*, as well as some rewritings of virgin martyr stories, far from requiring the denial of desire, imagined that the rapturous devotion of the nun toward God could easily, and happily, be shifted to a male object of desire. Finally, the explosion of continental pornography set in monasteries, represented most infamously by Jear Barrin's *Venus in the Cloister*, imagined that Catholic sexual excess was a perverse development unattractive to women. Given the choice, women would always choose chaste marriage over either sexual asceticism or extreme libertinism. All of these texts imagine that the privileged devotion of the nun will serve, rather than impede, the sexual, procreative, and political desires of men and that the nun's conversion, and the purging of Catholicism, will contribute to social stability by redirecting female desire and will to ends that are socially useful to a Protestant state. The second half of the chapter, "Desire, Secular and Sacred" focuses on two late seventeenth-century female writers, Mary Astell and Aphra Behn, who foresee that the nun's conversion has the potential to create social instability. These writers—who share conservative politics but whose lifestyles and writing are vastly dissimilar—focus on the problems around female will, female desire and social ethics that emerge with the abdication of absolute and divinely ordained patriarchy. In linking these writers via their representations of Catholic spirituality, this chapter makes it possible to view the relationship between their political conservatism and their feminist politics in a new way. I argue that both writers, albeit from different perspectives, critique the ideologies of romantic love and moral heterosexuality upon which the emergent political system of England rests.

THE NUN'S CONVERSION

Some Nunneries are such public Bawdy-houses, that they seem liker the Temple of Venus than the Sanctuary of God.

Lowe, 181

While modern images of the cloister often depict ascetic practice as a ruthless form of oppression of women via repression of their sexual desires, many seventeenth-century representations of convents imagine that the cloister is attractive to the libertine, if not explicitly sexual, desires of women. Marvell's "Upon Appleton House" (1681), for example, associates the cloister with Catholic sensual excess. This famous allegory of England's providential Reformation—and its defeat of Catholicism—imagines that England's future depends upon building Protestant estates on the ruins of Catholic convents. It depicts England's move to Protestantism as contingent upon securing alliances with virgins by staging a competition between a Catholic nunnery and a male suitor for the affections, and the inheritance, of the beautiful Isabel Thwaites. The first action of the poem, and the beginning of the narrative of England's providential march toward Protestantism, is a nun's speech to Isabel about the attractions of the nunnery. The nun-seducer depicts the convent as a place of beauty, over which Isabel will have dominion, where flowers and luxury abound. The choice of the "great *Bridegroom*" over an earthly spouse, does not, in this seductive nun's depiction, entail an estrangement of sensual pleasure and sanctity:

> Nor is our *Order* yet so nice,
> Delight to banish as a Vice.
> Here Pleasure Piety doth meet;
> One perfecting the other Sweet.

The nun's promise of a life filled with art, flowers, "crystallized fruits," and (chaste) lesbianism seems to appeal to Isabel's desires. In fact, the nun speaks to Isabel, as if "by chance" precisely the "thoughts" that Isabel herself had "long conceiv'd."

Fairfax, the suitor who will found a Protestant dynasty on Isabel's body, does not try to entice Isabel—or counter the offer of the nun—with either logic or luxury. Instead he relies on law, by claiming Isabel is betrothed and cannot divorce him, and force, that is kidnapping her, to deter Isabel from taking orders and thus to win her—and the nunnery that will become the Fairfax seat, Appleton House—for the patriotic cause of the puritan revolution. Rather than setting up a choice between Catholicism and Protestantism for the virgin Isabel to make, the poem rather unexpectedly hinges upon linking the cloister to the male military effort. The nunnery and Fairfax, as Anne Coterill has argued, both need the young virgin, since neither can produce heirs alone, and thus they share similar goals, crystallized fruit and Isabel's own desires notwithstanding. Later in the poem this pattern is repeated, as the "sacred bud" of the virginity of Maria, Isabel's descendent, must be destroyed in order to further Fairfax succession. Neither Isabel nor Maria are granted agency in making a choice between the luxury of the cloister and the patriotism of reproductivity. The competition between virginity and the Fairfax dynasty—and between Catholicism and puritanism—thus must be won with force and law rather than seduction. Rogers argues that Marvell's poem is haunted by the possibility that revolutionary violence could have been avoided (1996, 78–79). But my point, rather more skeptical of the poem's patriotic/puritan credentials, is that the poem reveals that Catholicism might in fact be more attractive to Isabel, as well as to Maria and to Fairfax, than the puritan Marvell might like to admit, only partially because it is the religion of seduction rather than force. The poem intimates that Protestant England is not merely haunted by its Catholic roots, but in fact that Catholicism provides most of what is valuable to the Fairfax dynasty—both its country houses and its fertile virgins.[15]

Margaret Cavendish's play *The Convent of Pleasure* (1668) makes a case for the attractions of the virgin cloister even more explicitly. Like Marvell's poem, it counterposes a space of female libertinism with the threat of male violence in order to enlist a virgin heiress in a political cause. Though Lady Happy spends most of her time in the play articulating her theory of female retreat as the route to female happiness, in the end, she marries. As with the virgins in Marvell's poem, the heroine of Cavendish's text does not make a clear choice for marriage and a political cause over libertine, though not necessarily unchaste, seclusion. The play ends with the prince, who has won the heart of the Lady Happy while crossed-dressed as a princess, promising to take her by "force of arms." Like Isabel Thwaites, Lady Happy never speaks after a male declaration of force against the allure of the convent. Both "Upon Appleton House" and *The Convent of Pleasure* stage a competition between Catholic excess and Protestant marital and political duty, and in each case seduction, luxury, and femininity are on the side of Catholicism, while force and masculinity effect the Protestant victory.[16] I do not mean to suggest that the texts invite similar readings of their attitudes toward these events: no doubt the play by the Catholic/royalist/female Cavendish celebrates the attractions of the nunnery while Marvell diminishes them, and Cavendish takes much more seriously the desires of her female protagonist, but in both cases, convents and virginity are portrayed as plausible sites of female desire, and both leave no space for a female will that is able to enact those desires. Despite Marvell's obvious anti-Catholicism and Cavendish's Catholic affiliations, convents in both these texts are rendered as plausibly attractive to young women—a decidedly appealing option, should their desires be consulted. The silencing of the virgins in both texts implies that if female desire, buoyed by seduction or rhetoric, was accounted for, the Catholic side would surely win. They both portray the passing of the all-female convent as a necessary, if lamentable, fact; women must give up their sensual pleasures in the service of political causes. However, both Marvell and Cavendish's texts found their descriptions of the attractions of the convent on mere materiality: luxury items and the libertine pleasures of the world. What these texts repress is the possibility that the virginal religious life offers something beyond individual material pleasure, for example, religious transcendence or legitimate social benefit. They neutralize the attractiveness of Catholic views of virginity by secularizing and disempowering virginity, representing the choice of a cloistered life as a self-interested one that cannot be made by the female protagonists who ultimately have no say in their destiny.

While Marvell and Cavendish's texts imagine that the cloister could be attractive to women, other English texts on convent life, quite to the contrary, imagine that the female cloister will satisfy male, not female, desires. They co-opt the story of the Catholic virgin for the purposes of Protestant male desire. One example is Daniel Pratt's *The Life of the Blessed St. Agnes, Virgin and Martyr* (1677), which recounts the story of the sixth-century Roman virgin who renounces marriage because of her commitment to Christianity.[17] The pagan Roman authorities finally send Agnes to a house of prostitution, but her supernatural virginity blinds the men who come to debauch her. Virgins like Agnes, one of the many virgin martyrs credited with the establishment of early Christianity in defiance of pagan persecution, have spiritual knowledge and faith that induce them to defy male authorities. In his dedication, the author Daniel Pratt, of this seventeenth-century English version of the story, argues that Agnes is meant to serve as an exemplar of ideal femininity and thus, rather unpredictably, to induce his friend Robert Stafford to marry:

> the noble Agnes will revenge all those fair Females; whose charms you have hitherto so stoutlie resisted. I do not hereby intend to make the Chast Saint a Bawd to any impure Love (for although in her life time she professe'd Virginity, yet she never question'd the lawfulness of the Marriage Bed,) but only to animate you to the search of some Heroine, who hath all those Virtues you see that the Sex is capable of. (A4–5)

Through this dedication, Agnes's own profession of virginity is ignored, buried in parentheses, and deemed irrelevant to her status as exemplar. Her virginity serves as a signifier of her virtue and thus, for a Protestant male, of her marriageability, not as sign of her sanctification and permanent commitment to avoid sexuality. She is a paragon of female virtue, both because of her virginity and despite her commitment to maintaining it, which the text diminishes.

This version of Agnes is a complete revision of the traditional virgin martyr story, which imagines that the sanctified virgin martyr has access to privileged information that supersedes temporal male desire and will. Under a model of revelation that the virgin martyr experiences, God's will supersedes man's will, including the temporal needs of succession, procreation, and so on. The Virgin Mary, though not a martyr, is a prime example of this mechanism: God's will works through her virgin body, nullifying Joseph's sexual right to her and to legitimate heirs by her. The subversive potential of this possibility is of course limited under early modern Catholicism: the truth of revelations made to religious women like St. Teresa had to be authorized by their male confessors/superiors. But many times the skeptical men are proven wrong in their estimation of female revelation by rapture, thereby creating martyrs like Dorothea and Agnes, as well as providing evidence that women are sometimes the privileged recipients of God's will. This ecclesiastical view of virginity circumvents the problem, articulated in the works of Marvell and Cavendish, that female libertine desires will be made subservient to male will. In the strongest ecclesiastical argument for virginity, St. Jerome makes the perplexing suggestion that virginity may actually transcend divine power: "I tell you without hesitation, that though God is almighty, He cannot restore a virginity that has been lost."[18] I am suggesting, of course, that female asceticism imagines a way around male (parental, spousal, political, and perhaps even divine) will and authority. The seventeenth-century English version of *The Life of the Blessed St. Agnes* imagines, conversely, that the privileged devotion of the nun will serve, rather than impede, masculine sexual and procreative desires.

I have been arguing that depictions of convents often reconfigure Catholic ideals of virginity for Protestant causes by demythologizing virginity and putting it in the service of reasonable and desirable Protestant femininity. The wildly popular and influential *The Portuguese Letters* relies upon a completely different notion of the attractions of convent life, positing irrational and self-destructive female emotional desire, rather than libertine material pleasure or pious virginity, as the source of the cloister's attractions. *The Portuguese Letters* fantasizes that sexual rapture for a man may mimic spiritual rapture by God and thus that rapture is the foundation for chastity. The passionate nun seems to effortlessly transfer her ecstatic devotion from God to her lover and back again. Even in the absence of the French lover, the nun's irrational faith keeps her chaste, and when her faith in him has disappeared, her faith in God ensures that she will take no other earthly lovers. Rapturous spiritual absorption thus provides the foundation for amorous devotion and chastity, and amorous devotion provides the basis for virtue, as well as for readerly interest. Other critics have noted the link between female religious rapture and amorous devotion in this text. For Rosalind Ballaster, the conflation of these modes of devotion constitutes the desirability of the Portuguese nun (and of *The Portuguese Letters*) (100–101). I argue, conversely, that this text, like other such texts linking female sexuality and spirituality at this time, degrades (or secularizes) Catholic female spirituality by linking it to sexual materiality. The Portuguese nun's rapture produces no special spiritual knowledge or political powers. The connection between religious and amorous devotion in *The Portuguese Letters* is not natural in that it is not an accepted historical convention, but it rather functions to secularize Catholic ideas of feminine spirituality: it converts spiritual experience to sexual desire, sanctification to consummation.[19] If so, then the demystification (de-Catholicization, depoliticization) of the nun in this text perhaps forms the foundation of its popular appeal in England.

Catholic mysticism is sometimes linked to the Church of England's other antagonist: radical Protestant sects whose claims to direct experience of God were derided as "enthusiasm."[20] When the third Earl of Shaftesbury tries to recuperate enthusiasm in *Characteristics of Men, Manners, Opinions, Times* (1711), he explicitly distances his positive and secular brand of enthusiasm from suspicious and feminized spiritual practices:

> Mysticks and *Fanaticks* are known to abound as well in our *Reform'd*, as in the *Romish* churches. The pretended Floods of Grace, pour'd into the Bosoms of the *Quietists, Pietists* and those who favour the exstatick way of Devotion, raise such Transports as by their own Proselytes are confes'd to have something strangely agreeable, and in common with what ordinary Lovers are us'd to feel. And it has been remark'd by many, That the *Female* Saints have been the greatest Improvers of this *soft* part of Religion. What truth there may be in the related Operations of this pretended Grace and *amorous* Zeal, or in the Accounts of what has usually passed between the *Saints* of each Sex in these devout Extasys, I shall leave the Reader to examine: supposing he will find credible Accounts, sufficient to convince him of the dangerous progress of ENTHUSIASM in this amorous *Lineage*. (Volume 3, 38)

In depicting religious rapture as mere sexual rapture and in locating the susceptibility to such confusion in women, Shaftesbury, like the author of *The Portuguese Letters*, transforms ecstatic female spirituality into mundane sexuality. Like the devotion of quietists and pietists—and like papists—sexual enthusiasm is politically irrelevant, "ordinary love" that passes, in the eyes of the ignorant, for something meaningful. The popularity of *The Portuguese Letters* may demonstrate an ambivalent English desire for its Catholic past and for the irrational rapture associated with it. But it also suggests a strategy whereby that nostalgia was managed, in that the ideals of Catholic femininity serve Protestant ideology: the Catholic nun's rapture is paradoxically her recommendation for ideal Protestant femininity. By downgrading rapture from a spiritual experience to mundane sexual pleasure, and thus amenable to chaste marriage and antithetical to lifelong virginity, this view of female rapture upholds Protestant sexual politics and a political structure that excludes females as well as Catholicism, which is at this time, as Frances Dolan has persuasively argued, feminized.[21]

The infamous *Venus in the Cloister* (1683), by Jean Barrin, even more obviously denigrates religious rapture by suggesting that sexual rapture will actually cure religious rapture and irrationality.[22] The two nuns whose conversation structures the pornographic narrative, both named after famous virgin martyrs, Angela and Agnes, describe their sexual experiences as a process of initiation into reason and out of ignorance and superstition. Angela, the more experienced of the two, recounts the story of Dorothy, also named for a famous virgin martyr, whose brutal self-mortifications induce an "amorous trance" and sexual orgasm rather than religious rapture (145). As a result of this experience, the young nun, who has been distracted nearly to insanity by her spiritual efforts, finds herself enlightened: "her mind which was before clouded and buried in thick darkness, found itself unveiled at the very instant of all its obscurity (146). Unlike the virgin martyr Dorothea, this Dorothy's enlightenment comes from finally capitulating to sexuality. But *Venus in the Cloister* is no libertine text. Although it is pornographic and extols the virtues of sex, it ultimately valorizes chastity over the excesses (and Catholicism) of libertinism. Catholicism is portrayed as a religion of sexual extremes: ascetic renunciation or perverse debauchery of natural sexuality. Over the course of their dialogues, Agnes, under Angela's tutelage, dallies with libertinism. The evidence that Agnes's initiation is complete is her realization that excessive libertinism is perverse, but moderated pleasure is not profane: "For what hurt can there be found in pleasure when it is well regulated?" (159). Agnes's narrative thus converts her from a virgin to a libertine and finally to a woman capable of chaste sexuality, that is, from a Catholic to a Protestant. Catholicism perverts the nuns' sexuality, but through education and experiment, both nuns find their way toward the moderate and chaste Protestant path.

These nuns are thus potentially perfect Protestants, who engage in extramarital sex and live in a nunnery only because the abusive Catholic system has forced them there, making them "slaves" who must renounce their "rights" and suppress "Love, Interests, Desires, and Wills" due to the tyrannical needs of their families and the Catholic Church (24, 132). Angela's parents, for example, compel her to take orders so that her brother can claim his "right of nobility" and inherit all of the family's estate. This configuration of female monasticism and patriarchal inheritance completely reverses the one found in Marvell: instead of the sexually mature virgin being necessary for a Protestant dynastic cause, her claims to an inheritance represent an impediment to a Catholic one. Both texts, though, make a case for aligning the virgin/nun with Protestantism: "Upon Appleton House" because she must renounce libertinism in support of the just puritan cause, and *Venus in the Cloister* because only Protestantism offers regulated pleasure and any possibility of female self-definition. The Protestant agenda of *Venus in the Cloister* is quite explicit. For example, Agnes's sexual and philosophical conversions lead her to the following insight:

> We must own, that there are many abuses practiced in our Religion, and I am not now at all surprised, that so many Nations have separated themselves from our Church, to apply themselves literally to the Scriptures. (81)

While some critics, Alexander Pettit for example, find the Protestant rhetoric in the text merely a ruse for its pornography, I argue, conversely, that its pornography is crucial to its Protestant agenda.[23] The pornography provides not only a salacious motivation to read the text but also a critique of perverse Catholic men and the Catholic system that produces them and thus offers a rationale for Protestants to appropriate the Catholic nun. It is true that Catholicism provides an alibi for the pornography (this is why it is important that the nuns are at least nominally Catholic), but it also true that patriarchal and perverse Catholicism produces the pornography, and thus anti-Catholicism is one of the main effects of the pornography.[24] The text's attitude toward sexuality naturalizes conjugal marriage and the bourgeoisie, and thereby subordinates the erotic to the political, as Donna Stanton argues (75–79). In short, the Protestant critique of Catholicism in *Venus in the Cloister* simultaneously produces pornography and promises to eradicate it via marriage.

Thus far I have been discussing two kinds of representations of convent life: those, like "Upon Appleton House" and *The Convent of Pleasure*, that suggest that the convent offers material pleasures and that women must forgo those pleasures in the service of male political and reproductive goals; and those like *The Life of the Blessed St. Agnes*, *The Portuguese Letters*, and *Venus in the Cloister* that imagine the Catholic nun, whether chaste or rapturous, as an exemplary—if not fully compliant—candidate for Protestant marriage and procreation. In the texts I have discussed, commitment to virginity is repeatedly found in conflict with male dynastic schemes, and female desire for virginity obstructs rather than facilitates male interest in legitimate procreation. Lawrence Anderton's *The English Nunne*, one of the few texts that countered, from a Catholic perspective, the onslaught of English anti-monastical literature, specifically addresses this aspect of the convent's politico-social impact. A potential nun, contemplating parental disapproval, easily recognizes the greater authority of God, saying,

> My *Father* gave a being to my body in this world; *God* is the supreme agent, giving creation to both of my soule and body; My *Father* intreats, but *God* out of his irresistible power, commands. . . . Why should my Soule be so trayterous [*sic*] to his divine Majesty, and so hurtfull to it selfe, as to prefer a temporall Father, before a divine Father. (24)

This text is interesting to me because it explicitly pits the authority of the father, and by the use of "trayterous," of the king as well, against the authority of God in order to argue that devoting one's life to reproduction of mortal dynasties is a decidedly inferior goal to cloistered spirituality. The young nun's male confessor asks her whether "the Sanctity of a Soule doth not incomparably exceed the benefit of Posterity?" (32) and denigrates the pursuit of biological heirs by suggesting, much like Richardson's Clarissa will, that Christ's sacrifice made familial distinctions irrelevant:

> Now these men (so much prizing posterity) need not to feare the want of an heyre; For who is he, that hath not many of his Kindred, though not many of his name? . . . Christ doth at that tyme remunerate, or repay a man (making him his heyre) with an eternall reward. (32)

The life of a nun, then, explicitly challenges the notion that virginity is valuable because it promotes patrilinear legitimacy. Catholic mystical virginity depends upon the supposition that God's will and man's will may diverge, thus providing a way for women to opt out of human authority and making virginity a threat, rather than an asset, to male schemes of paternity, dynasty formation, and so on.[25] The "thirsting and insatiable desire of continuing a descent in bloud," is, in this defense of nunneries, "most unworthy a Christian" (33). Catholic convents thus potentially pose a threat to all forms of political power that depend upon active female sexuality. Political philosophy during the Protestant revolution, exemplified by Robert Filmer's *Patriarcha* (1680) and John Locke's response in *Two Treatises on Government* (1690), focused on explicating the analogy between the family and the state. This is one reason that a commitment to virginity, which (combined with an option of convent life) allows a woman to evade paternal authority, similarly, at least by analogy, threatens the authority of the state. Indeed Margaret Ferguson has argued that the specter of female choice of virginity over marriage "haunted English Protestant discourses on the household and its theoretically analogous sphere, the state" (8).

Convents at this time, moreover, had a connection to politics that was more than just analogical. The Catholic loyalist cause on the Continent was associated with and supported by English monasteries abroad, which offered refuge as well as financial and logistical support to Stuart loyalists. Mary Knatchbull's convent, for example, loaned money to Charles I.[26] Moreover, Catholic obedience to the pope, and by extension to God, made them always potentially treasonous to the Protestant monarch of England. The Protestant Alexander Chapman, for example, claimed, "it is impossible to be of their religion and heere to be a true subject in civill obedience."[27] Monasteries and convents were seen at this time as dangerous breeding grounds for a continental Catholic political threat. Not surprisingly, then, virginity and religious seclusion became embroiled in the national cause as well as familial politics. One patriotic investigator published a *List of Monasterys, Nunnerys, and Colleges Belonging to the English Papists in Several Popish Countries beyond the Sea* (1700), which provided intelligence of at least 51 monasteries, both male and female, in order to "inform the People of England of the Measures taken by the Popish Party for the reestablishing of Popery in these Nations." There were also concerns, both from Catholics and Protestants, about the future of the property and wealth of the former monasteries in England, which represented a vast material support for England's economy, and which thus became a potent political lightening rod.[28]

The sexual depravity of priests and nuns is one of the most preva-
lent themes in seventeenth-century anti-monastical writing and was
one of the key weapons in the political struggle between English
Protestants and Catholics. In anti-Catholic literature, ascetic rejection
of sexuality almost inevitably leads to perverse sexuality, which can,
due to resultant illegitimacy and female debauchery, threaten political
power. For example, a pamphlet attributed to Daniel Defoe (1700)
proposes to castrate all priests found in England in order to protect
England and its virtuous women from Catholicism. In this tract, for-
bidding marriage is a "Doctrine of Devils" (5). Because of their
celibacy and their excessive access to women, the author argues, "The
Priests Testicles are the greatest Promoters of the Pope's Empire"
(15). In fact, this pamphlet argues, Rome insists on celibacy precisely
because it will lead priests to debauch women and thus will allow
Catholicism to "usurp the temporal as well as the spiritual sword" (5).
Texts like this make clear the link between sexual and national politics.
The theme of Catholicism, especially monasticism, as sexually perverse has a long tradition but repeatedly gets recycled in the service of
particular political struggles.[29] And this is especially true at the end of
the seventeenth century, when English audiences are inundated with
tales of the depraved sexuality of the monastery.

In Protestant representations of monastical life at this time, nuns
can be recuperated (converted) but male Catholic ecclesiastics, that is,
Catholics who represent a real political threat, are irredeemable repro-
bates. *The Monk Unvail'd* (1678) excoriates monks as "Dogs, Goats,
Monsters of Adultery," who "go beyond whatever *Petronius, Bocacius*
or *Aretine*, have described (24)." [30] This focus on the male Catholic
as irredeemable, while the female Catholic is converted into the
exemplar of Protestant piety, underscores the extent to which the virgin was crucial to the Protestant political cause. One final contributing factor to making the nun's conversion highly politicized is that
Protestant political aims at this time were plagued by problems of the
legitimacy of monarchical heirs: the Duke of Monmouth's literal illegitimacy and William's link via marriage to a tenuous claim. By transferring illegitimacy onto Catholics (the supposititious heir scandal
being one example and Catholic pornography being another) anti-
Catholic polemic claims chastity and legitimacy, and even virginity, for
Protestantism and thus supports the Protestant "destiny" of England.

In this campaign to root out a continental Catholic threat against
English Protestantism, Antonio Gavin makes his triumphant entrance
as an informed defector. In 1691, he published *The Frauds of Romish
Monks and Priests* (and a second volume in 1725), and in 1693,

A Short History of Monastical Orders, both of which criticize the abuses of the monastical system. But it is his *Master-Key to Popery*, which was first published in 1724 and which was repeatedly reprinted into the nineteenth century, that seals his claim as one of Protestant England's key weapons in the struggle against continental papacy. His anti-Catholic exposés, claiming to be true but hardly conforming to our modern standards of evidence, were wildly popular and controversial—so much so that he claimed to have been threatened by the pope.[31] Like much anti-Catholic propaganda, Gavin's texts impugn the virgin birth, virginity, and celibacy as contrary to nature. His propaganda links the dangers of Catholic femininity, virginity, and irrationality and depends upon the stereotype of Catholics as both ignorant and deceitful, equally capable of naively believing in miracles and cynically faking them. A long section of the three-volume *Master-Key to Popery* is devoted to debunking the purported "miracles" of three nuns as nothing more than simple fraud foisted upon an ignorant audience of believers. Gavin provides many examples of deceitful nuns and priests, but I want to focus on one that underscores almost every aspect of this particular brand of anti-Catholic vitriolic.

"Sor Valera," a young girl from Zaragoza, falls in love with someone considered unsuitable by her family and enters a Domincan convent in order to avoid marrying the man chosen by her father.[32] Valera is not attracted to the convent but rather forced to go there by unscrupulous familial tyranny. Her story thus predictably pits the nunnery against family procreative schemes. While in the convent, Sor Valera learns to feign virtue, and her seeming piety and austerity incite people to admire her as "a second Virgin Mary of our time" (205). Her lover, Don Christoval, becomes a war hero, thereby challenging the judgment of Valera's Catholic parents in rejecting him, and returns to live near her convent. They contrive to see each other repeatedly until Valera becomes pregnant, which threatens to expose them. Pregnancy is often represented in early modern texts as the one thing that will reveal the perfidy of women, but Catholics, perhaps through the inheritance of the Virgin Mary, can frequently circumvent this truth of the body. The reprobate nun sends her hapless lover to a Jesuit priest in order to procure, "Pristina Virginatis" a "wonderful" remedy, "so necessary and beneficial" for their troubles (207). The lover fears that it is an abortificant, for Catholics specialize in such profane things, but the young nun assures him that the 50 pistoles he pays will procure not a sin, exactly, but rather the illusion of a miracle.[33] This is another stereotype prevalent in anti-Catholic propaganda: Catholic belief in miracles is portrayed as ridiculous, and yet

Catholics often have unholy access to medicines and potions with miraculous properties. "For you must know," one anti-monastical treatise asserts, "all Monks are Physitians [*sic*]."[34] Valera tells the mother prioress and elder nuns that she has had a revelation that she is miraculously with child. Her faith in the efficacy of this miracle brew is total, and she assures her lover, "The Operation of the Remedy being Infallible, they will find me so, and both midwives, Physicians and Nuns, will give the Thing out as a Miracle" (208).[35] Upon finding herself "fit for the Tryall," her predictions prove accurate, as eight midwives say she remains "as good a Virgin as the Day she came into the World," and notarized announcements about her virginity are sent all over (209, 210). After the birth of a boy "prophet," which she endures alone and then claims to have slept through, the "foolish, infatuated" Catholics come from far and wide to idolize her and the child, greedily absconding with whatever might be converted into a relic (212). The story thus criticizes Catholic idolatry and Catholic belief in miracles, which are supported by their adherence to the doctrine of infallibility and exemplified by their belief in the possibility of another prophetic virgin birth.

While Gavin's text does not limit its excoriation of Catholic abuses to women, this is a particularly female kind of scandal. It is Valera and not her lover who manages the whole affair, while throughout the narrative, many men suspect her. Her confessor insists that he "never will believe" her pregnancy is a miracle, while another priest confidently asserts, "Time will be against false Virginities" (209, 210). And the archbishop, being "a very good man," suspects something more than the ignorant, and mostly female, populace and thus demands an inquiry (212). The ruse continues as long as it does because of cultural practices that give privacy and authority to women: the nuns are cloistered in their convent and the midwives allow no physician to be part of their investigation by insisting that such inspections are the midwives' "Right and Property . . . by a Possession from the beginning of the World" (210). In this way, the text argues against female seclusion: without the watchful and skeptical eyes of men, it implies, females will fall from virtue into ignorance and corruption. The Catholic belief in things like infallibility, virgin powers, and miracles is countered by Protestant skepticism, including a sense of human limitation. This text suggests that Catholicism is dangerously attractive, not only because it facilitates debauchery but also because it provides false simplicity and thus relief from a more complicated worldview: a world difficult to read, where material pleasures are limited and dangerous. Feminized Catholics are attracted to simplicity and thus susceptible to corruption.

Sor Valera is surely a great degenerate, but in a strange twist of moralizing, she is not the one ultimately culpable for her sins. This story suggests that while it is female virtue that is at stake in Catholic abuses, it is ultimately men who bear the burden of responsibility. Referring to the medicine that allows her to feign the miracle, the narrator tells us "by this Remedy, the Jesuits have got great Riches . . . they ought to consider that by it they encourage Vice; and it is certain that if there was not such a Remedy, many young Ladies would be more Vertuous than they are" (215). This link between female lewdness and male responsibility is often echoed in anti-Catholic propaganda. In many anti-Catholic tracts at this time, women are the site of irrationality and vulnerability, and thus it is not totally their fault that they become ensnared by Catholicism. The story of Sor Valera suggests that it is often difficult to tell the difference between sin and sanctity and between good and evil, since something may appear to be its opposite. In the case of Sor Valera, both a madman and the archbishop worry that Valera may in fact be the object of supernatural intervention, but that it might be Satan instead of God who has impregnated her. Whereas a virgin gave birth to Christ, it is also possible, according to these men, that "the Antichrist [will] be born by a nun" (214). It is only men who recognize how difficult it is to tell God from the devil, good from evil. Thus, while men, mostly Jesuits, get the blame for the abuses that result from this complexity, it is also men, Protestant ones, who bear the burden of responsibility for reforming these abuses. The text, then, locates its theological and epistemological struggles "between men," to invoke Eve Kosofsky Sedgwick's famous formulation.[36]

Gavin's story draws on elements of the convent stories discussed earlier, but it combines them in a way that eliminates nostalgia for Catholicism, especially in terms of a model for English femininity. Like the convents of Cavendish and Marvell, the one in Gavin's story allows women to pursue libertine desires, but there is no wistfulness here: the libertine desires of the women are not natural but perverted by Catholicism, which also prevents rational male intervention. Gavin's story likewise locates rapture and irrationality in women, but the rapture is faked, rather than genuine, and it serves female interests rather than male. The notion that rapture allows a young female to pit God's will against the demands of her earthly male authorities naturally invokes the possibility that she could manipulate this belief in order to defy men, as Peter Brown has argued (80–81). And sure enough, the Catholic belief in miracles means that Valera can dupe ignorant believers and thwart rational male efforts to expose her.

Gavin thus suggests that the monastical system allows both irrationality and ruthless self-interest to thrive because they mutually reinforce each other. In this, as in much anti-Catholic writing at the turn of the eighteenth century, nuns are not really virgins, and Catholic miracles are evidence of both corruption and naïve among Catholics. Protestantism, by contrast, is the truly chaste and truly reasonable religion.

While Gavin is clearly a polemicist, his arguments are similar to those of the serious Protestant historian Gilbert Burnet (1673). Early in his career, Burnet compiled a list of the "ridiculous stories" of saints' miracles that the Church of Rome "compel[s] her members to believe," including the story of a counterfeit virgin birth.[37] His *First Part of the History of the Reformation of the Church of England* (1681) credits the infamous story of the Maid of Kent, who faked revelations, with paving the way for the seizure of the monasteries. The "Monstrous Disorders" and "abominations" that reformers found in the monasteries were, according to Burnet, "equal to any that were in *Sodom*" (190–191). Burnet leaves the details of these monstrosities vague and ripe for speculation, since they are "not fit to be spoken of, much less enlarged on, in a work of this Nature," but he shares a perspective, if not a rhetorical strategy, with Gavin (191). Writing after the Restoration and during the period of Jacobite uprisings, writers such as Gavin and Burnet reached back in history and across the Continent for stories of Catholic abuses, as a way of reconciling the English to Protestant rule.

In general, Catholics at this time defend monasticism by claiming that it is not a corruption of the early church but rather a central component of it.[38] Protestants, for their part, stake their claim to superiority based on their own adherence to the ancient church, arguing that monasticism is a perversion of early Christian ideals.[39] One particularly relevant, for my purposes, example of this argument comes in a tract by Gregory Hascard called *Discourse About the Charge of Novelty* (1683), which argues that the Protestant goal is merely to

> [r]eform the *Romish* corruptions, which had tainted the Vitals of Christianity an indispensable Duty it *was* to preserve the Primitive faith, *like a chast Virgin*, and not suffer it to be longer prostituted to the Designs and Passions of Men by a Solemn Vow. (35–36)

This text metaphorically links Protestantism to virginity even as it derides the Catholic attachment to the Virgin Mary and deems the Catholic mandate of clerical celibacy to be "novelty."[40] In short, it simultaneously manages to criticize the Catholic ideal of virginity and to claim its symbolic capital for Protestantism. By impugning Catholic models of sexual abstinence as unnatural, productive of perversity, and impedimentary to reason, such anti-Catholicism, like the many versions of the nun's conversion that I have been examining, claims for Protestantism the virtuous, attractive, and temporarily virginal nun.

DESIRE, SECULAR AND SACRED

In the last section I argued that emergent Protestant political ascendancy required a derogation of Catholic models of sanctification and a conversion of the figure of the virgin from sanctified and ascetic nun into the chaste and fertile wife, the paragon of Protestant virtue. This conversion of the nun depends upon the reconfiguration of her desire and her will, since she must turn one, or preferably both, toward mortal objects of desire.[41] There are several reasons that this reconceptualization of female subjectivity happens, at least partially, via imaginative writings about convents. One reason is historical: convents as sites of female desire and of desirable females were very nearly eliminated in seventeenth-century English society, and yet they remained temporally and geographically proximate and thus readily available as imaginative sites for the reconfiguration of female desire and desirability. Moreover, as I suggested earlier, the fundamental purpose of the monastic routine is the manipulation of individual desire and individual will. And finally, since the figure of the nun had a nearly iconic power, her virtue provided a stock of symbolic capital in the form of a connection to sanctification that could legitimize a fragile authority structure. She therefore had to be eliminated or converted—or both, as things turned out. The convent narratives discussed thus far imagine female desire in several different ways: as self-interested libertinism and thus as dangerous to male political and procreative schemes, as irrational rapturous self-denial, or as ruthlessly rational self-interest. All of these representations of female desire can be made to serve emergent Protestant ideology: the libertine desires of women can be forcibly subject to repression, or wistfully forsaken, for greater political needs, and the rapturous or abstemious virgin can be imagined as the ideal Protestant wife. In these versions of the nun's conversion, the purging of Catholicism will inevitably contribute to social stability by redirecting female desire and will to outcomes that are useful to an Anglican state.

I turn now to two female authors of the late seventeenth century—Aphra Behn and Mary Astell—who imagine that the nun's conversion from ascetic or depraved Catholic to socially useful Protestant might be rather more complicated, in terms of its implications for both female desire and social order. The differences between these two writers are more obvious than their similarities: the withdrawn, intellectual, and proper Astell and the public, popular, and bawdy Behn are not typically discussed together. Behn wrote "libertine" poetry, scandalous plays, and amatory fiction, while Astell committed herself, anonymously for the most part, to the lofty philosophical debates of the age. Their philosophical inclinations mirror these generic and personal differences. Behn's allegiances to Rochester and to Charles II suggest a libertine/materialist bent, which is quite the opposite of Astell's Platonic/Cartesian inclinations.[42] From these very different personal, literary, and philosophical perspectives, Behn and Astell use the convent for thinking about the very real effects on women, and on society, of the paradigmatic, national, and ongoing conversion of the virgin. Moreover, they come to share a belief in the dangerously antisocial implications of an emergent model of female desire that depends on a separation of religion and ethics. This accounts, I will end by arguing, for their shared, and seemingly paradoxical, allegiances to both feminist and politically conservative causes.

Little can be said definitively about Aphra Behn's theological inclinations: probably raised Catholic and definitively a Stuart loyalist, her writing nonetheless evidences some freethinking tendencies, although she never, as far as we know, publicly declared religious allegiance.[43] Aligned philosophically with her mentor, Rochester, whose libertine career culminated in an embrace of Catholicism on his deathbed, Behn has typically been associated more with libertinism's iconoclastic derogation of secular and religious hypocrisy than with any positive theological purpose. Nonetheless, Catholicism—and monasticism in particular—figures prominently in her writing: *The Rover, The Feign'd Curtezans, The Fair Jilt*, and *Love Letters Between a Nobleman and his Sister* all feature monasteries as alternatives to romantic or sexual love. Her amatory fiction frequently deploys the figure of the nun for the purposes of political critique. My own fascination with amatory fiction, and with Behn's in particular, has to do with the fact that nuns and convents appear so frequently in this genre that is generally understood to be about female sexual desire and that at the same time is so often read as political allegory. The links, in Behn's amatory fiction, among sex, politics, emergent philosophies of desire, and convents suggest that the late seventeenth-century fascination with nuns was crucial to working out England's theological-political future and the theory of desire that would form the foundation of its secular ethics. It is not my purpose to argue for Behn's Catholicism. Rather, I argue that she employs a Catholic-based critique of emergent Protestant society for ends that are simultaneously feminist, political, and generically innovative.

Behn's fiction interrogates the links between father, husband, monarch, and God that were at the heart of late seventeenth-century political philosophy. The identity of the patriarch in all his incarnations suffered a profound period of instability in the latter half of the seventeenth century, and this instigated an unprecedented revitalization of English philosophy regarding the nature of political, spiritual, and affective allegiance. Hobbes maintained the need for subordination to a central authority, but he scandalously discredited the divine right of patriarchs. Filmer articulated the conservative position that the authority of the patriarch, both king and father, is divinely ordained through the inheritance of Adam and thus that there is a seamless chain of authority, to which the individual will should be subordinated, from God to husband. Locke's famous reply in the *Two Treatises on Government* denied a natural right of authority for both kings and husbands/fathers and invested the power of consent in the governed. Beginning with *Love Letters Between a Nobleman and his Sister* (1684–7) and continuing for the rest of her life, Behn wrote amatory fiction that intervenes in this debate by recounting the repeated failure of sexual, political, and spiritual commitments. Her heroines, often in and out of convents, repeatedly make vows, to God and to husbands, that they cannot keep. In an important argument, Susan Staves reads the failure of these religious and romantic vows as allegories for thinking about the problem of political vows and thus as a masculine, or gender-neutral, problem (1979, 191–252). In fact, there is a long scholarly tradition of reading amatory fiction, including Behn's, as political allegory. Ballaster, for example, argues that the interest in feminine subjectivity in Behn's fiction is a "serviceable fiction" that provides "a means of articulating party politics through the mirror of sexual politics, in which the feminine acts as substitute for the masculine, signifier to his signified" (84).[44] But I want, instead, to take at face value the issue of the vows of Behn's heroines as a female problem, because the object of all vows except romantic is, at this time, invariably male, which puts female vow takers in a rather different position than men. During the late seventeenth century, men were not merely allegories for God, but under both residual and emergent ideology, men and God were inherently linked. Under patriarchalism, men are God's agents, and under a theory of companionate marriage, men are God's substitutes. Though idolatry is derogated by Protestant theologies, Protestant society requires a kind of secular idolatry of women in that they must submit their will, and their property, to their husbands. They must do this, however, without the patriarchal theory that links the husband to the divine: without, that is, any reason for faith. Even Locke, the strongest proponent of contractual relations and liberal rights, argues that, as the "abler and stronger" of the two, the husband's will must prevail in cases where husband and wife have "different wills" (1967, 321). Given the fact that debates over patriarchy were exactly about the literal relationships among sexual, spiritual, and political allegiance, it seems important to attend to the differences and connections among these modes of allegiance, rather than to conflate them, in our critical practices.

I turn now to one exemplary instance of the way that Behn's fiction imagines the de-sanctification of the nun and its subsequent reorganization of female desire and vows. Isabella, the pious and beautiful young heroine of *The History of the Nun* elopes from her nunnery with a charming aristocrat who soon after reported dead in battle. After three years in mourning, Isabella marries again. When her first husband returns, Isabella kills him with a pillow and then, with perhaps the most subversive representation of female domesticity in English fiction, engineers the murder of her second husband with just a couple of stitches from her sewing needle. From pious nun, to sexually desirous virgin who becomes a virtuous wife and finally a murderess, Isabella's story is exemplary of Behn's investigation of the links between sacred and romantic devotion and between female desire and social ethics.

Isabella's conscription to life as a nun is portrayed as a choice of reason. Her "evenness of mind" is highly praised, and she views not only the world, but also her devotions, with a mien that is "far from transport" (144). Although she desires to be virtuous and although she performs her duties in an exemplary manner, Isabella's ruthless ascetic regime does little to mitigate her nascent attraction for her first husband, Henault. The Catholic nun's life is portrayed, contrary to representations like those in Marvell and Cavendish, as a regime of repression without material or spiritual attractions for a young woman, and thus her escape, based on sexual desire, can be seen as liberating her from this oppression. I want to argue, however, that Isabella's sexual passion, far from liberating her from ascetic repression, in fact winds up repeating the pattern of disillusionment with devotion. Isabella's rapturous devotion to Henault, in contrast to her religious vow, is depicted as a product of idolatry. She maintains her determination to keep her vow of chastity, despite her increasing sexual attraction for Henault, until Henault's sister surprises Isabella by showing her a picture of him: "at the first sight of it," Isabella "turns as pale as ashes" and "almost faints" (150). After this idolatrous, that is Catholic, introduction into the rapture of love, Isabella is soon enough breaking her vows of chastity, stealing money from the nunnery and running off to marry Henault. Much misfortune ensues, including their struggles with infertility and the reported death of Henault in battle. Despite her vow of devotion to him, Isabella, in the absence of his physical form or at least the credible possibility of his existence, cannot maintain her rapture. Isabella marries again, this time motivated by rational self-interest rather than by a self-destructive sexual obsession. In short, Isabella's devotion to God falters with the idolatrous emergence of Henault, and her devotion to Henault falters in his absence. Although they emanate from opposite motives, her vow to God and her vow to Henault prove equally untenable, as reasoned devotion and idolatrous passion both ultimately fail Isabella.

The convent grate that initially separates the lovers is a metaphor for the relationship of God to humans and monarch to subjects. In seducing Isabella, Henault makes a compelling case that remaining outside the grate, that is, being forced to undertake devotion that will be "eternal without hope," is dangerous and oppressive to humans. He seduces Isabella by suggesting that because sexual passion, unlike Catholic spirituality, is within the realm of human will to satisfy, it should be privileged. He proves, however, to be an inadequate object of worship because of his own humanity. When Isabella is ready to "give herself up to love and serve him" as "her monarch" with "no other consideration in the world," Henault realizes that he cannot function as a God or a monarch because he is beholden to his own father and to his country's political cause (169). Henault's love asks to be treated like the Catholic God; for example, Isabella must abandon the world for him, just as a nun would. But, leaving aside the question of what God can deliver, Henault does not have the power to fill that role for Isabella. As a worldly patriarch, he fails because his power is limited; he leaves Isabella in order to satisfy the demands of his own political and familial duties. As a comment on the connections between faith and love, Isabella's history suggests that neither spiritual nor sexual absorption can be sustained in the absence of evidence and visual reinforcement. As such, *The History of the Nun* invokes a key component of the seventeenth-century theological debates: is faith maintained by idols, mysteries, revelation, and rapture—or, as the Anglicans mostly argued, should religious belief be only based on verifiable probabilities? The debate, of course, hinges on the absence of God and the possibility of belief in the absence of sensual evidence. Henault's absence functions as a metaphor for God's absence. Similarly, since the problem of allegiance to the king during absences like death and exile had been paramount to loyalists like Behn for several decades, Henault's absence does function, as Staves argues, to raise questions about political allegiance. Isabella's failure to maintain her faith in and love for Henault is a comment on the difficulty of maintaining belief in an absent God or an absent king. But it is also, unquestionably, a comment on the inadequacy of sexual passion as a substitute. *The History of the Nun* suggests that even if nuns make the most desirable women, the nun cannot be easily converted into the wife because the husband cannot easily be substituted for God.

A major shift in ideas about the relationship between sexual and spiritual love occurs, according to Debora Kuller Shuger, in the late seventeenth century. She argues that before the Restoration and the ascendance of Protestant theology, spirituality and sexuality are not seen as antithetical impulses (1994, 179–182). With the revolutions of the latter seventeenth century, eros and agape are separated by a failure of agape. Because God, and his agent the king, have abdicated, there is, according to Shuger, an increasing emphasis on sexual and romantic love. This may account for the popular fascination with both *The Portuguese Letters* and the story of Eloisa and Abelard— Pope's poem on that subject being only the most prominent example—in which the monastery is imagined as an impediment to sexual fulfillment. Pornographic and romantic images of nuns de-sacramentalize love even as they exalt it as more physically and spiritually satisfying than religion. Romantic lovers, no matter how fickle, are more present and faithful than a silent God and a church structure that represses passion. By contrast, Behn's amatory fiction, far from celebrating sexual desire, predicts that eros will be an unsatisfactory substitute, in terms of both female happiness *and* social stability, for love of, and faith in, God. Had she been born earlier, then, Isabella would not have had to choose between sexuality and her vow, and she would need only love, not faith, to sustain her. But in Behn's world, just as love may initially induce the feelings of truth, enthusiasm, or revelation—and the social benefits of those feelings—that the civil wars and Restoration have made difficult to feel about gods or kings, it similarly causes disappointment.

The irony of *The History of the Nun* inheres in the fact that in pursuit of virtue as defined by the admiration of men, as a virtuous daughter, nun, and wife—that is, in trying to align her will and her actions to be in accord with the desire of the figures to which she vows devotion—Isabella becomes a sociopath. Throughout Behn's amatory fiction, the failure of sexual rapture and monogamy to maintain female desire frequently results in inadvertent, in that they are not consciously willed, criminal actions. Behn's reader repeatedly encounters women, frequently nuns, turning adulterous, murderous, libelous, and generally menacing in the face of the failure of their love object. For women in the disenchanted world of Restoration England, the only arena of vows or faith is romantic love, and the failure of these vows, like the failure to comply with political and spiritual vows, has social and ethical consequences. If political vows are meant to maintain social stability, and if spiritual faith, at least under Catholicism and Anglicanism, mandates secular ethics, these social controls only work, Behn's fictions suggest, if the object of vows can sustain the faith of the vow taker. The central political question raised by Behn's amatory fiction is as follows: how does a woman (or a subject, if one is reading allegorically) maintain a stable identity and contribute to a stable society if her object of desire, whose will she tries to divine in order to align her own with it, is unreliable? This question, raising at it does the specter of inevitable male fallibility, goes some way to explaining the later eighteenth-century obsession with the figure of the virgin as one who resists aligning herself with unworthy men and who becomes, in a way, a figure of stability and sanctity *for* men. For this is finally Isabella's dilemma: she has no one to venerate, and yet she stands as the object of devotion for countless people. So important is this role that even after her double murder, bigamy, and execution, Isabella is still venerated as the epitome of female virtue: she is "generally lamented" and "honorably buried" (190).

Critics have noticed that Behn's heroines do not suffer excessively, or even adequately, for their crimes. This results not from Behn's amorality but because it is not women, after all, who are the focus of Behn's social critique. Isabella's unsuccessful conversion from nun to chaste wife is attributed, by the narrator at the beginning and by Isabella at the end, to her initial vow breaking. But ultimately the story is morally ambiguous. At the crucial moment of the execution, the narrator abdicates, as she so often does in Behn's fiction, leaving us only with the image of the radiant Isabella and the reactions of the sentimental and perhaps naïve spectators. As Isabella's "beautiful head" is severed from "her delicate body," the heroine appears both repentant and possessed of a species of calm that is usually only associated with religious certainty (190). While Isabella goes to her death almost sanctified, her two devoted husbands share the ignominious fate of drowning while sewed together to a burlap sack. This moral ambiguity makes more sense if we see the novella as enacting a critique of a society in which nothing is worthy, for women, of faith and vow taking. If a key politico-theological question pertained to the relationship between spirituality and ethics, Behn seems to be suggesting that without spirituality—or in a society in which the only thing worthy of veneration, if anything is at all, is mortal and unstable—social ethics will suffer. As such, sexual desire in Behn's fiction is not an allegory for political desire, but it is a causative actor in social stability. This is why Behn's plots of female desire are political.

In *The History of the Nun*, ethics and religious faith have been divorced from each other in ways that they would not be under Catholicism. This imaginative divorce of ethics from spirituality—and even from desire—leads to neither social nor individual good. Female virtue's failure to produce social good functions as a critique of an emergent, disenchanted ideal of feminine subjectivity, on the basis that it is ultimately detrimental to society. This is why the heroines suffer less than their "victims." It must be noted that this is almost necessarily a critique of Protestantism. It is certainly possible to read Behn's reprobate nuns as evidence of a strain of Catholic nostalgia in Behn. For example, Isabella's most radiant moment occurs in the decapitation scene, which suggests that death brings religious certainty and happiness to this ill-fated nun. Perhaps the most sentimental and nostalgic scene in all of Behn's work is the ordination of Octavio in *Love Letters between a Nobleman and his Sister*. "Never was any thing so magnificent" as this ritual that removes Octavio from the world, which "has nothing in it which can really charm" (379, 383). So moved by this scene, which "gives us a real idea of heaven," the narrator (most atypically for a cynical Behn narrator) exclaims "I fancied myself no longer on earth." (381–382). I hesitate to make too much of the limited nostalgia for Catholicism in Behn, but I do think it is significant that Behn portrays such religious certainty as being available on this earth only for men (a pattern that is repeated in *The Fair Jilt*). By contrast, female pursuit of ecstasy or truth always results in disappointment that rebounds into social crimes. For Behn, the problem of female desire in a disenchanted world portends social chaos.

The historical extinction, evisceration, and inadequacy of various objects of female desire and devotion provides a way of accounting for the generic innovation (or instabilities) of Behn's amatory fiction, the plots of which, exemplified by *The History of the Nun*, can only be described as hyperbolic and the heroines of which, Isabella being a prime case, manifest almost farcical inconsistencies between intention and action. The volatility of female desire in amatory fiction has been the source of great critical interest. John Richetti argues that the "natural instability" of the female heroines of amatory fiction "helps to move the plot along" and helps the characters survive (23). Robert Markley and Molly Rothenberg begin with the assumption that Behn's work is devoted to a critique of repression and argue that the lack of formal unity in Behn's work results from the fact that she draws on a number of "incommensurate discursive strategies" to make this critique (303). But my point is that the formal and subjective instabilities that permeate Behn's fiction—the excessive and erratic nature of both her plots and her heroines—are not motivated by chaotic female desire or its repression but rather by a paucity of faith due to the inadequacy of the object of desire. From this perspective, Behn's "female libertinism" can be seen as a comment not on the strength of female erotic desire for men, but rather on the instability and inadequacy of male objects of desire in the wake of theological and monarchical, not merely sexual, abdications.

My reading of Behn's fiction reveals that the figure of the nun and the problem of female desire were intimately connected to political questions facing England at the end of the seventeenth century. I turn now to the most important female political philosopher and the most famous female Anglican of this period, Mary Astell. Astell's *A Serious Proposal to the Ladies*, which promotes the idea of a Protestant cloister, obviously hit a nerve with the English reading public when it was anonymously published in 1695. This is partially, as Ruth Perry has argued, because it offered a solution to the historical oversupply of marriageable women (105). It also struck an opposite nerve in its critics, who saw in the proposal a potentially pernicious infiltration of Catholicism into Anglicanism. I want to suggest that the proposal also hit a nerve because Astell, like Behn, understood that emergent models of female desire, by-products of the nun's conversion, were both socially dangerous and detrimental to women. While Behn explores the chaos that happens when one treats love as an "Almighty God," Astell sets her task, in *A Serious Proposal to the Ladies*, to rectifying the problem via a philosophical system that imagines a way around mandatory heterosexuality based on the argument that its promise to provide a moral foundation for social stability is bogus.

Astell grounds this most famous proposal for a Protestant nunnery on reason: in particular, on the importance of reason to society and to spirituality and on a woman's reasonableness. She argues for the commonly held conception that Protestantism is the reasonable choice over mystical Catholicism and against the commonly held notion that women are less reasonable than men. This allows her to be simultaneously feminist and staunchly Anglican. Astell figures reason's chief opponent to be the desires of the body, which she variously calls "affections," "passions," and "inclinations." A "Christian Life," according to Astell, "requires a clear Understanding as well as regular Affections, that both together may move the Will to a direct choice of Good" (16). Her philosophical view is rationalist, depending upon a mind/body separation and upon venerating reason and the mind over the body. As such, her argument for a Protestant cloister rests on transcending the material world as much as possible. Her monastery will allow women "to withdraw our selves as much as may be from Corporeal things, that pure Reason may be heard the better" (115). Astell famously and vehemently disagrees with Locke's empiricism and argues that true reason transcends the body rather than depends upon it. Her other antagonist, at least on the surface, is Catholic spirituality, because of its idolatry. As I argued earlier, rapture and revelation—associated with both Catholic mysticism and with dissenting enthusiasm—are models of spirituality that exceed human reason. As such, Astell's proposal depends upon aligning itself with reason and against both Catholicism and radical Protestantism.

Despite her explicit theological commitment, Astell proposes an overtly secular institution. Although she denigrates material satisfactions in favor of philosophical and theological pursuits, Astell's arguments for a female community are secular, based on the "real interest" of the potential members but also on larger sociological grounds. Her convent will, she claims, "amend the present and improve the future age" (6, 18). Astell's proposal is based on the kind of political reform characteristic of, as Defoe terms it, "a projecting age" (1697, 1). Bridget Hill argues that interest in a Protestant nunnery at this time arises from the belief, which may or may not have a basis in fact, that convents were sites for training women in education and piety and thus that their closure in the 1530s led to degradations in female development and an increase in social problems. Astell's scheme, like most seventeenth- and eighteenth-century schemes for Protestant convents, promises earthly benefits like female education. She conspicuously denigrates the Catholic justification for convents and virginity, which holds that the cloister is a place for women who want to pursue spiritual rather than social and political benefits and that sexual abstinence, rather than an act of renunciation, is simultaneously a source of physical stimulation and a vehicle for transcendence. Astell, like Protestants from all ends of the spectrum, imagines that humans, whether elect or reprobate, have to live in the world and that secluding oneself from the world for religious purposes procures neither spiritual nor social benefits.

Astell's proposal for a secular nunnery distances itself from any association with mystical Catholicism by representing such spirituality as, paradoxically, the route to a crippling attachment to the debased material world. For Astell, it is reason, not rapture, that will lead to transcendence of the physical world. She finds no conflict between reason and spirituality; in fact, "understanding," she claims, is the "noblest faculty" of the soul (16). In making her case for the rational bases of Anglicanism and of female equality and for the social benefits of the Protestant nunnery, Astell decries the Catholic model of the nun as both unspiritual and socially dangerous. "Indecent Raptures" will have no place in her female monastery, nor will the "ricketed, starv'd and contracted" devotee who, being "often at her knees," "petition[s] for those Graces which [she] takes no care to Practice" (17). Astell implies that the Catholic view of female sanctity, because it is tied to bodily experience, presents material dangers. Like many of Behn's heroines, such persons are, according to Astell, "always in extremes" and "a perpetual trouble to themselves and others" (17). Astell's high church Anglicanism seems inflected with latitudinarianism, in that it emphasizes reason and implies that sacred goals are indistinguishable from secular goals, like personal happiness and social stability.

Despite her efforts to distance herself from Catholicism, Astell's proposal did not escape the charges of popery and enthusiasm. Patricia Springborg and Perry report that Burnet convinced Queen Anne not to fund Astell's monastery because it threatened to lead to "Popish Orders."[45] The social benefits of her plan were also challenged, most famously by Damaris Masham, who insisted that Astell's cloister was an insidious form of quietism. Astell never developed a proposal for the practical details of her monastery. "To enter into the detail of the particulars," she assures her readers in the first part, "is not now necessary" (24). Nor, it seems, was it necessary two years later when Astell wrote, in response to her critics, a second part of her *Serious Proposal to the Ladies*. In this enigmatic and usually overlooked sequel, which is much more densely philosophical and radical than the first part, Astell articulates a theory of desire that intervenes in the seventeenth-century debate over free will, which developed from the central theological problem of the day: how does one reconcile belief in God's omnipotence with the absence of sure evidence of God's will? And how does one conform to God's will in the absence of knowledge of it, or in the face of selfish desires for something different?

These questions link problems of epistemology with theology, psychology, and ethics.

Early Protestant reformers had challenged the Catholic belief in free will and in the importance of good works (as well the humanist theory of the unbounded human will). Luther, for example, argued that the human will, by itself, is in bondage to sin. In arguing for justification by faith alone, Luther claimed that "without the grace of God, the will produces an act that is perverse and evil."[46] In its most radical forms, like Antinomianism, Protestant theology's rejection of human free will lead to a rejection, at least in the eyes of its detractors, of any ethical code. The relative importance of—and the relationships among—reason, grace, faith, and morality formed the foundation for most of the theological theory of the seventeenth century, with latitudinarians stressing the harmony of reason and morality, while the nonconformists continued to insist, to varying degrees, on the priority of grace over both reason and morality.[47]

If, very generally, Catholics argued for free will and radical Protestants for depravity of the will, the Anglican compromise of the late seventeenth century, propounded by people like Joseph Glanvill, John Wilkins, and Henry More, argued that humans, endowed with innate ideas and reason, have a natural tendency to desire the good, an argument that, at least superficially, circumvents the problems of tension between human will and God's will and between morality and spirituality. A key impetus for much of the compromise of Anglicanism was its ongoing commitment to maintaining the connection between church and state; in propounding their theology, Anglican theorists had to consider earthly political order as well as a future spiritual state. Theories of the will and desire were central to sorting out an Anglican middle way because these problems were central to debates about human morality and thus to theories of governance. The Anglican concept of "laws written into the heart," based on Pauline doctrine, directly challenged Hobbes's argument for the necessity of arbitrary and absolute power, radical Protestant claims that spirituality was virtually irrelevant to secular ethics, and the Catholic emphasis on the importance of freely choosing moral actions as the route to salvation. Moreover, it would be a chief instigator and a central antagonist for Locke's critique of innate ideas and his sensationalist epistemology.

The latitudinarian roots of "laws written into the heart" emphasized reason: the "heart" was seen as synonymous with the mind. But as this doctrine developed, and as the heart (a point that I discuss further in chapter 4) came to take on its modern connotation, as the site of both moral and romantic feeling, a philosophical theory of love became crucial to resolving these debates over free will and episte-mology.[48] That is, while latitudinarians emphasized reason, their descendants, which included both freethinkers and some high church Anglicans, became more divided over the relative importance of the affections to morality. This is the debate into which Astell, following John Norris, entered. Norris's *The Theory and Regulation of Love*, which appeared perhaps not insignificantly in 1688, links love of God with secular ethics. Claiming that, though "obvious enough to any one that will consider," this is an original way to think about morality, Norris argues that "all Virtue and Vice" can be reduced to "the vari-ous Modifications of Love." Norris explicitly links love of God with secular or "corporeal" love. Though the former is "simple desire" and the latter "wishing well to," nonetheless, for Norris, love of God and love of humans are both aspects of the "motion of the soul towards Good" (9). Although the Anglican notion of "laws written in the heart" as a mode of knowing would lose out, as the eighteenth cen-tury progressed, to empiricism, the idea that virtue inheres in secular, especially romantic love, would of course be the foundation for com-panionate marriage and the sentimental novel and thus a crucial com-ponent of secular ethics. It is also, of course, the ideology that Behn's amatory fiction challenges.

Intrigued by Norris's arguments, Mary Astell undertook a corre-spondence with him on the question of God's love. In *Letters Concerning the Love of God* published in 1695 shortly after the first part of the *Serious Proposal*, Astell pushes Norris to consider that God may be equally the author of human pain and human pleasure, chal-lenging Norris to integrate a response to Locke's sensationalist episte-mology—and the realities of a life of pain—within his Anglican theology. But it is in the second part of her *Serious Proposal to the Ladies*, along with the subsequent *Some Reflections Upon Marriage* (1700), that Astell's most significant deviance from Norris occurs. Whereas Norris, as part of his ethical program and an emergent Anglican theory of governance, diminishes the distinction between secular and sacred objects of desire, Astell, for the rest of her career, insists upon the vast dissimilarity between them, especially for women. While Hobbes implies that people are incapable of guiding themselves to follow God's law and Anglican orthodoxy claims that people would naturally do so, Astell, especially in the second part of *Serious Proposal to the Ladies* endeavors to demonstrate the difficulty that inheres in directing one's will, and one's love, toward God. For Astell, the world of sexual desire and procreation presents the largest obstacle to this spiritual goal. In a telling example of the way she sees secular and spiritual mandates in competition, Astell describes the procreative activity of producing heirs as conflicting with spirituality: "No Posterity" she declares, is "so desireable as the Offspring of our Minds" (151). For Astell, the key to happiness and to spiritual fulfillment is a correct understanding of God's nature as benevolent, and of our nature as reasonable but much more limited than God's. This is why "understanding" leads to a desire to do God's will and why doing God's will makes us happy. If we misunderstand our nature, or God's, our "inclinations take a wrong bias" (210). If our "understanding" is not developed, as it is not in women, then our spiritual destiny and our happiness are thwarted. Because women are encouraged to make themselves materially attractive to men, and because society encourages them to keep their desires focused on men and material objects and their energies focused on reproduction, women in particular, Astell argues, are spiritually imperiled by late seventeenth-century secular society.

I am suggesting that Astell moves away from Anglican orthodoxy in the second part of the *Serious Proposal to the Ladies*. In this, she shares something with Locke, who is otherwise an important adversarial impetus for her emergent theories. Locke's theory of the will developed over the course of his revisions of the *Essay Concerning Human Understanding*. In the first edition (1690), Locke accepts the Anglican orthodoxy that humans have a general tendency to desire the good. Given freedom of action (as opposed to freedom of will), humans will make choices toward future good. That is, in the first edition, the will tends toward moral, spiritual, and social good. The second edition of the *Essay Concerning Human Understanding* (1694), while maintaining faith in the essentially virtuous character of humanity, shifts emphasis from the (ethical) will to the (morally neutral) concept of desire, as both Jonathan Brody Kramnick and John Sitter have shown. In this revision, Locke relocates morality from the will to the understanding: instead of an essentially good human who sometimes errs, unavoidable defects of desire can be compensated for by reason. Locke argues that an agent has the "power to suspend determination"; that is, humans can withstand immediate pleasures in order to regulate our conduct to God's law (271). The moral sense is thus mainly a negative force: the power to suspend and repress desires. In this way, Locke's nascent theory of human psychology challenges the Anglican notion of "laws written into the heart," the radical depravity of the reformed will, and the pessimistic Hobbesian view that people are doomed to be ruled by an amoral and mortal power. The revised *Essay Concerning Human Understanding* depicts a conflict between human desire and human will that will become the key to modern notions of subjectivity.

The second part of Astell's *Serious Proposal to the Ladies* responds rather directly to Locke's theory of the will. Much has been made of Astell's rationalist critique of Locke's epistemology (his notion of "thinking matter"), but less attention has been paid to this aspect of her response to Locke. Astell's philosophy of the will follows Locke's developing theory, as well as latitudinarian theology, by making the understanding a key to morality. Portraying the human as torn between the desires of the body and the truths of the understanding, Astell makes a case for learning as a key to morality. Anticipating by about a century Mary Wollstonecraft's argument that women are corrupt due to their education, Astell's version of an Anglican compromise, like Norris's, is rooted in the belief that humans are essentially good. One difference between Locke and Astell is that Astell believes that reason needs nurturing from within the mind itself: seclusion rather than experience will promote reasoned morality, which follows from the fact that she is a rationalist rather than an empiricist. But the biggest difference between Locke and Astell is that Astell, especially in the second part, retains a sense of the significance of desire to moral goodness. For Locke, desire must be checked in order for the moral faculty of understanding to take over, but for Astell, desire is a critical component, in fact the end point, of reason and the key to spirituality.

In asking her female audience "Can you be in love with servitude and folly?" Astell begins the second part of her *Serious Proposal to the Ladies* with a decided emphasis on desire (72). In admonishing her audience "If you *Wish*, Why shou'd you not *Endeavor*?" Astell encourages women to yoke their will to their desire, which would lead them to follow her plan (72).[49] In language that provides ammunition for her critics to charge her with enthusiasm, Astell diminishes the role of reason by suggesting that it is, though crucial, merely a tool for passionate devotion to God. Reason allows us to "draw aside the clouds" that "hide the most adorable Face of GOD from us" so we can "lose our selves with Wonder, Love and Pleasure! Somewhat too ineffable to be nam'd, too Charming, too Delightful not to be eternally desir'd" (160). Astell explicitly contrasts this love of the divine with the demands of corporeal objects of desire, which keep us "sunk into Sense, and buried alive in a crowd of Material Beings," preventing, rather than facilitating, our spiritual development (160). For Astell our desire and "adoration" should turn toward God, not things of this world. We do not have "narrow groveling hearts" capable of only base objects of desire but rather are "all on Fire," and thus we do not need to enervate our desire but rather to direct it to the correct object (89). Thus, despite Astell's commitment to reason as a crucial component of morality, she insists that it is not our "sentiments" that must be censured, but rather our understandings, which "wilfully and unreasonably" allow us to adhere to material objects of desire (91). For Astell, the function of reason is to direct passion toward God, not to suppress passion. The second proposal, dedicated to the happiness of its adherents, will replace the "Pleasures of our Animal Nature" with the superior and "unspeakably delightful" pleasure of aligning our desires with God's will (98).[50]

While the revised version of Locke's *Essay* evokes an increasingly depraved desire, Astell's proposal develops in completely the opposite direction. In positing depravity of desire as a problem of understanding that can be rectified—if we understood our divine possibility, we would desire it—Astell posits desire as something to be cultivated, rather than repressed. Whereas Locke asks us to use our will to suspend our desires so that we may act as moral agents, Astell implores us to suspend our "assent" and to train our understanding so that love of God, and of truth, can take over (110–117). From this perspective, it looks like Locke, not Astell, is the proponent of repression and the pseudo-idealist. While the first part of her proposal claimed social benefits, in her response to her critics (and to Locke), Astell focuses instead on the problem of female pleasure and makes her case to women by arguing that in aligning their wills and their desires, they may be happy, virtuous, and spiritually purified. This may be a rhetorical strategy, aimed at convincing her original audience rather than her critics, but in the process Astell significantly challenges Anglican, and Lockean, philosophy.

Astell's works, especially the second part of *Serious Proposal to the Ladies* and *Some Reflections Upon Marriage*, point to a conflict in society: the needs of society and the standards for female virtue inhibit the development of real social virtue in women by perverting their desires away from God and toward men. Although Astell adamantly maintains the equality and fundamental similarity of men and women, in thinking about the lack of parity in social experiences of men and women—the marriage contract in particular—Astell theorizes the relationship between desire and spirituality in a way that predicts problems for a society organized to prevent the development of female happiness by limiting female desire to mortal objects and by discouraging the development of the "understanding" that would correct that desire. Astell's feminist perspective—that is, her interest in theorizing the problem of desire from a vantage point that accounts for the material conditions of women (as opposed to the abstract perspectives of Locke and Norris)—allows her to elaborate a philosophy of mind that neither naïvely believes in the essential harmony among individual desire, God's will, and political stability nor cynically insists upon their inherent antagonism.

Astell's proposal, of course, was never implemented, and I am not sure that anyone read her second proposal as critically as, for example, she read Locke. Even those who gave nominal support, like George Wheler, seem to have willfully missed the point. Wheler's treatise *The Protestant Monastery* (1698), though nominally supportive of her plan for sex-segregated female communities as "no ways prejudicial, but many ways profitable to the State, and creditable to the Church," argues against implementation on the grounds of impracticality (17). In a very telling misinterpretation of Astell, Wheler devotes the vast majority of his text to explicating an analogy between the nuclear family and a monastery. In Wheler's "Protestant monastery"/nuclear family, the women shares authority and honor with the husband; however, it is the man, because he is the unquestioned inheritor of God's will, that is "master" of his private monastery. In arguing that the monogamous nuclear family can mimic Astell's female retreat, Wheler entirely misses her critique of Anglican secular society. For Astell, individual desire is the route to doing God's will, and thus any model that requires a woman to please her husband and to subordinate her will to his is a route to both secular and spiritual degradation. Thus, even though Wheler accepts the premise of a female monastery, he rejects Astell's more radical premise about female equality and her argument in the second part about the relationships among human beings (including women), human desire, and God's will.

I argued earlier that Behn's fiction often represents a world made chaotic, not necessarily by erratic and libertine subjects of desire, but rather by unstable objects of desire. Similarly, Astell's writings about monasteries and marriage express profound concern that women must be prepared for multiple and various kinds of failure on the part of their husbands. Both, that is, depict men as unworthy objects of desire and inadequate substitutions for God. Theological arguments that dominated skeptical and libertine philosophy—God is either inscrutable or indifferent—effectively put their adherents in identical positions as the woman who loves a libertine, profligate, or unreasonable man, forced to swear allegiance in the face of epistemological uncertainty about the object of desire or indifference from that object. Astell and Behn are interested in a world in which all objects of desire presented to women are unsatisfying substitutes for God, and they similarly argue that social ethics, as well as female happiness, will bear the burden of this social transformation. I have been aligning Behn and Astell on the problem of desire, but of course this comparison elides an important theological difference: Astell clearly and unequivocally imagines God as a satisfying object of desire whereas the nuns in Behn's fiction, no matter how pious and diligent in performing the rituals of Catholicism, find no satisfaction in devotion. Astell might say that this is precisely because Behn's vision is too Catholic and thus full of empty ritual. As I argued earlier, it is in fact possible to read a significant strain of Catholic nostalgia in Behn. But I am suggesting that Astell, like Behn, evidences, if not nostalgia for Catholicism, at least nostalgia for an ecstatic spirituality available to women. I am also arguing that these two very different women similarly link the problem of female desire to questions about political and social stability.

On the surface, Behn and Astell share little other than gender, historical period, and the dubious distinction of title to that most illogical of categories, the Tory feminist. Scholars have recently expressed interest in this seemingly paradoxical combination of ideological allegiances: the peculiarly late seventeenth-century phenomenon of a feminist conservative politics. Behn's feminism has often been read allegorically, as an agent of her Stuart leanings, and the relationship between Mary Astell's two strains of philosophy—her feminism and her Anglicanism—has puzzled critics. In both cases, the relationship between feminism and conservative politics has typically been accounted for by assuming that one or the other is the predominant motivating force. So we can have either Astell the Tory apologist or Astell the first English feminist, and we can have Behn, cagey political player, or we can embrace the erratic, incoherent feminized version. If, however, we read Behn and Astell as theorists of an emergent model of female desire and its relation to political theory, their conservatism appears not reactionary, but rather a means to critique the emergent system—with its illogical and unevenly distributed combination of liberal and republican elements—from a contemporary female perspective. The representations of nuns and convents in both writers evidence concern about the psychological, social, and (at least for Astell) spiritual implications of the permanent loss of models of female desire that are based on ascetic, individual, or communal, rather than romantic and sexual, means and that grant epistemological or political authority to female subjects. From this perspective, it is possible to see the "Tory feminism" of such different women as Aphra Behn and Mary Astell as neither oxymoronic nor anachronistic, but rather as a set of calculated and prescient critiques of Anglican England and its vexed dependence on a model of female desire that disavows its Catholic provenance and thus that does not anticipate the problems, both for women and for society, that will accompany the conversion of the nun into the chaste and virtuous Protestant wife.

CHAPTER 2

The Hymen and
Its Discontents: Medical Discourses
on Virginity

If both the beginning and end of my story find the virgin idealized—sanctified under Catholicism and immortalized as the virtuous protagonist of sentimental fiction—the majority of her experience is marked more by peril than by admiration. Throughout this book, we find her exposed to depredation by theology, pornography, and satire. In this chapter, it is science that endeavors to deflate—and appropriate— her iconic power via the dual methods of objectification and pathologization. In what follows, I trace representations of virginity through three different kinds of medical discourse: the early modern midwife manuals whose immersion in humoural medicine mark them as old-fashioned almost as soon as they appear; the anatomy texts that, beginning in the seventeenth century, represent the vanguard of the new science; and the eighteenth-century midwife manuals that bear the stamp of this new science. Humoural medicine, which dominated medical discourse on women in the sixteenth and throughout most of the seventeenth centuries, treated prolonged virginity as pathological and thus de-sanctified it. Later, the new science, with its empirical epistemology, subjected the hymen to the same objectification as other body parts, contributing to the demystification of virginity. But the hymen resisted empirical investigation and ultimately science, that is, both anatomy texts and the new midwife manuals written by men, abdicated authority over female virginity, thereby creating a void that would be filled by literature. This trajectory of scientific texts on the hymen, which roughly follows the literary and political chronologies mapped out in the introduction, bears witness to a shift in sexual politics from a view that virginity is pathological to the eve of its re-idealization in sentimental literature. I argue that the scientific, disinterested analysis of the hymen failed to produce a stable object, which threatened scientific authority itself. I end by suggesting that imaginative literature, specifically the sentimental novel, became the new locus of discourse on female virginity because male power over female virginity was in fact an act of the imagination.

Midwives in England were originally licensed, pursuant to an order by Henry VIII, by the church. Although the order originated in 1512, before the beginning of England's official turn to Protestantism, I nonetheless begin here in order to suggest that early modern midwifery was intimately connected to religious politics. The first chapter examined Protestant critiques of Catholicism and the demise of an ideal of permanent virginity. This chapter begins by arguing that the revival of humoural medicine, roughly coincident with the Reformation, provided a medical explanation for the Protestant critique of celibacy. The Galenic/humoural system of medicine, which had been resurrected in the sixteenth century and which dominated early modern English medicine, is founded on the notion that the body continually produces and balances humours and that these liquid and vaporous entities assume responsibility for both physical health and emotional temperament. Under humoural medicine, almost all pathologies are due to "obstruction," and the mode of cure typically involves some type of purging. Disease begins in the body and the body is responsible to expel it. Mikhail Bahktin recognized that this system is based on two bodily canons: the grotesque, or the open body that cannot control its evacuations, and the "classical" body, which is structurally closed and which has control over its evacuations and ingestions. Critics such as Caroline Walker Bynum, Patricia Crawford, Gail Kern Paster, Audrey Eccles, and Peter Stallybrass have shown that humoural medicine imagines the female body as naturally grotesque or less well developed due to its inability to control excretions. While men can control their evacuation of semen, women involuntarily evacuate menstrual blood, their analogous fluid. Humoural medicine views physical virginity as pathological, because the hymen presents an unnatural barrier to evacuation of fluids. In the seventeenth century, greensickness (virgin's disease, or chlorosis) became a well-known condition, in which the hymen dangerously obstructs the evacuation of fluids.[1] The pathological hymen reflects a major inconsistency in the humoural view of female embodiment: women are both more leaky than men, and, in the case of virgins, more obstructed. Humoural medicine requires the evacuation of fluid from the body, and it pathologizes the way that the female body does this, thereby providing support both for the belief in the physical inferiority of women and for the undesirability of prolonged virginity. In short, it is a good adjunct to Reformation sexual politics.[2]

Seventeenth-century midwife manuals were steeped in both Galenic medicine and Reformation sexual ideology. Although women controlled the practice of midwifery, the written discourses of sex and midwifery, which were based in humoural medicine, were mostly written by men, often for a general audience. The first editions of such texts as Nicholas Culpeper's *A Directory for Midwives* (1651), William Sermon's *The Ladies Companion, or The English Midwife* (1671), Jane Sharp's *The Midwives Book* (1671), and *Aristotle's Master-Piece* (1690) arrived in England during the first big explosion of medical-sexual handbooks in the seventeenth century and were the principle written resource for information about female sexuality, including virginity.[3] The pseudonymous "Aristotle" texts were by far the most popular medical and sexual handbooks throughout the seventeenth and eighteenth centuries, and in fact they were published into the twentieth century.[4] There are versions directed at midwives (*Aristotle's Midwife* [*1711*]) and others directed at general readers (*Aristotle's Master-Piece*), who might be getting married or wishing to have children. These books provide advice about the proper time to get married, how to choose a partner, conception, pregnancy, and childrearing. As such, they naturally link medical advice with sexual politics.

Since originality was not prized in these texts, many of them repeat the same content and tropes. Following is an example, from *Aristotle's Midwife*, of the way that virginity is typically described in humoural-based midwife manuals:

> The *Caruncles* . . . in Virgins are reddish, and plump, and round, but hang flagging when Virginity is lost. In Virgins, they are joyned together by a thin and sinewy Skin or Membrane, which is called the *Hymen*, and keeps them in Subjection, and makes 'em resemble a kind of Rose-bud half blown. This Disposition of the *Caruncles* is the only certain Mark of Virginity; it being in vain either to search for it elsewhere, or hope to be informed of it in any other way. And 'tis from the pressing and bruising of these *Caruncles*, and forcing and breaking the little Membranes (which is done by the Yard in the first Act of Copulation) that there happens an Effusion of Blood; after which they remain separated, and never recover their first figure; but become more and more Flat, as the Acts of Copulation are increased. (10–11)[5]

This is a description of a virginity approaching its inevitable demise. The virgin vagina is "reddish and plump" suggesting good health, but also indicating that blood had built up and will need to be released and thus that the virginal state is naturally temporary. The "Rose-bud" simile supports this, as the flower has an inevitable teleology: it cannot stay a "bud" forever. Moreover, this hymeneal rosebud is already "half blown," indicating that the hymen itself prefigures, even causes, its own demise. The analogical association of virginity with vegetation supports an ideal of virginity as a natural but temporary stage, a healthy condition if not unnaturally extended.

If the natural call to end virginity was not heeded, a virgin could become ill with greensickness. Seventeenth- and eighteenth-century midwife manuals—as well as other medical texts—are replete with examples of the hazards of virginity. The French doctor Nicolas Venette, for example, recounts numerous cases of imperforate hymens that cause "Belly-Ache[s]," "Vertigoes," "Epilepsies," and the evacuation of blood from the nostrils and ears (45).[6] Considered a life-threatening condition, greensickness was cured by facilitating the release of fluids: purgation and bloodletting were sometimes suggested, but the most effective cure was sex.[7] Greensickness affected not only the virgin's health but also her appearance. Her illness made the virgin pale, or even green, in color. *Etmullerus Abridg'd* (1699), for example, describes the appearance of the virgin with greensickness as "the colour of the skin is pale, or somewhat livid and ugly" (597).[8] The healthy virgin, by contrast, is robust. Blushing, which suggests that blood is still contained in the female, and paleness, which suggests a sickness from lack of sex, were, paradoxically, both signifiers of virginity in the eighteenth century: the healthy virgin would blush, while the sick virgin, that is, the one whose virginal state was prolonged for too long, would become pale. In the excerpt above from *Aristotle's Midwife*, the hymen functions synecdochically for the woman: the simile "like a Rose-bud half blown" links the hymen to a rose, suggesting that the rosebud contributes to the "reddish and plump" aspect of the hymen and, by extension, the virgin. Oppositions suggest that this reddish and plump "figure" is preferable to the "flagging" and "flat" postcoital appearance. The passage thus suggests that the loss of the hymen will diminish the woman's beauty, even as retention of the hymen would threaten both her life and her appearance. It thus implies that virginity retains some cultural value even though it is fragile, transient, and prone to pathology.

This pathologization of virginity was motivated by the increasingly anti-Catholic, and thus anti-celibacy, climate in England. These medical texts de-sanctify virginity by treating virginity as a medical, not a theological, issue and by demonizing extended virginity. By the late seventeenth century, the religious implications of virginity were almost completely erased, and it was treated mainly as a medical topic. Sharp's *Midwives Book*, one of the very few midwife manuals written (not insignificantly) by a woman, makes a very rare case for lifelong virginity as a possible religious ideal.[9] Lifelong virginity is, she asserts, "a singular blessing and a gift of *God*" (165). But nonetheless Sharp clearly emphasizes her anti-Catholicism: "Let the Votaries of the *Roman* Church look to it, when they make vows of chastity, which the greatest part of them doubtless are never able to keep but by using unlawful means" (165). By the end of the seventeenth century, references to lifelong virginity as either a spiritual ideal or a medical possibility for women are almost nonexistent in Protestant texts, medical and otherwise, and the term "spinster" first assumes its negative connotation.[10]

In the eighteenth century, by contrast, virginity becomes idealized once again, and greensickness both diminishes as a pathology and becomes a fashionable disease to have, as it signifies extended and thus well-managed virginity.[11] For example, John Maubray, who was an early advocate of male midwifery and teacher of other midwives in London, satirically decries this emergent change in the standards of female beauty and sexuality in his description of the visual symptoms of greensickness:

> However, yet I have known many *Women*, in *France* and *Germany* who have been so far from thinking it an ugly *Colour* that they have esteem'd it most *beautiful* and used very *pernicious things* to gain and appropriate this *Colour* to themselves. (43)

Although Maubray is obviously against this change (and argues that English virginity figures differently than French or German), he hints at the notion that the very thing—prolonged virginity—that is viewed as pathological in the seventeenth century will become, by the end of my period of inquiry, once again a signifier of female virtue.[12]

Some of these changes are reflected in the Aristotle texts themselves. In 1695, *Aristotle's Master-Piece* offered this counsel about the appropriate conditions for loss of virginity:

> 'Tis a Duty incumbent upon the Parents, to be careful in bringing up their Children in the ways of Vertue, and have ever a regard that they fully not [*sic*] their Honour and Reputation, especially the Females, and most of all Virgins, when they grow up to be marriageable, for if through the unnatural severity of rigid Parents they be crossed and frustrated in their love, many of them, out of a mad humour, if temptation lies in their way, throw themselves into the unchaste Arms of a subtle

charming Tempter; being through the softness of good Nature, and strong Desire to pursue their Appetites, easily induced to believe Men's Flatteries, and feigned Vows of promised Marriage, to cover the shame; and then too late the Parents find the effects of their rash Severity, which brought a lasting stain upon their Family. (63)

This excerpt exemplifies the text's—and to some extent the late seventeenth-century's—attitude toward female sexuality. Parents are encouraged not to protect their daughters' virginity but rather to refrain from protracting it unnaturally. Female sexuality is, in its "nature," "good" and marked by "strong desire." The female is fully embodied and ruled by physical inclinations, which in general are healthy but which can degenerate into a "mad humour." It is only the tyrannical, and rather anachronistic, rigidity of parents, combined with the male suitor's unchastity (interestingly not hers), that cause the perversion of the girl's natural humour and her untimely and socially destructive defloration. The text depicts sex as natural, especially for the woman. The male is calculating, "feigning," and "flattering" in order to get what he wants, but ultimately the blame rests mostly on the parents, whose "unnatural" and "rash" severity directly causes these unnaturally contentious sexual relations.

A parallel admonition in the 1741 version of *Aristotle's Master-Piece* reflects some of the changes that have taken place in the intervening half century:

And the Use of those so much desir'd Enjoyments being deny'd to Virgins, is often follow'd by very dangerous and sometimes dismal Consequences, precipitating them into those Follies that may bring an indelible Stain on their Families, or else it brings upon them the *Green Sickness* or other Diseases. (28)

This explanation of the causes and the consequences of the untimely loss of virginity eliminates the harsh language of criticism directed at the parents in the earlier passage. Here, the agent of the "stain," is, due to the heavy use of the passive, much harder to pinpoint: "use," "consequences," and "follies" act as grammatical agents, while the woman herself and the parents who presumably deny her the "use" of her "desired enjoyments" are not named. They are, instead, the objects of the action: the family may gain a "stain" or the woman herself, if denied such "use," may get sick. The undesirable consequences can, paradoxically, include both loss of virginity (and the stigma attached to it) and prolonged virginity (and the medical threat of greensickness that is associated with it). On balance, the 1741 version shifts more of the agency and the consequences for poorly managed virginity from the family to the woman herself. For example, the later text mentions female masturbation as possible cause of virginity loss, while the earlier does not, and the 1741 version enjoins young women "to take all imaginable Care to keep their Virgin Zone intire" (34). The move toward making the woman herself responsible for her own virginity makes the 1741 virgin, unlike the virgin of 1695, a sentient agent responsible for controlling her bodily desires.

The differences between these two texts provide, in microcosm, a version of larger shifts in thinking about virginity, in which virginity ceases to be aberrant and instead becomes a defining stage of a woman's life. Overall, the later text de-pathologizes virginity and legitimizes it as a prolonged stage in a woman's life, although it certainly does not depict lifelong virginity as medically or culturally desirable. These changes are reflected in the most striking difference between the two versions of *Aristotle's Master-Piece*: the order in which the chapters are organized. While the chapters are largely the same and their content does not vary much, the chronology of the two versions differs dramatically. The 1695 version begins with marriage and later backtracks, in the sense of the chronology of a woman's life, to a discussion of virginity, which focuses on pathology and argues that virginity should not be artificially prolonged. The chronology of the 1695 version reflects a sexual politics grounded on the idea that virginity should be dispensed with as quickly as possible. The 1741 version, by contrast, begins with a discussion of male and female anatomy. The second chapter discusses when a virgin is ready for marriage, and the third chapter centers on virginity "proper." The rest of the 1741 version proceeds roughly in chronological order of the "standard" history of a woman's life: from virginity to marriage, conception, and childbirth. In mimicking the chronology of a woman's life, this text reinforces its desirability, allowing for virginity as a legitimate—in fact the first and perhaps defining—stage of a woman's life, rather than an ambiguous and hazardous precipice ruled by nature rather than culture.

The different treatments of greensickness in the two versions underscore my argument that virginity becomes de-pathologized in the eighteenth century. The 1695 text has a separate chapter on greensickness that precedes the chapter on virginity; thus, the pathology of virginity introduces the topic of virginity. The 1741 text, by contrast, does not have a separate chapter on greensickness, and it reverses the chronology: greensickness is discussed after the general discussion of virginity, thereby suggesting that greensickness, but not virginity, is pathological. By delaying its discussion of the possible pathology of virginity and by downplaying its significance (since it does not have its own chapter) the 1741 text offers a significant narrative space for being a virgin in a non-pathological way. In sum, the later text represents virginity as a stage of a woman's life that is properly protracted and that has its own rules. This stage is the one about which fictional accounts of women become, for a time, almost exclusively interested. In its chronology, the 1741 version of *Aristotle's Master-Piece* reflects the way that discourses of virginity could become about being a virgin rather than losing one's virginity. In this way, it makes the literary figure of the virgin possible. The rest of the sections in this chapter analyze the discursive hymen of scientific texts in order to show how scientific representations of virginity contributed both to the reformation of the virgin and to the generic and epistemological imperatives of the sentimental novel.

* * *

Greensickness ascribes a physiological purpose, albeit a pernicious one, to the hymen, but the hymen has more commonly been treated as a sign than as an organ, and it has long presented epistemological and semiotic problems, repeatedly producing questions like: does the hymen exist? how does one prove it? what signifies virginity? and what does virginity signify? Historically, blood at coition has been the dominant way of determining loss of virginity, but blood provides only retrospective knowledge of virginity; its absence may not signify as solid evidence; and it is easily faked, thereby creating anxiety that men will be subject to deception about a woman's virginity. The intact hymen has long been a source of interest as a more reliable signifier of female virginity, but its fragility, variability, and inaccessibility make its secrets elusive. In suggesting, as I do in chapter 1, that ideals of virginity are subject to the vagaries of localized politics, I am attempting to historicize virginity. This is an important goal of this book because all too often the relationship between virginity and patriarchy has been naturalized. One of the interesting problems in such a project (and thus a reason, perhaps, that virginity has often been treated as an ahistorical concept) is the ahistoricity of the hymen itself. From ancient Greece to our own present day, discourses on the physical properties of the hymen have changed very little.[13] Though it is a simplification, one might say that the technical view of the hymen has almost always been: It exists, though not in all women. It is broken on first intercourse, though may be broken in other ways as well. Different ages and different writers have theorized the significance of these physical properties differently, but the physical properties of the hymen survive changes in medical practice and account for the fact that discourses on virginity are dogged by anxiety over semiotic and epistemological reliability.

Early modern midwife manuals generally assert the semiotic and epistemological reliability of the hymen, at least in general terms. Francois Mauriceau says that the disposition of the hymen and caruncles is "the very certain Mark of Virginity" (36); Maubray claims that the hymen is the "real sign of virginity" (38); and Culpeper, whose early book on midwifery was famously followed by one of the first books about herbal medicine, concurs that "where ever it is found" the hymen is "a certain note of Virginity" (29). The excerpt above, from *Aristotle's Midwife*, depicts the female body as a legible and reliable indicator of a moral or social truth about her sexual experience; it is easy to distinguish the virgin from the nonvirgin. To some extent, her body even signals the amount of sexual experience she has had, since the caruncles "become more and more flat as acts of copulation are increased." "Aristotle" acknowledges that the hymen could break without intercourse but says "these things happen so rarely that those virgins to whom it so happens do thereby bring themselves under just Suspicion" (11–12). Moreover, the Aristotle texts imply that women who try to deceive men about the status of their virginity can be found out. For example, *Aristotle's Master-Piece* (1695) recounts a case in which a woman's claim of rape is invalidated by the examination of a surgeon and two midwives, who find her hymen intact.

Nonetheless, these midwife manuals belie anxiety about their epistemological authority over the hymen. Though the hymen is usually claimed as a reliable sign, other body parts are often discussed as signifiers of virginity, indicating a lack of collective certainty about how to confirm virginity. Many authors claim that various areas of female anatomy, including the womb, the cervix, and the vagina, are physically and visually different in virgins and nonvirgins. But other writers warn that that these reputed signs of virginity might be faked. Sharp's skepticism is typical: "Amongst those signs of Maidenhead preserved, is the straightness of the privy passage. . . . But it can be no infallible sign because unchaste women will (by astringent medicaments) so contract the parts, that they will seem to be maids again." (267). In typical fashion for these texts, Sharp debunks other signs of virginity because they too can be counterfeited. Her definition of the hymen is particularly skeptical:

> it is broken at the first encounter with man, and it makes a great alteration; it is painful, and bleeds when it is broken; but what it is, is not certainly known. (265–266)

In this description Sharp extends the epistemological problems presented by the hymen, suggesting that they transcend questions about its pervasiveness and reliability and intrude even upon its essence. But overall, early modern midwife manuals address the epistemological and semiotic problems presented by female sexual anatomy in a rather consistent way: by suggesting that there are epistemological limitations but at the same time insisting that, at least in general terms, the hymen does not escape their field of understanding and that their understanding is superior to all others. Their emphasis on the pathological nature of female virginity is, as I stated earlier, connected to Reformation sexual politics. But it may also be a form of displacement: their focus on the physical pathology of virginity de-emphasizes its epistemological incorrigibility.

Given the ultimate uncertainty about how virginity can be determined, it is not surprising that the possibility of deception with respect to virginity is a prominent concern of the culture. The "virginity test" has long been alluded to in literature and in medical texts, but there is little agreement about what kind of test works and a good deal of anxiety about the possibility of faking it.[14] Roger Thompson has shown that the art of reconstituting lost maidenheads was a typical trick in pornographic literature (72) and Michael Ettmüller actually gives a recipe for doing it (594).[15] Such admission of the possibility of deception, though, is rare in early midwife manuals and, where alluded to, these manuals imply that it is not the author but the layman who may be deceived by the woman's body. Maubray makes this explicit when he declines to publish a virginity test because what he intends "for the *Benefit* of All in *general*," might instead lead to "the *Detriment* of some in *particular*" (42). By claiming that, though recalcitrant, female sexual anatomy does not escape their expertise, early modern midwives maintain authority to speak about women, but they constitute their own authority at the expense of the authority of male sex partners. A key problem with the hymen as a certain sign of virginity is that it is available only in general terms or in extremely unusual cases, such as fraudulent charges of rape or annulment due to impotence. It seems manifestly unlikely that anyone interested in the virginity of a particular woman could examine her anatomy in such detail. This "certain sign," then, would be available only to doctors, and only in very rare circumstances. Laypeople are left only with the overdetermined and notoriously unreliable sign of blood.

The hymen's availability as a sign manifests most commonly—as blood—only upon its demise. Blood at first coition is usually described as an unproblematic sign of the former presence of the hymen. Maubray, for instance says that an effusion of blood at coition is "a certain Sign of VIRGINITY" (39). The Aristotle texts also repeatedly assert that blood at coition is a fairly reliable indicator of virginity. Although blood has its own epistemological problems, it is, unlike the hymen, highly visible and available. What this means is that while virginity is very hard to confirm, signs of defloration are much more available for visual confirmation. While a man cannot ever be sure that a woman is a virgin, her defloration can be confirmed by the sign of blood. The posture of certainty—common though not universal—about such an overdetermined sign as blood is unaccountable, because many parts of the body, especially the humoural body, bleed. And the usefulness of this information is unclear, as blood is only a retrospective sign, one whose presence or absence manifests only when the information is no longer very useful, that is, after marriage, sex, or rape. Furthermore, for most of these writers, the *lack* of blood has no meaning. Since the hymen may not be present in all women and since it may be broken in "innocent" ways, lack of blood does not necessarily signify lack of virginity. Like Sharp, who calls the absence of blood "not so generally sure" a sign of defloration, most of these texts admit that the absence of blood is a more difficult sign to interpret than its presence (266). *Aristotle's Master-Piece*, for example, insists that husbands whose brides do not produce the bleeding "token of virginity" should not censure them: "*Unless the contrary they plainly know / for they may yet unspotted virgins be / Altho' their Virgin Tokens none can see*" (1741, 34). For "Aristotle," the woman's production of blood is a purely performative and gratuitous sign that will please her husband but that he cannot require.

Blood is an even more highly charged sign of virginity (or, more specifically, virginity loss) than the hymen precisely because it manifests in private, to the sexual partner of the woman, not to the scientist. But, ultimately, both the presence and absence of blood are signifiers that refer more to men than to women. I am suggesting that the virgin anatomy becomes a way of working out power/authority issues between men, specifically between those who have access to the anatomical secrets of the female body and those who have sexual access. Blood is a sign of male sexuality, and the lack of blood is a challenge to the ability of male sexuality to signify and to matter. Writers who insist upon the verifiability of female virginity are insisting upon the importance of male sexuality. Maubray, for example, bolsters his claim to the ontological reality of the hymen by arguing that since "something *extraordinary* happens in the first COITION" there must be a signifier for it (39). From this perspective, which reveals epistemological debates over virginity to be implicated in competitions between various systems of male authority, interest in resolving the semiotic and epistemological problems presented by virginity can be seen as a fantasy of successful competition with other men.

This point is supported by the emphasis on the irrevocability of the loss of the hymen. Venette, the French writer who rivaled "Aristotle" in popularity, says,

> As there are no Signs that can clearly discover it, so there are no Medicines that can restore it when once lost. It may be in our power to mimick Nature, and to produce a counterfeited one, but all our force will not reach so far as to re-establish the Natural, which is the most precious, and most valuable. (56)

For Venette, the hymen forces humans to consider the outer limits of their knowledge. Not to be outdone, a contemporary religious/legal tract, *A Treatise Concerning Adultery and Divorce* (1700), ups the ante even further, through a comparison with divine power:

> though God can do every thing, I am bold to say it, He cannot restore *Chastity* when a woman has lost it: And who will go about to propose an Equivalent for an inestimable Loss, never to be recovered? (34)

This text echoes an argument made by Saint Jerome (discussed in chapter 1), one of the most influential ancient writers on virginity. According to Jerome and this treatise, God, who created the world and who can raise the dead and forgive all sins, cannot restore chastity.[16] The sign of blood thus signifies the power of masculine sexuality, as it can do something that God cannot undo. With the introduction of God, we have a trio of masculine authority figures—romantic, scientific, and religious—whose authority is implicated in female sexuality.

*　*　*

Early in the seventeenth century, William Harvey (1958), the most celebrated doctor of the seventeenth century, discovered the circulation of the blood, a discovery that would, theoretically, undermine the entire system of humoural medicine. But since humoural medicine accounted for so many interlocking systems of belief—for example, medicine, sexual politics, and psychology—its demise was slow and uneven. In Europe, major advances in the fields of anatomy, embryology, and gynecology occurred during the seventeenth century. These advances made their way to England in the late seventeenth century and brought standards of both epistemology and rhetoric that would supersede old ways of writing about the body. Anatomy in particular represented an immense challenge to the humoural system because it focused on discrete body parts rather than seeing the body as one organic system. The seventeenth-century anatomy theaters discovered, or at least publicized, these newly emerging body parts. Anatomy participated in a larger rethinking of the physical body during this time period, in which the body was broken down, and its parts were fetishized, functioning as synecdoches for the bodies and the personalities associated with them.

A most contentious aspect of anatomy was the effort to explain, describe, and differentiate male and female reproductive anatomy. In this process, the hymen had a special place: an organ whose existence was long debated and that disappears as it reveals itself, its status as available only in a very limited class of bodies, virgin women, and only in some nondeterminable subset of them, made the hymen a highly sought-after physical entity and at the same time allowed it to bear the weight of competing cultural discourses about the differences between women and men and between one kind of woman, the virgin, and other women. As my analysis of the midwife manuals suggests, it was also highly implicated in mediating issues of authority between men. With the new science and new modes of establishing authority, a new truce had to be enacted between the hymen and the various men whose authority was implicated in it.

In terms of this contest for authority, the "Aristotle" texts, as their pseudonym indicates, rely upon wisdom of the ancients to establish their superior authority over female anatomy. Their debt to ancient sources, though, is mostly unacknowledged in the early editions; the 1695 edition of *Aristotle's Master-Piece* presents all of its material as fact; it makes no explicit claims about the source, the authority, or the authenticity of its ideas except to begin by asserting that its information "plainly appears in Holy Writ" (A3r).[17] By contrast, editions beginning in 1741 have a preface from the editor stating that Aristotle's name and the authority it confers need not be explained: "*To tell thee, that Aristotle, the learned author of this Book, was generally reported to be the most knowing Philosopher in the World, is no more than what every intelligent Person already knows*" (A3r). My implication, of course, is that this disavowal protests too much. Given the revolutions of the new science and empirical philosophy, not to mention Protestant theology, Aristotle's authority as well as that of "Holy Writ" (i.e., any inherited authority) would be less clear in 1741 than it had been in 1695. Other early midwife manuals similarly rely primarily on the authority of the ancients. Sharp supports her argument with both Protestant scriptural interpretations and a survey of ancient thinking on the subject.[18] Regarding questions about the existence and function of the hymen, Sharp first reviews the debate among ancient authorities and ancient cultures and then proceeds to announce her position on the debate, which is that there is a hymen in all virgins. Her authority, then, comes from having personally read the ancients, not from any one ancient author's opinion. Her own discrimination as a reader authorizes her, which is evidence of the impingement of neoclassical epistemological modes into the humoural-based midwife manual.[19]

The epistemological standards of the new discipline of anatomy challenged ancient authority—and thus authority of midwife manuals— by requiring claims to be supported by firsthand visual evidence and corroborated by objective witnesses. The forum for this new discipline was the anatomy theater. T. Hugh Crawford argues that since Vesalius held the first public dissection, the production of medical knowledge—and the authority of the scientist—has depended on the exposure of physical detail.[20] Virtually all English anatomy texts reflect this new standard. The London physician Thomas Gibson, for example, in his *Anatomy of Humane Bodies* (1682), identifies himself as a doctor and claims to have knowledge of female anatomy and conception based on his experiences in dissecting rabbits. He explicitly asserts his superior authority to Galen, based on the fact that Galen "never Dissected any woman" (185). The French anatomist Pierre Dionis, who also wrote a midwife manual, credits neither the Bible nor the ancients; instead he relies on the knowledge of "modern discoveries" and his own publicly performed anatomies. Having "dissected Girls of all Ages" in his "diligent Pursuit" of the hymen, Dionis arrives at the unusual position that the hymen does not exist, except in cases of "Particular and extraordinary Accidents" (192).[21] Early anatomy texts (those of the seventeenth or early eighteenth centuries) place more emphasis on the availability of all body parts, including the hymen, and the authority of the scientist to touch them than any of the early midwife manuals did. The drawings in anatomy texts are intended to recreate the feeling of firsthand visual knowledge: they depict body parts splayed open, as they would be after a dissection, rather than as they would be in the body, suggesting, according to Ludmilla J. Jordanova, that anatomy can lay open the secrets of the closed body.[22] Dr. Gibson's anatomy text is contemporary with "Aristotle's" and Venette's midwife manuals, but its sensibility is more modern. In his text, the woman's whole reproductive system becomes available to the male medical gaze. If the hymen be found "in the form described," according to Gibson, "it is a certain note of virginity" (154). The language that accompanies the drawings is more technical, more concrete, and even more masculine than earlier midwife manuals. For example, he describes the cervix as the size of a "quill" (151). This analogy suggests that a quill, wielded by the male, can be inserted into the women's reproductive system. By contrast, in the "rosebud" simile cited earlier, the naturalness and delicacy of the bud about to flower imply an injunction against interference with the woman's body. Where the hymen of early midwife manuals might have kept the female body closed and unavailable, anatomical methods promise to open it.

But the methodologies and discursive standards of anatomy presented problems for anatomists in terms of the virgin body. First of all, the trend toward authority derived from repeated personal experience was hard to claim for virginity. In addition to the resistance that any radical rethinking of the human body encounters, the development of the understanding of the female body may have been slowed by the lack of available female cadavers for dissection.[23] Questions about female virginity were especially problematic since virgin females would have been even less available. While anatomists regularly call attention to the specific circumstances that lead to the specific information they present, they rarely (and I will discuss one exception shortly) can produce this kind of authority when speaking about virginity. This is the source, one might guess, of Dionis's unusual position that the hymen does not exist at all.

Moreover, the new science, with its injunction to rely on visual evidence, was monitored by the Royal Society, which made a concerted campaign to reform and regularize scientific language. One of its main mandates was to strip scientific language of poetic devices.[24] This imperative meant that many of the tropes used earlier to describe virginity had to be abandoned, at least in scientific texts (though an allusive and euphemistic style would be reactivated in pornographic descriptions like John Cleland's *Memoirs of a Woman of Pleasure*, a point to which I will return). Whereas earlier midwife manuals could invoke ancient authority, literary tropes, and the subjunctive mood (the hymen "may" or "may not" always be present), anatomists have to provide illustrations of their objects of study, and their descriptions refer to the illustrations. Thus, while Gibson could replace a masculine metaphor, the "quill," for the feminized rosebud, this strategy became less available as anatomical discursive standards permeated writing about female virginity.[25]

One important goal of the new anatomy was to discover the purpose of body parts, and here, again, the hymen is anomalous, as it does not easily lend itself to claims of physiological usefulness and thus has rarely been attributed a function in medical texts. Midwife manuals like that of "Aristotle" had ascribed semiotic and social—but not physical—usefulness to the hymen. Venette provides a rare example of a hymen credited with a medical purpose:

> sometimes it happens, tho' very seldom, that Nature being willing to preserve the Womb of some tender Woman, produces a Membrane above the Urinary passage, that Air, or other extraneous matter, may not disorder the interior parts; and this Membrane is properly called *Hymen*. (14)

For Venette, nature has agency in constructing women's bodies not only as signifiers of their moral qualities but also as safeguards of morality: the "tender" woman is provided with a hymen to protect her.[26] But this discussion of physical usefulness for the hymen is rare in midwife manuals and does not lend itself to the standards of anatomy, which generally do not ascribe agency to "nature" in terms of particular people, instead searching for generalities. Moreover, Venette in general finds the hymen to be "contrary to the Laws of Nature" (14).[27] The hymen has never been assigned a general, salutary purpose, a circumstance that may, in fact, partially explain the obsession with the usefulness of the hymen as a sign, a function, incidentally, that Venette denies, insisting that "nothing in all Physick is more difficult to know than a Maiden-head" (51).

In anatomical discourses on virginity, the unavailability of the hymen is frequently represented as a failure not on the part of science but rather on the part of female bodies. While scientific methods provide reliability, female bodies are unreliable and potentially deceptive. For example, as mentioned earlier, Dionis states unequivocally, based on his dissections, that the hymen does not exist. The woman's body, in his account, can sometimes signal her virginity, but "this feeble Testimony of Virtue is not to be met with in all Maids" (193). This empirical scientist takes great pains to establish his authority based on his inspection of many female bodies. Those same physical details, however, are not in the control of the woman and are not accessible to the nonprofessional. His position on female anatomy, representative of a larger trend, substitutes the truth that the body of any given woman might reveal for the truth about women in general—that their bodies are unreliable and potentially deceptive sources of information. This might explain why anatomy books generally do not discuss blood as a signifier of virginity, since they are not interested in the signs of sexuality, but rather in the signs that provide evidence of their own authority over the body. Despite its failure in certain respects, anatomical discourse on the hymen accomplishes several things. It constructs a kind of knowledge that is about women in general rather than about any one woman; it makes that knowledge confirmable only by doctors and medical methods; and thereby it institutes a significant kind of knowledge that can be gained only by giving men access to women's bodies. At the same time, it supplies an alibi for the failure of scientific methods, since it is women's bodies, not scientific methods, that bear responsibility for epistemological failure. Anatomical discourses on the hymen exploit the semiotic unreliability of the virgin body by synecdochically linking it to the woman: like her body, the woman's claims about herself may be deceptive. In short, science places the blame on women for its own failures.

Before 1700, practicing midwives had been almost exclusively women, even though men had generally written the books about midwifery. As direct observation and comprehension of the body's physiological purpose became standards for scientific authority, one might have expected that female midwives, who had great experience with the reproductive systems of women, would become the authors of midwife manuals. But the opposite thing happened, in that men took over the day-to-day practice of midwifery. With the emergence of new standards of epistemology, if men were going to continue to be the authorities on women's bodies, that is those authorized to write about them, they needed also to be the practitioners. The right to write about midwifery had to be supported by experience in midwifery, so the split between men writing about and women practicing midwifery could not continue.[28] Practice would hereafter constitute the authority to write, and men began practicing midwifery in much greater numbers than female midwifes (Sarah Stone being an exception) who also wrote manuals.[29] The midwife texts published by English midwives in the 1720s and 1730s represent a radical break from the earlier midwife texts both in terms of subject matter and in how authority is constituted.[30] Such authors as Edmund Chapman (1733),

William Giffard (1734), and Stone (1737) claim authority to practice midwifery and to write about it by virtue of clinical practice.

Scholars such as Lisa Forman Cody, Robert Erickson (1982), and Adrian Wilson have noticed this shift to man-midwifery and have debated how and why it happened and what its implications were for obstetric care. However, scholars have not noticed the important implications that this transition had for virginity, which is that increasing authority over female bodies in general meant decreasing scientific authority over the virgin body. This is because experience as a "practitioner" could not be invoked for speaking on virginity. The only legitimate arena for inspection of the female genitals was childbirth, where, of course, there are no virgins involved. As noted earlier, the treatment of sick virgins consisted of various kinds of purgation and bloodletting, though the preferred cure was marriage. These practices do not lead to direct observation of female sexual anatomy. While some critics claim that midwives may have occasionally masturbated virgins ailing with greensickness, the written medical treatises do not support this claim.[31] Nevertheless, according to Lois Chaber, the male takeover of midwifery was partially accomplished by impugning the moral attributes of female midwives for just such indiscretions (219–220). Moreover, the standards of the new science led to an increase in specialization, which meant that midwifery and anatomy became wholly different fields: the practice of treating and speaking about live women became divorced from the practice of dissecting dead bodies and describing anatomy. Saran Stone, for example, says, "I shall not fill any part of this Book with needless discourse on the Parts of Generation" (xviii), and Chapman concurs, "I think that such as never saw the *Dissection* of a Human Body, will be but little the better for a bare Description of those Parts," insisting, by way of explanation, "it is enough for one Man to act well in one Capacity" (preface). In short, there emerged, in the early decades of the eighteenth century, a new class of professional, mostly male, whose purview of specialization was midwifery. For reasons of propriety and their fragile authority, the new breed of midwife focused almost exclusively on pregnancy and infant care, virtually ignoring unmarried women.

Traditional female midwifery had cultural and legal authority over the female body, including virginity, but as modern (i.e., male) midwifery emerged, this authority diminished, as Mark Jackson has argued.[32] Whereas midwives previously had been called in by courts to confirm pregnancy, virginity, and even impotence, this function of the traditional midwife disappeared, as women gradually lost authority to testify about women's bodies. A popularized account of the divorce case

of Catherine and Edward Weld (1732) illustrates this phenomenon.[33]
Catherine sued for divorce based on Edward's impotence, resting her
case on sworn affidavits from "Three experienced Midwives" that she
was "*Virgo intacta*" (31). But surgeons for the husband argued, and
the court agreed that Midwives are not "*competent Judges of a
Woman's Virginity*" (33). Citing many sources, including Dionis's
"most curious *Dissertation*," the text argues that divorce cannot
depend on virginity, as this kind of evidence is "altogether uncertain,
and the most defective of all Proofs" (33, 61).[34] Noting that "there
are a thousand Ways of losing the Marks of Virginity, without having
to do with a Man; there are, in like manner, a thousand Ways of recov-
ering them again," the text argues against the ability of the female
body to testify to anything, especially male impotence (46). The text
goes on to claim that any inspection itself would violate a woman's
honor, providing more evidence for its admonition against investigations
of virginity by arguing that such investigations prove nothing and in
fact threaten the very thing they set out to prove.

I am suggesting that as newer methods of establishing authority
over the body take over, the hymen begins to disappear, either, as is
the case with Dionis, physically, or, as with the midwives, practically,
and rhetorically. The midwife manuals of the 1730s totally ignore
both the topic of virginity and the anatomy of the hymen. While
anatomists continue to describe the hymen, they do not engage any of
its controversial aspects and they rarely attach significance or usefulness to the hymen. The prevailing beliefs about the hymen confronted
anatomy with the limits of its field, and most eighteenth-century
anatomy texts, like those of William Cheselden (1713), James Keill
(1718), and Lorenz Heister (1721), radically de-emphasize virgin
anatomy. The most important figure linking midwifery and anatomy
was William Smellie; in his *A Set of Anatomical Tables with Explanations
and an abridgement of the Practice of Midwifery* (1754), there is
only one illustration of a woman who is not pregnant, and no hymen
is present. The difference between virginal and maternal bodies does
not seem to interest this midwife and anatomist, as was increasingly
the case with other anatomists. Neither the newer midwifery texts
nor anatomy ever gained the kind of cultural authority over virginity
that the earlier midwife manuals had. The injunction to direct
experience, the mistrust of the evidence in any one woman's body,
and the interest in defining and revising the category of woman
created a social climate in which a fascination for the hymen
flourished, but in which medicine and science had to abdicate
authority.[35]

The argument of this book as a whole hinges on the fact that just as medicine loses interest in virginity, we see an obsession, in literature, with virgins. I am linking the absence of virgins in the midwife manuals of the 1730s with the emergence of English fascination, in the 1740s, with literary virgins like Pamela. In the rest of the chapter, I examine one anatomy text, William Cowper's *The Anatomy of Humane Bodies* (1698), at some length because its bizarre story about the hymen is exemplary of the crisis of authority around the hymen that I have been describing. Cowper was a member of the Royal Society and one of the most important medical writers of his day; he was also, incidentally, involved in a well-known plagiarism case.[36] A fascinating product of the early anatomists' efforts to bring the hymen under the purview of anatomical methods, Cowper's anatomy text provides insight about how the epistemological, semiotic, and generic problems that medicine found in virginity set the stage for the particular form taken by the eighteenth-century literary obsession with virgins.

Dedicated to the president of the Royal Society, Cowper's text very deliberately tries to conform to the new standards of experimental science.[37] Drawings are the foundation of Cowper's anatomy text. The large drawings are accompanied, as is standard in such texts, by textual explanation. The hymen is drawn into one of the figures of female sexual anatomy, but the text accompanying the figure describes the hymen in terms that are ambiguous and changeable. "Traverse" in girls of 7 or 8 and "valvous" in virgins above 16 or 17, the hymen, once broken, becomes a set of caruncles, whose figure and number are variable.[38] Cowper's use of adjectives, multiplying due to differences among women, and his attempt to describe the hymen scientifically, do not lead to a coherent position on the hymen or on virginity. The text downplays the controversies over the hymen, and thereby it strategically avoids drawing attention to the limits of anatomy, but this means that his text cannot elaborate much about the hymen or about the nature of female virginity. His claims about the hymen are stated less authoritatively than his claims about other body parts, and they are much less authoritative than the earlier midwife manuals' discussions of virginity. Cowper assumes that there is a hymen in all women but does not acknowledge that the point is controversial. He avoids the controversy of a virginity "test" by stating, in an aside, that the hymen may be broken "in Coitu or otherwise.[39] Whereas Cowper often claims firsthand knowledge from viewing dissections of other organs, he does not claim such experience with the hymen, and, more than usual, he resorts to citing other anatomists. On the topic of purpose,

Cowper is uncharacteristically silent about the hymen. The standard, intact hymen of his drawing functions neither semiotically, as a reliable and accessible sign of virginity, nor physiologically, and the descriptive text that accompanies it similarly fails to establish the norms or functions of the hymen. Cowper's description is inadequate with respect to anatomical standards, including his own, because it fails to successfully generalize about all hymens and because its relation to the figure it illustrates is unclear.[40]

Without recourse to poetic tropes or to the authority of ancient sources made ineligible by Royal Society standards, Cowper resorts to a narrative form: the individual case study. The illumination of pathologies was a major goal of the new anatomy, and it is in the narrative form of the individual pathological case that Cowper's text achieves some mastery over the hymen. After the description, which I have argued is inadequate to social questions about the hymen and to the standards of anatomy, Cowper offers this narrative of a perversely imperforate hymen, a story that is punctuated by reminders of the inadequacy of simile and the visual deceptiveness of female bodies:

> Some years since I was call'd by my Ingenious Friend Dr. *Chamberlin* to see a Marry'd Woman of above Twenty Years of Age, whose Lower Belly was very much Distended, as if with Child. Upon Examining the *Pudendum*, we found the *Hymen* altogether Impervious, and driven out beyond the *Labia Pudendi* in such Manner, that at First Sight it appear'd not unlike a *Prolapsus Uteri*. In the Upper Part towards the *Clitoris* we found the Orifice of the *Meatus Urinarius* very open, and its Sides Extruded not unlike the *Anus* or *Cloaca* of a Cock, and without any Difficulty I could put my Fore-finger into the Bladder of Urine. On dividing the *Hymen*, at least a Gallon of Grumous Blood of divers Colours and Consistencies came from her, which was the retain'd *Menstrua*. The next Day, no less a Quantity of the same Matter flow'd after removing the Pessary which I had put in the Day before. After Three, or Four Days she was easie, and soon after recover'd, and within a Year was deliver'd of a healthful Child. Her Husband told us, Tho' lying with her at First was very painful to himself as well as to her, yet at last he had a more easie Access which could be by no other Way than the *Meatus Urinarius*.[41]

In this passage, the anatomist and a famous midwife, joining their authority together, examine a married woman who displays all the signs of normal defloration and pregnancy.[42] These illustrious medical men, not deceived, discover that her intact hymen has been obstructing the menstrual flow. They break the hymen, drain the uterus, and the couple goes on to a happy ending, a "healthful child." By way of explanation, both anatomical and psychological, Cowper claims that the couple had been having intercourse through the wife's urinary tract. This experience of sex might not have been quite as pleasurable as they would have expected ("at First was very painful to himself as well as to her"), but the experiences of penetration and decreasing pain, as well as the signs of pregnancy, led them to believe that they were having standard sexual intercourse. The hymen in this story presents a pathological obstruction to the desirable functioning of marriage and procreation; the signs provided by the woman's body are deceptive; and the couple needs the authority of the medical men to understand her anatomy and to procreate successfully.

This narrative accomplishes several things that the drawing and description do not. First of all, it places Cowper and a qualified corroborating witness (a Chamberlen no less) as eyewitnesses to an intact hymen. As the woman is ill and not a virgin, both their presence and their medical intervention are authorized, and their success confirms their medical legitimacy. As for objectivity, Cowper assumes the consummate position of disinterestedness: far from seeking out the truths of the hymen, he is called in by another doctor, who seems himself to have simply stumbled upon this virgin anatomy in the course of normal midwife duties.[43] The fact that the woman is married, the presence of the husband, and, perhaps, her unnatural disfigurement diffuse the possibility of an erotic response on their part and thus bolster an implicit claim of objectivity. Furthermore, the anatomist's specialized understanding of body parts leads to a beneficial medical effect. This narrative of an extremely unusual hymen, then, helps Cowper bring the hymen under the authority of anatomical discourse.

This anecdote authorizes the medical men, specifically men of the new science and its new discursive standards, through the perverse deceptiveness of the woman's body. The text signals the deceptiveness of her body through analogy: her hymen is "not unlike" a prolapsed uterus, and her grossly enlarged urinary tract, which her husband mistakes for a vaginal canal, could also be mistaken for the anus of a cock and thereby, presumably, the anus of a human. These comparisons are not figurative similes. They are visual comparisons, and thus, far from helping to clarify the deceptive visual evidence of the woman's body, they suggest that the female body is fundamentally untrustworthy. In suggesting that the virgin cannot be distinguished from the woman whose uterus could fall right through her vagina and that the three apertures of a woman can all be confused, this text authorizes the intervention of the medical men by suggesting that they are the only ones not deceived by these ambiguous visual signs. The women's body is both semiotically and physically pathological, and these pathologies allow the medical men access where there would not have been access under normal circumstances.

Although a rare medical curiosity, this narrative of a perversely imperforate hymen shares a number of qualities with "normal" hymens and thus implies some general truths about the female anatomy, to wit: the woman's body produces false signs, and the hymen is dangerous both to her health and to procreation, as well as to the man, who suffers pain and is threatened with lack of an heir. Though this story seems anomalous, it reinforces the generally pathological nature of the hymen and the salutary effect of sex and men. This narrative is, ultimately, merely a story of defloration and, as such, has something to say about norms of defloration. Blood is the sign of normal defloration, and this medical procedure elicits a colorful gallon of "grumous blood," a sign of both the pathology of the hymen and the efficacy of male intervention. The problem in this case is the hymen, and the solution, one which is far from necessarily medical, is defloration by a man. Though the hymen in general resisted the visual standards of anatomy, the male scientists in this case can, like sexual partners, produce unambiguous evidence of their effect on the woman. This anomalous case superimposes a traditional defloration narrative on a pathological medical defloration; the shared properties of these narratives of physical defloration include delay, epistemological uncertainty, obstacles (both physical and social), pain, blood, and a resolution that rewards all participants with happiness in the form of sexual, genealogical, or epistemological satisfaction. Thus, while the hymen itself may be elusive, changeable, and pathological, as the hymen in this case is, the narrative of defloration by a man is established as normative, salutary, and available for scientific observation. Moreover, this narrative of the hymen, in both normal and pathological versions, functions analogically for the emergent narrative of the virgin herself. Like this hymen, the eighteenth-century virgin will display ambiguous signs, will suffer pain and misunderstanding, and will be cured by male sexual/romantic intervention. The narrative of defloration reveals itself to be the plot that structures so many domestic narratives even today, a point I will develop further.

Cowper's recourse to the case study is marginally adequate to anatomical discourse. At this time, the case study was typically used to illustrate a specific point, and it appeared more commonly in medical texts, like the newer midwifery texts, than in anatomy texts. Nonetheless, it was still an acceptable form in anatomy texts, and Cowper himself uses the form in other instances. But narratives are rare in Cowper's text, and this one is unique in that Cowper does not explicitly state its purpose. Furthermore, this is the only narrative that he refers to as a "history" rather than a "case", that is, by a literary term rather than a medical one.[44] As such, it is neither the kind of truth nor the kind of evidence upon which the rest of the text relies. Ideally, an "experiment" on virginity would have, like a dissection, taken place in a social space and would be replicable.[45] This case is unusual and medically urgent, so repeatability is not possible here, and the possibility of finding such a case to dissect would have been slim.[46] Cowper's text makes a case for the propriety, legitimacy, and plausibility of this case study, but the case itself is extremely specific, unusual, and non-replicable. Since it provides no "virginity test," such a narrative is not useful for laypeople who might have a question about a particular woman's virginity. Moreover, the knowledge that Cowper has access to depends on separation of knowledge and erotic satisfaction. The doctors in this case have access to both medical knowledge and to the action of defloration, and thus the case study puts medical authority over the husband's, whose naïve drives the story.

This narrative, then, fulfills certain epistemological and generic demands, but it produces more problems than it solves. Since the woman is physically virginal, despite her marriage and her intention to have sex, the story detaches virginity from chastity. As such, this case suggests the very problematic notion that virginity could signify nothing about the actions or intentions of a particular woman. Further, it suggests that virginity is not material at all, but rather a fully symbolic identity, since the woman has a hymen but is not a virgin. With Cowper, we have arrived at a massively overdetermined hymen. Unavailable to empirical epistemology, it nonetheless contributes to authorizing scientific endeavors. Putatively a sign of female virginity, it comes to signify something about men rather than women. A way, perhaps, of disciplining female sexuality and of separating women into two categories, it miraculously rebounds to become a sign of male sexuality and a manner of distinguishing between men: between those who have access to its secrets and those who do not, or between men who know women and men who have sex with women, or between men who have authority and men who are subject to satire. Out of these crises of evidence and significance, certain kinds of generic quandary emerge. Cowper's text demonstrates what these quandaries are and suggests that they are better addressed not in scientific texts, but in the discursive modes of narrative and fiction (if I may be so bold as to challenge his story's authenticity). Cowper's fabulous narrative of the "strange but true" hymen is tightly constructed to fulfill the epistemological imperatives of anatomy through a slightly unorthodox methodology, but in fact it ends up revealing the fissures and limitations of this method and thus offers an explanation for why we get narratives of virgins in literary texts rather than representations of virginity in medical texts. Cowper's story reveals the fact that emergent ideals of virginity are more suited to a narrative mode than to visual description or poetic tropes, because interest in virginity is, at least in Protestant England, motivated by interest in defloration rather than in the facts of physical virginity and because embedding the hymen within a narrative creates formal authority where scientific authority is lacking. Moreover, my analysis of the hymen of seventeenth-century medical texts suggests that fiction is the appropriate mode for discursive representations of virginity, because epistemological and semiotic authority over virginity can be, at least at this time, only an act of the imagination.

Although the virgin disappears from science, there remained a profound interest—both in literature and in real life—in virginity and the hymens of women. This is evidenced by the novelistic obsession—sentimental, satiric, and pornographic—with virgin protagonists and by the "defloration mania" that reached its height in the second half of the eighteenth century and continued well into the nineteenth century.[47] Medicine, though, is not driving this new obsession with virginity, which is fueled by lack of knowledge and by the kind of energy that circulates around an object that is threatening. April Alliston has argued that the hymen's inaccessibility creates a situation wherein men are forced to rely on a woman's "word" about the status of her virginity.[48] The new science may have promised to substitute its own authority for women's physical and linguistic inscrutability, but that effort ultimately failed, leading, I suggest, to the obsession with woman's "words" in epistolary novels featuring virgin protagonists. Kathleen Coyne Kelly describes physical virginity as an "abstract idea residing in an anatomical metonym" (7). What I have been tracing is the way that new models of science attempted to make the abstract qualities of virginity concrete and why that effort was doomed to fail. One reason, implied by Kelly, is that virginity never did really reside in the body. In arguing for an epistemologically unstable hymen, this chapter contributes to ongoing work that challenges the idea that neoclassical thinking insisted on the passivity of the object of analysis.[49] In fact, I suggest that the pervasive instability of the material hymen may be part of the reason for its ongoing attraction and power as a sign. I do, nonetheless, argue for a kind of failure on the part of scientific discourse with respect to the hymen. Late seventeenth-century science subjected the hymen to new epistemological and rhetorical standards and deemed the hymen—and women—to be simultaneously inadequate and incorrigible. But the hymen had its revenge, in that it refused to make itself fully available for scientific exploration, thereby exposing those who pursued its secrets to satire and maintaining a good deal of its symbolic power. In demonstrating that the early modern hymen could not be maintained as a material object, I suggest that the dematerialization of virginity into "virtue" was motivated to some extent by the failure of empirical epistemology. I am proposing that the hymen's resistance to objectification was in fact what made it the perfect object for skeptical neoclassical analysis and may partially account for the enduring interest in the figure of the virgin after she has been defrocked, pathologized, and dissected.

CHAPTER 3

Hymen Humor: Ballads and the Matter of Virginity

At the same time that acolytes of the new science were wrangling with the materiality of the hymen and propagandists for the Protestant cause were maligning the motivations and material practices of the cloister, the material reality of virginity was being meditated upon in a very different realm. On the streets of London and throughout other English cities, ballad mongers sang and sold songs about sexuality and courtship in which virginity figures prominently. Although scholars assume that ballads were written mostly by men, they were performed in public for an audience that would have included women and that would have been lower class, or at least more economically diverse than the audiences of any of the other literature that I examine.[1] As such, they offer a perspective on virginity in which both class and gender figure differently than the mainly middle-class and masculine texts that I deal with elsewhere. Printed quickly and cheaply, they were repeatedly copied and recycled. The street ballad flourished when it became feasible to publish short pieces quickly and inexpensively, and it declined when the publishing world began to move toward longer works. Their heyday was the early sixteenth century, but they were an extremely important form of popular culture throughout the seventeenth and early eighteenth centuries.[2] Most importantly for my purposes, these broadside and broadsheet ballads, more than any other genre that I am looking at, with the possible exception of novels, are obsessed with female virginity; certainly the explicit acknowledgment of virginity as the subject of these ballads is unparalleled in other forms.[3] The emphasis on virginity is also unparalleled, as far as I can tell, in ballads of other historical periods. Sixteenth- and early seventeenth-century ballads about sex focus on cuckoldry and marital strife but not so much on virginity, an equation that seems to have reversed itself toward the end of the seventeenth century.[4] What distinguishes the ballads from other discourses of virginity is their emphasis on wit, rather than epistemology, sexual desire, or virtue. This focus may account for their unprecedented multiplicity of plots and their lack of explicit moralizing. Virgins make their appearances in these ballads as seduced maidens, as cunning tricksters and naïve romantics, as lusty sufferers of greensickness, as spiritual martyrs, and as market-economy barterers, both successful and unsuccessful. That is, "virgin" is not an identifiable identity. Rather, these ballads represent a myriad of narrative and representational possibilities for virginity.[5] At the same time, they use virginity as a heuristic device for deception, loss, death, the coinage crises, and the marketplace. In short, these ballads, though in a lower-rent district than the Royal Society, the pulpit, the theater, or even the emergent culture of coffeehouses, are hardly removed from the events in other realms. As a matter of fact, they comment upon their higher-class counterparts in extremely witty ways.

The previous chapter, which discussed the way that the scientific revolution's emphasis on investigating the material reality of the body impacted both representations of virginity and the Reformation project to convert England, revealed that virginity was hard to maintain as material object. In this chapter, I argue that the immateriality of the hymen forms the foundation for almost all of the humor around virginity in street literature. The publication circumstances of the ballads—their ephemerality, performativity, overt consummability and very public status—mean that they are perfectly situated to offer a critique of emergent ideas about virginity and materiality. This is because their genre discouraged the development of individual subjectivity and precluded investigation—even imaginatively—of physical interiority. As a performative, public genre like the theater, ballads access virginity only imaginatively, via representation. Precisely because the material reality of the hymen is generically unavailable in ballads, the form invites meditation on the relationship between the materiality of virginity and its representations. Whereas scientific discourse stages a crisis about the materiality of the hymen, and thus the more general availability of the body to empirical epistemology, these ballads, in response, satirize the scientific revolution and other middling pretensions, such as marriage, virginity, and virtue, that hinge upon complex and overdetermined oscillations between abstraction and material reality. In ballads about virginity, the joke, almost invariably, revolves around the materiality and linguistic comprehensibility of virginity. Over and over again, we find the ambiguously material word at odds with the even less material hymen.

Many of these issues are played out in one of the wittiest ballads of virginity, "The Fair Maid of the West, who sold her Maidenhead for a high-crown'd Hat," in which a young virgin makes an even trade of her maidenhead for a hat that she desires.[6] She negotiates with the haberdasher, who originally stipulated for her maidenhead plus a crown, and feels that she made a good "bargain":

> With a fine Hat I now am sped,
> And all for a silly Maidenhead.

She then reports this transaction to her mother:

> He had my Maidenhead said she,
> Which was a great plague unto me.

The industrious young woman's mother is incensed and insists that she cancel the deal, return the hat, and "retrieve" her maidenhead. The haberdasher is only too happy to reverse the trade, and he "restores" her maidenhead. On the one hand, this young and now former virgin seems to be the object of satire because she has absorbed the notion that her hymen's value inheres in its materiality and thus that it can and even should be traded for other materially valuable items. She also misunderstands its value, in that she does not realize that it might be more valuable than a hat, no matter how fashionable. Her mother is even more worthy of ridicule because she seems to believe simultaneously in the materiality of the hymen (it can be restored) and in the hymen's fundamentally abstract nature (since the "restoration," one can only assume, is a purely linguistic act). Both women foolishly accept the false notion that the maidenhead is a tradable item, one whose trade can be revoked and one that can circulate, and recirculate, like other material consumer items. The haberdasher appears to be the lucky beneficiary of the women's consumer desires and their naïveté: he winds up with both the maidenhead and the hat.

The joke, however, is not entirely on the women. In the absence of a pregnancy, these women really can decide whether the maidenhead has been "restored," since men have no reliable way to test claims of virginity. Hence, the women will probably fairly easily be able to conduct another, more advantageous, negotiation for the younger woman's maidenhead in the future. Although the daughter returns the hat, the implication is that this is entirely unnecessary: with or without the hat, the women are the ones who will testify to the material reality of her hymen. In general, women get to decide the status of the hymen, and thus they are in a position to dupe men about it. In fact, it is precisely because they understand how to take advantage of the hymen's ambiguous materiality that the women emerge here, at least potentially, as better positioned than men to exploit the market for maidenheads. This is also why the mode in this, as in most ballads, is comic rather than satiric: no didactic lesson can be discerned here, since no participants are harmed. As an ephemeral thing, the maidenhead is productive of the silly, not the tragic or the moral. This ballad exhibits virtually every aspect of humor in the ballads about virginity; there are aspects of the humor that relate to the materiality of hymen and to how this materiality positions the hymen in a market economy. There is also a tension between the material reality of the hymen and its discursive reality: what does it mean to say the haberdasher "had" a maidenhead? And what does it mean to "restore" it? In short, materiality, economics, and linguistic deception are the centerpieces of hymen humor in these street ballads.

This ballad is also at least marginally an example of a subcategory of virginity ballads: ballads about greensickness that respond directly to the medical hymen discussed in the previous chapter. Far from being materially valuable or salutary to this young virgin, her hymen is described as a "plague." As I discussed earlier, greensickness was considered a serious, even critical, disease in which the hymen pathologically obstructed the menstrual flow. Coincident with the medical community's burgeoning interest in this disease, we find an explosion of ballads on greensickness. Many of the ballads I examined in researching this chapter persisted in different forms for centuries, but the greensickness ballads have a much shorter lifespan: the vast majority of them were published between 1670 and 1695, right at the beginning of the scientific revolution.[7] Unlike its contemporaneous medical community, ballad culture did not take greensickness seriously, frequently playing on the ephemerality and ambiguity of the hymen in order to comically criticize the idea that it could have the power to threaten a woman's life—or a man's masculinity. "Dick the Plow-Man" provides a particularly apt example of a greensickness ballad, since the female suffering from greensickness is an especially extreme caricature of female aggressivity and the male is an exceptionally extreme dupe.[8] This ballad tells the story of Betty, who is "very sick" and in need of "something Dick has got." Betty's illness is construed as purely physical, and she intuitively understands both what her problem is and what it is that "Dick has got" that she needs. Dick, however, does not understand her when she explains that she is sick and that only he can cure her. Though written in the third person, Betty's voice dominates while Dick's lack of understanding is exploited for comic effect:

> Prethee *Betty* how should I know,
> What the thing is that you mean;
> Then she sighed, and cry'd Hi-ho,
> Such a Fool was never seen:
> I must languish here and dye,
> Here and dye, here and dye;
> And can't have a Remedy,
> For my grievous mallady;
> *Was ever there so dull a Sot,*
> *That knows not yet what he has got.*

The humor in this ballad derives from the fact that the male sexual organ is not named directly: metaphorized as a "thing" and a "remedy" and providing a synecdochical source for our hero's name, the penis nonetheless has no material reality for Dick because of its lack of linguistic presence.[9] The only reason that Betty is sick, actually that Betty is even *speaking*, is because of Dick's lack of comprehension—a fault that links linguistic and physiological inadequacy. Part of the joke comes from the immateriality of the hymen: it really should not be able to cause such problems, since the much more material penis can easily correct the problem. Even though Dick is extremely dense, he also possesses something that is valuable, even critical, to the virgin Betty. The joke is funny only because of its manifest absurdity: the normally and appropriately ephemeral hymen is asserting itself more forcefully than the penis, whose material reality is never in question. The joke works by imaginatively linking the hymen and the penis: while one is manifestly visible and material, their shared properties, in terms of gender identification, suggest that the properties of one might infect the other. The "thingness" of the penis is at issue precisely because the metaphorical weight it carries, as a thing that differentiates sex, links it to the ambiguously material realm of female sexuality. As a disease of the hymen, greensickness in this ballad is revealed to be a complicated joke, one that revolves around the absurd notion that the male sexual organ might be as immaterial as the hymen. What is at stake here is the fundamental dissimilarity between the hymen and the penis, and between the man and the woman in terms of how the alienability of their sexuality is theorized. Women can lose, trade, or give away their virginity; they can be made ill by it and they can be victimized by its theft. But the male's sexual organ and very sexuality cannot be alienated from him, do not degrade with use, and are not typically metaphorized as part of an economic system.[10] Thus Dick's obtuseness—the fact that he does not understand how his sexual organ can be a "thing" and so misunderstands its value and its usefulness—can also be read as a sophisticated resistance to seeing his penis in terms similar to the hymen. The hymen's special status derives from the fact that it is simultaneously a material object, a sign of something valuable and, unlike the penis (at least in this account), alienable from the body, at least conceptually. John Sitter argues that in witty Augustan writing, the body is often seen as a "corrective to abstraction" because ignorance of the body is the root of abstraction (5). In this and other ballads, however, the hymen is revealed to be unlike other body parts in that its ambiguous materiality and fundamental metaphoricity make it ripe for abstraction, rather than allowing it to act as a corrective to abstraction (5). Sitter argues that "writers of the period tend to assume that the ability to recognize and use metaphor reflects a proper recognition and use of the body" (130). But the hymen of this study usually manages to maintain its connection both to abstraction and to the material reality of the body.

I have been using Marxist terms in an effort to uncover the economic "joke" about the hymen. But the hymen does not, it seems, fit nicely into Marx's economic lexicon. This might be taken as evidence for the historical anachronicity of using Marx to talk about eighteenth-century culture. However, this critique would then leave us without a joke. For just as the hymen cannot be compared to the penis without significant destabilization of both terms, so too the hymen cannot easily be regarded as a commodity. In fact, the misrecognition of the hymen as commodity offers many comic possibilities in these ballads. Many years later, Karl Marx will describe the commodity in terms that sound uncannily like the hymen that this project has been describing:

> A commodity appears at first sight a very trivial thing, and easily understood. But its analysis shows that it is, in reality, a very queer thing, abounding in metaphysical subtleties and theological niceties (I.4, 81)

While part of the goal of this book is to complicate the feminist truism that women are objects of exchange, I might be willing to admit here that the hymen could be the paradigmatic commodity precisely because of its immateriality and its resultant ability to support abstract structures. Except that the young virgins in the two ballads discussed thus far refuse to recognize the "metaphysical subtleties and theological niceties" of the hymen. Their virginity is an obvious and trivial thing without metaphysical, metaphorical, or ideological weight. In sum, ballads about virginity reveal the very immateriality of the hymen and then use that immateriality as the basis for a series of jokes in which the hymen gets mistaken for a commodity. Pre-Marx, these ballads offer a proleptic critique of an emergent economy in which virginity will come to have both material and metaphorical weight.

Some ballads do treat the hymen as an object of exchange. However, they also quite frequently embed a self-reflective critique of this idea. A good example is "The new Irish Christmas Box. Or, the Female Dear Joy Trick'd Out of her Maiden-head."[11] A virgin sleeps with the first person speaker, who is bragging about this escapade, because he promises her a number of popular consumer items: a bottle of claret, a rigging, a top-knot, and some new gloves. When she subsequently gets pregnant, he happily insists that they will be married "When the Devil is Blind." But this is not represented as heartless cruelty. The male speaker's poor treatment of the virgin seems justified by the combination of her obvious naïveté about the economic system and her class aspirations. The items that she trades for her hymen belong properly to a woman of a higher class. Her attraction to these consumer goods sets up and justifies her downfall. The implication is that the speaker has made a good deal, and the maiden's inability to see the value of her maidenhead allows her to become the satiric object: she simultaneously overvalues herself by aspiring to a higher class, and undervalues her virginity, which would allow her to maintain her current class. The woman fares especially poorly here, since she gets nothing that she wants in the trade—there is no indication that she wants sex, and she does not even get the items that he promises her. If we assume that the "Irish" in the title refers to the poor girl's nationality, she is, according to the codes of virtue set up by this study, doomed: as an Irish (i.e., not British), Catholic (i.e., not Protestant), lower- (i.e., not middle-) class figure, she is predictably overinvested in the material world. In any case, the conflict in "The new Irish Christmas Box" comes from the fact that the maidenhead is not a commodity in the same way that other items are. It is both more perishable and less mobile than most commodities: it cannot really be traded because it cannot continue to circulate. Marriage is typically depicted as the only good investment to be made with the only capital a poor woman has. The female in this ballad, unlike the ones previously discussed, finds herself in the satiric mode rather than the comic because she refuses to accept the hymen's special status, and she does not appear to have a mother who will teach her. This ballad suggests that ultimately the hymen does not conform to the laws of commerce because its exchange value is limited to exchange in marriage or prostitution. As such, this ballad both contrasts the marriage market with the consumer market and simultaneously reveals some fundamental, and unsavory, similarities. The idea that the hymen cannot be subject to the vagaries of the capitalist system is, after all, the fundamental idea supporting companionate marriage. What these texts are doing is making explicit both the ideal and the impossibility of seeing virginity as a value that lies outside of economics. As a kind of symbolic capital, in Pierre Bourdieu's terms, the hymen produces economic relationships disguised as moral relationships (120–123).

Whereas traditional feminist arguments about women and exchange almost always position the woman as a passive object of exchange, these ballads often rely, for their humor, on the notion that if the hymen is a valued object of exchange, then the woman is positioned to be an agent in the marketplace.[12] This is why the women in the first two ballads discussed are the sources of wit. But in any case, or perhaps as a result, most ballads reject the idea that the hymen is a commodity that can be traded. For example, in "My Thing is My Own"[13] the female speaker takes the materiality, and the valuability, of her hymen very seriously indeed, in that she insists that her "thing" cannot be traded or sold:

> An Usurer came with abundance of Cash,
> But I had no mind to come under his Lash,
> He profer'd me Jewels, and great store of gold,
> But I would not mortgage my little Free-hold.
> My thing is my own, and I'll keep it so still
> Yet other young Lasses may do what they will.

This young woman insists (through the repetition of "my thing is my own") that her hymen is not a commodity that can be substituted for money or other commodities. Her virginity is a personal possession that she may choose, in defiance of laws of exchange, to maintain for life.[14] But this sense of jurisdiction over her body and decisions about her life is undercut by the suggestion that her virginity and sexuality are a "Free-hold." The ballad's ending makes the implications of this more clear:

> My thing is my own, and I'll keep it so still,
> Until I be Marryed, say Men what they will.

As a "free-hold," her virginity is the key to her lifetime maintenance. It is her inheritance from a patriarchal system, and thus it is not hers to sell or develop. It is also not hers to keep. This young woman's virginity functions like a dowry; it does not make her economically independent but rather keeps her enmeshed within a patriarchal economic structure. Her maintenance is dependent on her getting married, and her husband will be responsible for managing her inheritance. This ballad, along with the ones previously discussed, get their comic energy from misapprehension of the hymen as an object of exchange. While they depend upon the notion that the hymen is a material object, they also depend upon the fact that its materiality is not obvious and has a special status. In other words, they rely on the notion that the materiality and the value of the hymen are frequently misunderstood. In all of these ballads, the hymen resists being fully implicated in capitalism.

Throughout this book, I discuss the anxiety that surrounds discourses on virginity, and I argue that satire lurks as a threat to epistemological and sentimental investments in the hymen's ability to signify virginity. Satires against virginity often function exactly as eighteenth-century satire is supposed to, in that they enact a skeptical critique of the effort to isolate the purely material from the purely abstract, or vice versa. What then, might we make of the predominantly comic mode of these ballads? What ideological, intellectual, or social work do they perform in this larger culture of discourses on virginity? The answers to these questions would seem necessarily to entail attention to the ballads' role as popular literature and thus attention to the problem of class. The "story" about virginity is that it matters mostly or literally only for a ruling class or at least for a propertied class. Virginity matters, that is, only if there are genealogical rights, divine authority, or real property at stake in biological birth. Scholarship about the relationship between sexuality and social class traditionally argues that the middle-class rise to power was related to its claims to sexual virtue, which are made by contrasting middle-class (and Protestant) sexual values with both naïve promiscuity on the part of the laboring class and self-indulgent aristocratic libertinism. My readings of the ballads support this division of the classes by sexual values; while laboring classes are frequently seen to be satirizing middle-class pretensions to sexual virtue, they are just as frequently satirized for pretending to those same virtues. So the ballads' trivialization of virginity can be seen as either conservative or critical. In a very influential argument about carnival and other types of popular culture, Mikhail Bahktin has argued that such witty, comic forms can offer a revolutionary critique of an oppressive seriousness. And many critics, for example Robert Markley, argue for the subversive potential of Restoration comic forms. But not all critics see comedy as radical. For instance, Sigmund Freud finds the genesis of jokes in child's play, arguing that the wit of jokes works as a screen that enables us to disable the functioning of reason and critique (1957b). Perhaps even more pessimistically, Samuel Weber, in his analysis of Freud, argues that jokes are even less defensible in that they always germinate from narcissistic desires.

Thus it seems crucial to emphasize that the ballads generally employ comic rather than satiric wit.[15] That is, they do not necessarily aim to "correct," or at least not explicitly. If the function of the satiric is to draw attention to problems that must be addressed, the comic is more commonly seen as a way to argue for the irrelevancy of its vehicle. The comic is usually seen as a much gentler mode, one that pokes fun at the irrelevant. And the hymen's material irrelevancy is what makes it, at least in the context of the ballads, a foundation for the comic. Thus when ballads treat the body, including the penis and especially the hymen, as comic they, in the words of Leon Guilhamet, reduce them to "things of no importance" (7). This is not to say that these ballads do not do ideological work, because the reduction of the hymen to a thing of no importance is undoubtedly ideological work of the highest order. In John Locke's famous, if by no means original, formulation, wit is distinct from judgment in that wit bring things together while judgment separates them (1975, 155–157). In some ways, then, these witty ballads bring together things that science and emergent discourses of sociability endeavor to separate: the hymen and the penis, the material and the immaterial, economic commodities and such invaluable abstractions as science and money. In Locke's formulation of wit, the one that points to and perhaps catalyzes the historical denigration of wit, these things should not be put together. But under the more archaic version of wit relevant to these ballads, the bringing together of material reality with the metaphoricities, metaphysical subtleties, and theological niceties that it screens is, in fact, exactly the point.

*   *   *

I have been discussing the ways in which the ambiguous materiality of the hymen provides the source of the humor in a number of ballads. Ambiguous materiality is why the hymen can be equated, for comic effect, with money—why, that is, the hymen both is and is not like other commodities. It is like other commodities in that it is subject to fetishization, but it is distinguished by the same thing: its role as commodity fetish is always made unstable by its exemplary ambiguous materiality. The hymen is, in sum, a funny, obvious, and ambivalent thing when it is seen to be operating in an economic realm. I turn now to ballads that deal more directly, and realistically, with a courtship situation and that address the hymen's naturalized role within the economy of sexuality and marriage, rather than its seemingly less natural role within blatantly economic transactions. Whereas ballads about economy lay bare the paradoxical nature of the notion of hymen as commodity, these ballads depend upon something altogether different for their comic effect. Rather than making obvious the immateriality of the hymen by revealing the comic possibilities that arise from a particularly naïve kind of misrecognition about the hymen's status as material commodity, these ballads about deception work in the opposite direction. They investigate the deliberate attempts, facilitated by the hymen's ephemerality, to exploit misrecognition via rhetorical deception. By undertaking an exploration of the analogical links between linguistic deception and the kinds of bodily deception made available by the hymen, these ballads reveal the extent to which the hymen's ambiguous materiality can be seen in antagonistic conflict with the ambiguous materiality of words. In short, instead of mining the hymen's relation to material things ("have you heard the one about the hymen the hat and . . . 'the thing'?") for comedy, these ballads work by putting words in competition with the hymen.

A huge number of ballads admonish women, both indirectly via their narrative and explicitly via moralization, to beware of the male rhetoric of seduction. The "dissembling cogging, / cunning, cozening young man" is a frequent antagonist of not only the women's virginity but also her wit.[16] Since it is young men's "constant trade to cog and flatter," young maids must "of flattering words beware."[17] Over and over again, ballads enjoin women not to find themselves in the situation of this poor girl, who addresses her seducer:

> First by deluding words thus to deceive me,
> Having obtained your ends scornfully leave me.[18]

Such outcomes and admonitions warn women to beware of male speech, and there are many stories of women learning from the mistakes of others and thereby resisting the deceptive advances of men.[19] These stories suppose a necessity of female alliance against the wiles of men and posit that the female who is motivated by her appropriate desire for marriage must take a skeptical approach to the language of men.[20]

Male deception in these ballads centers on the discourse of seduction. There is a long history of seduction poems in English literature, but the *carpe diem* poems of the seventeenth century (like Andrew Marvell's "To His Coy Mistress") are the immediate historical antecedent and influence on the literature discussed here. Seduction poems usually assume that the female's hesitancy comes from the conflict between her natural sexual desires and a cultural injunction against sex outside of marriage. According to literary critic Derek Connon, in a typical seduction, the man convinces the woman that he has some knowledge that she does not, and this justifies the breaking of convention. The seducer typically de-emphasizes the importance of the seducee's virginity, focusing on the pleasures of sex, based on his knowledge thereof, and making little distinction between the first experience of sexual intercourse and subsequent ones. In the late seventeenth and early eighteenth centuries, there were a number of ballads that followed such a conventionally successful seduction plot: the male instigates, the female consents and enjoys it, and virginity does not figure as especially important. A song from *The Musical Miscellany* (1729) offers an example. In this song, repetition follows consummation almost immediately:

> When, with a Sigh, she accords me the Blessing,
> And her Eyes twinkle 'twixt Pleasure and Pain;
> Ah, what a Joy 'tis, beyond all expressing!
> Ah, what a Joy to hear, *Shall we again?*
> Ah, what a Joy, &c. (101)

While there are a few such successful seduction ballads (in which the woman does not regret her seduction), and while there are also many cases of women victimized by male seduction, there is a much more striking trend in popular street literature, in which strong female characters mock the conventions and assumptions of seduction narratives. "In Cloe's Chamber" is a fascinating example.[21] It begins by claiming that it is a "relic" of a poem about three times as long. The ballad begins to describe a typical scene of female desire and consent:

> A melting Virgin seldom speaks.
> But with her Breasts and Eyes and Cheeks:
> Nor was it hard from These to find
> That CLOE had—almost a Mind.

Although it is the man who is driving the seduction in this description, Cloe is also sexually desirous and her body, which is presumably less deceptive than speech, reveals her desire or her "mind" to have sex. Before the consummation, which seems to be the direction in which things are headed, there is an abrupt break in the seduction narrative; the "Desunt Caetera" ("the remaining bit") continues:

> For CLOE coming in one day,
> As on my Desk the Copy lay;
> What means this rhyming Fool? she cries,
> Why some Folks may believe these Lies!
> So on the Fire she threw the Sheet.
> I burn'd my Hand—to save this Bit.

The depiction of the amorous couple after marriage, or even after sex, suggests that this ballad is a parody of carpe diem poem and marriage plots. In this scene, Cloe is far from the desirous and conflicted maid that the first part of the poem depicts, and "Damon" is far from the irresistible seducer—he is, instead, a pacified, even henpecked, husband (also a common convention of popular literature). By tossing his song of female desire and male seduction in the trash, Cloe exposes the story as fiction and leaves the man with a burned hand and a bit of a ballad, that is, with a wound and a fragment. Her actions suggest that stories of female desire and seduction are both fragmented and fictionalized. Instead of sexual pleasure, the ballad promises domestic authority to the woman who resists the fictional narrative of natural female—and male—sexual desire. This ballad thus parodies both female virtue and male libertinism, a discourse that claims to expose the artificiality of female virtue while upholding male sexuality as natural. Probably written by a man, John Banks, this poem exposes the conventions of texts of sexual desire, now past their heyday, as fictions that function to shore up masculinity.

Questions of fictionality often impinge upon the representation of virginity in this period. In many cases, virginity and fictionality are tropes for one another since authority over the hymen is frequently revealed to be an act of the male imagination. In this ballad, however, it is seduction and fictionality that are mutually implicated. The man's narrative of seduction is interrupted—that is, revealed to be a fiction—at the precipice of consummation. Ballads at this time frequently portray male sexual desire as an instrumental fiction in the service of other desires and not, as in *carpe diem* poems, a product of natural sexual urges. Men seduce women not for love or sex, but they do so often for material goods or for a story to tell their friends. In this ballad, Damon's desire to recount the story of the seduction of his wife is not diminished by the fact that the story is untrue, for he saves the "bit" of the story at the expense of a burn. For Damon, the story of seduction is perhaps more important than the fact of seduction. In another, especially bizarre, example of distorted male motivation, "The Country Maiden's Lamentation" recounts the story of a tailor who seduces a poor country girl merely to acquire her clothes, a plot that takes some time to execute: he seduces her, gets her pregnant, and then, when she begins to grow too big for her clothes, runs off with them, promising to alter them to fit her.[22] This ballad comically suggests the elaborate lengths that men will go in constructing fictions to seduce women, and it questions the male motivation for such fiction-making. There are thus two levels of fiction making at work in these ballads: fiction is a crucial component of seduction, and sexual desire can be fictionalized to serve other, more pressing, desires, including narrative desire as well as material (in this case, sartorial) desire.

Women are similarly implicated in fictionality and deception. In many cases, a woman deceives a man regarding the status of her virginity. Since the hymen's physicality does not lend itself to proof, the possibility exists for deliberate female deception about her sexual experience. Where a woman sells the maidenhead, it is usually a story that winds up poorly for her, and where she sells it more than once, the story becomes pornography. But where she simply tricks a man into marrying her—that is, when marriage, not money, is the motivation—the possibilities for comedy and satire make it a favorite story of popular literature. *The Richmond Maidenhead* (a chapbook from 1722) is a good example. A much-diseased fop decides that the country will provide a disease-free virgin that he can seduce without worry. He is apparently acting on a myth that sleeping with a virgin could cure venereal disease. Upon finding a likely suspect, the "maiden" of the title, he attempts to seduce her. He begins by assuming that she is a virgin, but he becomes impressed with her because she resists his advances. Rather than him convincing her to sleep with him, she ends up convincing him to marry her. After marriage, he admits to having planned to seduce and abandon her, whereupon she explains,

> The Dame reply'd, ay, so I thought,
> Old Birds cannot with Chaff be caught;
> *Twice* in this manner I've been bit,
> But the *third Time* have learnt more *Wit*.

The man is clearly the butt of the joke here, and it is his desire to deceive the woman that both allows him to be tricked and justifies his fate. In wanting to find a virgin, the male sets up evidentiary standards of virginity—presence in the country, lack of knowledge and understanding about sex, resistance to his advances—that are easy to fake and that cause him to misread the signs of virginity. His self-interested, and mainly nonsexual, desire for a virgin and his willingness to deceive her lead to his being tricked himself. The text is comic: it is not explicitly meant to instruct or to move the audience, except to amusement; there is no victim, and the message here seems to be that these two are equally matched. (Although I think she gets a poor bargain, in a diseased, deceptive, and easily fooled husband, I do not think the ballad is meant to be seen as moralizing).

Many of these ballads rely on population mobility as an accessory to deception, and they do not necessarily depict this as a bad thing. Since there is no way to physically determine virginity, men must rely on knowledge of the woman and her social circle for any information about her. They must rely, that is, on secondary signs. While women are easily seduced by men's words, men, not willing to believe testimony, are just as frequently deceived by their own beliefs about femininity. *The Richmond Maidenhead*, like William Wycherley's *The Country Wife (1675)*, suggests that men believed that women in the country were more likely to be virgins, though of course this belief turns out, in both examples, to be false. Similarly, "The Merry Hay Makers" suggests that geographic relocation, typically from the country to the city, was a manner of deceiving men about one's virginity.[23] It claims that young women enjoy sex in the country, "And when they are crackt, away they are packt, / For Virgins away to the City."

Because men are easily deceived about the virginity of a woman, the consequences of losing one's virginity are often depicted as minor and surmountable. Women's sexual activity and deception of men are all in good fun and often amenable to marriage rather than detrimental. Even pregnancy is not necessarily an obstacle. "The Witty Western Lass," though pregnant, does not despair:[24]

> And, as he hath cozened me,
> So will I, by cunning, gull another.

Another nonvirgin explains, "I can pass currant / and sell it again."[25] These women did not set out to sell their maidenheads, but the deceptions practiced on them by men have dragged them into the tricky marketplace of the sexual economy, and they often prove themselves to be better at the game than the men. Typically in these ballads, the woman has lost her maidenhead by some male deception via rhetorical seduction. Her ability to survive depends on her turning the tables on another man; her ability to do this depends on her having an understanding of the male investment in the hymen and of his belief system about how it signifies. Though she may not value her own virginity, she fares better if she realizes that men value the maidenhead as potentially a fair exchange for marriage. Selling a maidenhead will lead her astray, but tricking a man to marry her can have a good outcome. Most of these "counterfeit virgins" are not named, thereby suggesting that real men do not usually get hurt.[26] Men are tricked as often as women, women who have been deceived go on to justifiably deceive a man, while men who have been deceptive often find themselves justifiably on the receiving end of a deception. Mostly, it turns out that all these kinds of deception are essentially harmless. It is only the naïve virgins—those unwilling to engage in or to suspect deception—who end up in tragic circumstances. These ballads de-emphasize the importance of female virginity, and they even suggest that the male belief in virginity is a kind of fiction that engenders and justifies all kinds of deception. The ballads thus depict sexual politics as a relatively even playing field in which consequences are merciful and fair as long as both parties recognize the fictionality of their courtship.

Ultimately, though, male reasons for deception are less noble—for example, to steal clothes or to have a good story to tell—than women's reasons, which are typically to get married and find a father for her children, and the outcomes of male deception are more serious—pregnancy and poverty—than women's deception of men, where the deception itself seems to be the only negative consequence. While women are often witty, deceptive, and successful at manipulation, the ballads do not use these stories as an occasion to warn men. It is women who must be on guard, and it is women who can become tragic victims. Where the woman deceives the man in order to achieve marriage, the ending is usually portrayed as happy, even if the man is not the seducer or the impregnator. Where the man deceives the woman, the loss of virginity by itself is not depicted as the tragic consequence because she can deceive another or because more severe consequences—like pregnancy—loom larger. "A New Ballad Upon A Wedding" serves as interesting example.[27] It charts the story of male desire, female ambivalence, and the rush to marriage in a parody of the hyperbolic language of love poetry. The poem builds suspense through depicting the wedding as an unwelcome delay of defloration: "Thus envious Time prolong'd the Day, / And stretched the Prologue to the Play." The narrative follows the rhythms of courtship with a virgin, and the bride plays the part of the conflicted virgin about to have sex; thus, when at last the husband enjoys sex with his new wife, he does not notice that she is not a virgin. The poem ends as follows:

> But what was done, sure was no more,
> Than that which had been done before,
> When she her self was Made;
> Something was lost, which none found out,
> And He that had it cou'd not shew't,
> Sure 'tis a Jugling Trade.

The bridegroom's silly romantic notions about virginity, love, and marriage are what get him in trouble, in that he is tricked, but since he does not know it, there is little harm done: he is a happy groom. This story suggests that the male investment in defloration is not based in material realities but rather in a desire for a fictionalized narrative. Because the hymen cannot be put to a "trial"—its reality cannot be tested or proved—fictionality and narrativity are always involved in representations of female virginity. That is, virginity is valuable as a story, and the ballads depict a struggle over the events and retelling of the story, valuing wit and socially desirable outcomes, like marriage, over truth.

Many of these ballads survive in nineteenth-century collections, whose editors often feel the need to comment on the morality of the material they are presenting. A series of ballads on "The Lass of Lynn's New Joy" is a good example. The girl is seduced, impregnated, and abandoned.[28] With the help of her mother, she finds a husband and gives birth five months after marriage, whereupon the midwife convinces the husband that such things are normal. While the nineteenth-century editor, Joseph Woodfall Ebsworth, acknowledges that this is intended to be read as a happy ending and that his Victorian counterparts have no right to pass judgment, he nonetheless cannot resist an invective against this tale. Interestingly, it is the older women who bear the burden of his distaste:

> We have no doubt that she [the midwife] was a crony of that scheming mother-in-law, who had persuaded the lass into marriage. Our hope is that they were not often admitted into the house. There were no Mothers-in-law in the Garden of Eden: they are decidedly a product of the Fall, and one of its worst. (465)

The ballad is written from the perspective of the seduced maiden, but Ebsworth makes the story about the husband: about his being unfairly deceived by her rather than the reverse. For example, his use of "mother-in-law" shifts the perspective from the girl to the husband and, in so doing, creates a female culpability that does not exist in the ballad itself. As I have been saying, in this ballad and others of the period, the deceptions of women are portrayed as harmless or even productive while male deception is more heavily criticized. By the nineteenth century, however, female deception was in and of itself bad. In another example, John Holloway and John Black reproduce a ballad (unfortunately undated) in their collection of "later" broadside ballads that supports my claim that female deception becomes more of a concern later. In "The Country man Outwitted: or, the City Coquet's policy" (ballad no. 30), a nonvirgin woman tricks a man by offering him her maidenhead. She and a male accomplice then rob him, and she beats him viciously. The male speaker takes a "warning" from this. The editors remark that this is an "unusually vivid and detailed rendering of a stock situation" (76). But my point is that the bloody details and the unusual viciousness of the woman are later developments. In the heyday of the ballads, female deception was licensed by the man's overinvestment in the hymen and was an ultimately benign strategy, since deception about virginity, if it is filtered through the lens of wit, generates stories that provide comedy and facilitate harmonious sexual relationships.

The nineteenth-century editors' comments on these Restoration and Augustan ballads reveal changes in attitudes toward virginity and female sexuality, in that both premarital sex and female deceptiveness become de-legitimated, at least representationally. I have been arguing that there is a relationship between virginity and deception. These ballads of deception demonstrate that the more fictional deception is licensed, the more virginity is downplayed. The converse is also true: where virginity is important, deception is de-legitimized. It is possible to see the cultural obsession with virginity in the mid-eighteenth century as an integral part of a culture of sincerity and to see investment in virginity as a hedge against a culture of deception. It is precisely because virginity is so subject to deception that it gets to stand in for "virtue": virtue coming to consist, in a figure like Pamela, in being unwilling to deceive about the very thing, virginity, that is easiest to deceive about. In simple terms, changes in attitudes toward femininity, reflected in the nineteenth-century editors' moral condemnation of deceit over virginity, parallel changes in the literary sphere. These include the ballads' transition from popular street literature to collector's item and the decline in comic representations of virginity, a point that I take up in the next section.

*   *   *

I have been describing various kinds of incongruity as the source of comedy about virginity. Many theories of comedy locate incongruity as a primary source of the comic, and virginity provides several sources of incongruity for the comic ballads discussed thus far. Virginity's incongruity inheres in its ambiguous materiality and in its status, at this time, as a complex stage in which a woman is sexually mature but not sexually active. This quality of virginity, its intrinsic incongruity when defined as a stage, accounts for its ability to generate even more incongruous states: the pregnant virgin, the nonvirgin with a hymen, and so on. Comic ballads further exploit incongruity around virginity by highlighting the incomparability of the hymen with material objects and with male sexuality. I have been showing how virginity is generative of wit—that particularly linguistic form of comedy preva-lent in the Restoration and Augustan periods—because wit almost always revolves around metaphorizing the body, a problem that the hymen stages perhaps better than any other body part.

But comedy is not the only possible response to incongruity and thus to complex states of female being. In a study on creativity, Arthur Koestler has argued that there are three general responses to what he calls bisociation. The first response, represented in this study by both the scientific efforts to describe the hymen and the satiric efforts to deflate it, is objectification. The second, exemplified by the ballads discussed thus far, is the comic. The final possibility for Koestler is aes-theticization, in which one treats the complexity itself as a source of aesthetic pleasure. I suggest that another possible response is spiritu-ality, which helps humans understand or accept what seem to be incongruities in our experience. One of the things this study has been doing, then, is describing a contest between the ability of these modes to act as heuristic devices for thinking through complex ideas about female sexuality in a landscape that has shifted politically, spiritually, and materially. It has also been considering the ways that virginity itself acts as a heuristic device for thinking about this new landscape. In chapter 2, I talked about the objectification of virginity, and in this chapter thus far, I have been describing the ramifications of treating virginity as comedy. In this section, I take up ballads that treat virgin-ity in something other than a comic way. They aestheticize it, spiritu-alize it, or treat it in a mixed mode. My point here is to offer another way to think about the links between the history of sexuality and literary history, in particular the demise of ballads, a form dominated by the comic mode, and the rise of sentimental and satiric treatments of virginity in novels.

One of the most popular ballads, over many centuries, about female sexuality is "The Bride's Burial," which recounts the story of a woman who slowly dies during her wedding ceremony.[29] Her adoring husband laments the death of his bride, who perishes both "a maiden and a wife." The importance of this phrase in underscoring the tragedy of the events suggests that the incongruity of a woman having both titles is what motivates this ballad and its idealization of the bride's incongruous state. The extreme solemnity of the ballad contrasts sharply with the witty ballads discussed earlier, and the extreme adoration of the woman—by the husband, by the wedding guests, and, the ballad seems to presume, by the audience—imply that each title is quite valuable. By maintaining the virtues of both in perpetuity, the woman will be revered permanently. Deliberately maintaining one's virginity was considered socially criminal and medically dangerous, but this protagonist, who manages to maintain virginity while also embracing marriage, can, through death at this well-timed moment, be revered in ways that a deflowered bride cannot. This is perhaps why the virgin bride in this ballad is far from distraught. She calmly accepts her fate and, while dying, directs her funeral and makes charitable decisions about her possessions in ways that suggest that her death creates bounty ("My Wedding-dinner drest, / Bestow upon the (poore) / And on the hungry, needy, maim'd / that craveth at the doore"). She directs her husband away from thoughts of love to thoughts of God ("Now leave to talke of love, / and, humbly on your knee, / Direct your prayer unto God, / But mourne no more for me"), thus suggesting that the purpose of marriage (spiritual union and growth, and benefit to the larger community) can be fulfilled without sex. Theirs is a model of Protestant holy matrimony in that it manages to revere both virginity and matrimony while being socially productive. Her unusual and incongruous situation of being a virgin bride represents a standard of femininity that, while not tenable for long, is idealized. This is why her death is aestheticized rather than treated tragically or comically.

"The Bride's Burial" demonstrates the conflicts between the ideals of virginity ("a maiden") and marriage ("a wife") at this time, it and resolves those conflicts through its reverence of a woman who does not have to choose between them.[30] But the seriousness and reverence of the ballad is interrupted in the last stanza:

> In earth they laid her then,
> For hungry worms a prey:
> So shall the fairest face alive
> At length be brought to clay.

While this stanza can be read as a depiction of the tragedy of early death, it also somewhat undermines the rest of the ballad by suggesting, through the worms, that her virginity—which is emphasized symbolically by white maidens, lilies, and her coffin—will not survive death. The final lines invoke a common ballad theme, with a long history in canonical poetry as well, of arguing that women should not maintain their virginity because their beauty will inevitably fade, an argument against the kind of perpetual virginity that seems to be the basis of the dead bride's acclaim. The poem's putative admiration of the woman is further undercut by the tune to which it was, at least sometimes, sung: "The Ladies Fall," which invokes the unsanctioned loss of virginity.[31] The virgin bride's purity of mind and intention are tainted by her association with the fallen woman of the tune and by her decaying body. This ballad, then, manages to maintain several contradictory ideas about perpetual virginity and about the relationship between marriage and virginity, and it manages to embody both Catholic and Protestant ideals of virginity at once. The ballad seems amenable to both reverent and ironic interpretations. Its ambiguity and overdetermination, and thus its flexibility to multiple interpretations and varied representations, perhaps account for its sustained popularity in the long transition to a new Protestant ideal of virginity. And its popularity perhaps attests to the endurance of Catholic reverence for dying a virgin, a state that can be idealized and aestheticized not despite its contradictions but in fact precisely because of them.

The representation of a "virgin bride" could, and sometimes did, evoke comic representation. But in "The Bride's Burial," and actually in much sentimental literature, this incongruity is predominately aestheticized. It is the aesthetic response to virginity, rather than a comic one, or indeed an objective, empirical one, that will win out as the eighteenth century progresses and as ideas about female sexuality make both comic and empirical representations much less frequent. I develop this point by examining the history of one ballad, which persisted, and mutated significantly, over several centuries. In its early incarnation as "The Maid and the Palmer," the ballad, which is based on biblical stories of the Samaritan woman and Mary Magdalene and which was popular in the sixteenth century, recounts the story of a woman who claims to be a virgin but who is discovered, by either Jesus or the palmer, to be lying. Upon going to church in her maiden-wreath, the wreath withers and a trail of blood follows her, providing evidence of her fraudulence.[32] By the mid-seventeenth century, the story had been corrupted into a minstrel and renamed, in the only complete extant version, "Lillumwham." In this version, the woman does not bleed and in fact gives all signs of being a virgin: she is "lilly white" and the clothes she is washing are described as white three times.[33] Her dishonesty is thus more difficult to detect; absent blood, the supernatural powers of the palmer are needed to discover her perfidy. In "The Maid and the Palmer" the crime of falsifying virginity could be rectified with spiritual penance.[34] This later version also assigns a penance to the deceptive virgin: "When thou hast thy penance done, / Then thoust come a mayden home." The idea of a penance that could restore virginity contrasts with St. Jerome's argument—and mine of the last chapter—that defloration is usually seen in irrevocable terms. However, the penance assigned to the maid in "Lillumwham" is quite severe: seven years as a stepping stone, seven years as a clapper in a bell, and seven years leading apes in hell. The idea of an elaborate, and thereby impossible, "cure" for the loss of virginity is also invoked in a "A Marvelous Medicine to Cure a Great Pain, if a Maidenhead be Lost, to Get it Again" a seventeenth-century satiric ballad that is commonly attributed to Marvell (1657) and that prescribes a ridiculously complicated concoction of medicinal herbs to "restore" virginity. These texts suggest that the extreme lengths that religion or medicine would need to go to restore virginity make it practically impossible. They also, in contrast with the "deception" ballads, fantasize that loss of virginity leaves recognizable signs, even if those signs can only be read by a supernatural power. The impossibility of determining virginity is surely linked to the notion that restoring virginity is impossible, and the link prevails in both religious ("Lillumwham") and medical ("A Marvelous Medicine") ballads. By the late seventeenth century, such narratives have disappeared, so even these outlandish remedies are no longer available to the deflowered virgin.

The "crime" of loss of virginity before marriage becomes increasingly serious as the ballad develops. "The Cruel Mother" is a descendant of "The Maid and the Palmer" that emerged in the seventeenth century but that, unlike "The Maid and the Palmer," persisted into the nineteenth century.[35] The story is similar to "The Maid and the

Palmer" except that it is murder, rather than unchastity, that is the primary sin: a woman claiming to be a virgin (she is "wearing her maiden-wreath") is confronted by the children that she has murdered. The obsolescence of "The Maid and the Palmer" and the emergence of "The Cruel Mother" suggest that the implications for faking virginity have changed. As such, these ballads reflect, as Tony Conran has argued, changes in sexual politics that were wrought by the emergence of Protestant sexual politics. Where once the deceptive woman had to answer to God (and in the "Lillumwham" version, to a stranger), now she must answer to her family. In "Lillumwham," the woman has had sex and has murdered nine children, but, as her penance will return her to virginity, it seems clear that her crime is sex and deception, not murder and failure in her role as a mother. Many of the ballads that I discussed earlier in this chapter depict women who need to rely on wit to convince or trick men to care for them and their children. Those ballads suggest that, in the early eighteenth century, the choice of when and how to end a woman's period of virginity was largely up to the man, as were the consequences of that choice. Women were enjoined to make good choices for themselves, but the blame for poor choices and the responsibility for the consequences fell upon the man. "The Cruel Mother" points to a different emergent, idea: that a woman's virginity becomes a question of the life and death of others, not just the woman herself. Virginity becomes a question that is properly addressed in a social rather than a religious or a private forum; it also becomes an arena over which the woman is responsible and that—depending on how she manages this responsibility—will constitute her character. In combining the theme of death with the ballad of deception, "The Cruel Mother" returns a level of seriousness to the discourse of virginity that would make lighthearted narratives of silly economic exchange (like "The Fair Maid of the West, who sold her Maidenhead for a high-crown'd Hat") and of lusty virgins with greensickness (like "Dick the Plow-man") relics of the past. This ballad about virginity's relationship with life and death serve simply and ultimately to emphasize the high stakes involved in women's sexuality in the middle of the eighteenth century.[36]

This is not to suggest that only women are culpable. Although ballads featuring deceitful and murderous virgins seem to have been quite popular, there was also a counter trend, which similarly featured blood, in ballads that depicted wronged virgins returning to claim vengeance. In these ballads, the blood of a seduced woman confronts and accuses the man who seduced her. Her bloody image functions to create a conscience in him. "Fair Margaret and Sweet William," a ballad that existed from the seventeenth through the nineteenth century, is a typical example.[37] William seduces Margaret and then marries another. She appears to him in a frightful dream of revenge: "I dreamed my Bower was full of red 'wine,' / And my Bride-bed full of Blood." The ability of blood to create conscience suggests, as Elizabeth Bronfen argues, that men must view female suffering in order to be moved. But the preoccupation with blood in many ballads relates not just to spirituality and to morality but also to epistemology. The sight of blood is, of course, the sign that a woman's virginity has ended: as I explained earlier, the medical texts put immense emphasis on the reliability of this sign, though it generally could be seen as amenable to masculine control. If virginity, and its loss, create epistemological dilemmas, many ballads imagine that supernatural phenomena, especially dreams, can rectify that inadequacy. And if "The Cruel Mother" will be found out, so, it seems, will the deceitful seducer. The first person speaker of "The Bleeding Lover," for example, promises her wayward lover,

> In thy dreams I will affright thee,
> And appear in ugly shape;
> Care and sorrow shall betide thee,
> There's no hope for to escape.[38]

The fascination with blood and with dead virgins in ballad culture seems to reflect nostalgia for both Catholicism and for humoural medicine, systems of belief that were both highly associated with blood.[39] Several things may account for this. As I have suggested earlier, access to a dead virgin body was highly unusual and, in some circles, prized. It may also be that the fascination with dead virgins and with ruined virgins who return attests to the power of virginity: dead virgins gain a type of eternal virginity and people who ruin virgins gain a kind of eternal damnation. The texts that I discuss in this section, then, confront the problem of the spiritual powers of virginity. Some debunk it, some revere it, and, more commonly, most of these complex texts create a tension between these views, thus exhibiting the culture's love/hate relationship with virginity that is probably related to virginity's special powers over death. These texts show the conflicts being worked out as a new ideal of virginity emerges, and they demonstrate the high stakes—life and death— in this process.

The ballads that I have been discussing proliferated at a transitional moment in the ideology of virginity. Their radical multiplicity in representing virginity indicates a moment of possibilities for sexual politics, but they also belie an anxiety about those possibilities. In analyzing the variety of representations of virginity in these ballads, I have been trying to show how this transitional moment in the history of virginity allowed virginity to become inscribed in a number of other cultural forms: the conventions of fictionality, changing scales of value, the marriage imperative, and so on. The conditions of publication of these ballads as a genre—both their plasticity and their ephemerality—allowed them to expose and reflect the relationship of virginity to these other cultural forms. In the last chapter, I traced the resistance that the female body made to scientific discourse. This chapter does something very different, though not incompatible. Ultimately, my analysis of the vast variety of discourses in these ballads of virginity shows that, to a large extent, ideologies of virginity are constructs of the female body, rather than truths grounded in it. These ballads also reveal that the eighteenth century carved a space for a subtle and sophisticated critique of the desire to found abstract political structures, like patriarchy and capitalism, on a gendered body part of ambiguous materiality. In fact, that space is occupied by the most vulgar of its literary genres, the broadside ballad; the critique is rendered more sophisticated by its medium's very vulgarity. By dispensing, in the most casual, ephemeral, and constricted of forms, a proleptic critique of the foundations of both the sentimental novel and the materialist criticism that will become its symptom, these ballads offer a chastening rebuke to the scientist, and the scholar, who imagines herself/ himself to be pursuing a naïve object.

CHAPTER 4

Virgin Idols and Verbal Devices: Pope's Belinda and the Virgin Mary

True Poesy, like true Religion, abhors idolatry.

Edward Young, (1759), 57

Everyone knows that when the heroine of Alexander Pope's mock-epic *The Rape of the Lock* (1714) exclaims, "Oh hadst thou, Cruel! been content to seize / Hairs less in sight, or any Hairs but these" that she is talking about her virginity (IV.175–176). Most critics take Belinda's distress over losing a lock of hair to be indicative of her problematic privileging of reputation over virtue, or sign over referent.[1] The superficial Belinda values the hair on her head—a visible sign of her virginity—more than her pubic hair, which is presumably more connected to real virtue because of its physical proximity to her hymen. Pope's poem is often read as a critique of its characters' excessive investment in material objects, but Belinda, in the case of her virginity, is criticized for caring too little. Belinda's obsessions with visual signs and with her virginity link her to the stereotypically idolatrous and sexually deviant Catholic, a figure whose appearance in anti-Catholic propaganda (already seen in chapter 1) provides an important context for the poem. But Pope's poem can hardly be charged with anti-Catholicism or with promoting the cause of "real" virginity, and one can hardly make the case that it argues for an ethics founded upon mimesis and a coherent material or semiotic world. On the contrary, the poem satirizes all idolatrous desire for meaning in the material world. By analyzing *The Rape of the Lock* through the lens of anti-Catholic critiques of virginity, idolatry, and the Virgin Mary, this chapter makes it possible to read Belinda's outcry not as evidence of her problematic devaluation of virginity and overinvestment in visible signs, but rather as indicative of the poem's own skeptical attitudes about the sanctity of virginity and indeed about the semiotic value of the material world.

The first chapter of this book analyzed anti-Catholic propaganda against virginity and argued that the Protestant critique of virginity accomplished, among other things, an elimination of virginity's access to metaphysical authority. Chapter 2 discussed how the materiality and semiotic unreliability of virginity vexed scientific writing about female bodies, and chapter 3 showed how popular culture enacted a witty critique of these aspects of virginity and Enlightenment ideology. This chapter shows that virginity was a highly contested object at the center of eighteenth-century debates over theological semiotics, and it argues that it is therefore no coincidence that virginity is the vehicle for Pope's poem, which is both a critique of Enlightenment epistemologies and a dazzling experiment in neoclassical aesthetics.

The Rape of the Lock fictionalizes an incident that disrupted an elite Catholic community: a "well-bred" young man (Lord Petre, who supplies the basis for the Baron in the poem) clipped a lock of hair from a young woman (Arabella Fermor, who becomes Belinda in the poem) whom he may have been courting (I.8). As a satiric *poèm à clef,* the poem inherently raises questions about mimesis, or the relationship between referent and representation. Moreover, the central tension in *The Rape of the Lock* lies in the relationship between the literal and the symbolic. The action hinges on the connection of Belinda's hair to her actual, physical virginity, a crucial dimension of the poem that critics have often referenced but whose significance is commonly ignored.[2] The style in which Belinda wears her hair, mostly piled up but with two long curls on each side of her neck, was a customary fashion for young marriageable—that is, virgin—women. The locks are thus a material signifier of virginity, something whose material existence is otherwise difficult to determine. The cutting of the lock is, then, a symbolic rape, and the poem investigates the power and relevance of such a symbolic act.

Like the poem, the Church of England's critique of Catholics at this time centered on problems of signification and representation. Protestant theologians and propagandists excoriated the idolatry of Catholicism, in particular the worship of saints, especially Mary, and the doctrine of transubstantiation. From their perspective, Catholicism sacrilegiously privileges visual symbolic practices and propagates the erroneous notion that icons can stimulate spirituality. Protestantism, by contrast, prioritizes language; only words—specifically "the word" of the Bible—can lead to God. Protestant critics of mariolatry complained that Catholics worship Mary instead of God (the thing that she represents or mediates for) and thus that veneration of Mary is idolatrous. Protestants worried not so much that physical representations (of Mary or God) would be substituted for the real thing, but more that Mary would be substituted for God; that is, they endeavored to prevent the thing intended to represent God's goodness (Mary) from becoming the focus of worship.

In addition to idolatry, the issues of virginity and celibacy were crucial, as I argued in the first chapter, to the debates between Protestants and Catholics that I am proposing as a key context for understanding Pope's poem. As the quintessential virgin who attracts idolatrous worship, Mary is an important figure in the transition to a permanently Protestant England. She presented challenges to Protestant theologians, who denounced Mary's capacity for mediation, her perpetual virginity (as both fact and ideal), and the tendency of her worshippers to deteriorate into idolaters. Protestant writers criticized the manner and extent of Catholic worship of Mary but still upheld her as "Blessed among women." Mary's virginity at the time of her conception of Jesus was important to this status, just as a woman's virginity at marriage matters under Protestant ideals of femininity, but Mary's "perpetual" virginity, both as fact and as an ideal, presented more vexing theological problems. Mary's espousal to God is the model for the female commitment to life in a convent as a nun, something that Protestant theologians and their adherents clearly opposed. Protestant reformers were thus in the awkward position of challenging Mary's perpetual virginity, her divinity, and her capacity to become an idolatrous object of worship, while simultaneously advocating the importance of virginity at marriage.

Debates over the Virgin Mary at this time were, ostensibly at least, more about idolatry than virginity. But both virginity and idolatry were crucial for the Protestant cause. Moreover, they are inextricably connected, since idolatry is driven by the desire to materialize something—like virginity—valuable but unavailable to the eye. A popular, and often reprinted, tract from 1641 demonstrates just this relationship. The Protestant polemicist Thomas Master levels an especially strident critique of Mary that illustrates the connection between idolatry of Mary and Mary's virginity. Starting with a concept of "woman" as inherently debased, Master articulates the degradations that make Mary even more debased than other women, settling on virginity as the ultimate source of negation: "Virgin is below Woman. A Cipher bears no proportion with a Number, and Virgin is a very Cipher in nature, it hath no being nor name, God made it not (6)."

Invoking the definition of a cipher as something empty or void, Master argues that Mary and her virginity have nothing worthy of worship. "Cipher" can also mean something that is unclear, that needs a "key" or an interpretation.[3] In both cases, a cipher involves a crisis of significance: something that is meaningless can take on false meanings and something obscure may or may not have meaning. For Master and other reformers, Mary's virginity is precisely the reason that she should not be idolized. Nevertheless, my point is that virginity's status as a "cipher" creates the conditions for its idolization.

While Mary was controversial during the Reformation, debates about her flourished again beginning in the 1680s, when she became a focal point for anti-Catholic sentiment. In the sixteenth century, the Protestant Queen Elizabeth had been able to retain Mary as a figure for Protestant femininity through her self-presentation as the "virgin queen." But at the end of the seventeenth century, Mary represented an important dividing line between Protestants and Catholics, and she figured prominently in anti-Catholic writing. The most important stimuli for this renewed anti-Catholicism—and especially for critiques of marionism—were the revolution of 1688, sparked by the birth of a supposititious Catholic heir, and the Jacobite uprisings that followed. James II's Catholic tendencies had long been a source of concern for his Protestant subjects, but it was the immanent (and long awaited) birth of a child that sparked the crisis. Protestant fear of a Catholic heir, along with very real Catholic desire for such an heir, fueled suspicion that the queen would try to procure a male baby and pass him off as a legitimate heir by secreting him into her bed "reaking and hot from the Womb" via a warming pan.[4] The queen, Mary of Modena, was aligned with the Virgin Mary: rumors circulated that she claimed to have received a visitation from the Virgin and that the pope sent clothes of the Virgin Mary to her. As a result of these rumors, 40 witnesses officially testified to the genuineness of the birth, though of course it was the heir's Catholicism, and not his legitimacy, that concerned Protestants. The warming pan conspiracy theory depended upon the stereotype of Catholics as deceitful plotters, equally capable of naïvely believing in miracles and cynically faking them; it also depended upon impugning Mary and the virgin birth. The subsequent birth of a Catholic heir-apparent lead to the Protestant revolution of 1688–1689 and to periodic uprisings of his supporters throughout the first half of the eighteenth century. It also lead to renewed anti-Catholicism, which focused on Mary, on idolatry, and on sexuality.[5]

Pope was uniquely situated to exploit the highly charged debates around Mary, virginity, and Catholicism. Pope was born in 1688; in fact, he was born within 20 days of the anxiously anticipated heir. The members of his family were practicing Catholics, and consequently over the course of the next several decades suffered discrimination and deprivation. Pope himself never renounced Catholicism, although he was not fully participating in that faith by the time he wrote *The Rape of the Lock* and although such renunciation would have had significant benefits. As Catholics, Pope and his family could not vote, live within 10 miles of London, serve in Parliament, own a school, or travel abroad for education, among other restrictions. As a young Catholic born into this bitterly oppressive time, Pope's first exposure to reading was through his father's library, which included, according to Pope himself, "All that had been written on both sides" about the religious controversies of the time.[6]

Both *The Rape of the Lock* and the debates over Mary revolve around attractive virgins at the center of controversies involving the interpretation of bodily signs, problems of faith and secularization, and the fragmentation of a community. Like the debates about Mary, the poem investigates the danger of idolatry, the relevance of symbolic action, and the importance of female virginity. Both the poem and the religious debates address the anxiety of the loss of a signified once an object attains symbolic status, and thus both address the problem of idolatry in general and the specific dangers that inhere in idolizing virgin women. Like the debates over Mary, the poem links idol worship to representations of virginity: the lock—which should simply represent virginity, which in turn should represent virtue, future chastity, or sanctification— becomes a fixation in itself. In fixating on the lock, actual virginity becomes less important than evidence of virginity, and, even more problematically, virtue or inner qualities become less important than physicality. There are allegorical and parodic connections between Belinda and the Virgin Mary: both receive visitations that foretell a peculiar change in the status of their virginity; both become objects of veneration and stimulate idolatrous behavior; and both experience assumption. But I am not arguing either for direct influence or allegory. Instead, I read Pope's poem alongside critiques of Mary because they emerge from the same cultural moment: one in which female virginity was a contested ideal subject to accusations of idolatry, in which the sign of virginity was so highly charged that it could be used to debate the meaning of signs in general, and in which religious views on virginity, idolatry, and symbolic action would have important implications for literary history.

The Rape of the Lock engages debates about idolatry and representation on the level of both form and content. Critics of seventeenth-century poetry like Malcolm Ross and Barbara Lewalski have traced changes in English poetic practices that result from the Reformation. Ross argues that poetry was aesthetically debased as a result of the Protestant critique of transubstantiation. Lewalski, in response, argues that the Protestant revolution in poetics created a radically new poetic tradition, one in which spiritual truths could be represented in figurative language. While the idolatrous practices of the Catholic characters in *The Rape of the Lock* are clearly criticized for their lack of spirituality, the poem itself does not offer—on the level of either form or content—a meaningful alternative. The poem criticizes both Protestant and Catholic symbolic practices and, most radically, it is even skeptical about secular, poetic modes of meaning. There is ultimately no spiritual or symbolic truth behind the language or actions of the poem. *The Rape of the Lock* parodies the search for symbolic meaning in the material world, and it iconoclastically derogates both secular and spiritual things: the icon, virginity, and the "word." I argue that it is no coincidence that female virginity is the "material thing" that provides the vehicle for this critique.

The dates 1688–1714 provide the context for my reading of *The Rape of the Lock*; they encompass the time from the Protestant revolution through one of the most significant Jacobite uprisings; they also coincide with increased criticism of Mary; and finally, the dates book end Pope's birth and the publication of the full five canto version of *The Rape of the Lock*. In what follows, I analyze the poem alongside the theological debates over the Virgin Mary. My argument moves, like the Protestant critique of idolatry, from questions about mimesis to a crisis of meaning that verges on the abyss of skepticism. I begin by analyzing the poem's representation of Catholic characters. I then move to the poem's narrative structure and poetics. I conclude with a discussion of the poem's relationship to its critics, suggesting that this relationship is intimately shaped by the poem's idolatrous subject and its immersion in theological debates about signs.

* * *

The characters in *The Rape of the Lock* are based on real Catholic people, and the poem subtly satirizes their predictably Catholic over-investment in visual icons and their resultant inability to distinguish the literal from the symbolic. Though Belinda and the Baron champion opposite sides in the debate over the lock, they share a similar view of the relationship between the literal and the symbolic. Belinda confuses the symbolic with the literal, and she "overreacts" (according to most undergraduates and not a few critics) because her hair is not her hymen and thus her dismay, as if she had been actually raped, is unfounded and frivolous. Her oft-quoted exclamation "Oh hadst thou, Cruel! been content to seize / Hairs less in sight, or any Hairs but these" suggests that she has invested too much in the symbolic realm, being more concerned with her hair—and thus the appearance of her virginity—than with her hymen and her literal physical virginity (IV.175–176). The Baron, for his part, immediately invests his idolatrous desire on the lock itself and not Belinda ("Th' Adventrous *Baron* the bright Locks admir'd," II.29). He is a fetishist who habitually fixates on symbolic objects as a source of satisfaction and whose interest in the symbolic may well preclude an interest in the literal.[7] There is, for example, no indication that his desire for the symbolic representation of her virginity extends to an interest in Belinda's actual virginity. Like the stereotypically corrupt Catholics of Protestant polemic, Belinda and the Baron do not understand the limits on the representational function of objects. The poem opens with parallel scenes in which Belinda and the Baron engage in rituals that conflate physical or symbolic objects with writing, suggesting that their shared problem is their Catholic tendency to give priority to objects over words and to signs over meaning.

At her dressing table, Belinda lines up "Puffs, Powders, Patches, Bibles, Billet-doux" (I.138). Alliteration connects the three physical objects (Puffs, Powders, and Patches) and the two objects associated with words (Bibles, Billet-doux). The near alliteration of "p" and "b" and the fact that all these objects coexist on Belinda's dressing table suggest that Belinda treats the physical and the linguistic comparably; in fact, she has turned the linguistic into the physical, since she is reading neither the Bibles nor the Billet-doux. The multiplication of things reduces their specificity; their individual functions are subordinate to their collective augmentation of her attractiveness. Even the specificity of the Bible as "the word" is eliminated by the plurality of "Bibles" as well as the Bibles' alliterative association with love letters. From a Protestant perspective, of course, Belinda is a typically corrupt Catholic, turning words into icons, worshipping things, and worshipping herself, rather than the word of God.[8] Belinda's lock is the main icon here, and even this is implicated in her corruption of words. The letter talks of "wounds" and "charms"; that is, it speaks the language of symbols, idols, and fetishes, and Belinda herself may then, according to Geoffrey Carnall, use this already corrupted language to create another fetish, the lock (I.119).[9] The object of worship is thus several degrees removed from what began with only a loose—metonymic and alliterative—connection to "the word" (the Bible). Belinda's dressing table altar is the place where the lock is literally produced and also where it is turned into an icon. The poem shows us how the lock is physically made, and also, through metonymy and alliteration, how it is transported from a physical object into a representation of itself. And Belinda's focus on this fetishized physical object interrupts the speech of advice and warning given to her by her protective spirit, Ariel.

The Baron's parallel scene, in which he traffics in the symbols and words of courtship, demonstrates the effects of Belinda's construction: Belinda's careful preparation of her hair evokes an idolatrous response in him, as we are told "Th' Adventrous *Baron* the bright Locks admir'd, / He saw, he wish'd, and to the Prize aspir'd" (II.29–30). The Baron's idolatry figures him as a parody of a Marian worshipper, even more corrupt than Belinda. Like Belinda, the Baron has books at his altar, but his are "French romances," not the Bible (II.38). Though he is constructing a ritual, he is imploring "ev'ry Pow'r" for help, suggesting that he does not recognize one true God (II.36). Like a Mariolater, the Baron "gives the creature worship due only to the creator"; thus he is an idolater in both senses: he worships images and false gods.[10] His interest in Belinda's hair explicitly connects him with one of the most criticized of Catholic practices: the acquisition of relics, among the most sought-after of which were the hairs of martyred virgins. In the hopes of obtaining his idealized object, which is a symbol of virginity but not inherently valuable, the Baron sacrifices his previous objects of worship, "the Trophies of his former Loves," in a fire that he lights with "*Billets-doux*" (II.40). Through its visual impact on the Baron, the lock has become an idolatrous object of worship that loses its referent. From the Baron's perspective, the lock neither has a relationship to spiritual value nor is it connected to Belinda, as evidenced by his desire to detach it from her. Thus, his relationship to the Bible and the word of God is even further removed than Belinda's, and his investment in physical objects of idolatry is even more corrupt.

These Catholic characters are almost like Protestant caricatures of Catholics: their fixation on the symbolic causes them to misread, misvalue, and improperly worship. They focus their idolatrous energy on Belinda's lock, a material, visible sign of her virginity. The lock's visual attractiveness creates a desire for the lock itself and situates value in the lock but not in the virginity that it represents and not in Belinda as a marital or sexual partner. Visual signs create desire ("He saw, he wish'd, and to the Prize aspir'd") but also distort and divert desire along a chain of metonymy that dispossesses both religious and social symbols of meaning and thus that threatens both theological and

Enlightenment epistemologies. Belinda's iconic beauty, for example, has the potential to deceive its admirers regarding the status of her virginity. Her face could hide her faults, the poem tells us, "if *Belles* had Faults to hide" (II.16). The satiric "if" here of course suggests that whether Belinda or any other woman has a "fault" that her beauty might hide is an unanswerable question. The poem reveals that physical and visible idols of virginity (like the lock) are created, perversely, in response to virginity's lack of materiality and visibility and thus may bear no relation to empirical reality. When Belinda makes her resplendent entrance to the pleasure party decked with a "sparkling *Cross*," the Catholic investment in the visual demonstrates its dangerously sacrilegious power (II.7). The cross is the one visual symbol approved by Protestants, but this cross, despite its sparkle, cannot compete with Belinda's beauty, which she has deliberately constructed to be idolized. The proximity of the cross to her beautiful bosom invests the cross with erotic rather than spiritual power. "*Jews* might kiss, and Infidels adore" Belinda's cross, indicating that Belinda's beauty has the potential to divest religious symbols—not just secular values like virginity—of their significance and power (II.8). The speech of the prudish Clarissa attempts to inject a value system based on something other than physical beauty and visuality, but her words cannot compete with the frenzy created by the visual spectacle of Belinda's beauty and her distress. Murray Kreiger describes the characters' confusion of sign with referent as a "logical fallacy of metonymy" that creates errors in interpretation (203). My point is that their metonymic desire goes beyond error to the heresy, from the perspectives of both Christianity and the Enlightenment, of a meaningless world. Belinda's beauty, so dependent on idolatry, competes not just with her own virginity, a material reality, but also with religious meaning: it is a cipher in the sense that it divests of meaning everything with which it comes into contact.

While my reading so far positions the poem as an ideologically Protestant satire of idolatrous Catholicism, the characters can be equally faulted from the perspective of orthodox Catholicism. The Catholic defense of the use of idols is fragmented, but in its most vehement incarnation, it completely turns the tables on the Protestant critique. Lewis Sabran, for example, argues that religious and secular idols are no different. John Gother claims that Catholics do not worship idols; they merely use representations to bring to mind the original. One of the major interlocutors in this debate is France's Bishop of Meaux, Jacques Bénigne Bossuet, who was widely published in England and who was a major target of English Protestant critique.

Bossuet argues that the distinction drawn by the Protestant writers between words and idols is false in his *A pastoral letter from the Lord Bishop* . . . (1686):

> Are not Paper and Letters the Work of Mans [*sic*] Hand, as well as Sculpture and Painting? But who do's not see, that in all these things we regard not what they are, but what they signifie. (1686, 17)

Bossuet (echoing both St. Augustine and John Locke (1975) and thereby linking theology, epistemology, and linguistic theory) does not merely defend the Catholic implementation of visual idols. Instead he claims that words, and by implication the Bible, are just as symbolic and just as much a physical product of humans as any other object.[11] Bossuet directly attacks the Protestant belief that the imaginative use of physical objects is sacrilegious; on the contrary, he celebrates the spiritual and symbolic potential of the concrete.

Protestant writers claim that by focusing on words rather than objects, they create a spiritual communion with God that is not vulnerable to the aesthetic pleasure evoked by physical objects. Bossuet responds to this assertion by contending that the Protestant's literal approach is in fact more debased:

> But whilst they glory in being more spiritual than we, and of paying to the divinity a purer adoration; they are in effect carnal and gross, because they follow nothing but their sense and humane reason, which persuades them that a man cannot be a God. (1686, 23)

Bossuet here focuses on the problem of faith, arguing that imagination and symbolization underpin the religious beliefs of Christianity. On both sides of the debate, the spiritual reigns supreme over the physical, but for Bossuet, the physical icons of Catholicism, joined to the human imagination, can lead to spiritual truths. For Bossuet, the Protestant insistence on the physical as debased indicates that Protestants lack an understanding of the way that God is in all things. Catholic spirituality and faith, by contrast, rely upon the ability of humans to understand how physical objects can point beyond themselves.

From the point of view of Bossuet's Catholic doctrine, the problem with the Catholic community in *The Rape of the Lock* is not that they ascribe too much power to symbols, but that in fact they do not ascribe enough. Belinda values her lock only insofar as it relates to a physical ideal of virginity, her pubic hair, not to a higher ideal of virtue or devotion to God. Virginity is not a holy ideal in this English Catholic community, and the Catholic characters in the poem have lost the ability to see how objects and words can point very far beyond themselves. The poem's poetics reveal that Belinda can only move through alliteration or metonymy, linking her lock to her pubic hair and her Billet-doux to the Bible, but neither words nor images transcend the material world. The characters can thus be faulted from a Protestant perspective for their overinvestment in idolatrous objects. But they can also be criticized, from a Catholic perspective, for a failure of symbolic and spiritual imagination as well as for their denigration of virginity's spiritual potential. This is why readers can criticize Belinda both for undervaluing her virginity, by putting more value on her curls than her actual virginity, and for overvaluing it, by resisting its loss, as if it had transcendent value. The poem blurs the line between sacred and secular ideals of virginity and between Protestant and Catholic perspectives on idolatry, and this ambiguity is precisely what gives Pope's satire its double-edged subtlety.

* * *

If sacred hermeneutics endeavor to know something about God, narrative poetry, we might assume, will reveal intangible truths about its actions and characters. That is, both sacred and poetic hermeneutics strive to transcend the material. The problem with idolatry, from a Protestant perspective, is that it embodies the sacred rather than providing a means for transcendence of the material world. While *The Rape of the Lock* satirizes the idolatrous behavior of its characters, the poem's irony inheres in the fact that the poem itself never transcends the material world. In the last section I showed how the sacrilegious idolatry of the characters in *The Rape of the Lock* makes their world both superficial, in that it relies on visuals, and byzantine, in that Belinda's overdetermined virginity produces an untenable situation for her. In this section, I argue that the poem's iconoclastic project extends to secular and poetic modes of meaning, producing a superficial and bewildering world for the reader. The narrative structure and poetics of this mock-epic prevent the emergence of a symbolic meaning that would fill the void created by the poem's iconoclastic representation of its characters. As such, the poem is truly iconoclastic and profane, equally skeptical of both sacred and secular interpretive practices.

Virginity makes the perfect vehicle for a satire of theological and poetic hermeneutics, because it presents particular problems for theorizing the relationship between the mind and the body and thus between the material and the immaterial, the sacred and the secular. The original theological justification for virginity depends upon the notion that virginity of the body can lead to elevation of the soul. St. Paul, for instance, says, "she that is unmarried . . . may be holy, both in body and spirit."[12] Theological virginity is firmly rooted in the belief that there is an inherent connection between body and soul. But eighteenth-century anxiety about virginity depends precisely on its lack of physicality and visibility; the status of virginity is not visibly present on a body, and physically visible signs, like Belinda's lock, may lie by suggesting that a young woman is a virgin when in fact she is not.[13] Virginity's material inscrutability is the reason that it simultaneously attracts idolaters and iconoclasts. The Protestant critique of idolatry endeavors to sever the body/soul connection that veneration of virginity entails by decrying the worship of all corporeal images. William Sherlock, for example, argues "to worship such corporeal beings, as may be represented by Images, is to worship corporeal Gods, which is Idolatry" (35). Mary's very embodiment—her humanity, her maternity, and her virginity—make her more accessible to idolatrous representation than God. Furthermore, the ambiguity of her physicality—a pregnant virgin, mortal and yet assumed into heaven like a deity—makes her a special temptation to idolaters and a special problem for theological debates about the mind/body connection.[14] Thus Mary has particular relevance to questions, fervently raised at this time, about the body: What do the visible signs of the body mean? How does the body relate to a person's "character" or spirituality? What is the relationship between human corporality and divinity? Because her virgin (and arguably divine) body encloses secrets not visible to the eye, Mary epitomizes the danger of relying on visual signs. Yet this is precisely why she becomes the focus of idolatrous worship grounded in vision and visions.

It is a commonplace that Reformation theologians de-emphasized the body and the visible or tangible physical world; instead, they privileged the word of God as manifested in the Bible. The Protestants who write about Mary at this time de-emphasize the body of Mary by insisting upon the power and mystery of "the word" (as that which can impregnate Mary) and on the stability of the meaning of scriptural language. Their aim is both to prevent Mary's body from emerging as an icon to be worshipped and to question the value of a virgin body, of virginity, and of the body in general. The Protestant writer William Clagett illustrates this redefinition of virginity in a tract on Mary. In a revision of the Pauline formulation "both in body and in spirit," Clagett says that God has "No less regard to a holy Mind than to a pure Body" (3). Whereas Paul gives the body equal status with the soul and even an ability to affect the soul, Clagett's "no less" indicates a priority of intangible values over material ones. Moreover, Clagett shifts the inner quality at stake in Mary from the "spirit," to the "mind," that is, from a religious value to a secular one. Protestant discourse on the Virgin Mary thus devalues virginity as a spiritual ideal and denies a link between the physical body and subjectivity or spirituality.

The Rape of the Lock seems similarly committed to de-emphasizing the body, though, contrary to Protestant theology, it ultimately rejects the notion that something outside the physical can be known. Belinda hopes that she can control what is *seen*: she wishes that "hairs less in sight" had been violated. While the characters rely on such superficial visual symbols, the poem criticizes this emphasis on appearances and thus seems to promise a different system of epistemology and morality. The hymen is the physical object that is presumably most at stake in any discourse about the rape of a virgin, but as a strategy for uncovering the truth about Belinda, the poem's investigation of Belinda circumvents the hymen, an indicator of physical virginity, in favor of the heart, the place where emergent ideas about gendered subjectivity were being located exactly at this time.[15] And in fact the poem suggests that Belinda's heart is the key to her dilemma, as the "earthly lover" lurking there is what debilitates the sylphs who usually accompany and protect her and who provide another kind of icon of her virginity. From the physical icon of the lock, which can be made to lie, the poem moves metonymically, at Belinda's own suggestion, to her pubic hair, which adjoins the hymen but does not lead to it. Instead, the pubic hair is a liminal space, a way of suggesting that we are proceeding to the "inner" Belinda, an interior that promises to reveal subjective rather than physical truths. In short, we skip the hymen and head for the heart.

Although the heart promises access to nonphysical aspects of Belinda, it in fact turns out to be just another physical object. Belinda's heart is described as a physical space. We learn of the "earthly lover" just before the rape occurs, suggesting that Belinda's emotional state at least partially accounts for the violation. But the "earthly" lover lurks "at" not "in" her heart. The preposition "at"— along with the description of the lover as "earthly" and "lurking," which imply physical embodiment—indicates an actual physical space, not necessarily an emotional truth. Also, the fact that the lover is "at" rather than "in" the heart suggests a lack of completion. In the action of the poem, the revelation of the earthly lover "at" her heart is the fatal fact, the one that makes the rape possible. The Baron's action of cutting off her hair—authorized by the presence of the earthly lover—erases the visual representation of her virginity, including the sylphs, even though her heart has been penetrated neither by the earthly lover nor by the narrator and readers. The poem's pretension to transcend the physical thus turns out to be a form of coquettish striptease: the poem empties the idol (the hair) of meaning, and it entices the reader with a promise of a more veracious and important kind of meaning (the heart), but the poem does not fill the void created by its own iconoclasm.

Like the narrative movement toward Belinda's heart, the poem's figurative devices expose idolatry without attempting to fill the void of meaning created by this evacuation. For example, just as Belinda relies on what can be seen, many of the poem's verbal devices are linked to the visual. In addition to alliteration, two of the most important poetic devices of the poem are synecdoche and metonymy. Pope makes things that are visually connected to people, or a part of them, stand in for them. For example,

> Sir Plume, of *amber snuffbox* justly vain,
> And the nice Conduct of a *clouded Cane*. (IV.123–124)

Sir Plume's character is defined by the material and visible icons with which he is associated. According to Clarence Tracy, Pope gives his readers an "illusion of reality" by evoking character through objects associated with various people, and Ellen Pollak adds that the poem "criticizes the sterility and social vanity of a world in which appearances have actually become substitutes for the things themselves" (77).[16] The poem neglects to provide its characters with interior thoughts and feelings, and it even avoids describing their "real" physical qualities; for instance, we know Belinda is beautiful, but we do not know what she looks like. Instead, characters are constituted by the objects they possess: Belinda's icons make her beautiful and Sir Plume's snuffbox makes him vain. This quality of the poem is usually, and rightly so, considered to be a comment on the emergent world of consumerism—Laura Brown's argument is most influential on this point—or as evidence, as Pollak thinks, of its misogyny.[17] But the poetic devices of synecdoche and metonymy also relate to larger epistemological and theological questions about the possibility of reaching meaning through visual signs and verbal devices.

The poetic devices that are linked to the visual, and thus to idolatry—that is metonymy, synecdoche, and alliteration—are in conflict with two other important aspects of Pope's aesthetic: that is, couplets and zeugmas. The idolatrous verbal devices, which give an illusion of meaning and depth, are constantly interrupted by the poems' couplets and zeugmas, which audibly and cognitively interrupt the slippery forward movement of the metonymy and alliteration. In so doing, these verbal devices iconoclastically disrupt the poetics of the visual: they insist that contiguity and visuality do not constitute meaning. The following lines, which describe the strategies of the sylphs to keep the icon intact, illustrate this poetic tactic:

> With varying Vanities, from ev'ry Part,
> They shift the moving Toyshop of their Heart;
> Where Wigs with Wigs, with Sword-knots Sword-knots strive,
> Beaus banish Beaus, and Coaches Coaches drive.
> This erring Mortals Levity may call,
> Oh blind to Truth! the *Sylphs* contrive it all.
>
> (I.99–104)

Notice the sylphs' strategy: they constantly shift from object to object in order to maintain the icon of virginity intact. Alliteration ("Beaus banish Beaus") linguistically reinforces this physical movement, and synecdoche (especially "Wigs" for "Beaus") repeats the idolatry that has caused the conflict. But the couplet form, which insists on sending the eye and the mind backward in order to explore the relationships between things (in a telling example, moving backward from "Heart" to "Part"), rhythmically interrupts the idolatrous movements of the sylphs and of the poetic devices based on physicality. W. K. Wimsatt argues that Pope's rhymes "impose upon the logical pattern of expressed argument a kind of fixative counterpart of alogical implication" (153).[18] My point is that in the case of this poem, the couplets interrupt, and therefore foreground for examination, the alogical associations formed through the idolatrous practices of alliteration and metonymy. Whereas Wimsatt finds that rhymes, as an "amalgam of the sensory and the logical," are the "icon in which the idea is caught," I am arguing that Pope's rhymes are iconoclastic (165).

The main critical debates about *The Rape of the Lock* from the last 20 years have focused on the poem's obsession with materiality. For the most part, critics have come to the poem from a perspective that privileges the symbolic over the literal, subjectivity over objectivity, and the sign over the referent. For example, Laura Brown's influential argument that the tensions in the poem result from the paradoxes of early capitalism and its focus on material objects and Pollak's feminist critique of the poem for denying Belinda interiority both rely on a

Protestant and Platonic privileging of intangible value over the debased material world. My point is that, when viewed as a participant in these historically specific debates over idolatry, Pope's poem may actually be seen as enacting a critique of a Protestant semiotics that privileges the intangible over the tangible. Ross has shown how Protestant semiotics detaches the sign from any material or ontological reality (the Eucharist is not really Christ's body) and replaces materiality with psychology (Christ's body is present in the memory of the recipient of the Eucharist). That is, the reformers separated symbol from truth and transformed the Eucharist from a corporate act to an individual subjective recollection (35). The problem with idolatry, of course, is that it makes the opposite move: in separating the material from the immaterial, it retains solely the material. I am not arguing that *The Rape of the Lock* tries to recuperate idolatry, but neither does it try to replace materiality with a disembodied, transcendent value, whether spiritual or psychological. In fact, in its insistence on the limitation of meanings in the physical world (what Helen Deutsch calls its "continual dead-ends"), the poem parodies both the materiality of idolatrous Catholicism and the disembodied ideals of Protestantism (52).

The demystification of virginity by exposing the visual and verbal devices that construct it as an object of worship reveals the poem to be radically skeptical about virginity's relationship to spiritual practice or, in fact, to any nonphysical meaning.[19] In response to the issues, raised by the debates over Mary, that concern the linkage of female virginity, ideal femininity, spirituality, and interpretive practice, the poem offers a resolution that is based on detaching ideals of virginity from spirituality. In this sense, it supports the Protestant ideal of femininity, which is crucial to England's emergent Protestant identity and which is grounded in secular virginity and holy matrimony. But in its radical questioning of the capacity of secular things to embody symbolic meaning, Pope's poem takes iconoclasm beyond the single issue of virginity. Both the physical and the figurative function in the poem to resist rather than to create meaning: the verbal devices lay bare the process whereby visual things gain meaning in order to demystify secular things, like virginity, that have the symbolic charge of a sacred thing. This is why the poem ends with the parodic assumption of Belinda's hair; a meaningless and replaceable material object that has incurred sacrilegious idolatrous worship is the only thing eligible for (ironic) transcendence. In short, the poem's narrative structure and formal features continually deny the "leap of faith" required to believe that a human might be divine or that a lock of hair, or even a hymen, might reveal subjective character traits.

* * *

Because of the poem's pervasive thematic and structural resistance to spiritual and symbolic meaning, critics of the poem find themselves in the same position as Belinda, at risk of making too much of a symbol. For example, critics of the poem have alternately tried to discover subjective truths about Belinda and to criticize that project, a perspective that usually ends up, paradoxically, criticizing Belinda for not having any subjectivity. As Stewart Crehan suggests, the effort to analyze Belinda in a way that creates or completes her subjectivity inevitably feels stilted: Belinda is simply not real; her existence is only symbolic (55). Of course all literary characters are merely symbolic, but this poem, rather perversely, constantly debunks the power of symbols. Symbolic things like the lock or Belinda herself cannot, the poem implies, be subject to meaningful analysis. For Kenneth Gross, idolatry debates raise questions about human imagination and the limits of human reason: can humans know anything outside themselves or can they only remake the world in their image? (34–37). My point is that readers of *The Rape of the Lock* find themselves in the fun house of the latter option. Far from being able to distance ourselves from the frivolous characters in the poem, we find ourselves in the same position as those characters, unable to find transcendent meaning, left only with aesthetic admiration of the visual or verbal beauty.[20] Pope's mock-heroic elevates the frivolous to the level of epic in a parallel move to the action of the poem, Belinda's obstinate distress over a secular symbolic action. In both cases, anyone who ascribes religious or interpretive power to the secular symbol risks the charge of pride and thus risks satire. Pope himself in his satiric *A Key to the Lock* (1715) suggests that the attempt to read allegorically or symbolically will subject one to satire.[21] He specifically criticizes the search for allegorical meaning in the poem by mocking the idea that someone would take Belinda as representing "The Popish Religion, or the Whore of Babylon" (29). As we have seen, the effort to uncover subjective depth or symbolic meaning for Belinda can proceed only by analyzing visual and verbal symbols, which the poem insists is fraught with the possibility of frivolity. In short, this *poèm à clef* resolutely resists a key and, like Mary's virginity and Belinda's beauty, relentlessly ciphers meaning.

Thomas Woodman has argued that Pope makes a "religion" of poetry; that is, Pope has a moral commitment to the truth behind art. But this poem resists the kind of truth that the religious debates insist upon. In a religious semiotic, symbols, figurative language, and examples function to point to a higher truth, one that needs to be arrived at through interpretation but one that nonetheless has some unified, transcendent meaning.[22] As John S. Prendergast—as well as many Catholic defenders contemporary with Pope—argue, the positions of the two churches on the relation between the truth and its representations, whether linguistic or visual, do not differ significantly. Prendergast claims that the positions of both religions on transubstantiation "affirm the symbolic reality of mediation which allows signs to function in the first place" (65). Catholic and Protestant disputants may debate the use or meaning of symbols, but the presence of a higher meaning, and in fact the same higher meaning, is not disputed.[23] By contrast, Umberto Eco describes the attraction of human symbols as lying precisely in their vagueness: their "fruitful ineffectiveness" in expressing a final meaning (130).[24] This is why Mary with her paradoxical "fruitful virginity" is the patron saint of *The Rape of the Lock* and the central object of dispute in the theological debates about signs.[25] Although Pope's poem pretends toward a "moral"— this is why Pope claims to have inserted Clarissa's speech—the long history of debate over the poem's meaning, the inability of the signs and figures in the poem to construct stable meaning, and Pope's own resistance to such a "key" suggest that the poem is ultimately committed to resisting a unified interpretation. The icons of Belinda's virginity, as well as Belinda herself, are exposed by the poem's verbal devices as ultimately vacuous. The poem reveals metonymy, synecdoche, and alliteration as analogous to idolatry, ways of constructing meaning through physical relationships, and, as such, practices that can never be theological or even reliably meaningful. I am suggesting that the poem is radically skeptical, heterodox both to Christian hermeneutics and to Enlightenment epistemologies, though not, perhaps, to modern poetics. Years later, in *An Essay on Man* (1733–1734), Pope will argue, in accord with Enlightenment orthodoxy, that the human condition substantially limits human knowledge, but this earlier poem is even more skeptical. Fully ironic and fully iconoclastic, *The Rape of the Lock* implicates its readers, as well as the characters and its own narrative voice, in the attractions and the dead ends of any idolatrous search for meaning. This is why of all Pope's work, it is *The Rape of the Lock* that has sustained the most critical interest: a debate that remains mired in literal meanings and aesthetics and that rarely approaches consensus on the higher truths or symbolic meanings in which the poem may participate. Pope's renovation of the virgin idol shows why virginity was a likely vehicle for this critique of both sacred and secular epistemologies, as debates about the sacredness of words hinged on the sacredness of Mary's ambiguous and paradoxical virginity and because virginity's resistance to being "seen" meant that at this time (i.e., even before *Pamela* [1740]), nothing could be more "in sight" than the beautiful virgin idol.

CHAPTER 5

Faking It: Virtue, Satire, and Pamela's Virginity

Why is Nature so dark in our greatest Concerns? Why are there no external Symptoms of Defloration, nor any Pathognomick of the Loss of Virginity but a big Belly? Why, has not Lewdness it's [*sic*] Tokens like the Plague? Why must a Man know Rain by the aking of his Corns, and have no prognostick of what is of infinitely greater Moment, Cuckoldome?[1]

In this quote, the central satiric object of the Scriblerian farce *Three Hours After Marriage* (1717) laments his inability to verify his wife's claims to virginity. Fossile, a medical doctor, has recently married a hyperbolically unchaste and deceptive woman. The action of the play takes place while he delays consummating the marriage until he can determine whether or not his wife is a virgin. With its scientific language, its tone of profound disappointment, and the hyperbole that indicates the speaker is being satirized, this lament suggests the failure of the Enlightenment to answer a man's question about the sexual history of a woman. Fossile's desire for a "symptom," "pathognomick," "token," "prognostic," or a "mark" (or even the ability to make an "enquiry") suggests his obsession with the inscrutability of the female body and his frustration with the failure of science. His complaint is marked by a wistfully excessive desire for scientific evidence of virginity, by skepticism of the medical profession's ability to provide such proofs, by a lament for the incompatibility of knowledge and sexual pleasure, and by a fear that the deceptive and inscrutable female body threatens masculine dominion.

Though his scientific skills are inadequate, Fossile attempts to pursue evidence of his wife's virginity (or lack of it) throughout the play. He falls victim to a false virginity test, foisted on him by one of his wife's lovers, that purportedly works by invoking, in unchaste women paradoxically enough, a blush, which is an indirect, ambiguous, and overdetermined sign of female virginity.[2] In the absence of both method and justification for interrogating the condition of the hymen, Fossile tries to analyze other physical clues, even ones as ephemeral as a blush; as such, this virginity "test," in both conception and execution, mocks the doctor's claims to scientific authority. Even more perversely, Fossile then takes his wife's refusal to be tested as evidence of her virginity: that is, her symbolic opposition to medical investigation is proof of her resistance to males on all levels. He then performs the "experiment" of the virginity test on all the women in the play, at which point his standard then changes again, as those who refuse the test are presumed unchaste and labeled Cartesians (for "matter and motion"), while those who take it (presumably it has no effect) are deemed virtuous Platonics (for "ideas"). This division of women betrays Fossile's confused motivations for his virginity inquiry: it is not clear whether he is interested in virginity as a principle of the body or of the mind. He desires information about the status of the body, but he relies largely on verbal evidence. He wants to find out about his wife's virginity, but he accepts her refusal to take the test as proof of her virginity before proceeding to all the other women. His desires for repetition (repeating the experiment with many women) and objectivity (he wishes for a standard outside himself that he can apply to disinterested parties) derive from the tenets of the new science, but since it relies on a verbal rather than a physical response and since his administration is anything but controlled, the test proves completely ridiculous both as a scientific experiment and as evidence of what the rest of the play indicates is his real object of knowledge: his wife's sexual experience.

Like most comedy of the period, this play relies on wit and linguistic play to convey information and evaluate character. Fossile is the butt of the jokes because his skills at interpreting linguistic clues are as laughably inadequate as his medical prowess.[3] By contrast, the wife's lovers, skilled in the art of verbal play and interpretation, enjoy sex with Fossile's wife. The audience, because they see the interactions between his wife and her lovers, has access to the information that the husband is desperately in need of. But each time such evidence becomes available to Fossile, his reliance on certain kinds of information allows him to be deceived and satirized. Moreover, through its privileging of the libertine pleasures of wit and sex, the play implies that knowledge of virginity would, even if available, not be valuable. The play thus satirizes the pursuit of useless knowledge through ineffective means. More specifically, by suggesting that an interest in the facts of female anatomy and the consummation of the desire to enjoy that same anatomy are incompatible, it satirizes men who place knowledge before pleasure. The satirization of Fossile illuminates the stakes involved in the contemporary debates about virginity and about the legitimacy of the medical profession. Fossile's problems arise from his reliance on the methods of science: the injunction to repeat, the fixation on the physical and the visible, the difficulty of achieving "objectivity," and the tendency to distort the object of knowledge. His reliance on these methods opens him up to dramatic irony: he becomes the comic figure in this farce, and the medical community of which he is a part is satirized as a whole.

This play manages the anxiety that an interest in virginity will make a man ridiculous by compartmentalization: the doctor/husband interested in visual evidence gets neither knowledge nor erotic pleasure, while the wife's lovers enjoy sex and the audience enjoys the comedy and the pleasure of knowing more than Fossile. The play suggests that the key to knowledge of female sexual behavior lies in language, not in physical evidence, and it criticizes the possibility of a successful objective inquisition of physicality. When it comes to female sexuality, men are offered the options of erotic pleasure, if they relinquish both virginity and its scientific pursuit, or satiric derision, if they do not. Coming from the bawdy tradition of Restoration comedy, the play seems to suggest the silliness of interest in virginity. But even though Fossile is the satirized dupe, his lament about the inadequacy of information on female virginity does reflect a real obsession with identifying female virginity that marks the early eighteenth century. The woman in question here is not a virgin, and thus the play can only demonstrate that sexual promiscuity, but not necessarily virginity, may be confirmed. Satirizing Fossile on the stage illuminates the tension that revolves around female virginity and suggests that the answer does not lie in medical methods, yet the play does not, in the end, offer an alternative model for understanding female virginity. This play was a minor comedy at a time when the genre of the comic farce was in demise. The medical doctor's incomplete access to the truth of the bodies of women, especially virgin women, would have been underscored by the generic limitations of the theater: the impropriety of a man investigating a woman's genital anatomy—a real concern for doctors of the period—would have been especially clear in the public arena of the theater. The theater's ineffectuality with respect to virginity—that is, its confinement to the physical and linguistic exchanges that may plausibly take place in public spaces—may be an example of the kind of generic limitations that contributed to the demise of the genre. Beyond the obvious limitations, true for all types of drama, of exposing virginity on a public stage, the genre of the farce itself is antithetical to a serious, reverent representation of virginity. By examining John Gay's play—a discourse that exposes but does not resolve the problem of investigating idealized virginity—I am suggesting some of the imperatives that would shape the emergent discourse of virginity in the novel, *Pamela* in particular.

Samuel Richardson's sentimental novel *Pamela* (1740) revolves around the repeated attempts of the aristocratic Mr. B. to rape his servant, the exemplarily virginal Pamela. Mr. B's pursuit of Pamela's body instigates the narrative, but the novel's objective is the loftier, according to its own standards, investigation of Pamela's interiority. The narrative action converts Mr. B. from an admirer of Pamela's body into an acolyte of her virtue, and thus it relocates feminine social value from virginity and embodiment to virtue and interiority.[4] While Pamela's virtue depends upon preservation of her virginity while she remains unmarried, it ultimately transcends physicality and comes to represent the intangible qualities that make her suitable for the wildly implausible hypergamous marriage with Mr. B. This shift from virginity to virtue—or from a literal investment in virginity to a figurative one—can be seen as a response to the intransigence of material virginity that was discussed in chapter 3 and that provides the vehicle for the satire in *Three Hours After Marriage*. Though the epistemological problems presented by Pamela's virginal body do not at first appear crucial to *Pamela*, this chapter argues that they nonetheless shape the epistemological crisis—and generic resolution of that crisis—around Pamela's virtue. I have been arguing throughout this book that because of its inconstant materiality, virginity presented a particular kind of epistemological problem during the era of the scientific revolution. Virtue's very immateriality, by contrast, creates an altogether different kind of epistemological quandary in *Pamela*. Pamela's virtue, so unexpectedly extravagant for a servant girl, must be produced and proven for a skeptical audience that includes Mr. B. and the reader. Pamela's epistolary accounts of her heroic attempts to preserve her virginity produce evidence about her interiority and thus allow readers to evaluate her "virtue." Epistemological dilemmas catalyze the shift from virginity to virtue; they transform the narrative from a rape plot to a marriage plot; and they impinge upon formal elements of the narration.

Scholars have long acknowledged that the novel *Pamela* is obsessed with virginity and that epistemological uncertainty is endemic to its form, but no one has persuasively linked the novel's two obsessions: virginity and proof.[5] Whereas other critics have argued that novels absorbed scientific discourse, I argue that the sentimental novel's generic strategies and its valorization of interiority result from the *failure* of scientific methods. Whereas the virgin female body confronts science with the limitations of its methods, Pamela's virtue, paradoxically, proves more amenable to emergent epistemological standards than physical virginity is.[6] From this perspective, the heralded move of the novel toward psychological and moral investigation—and its application of empirical inquiry to subjectivity—are not evidence of generic and social progress motivated by science. Analyses of the links between epistemological dilemma and genre in medical texts and in *Pamela* suggest that the subjectivity that the sentimental novel investigates proves to be not more complex than physicality but merely more accessible to representation and verification by male authorities than physical phenomena were. *Pamela*'s strategies for containing the epistemological, representational, and satiric problems presented by femininity are largely generic and formal. In its focus on Pamela as the narrator of her own story, the novel displaces epistemological anxiety from the male to the female. As an epistolary novel, *Pamela* circumvents the problem of the body by suggesting that it is women's words, not their bodies, that may escape male investigative methods. Moreover, *Pamela* positions the reader—rather than the woman herself, a man who may be sexually interested in her, or a scientist—as the one with access to the most reliable evidence; as such, it creates a disinterested, nonscientific community that may debate Pamela's virginity and her virtue as "matters of fact."

In comparing the efficacy of the epistemological strategies of the medical texts and of *Pamela*, I do not conclude that the novel establishes Pamela's virtue as an unassailable truth. On the contrary, the rapid and prolific accretion of satires, defenses, and debates that followed the publication of *Pamela* depend for their effect on the instability of the evidence of Pamela's virtue; that is, they exploit the idea that virtue, like virginity, can be faked.[7] The most famous of these, Henry Fielding's *Shamela* (1741), satirizes Pamela's "vartue," thereby suggesting that Pamela's virtue is nothing more than a linguistic construction staged for effect and subject to fraud. Henry Fielding and other satirists deem Pamela's own account of her virtue to be an unreliable body of evidence. Richardson, in turn, responds with near obsessive revisions of *Pamela* that are, as T. C. Eaves and Ben D. Kimpel have argued, primarily aimed at making Pamela's virtue a more compelling matter of fact (1967, 61–88). The "Pamela controversy," though centered on the truth status of Pamela's words and virtue not her body and virginity, in fact emerges from anxieties about the epistemological reliability of medicine and thus about the possibility that women may elude male power/knowledge structures. In short, concern that Pamela's "virtue" can be faked results from displaced anxieties about whether virginity can be counterfeited, as well as from ambiguity about the meaning of virginity and its value. These anxieties over virginity and virtue are linked by their shared concern that women are privileged observers of themselves and are thereby in a position to deceive men. Thus, the *Pamela* satires represent an appropriate response to the representation of virtue in the novel, in that they rehearse—and thereby demonstrate nostalgia for—a situation in which epistemological anxiety can be located in female deceptiveness and not in a failure of male methods of empirical investigation. This chapter examines the ways that *Pamela* responds to both scientific representations of virginity and to the satires of that discourse by producing both a secular sentimental discourse on virginity *and* a new kind of satire of virginity.

* * *

One of *Pamela*'s most clever strategies, in terms of its response to gendered representations of virginity, is that it transfers the interest in virginity from Mr. B. to Pamela. By making Pamela the defender of her own virginity, more concerned with it and valuing it more highly than Mr. B. does, *Pamela* displaces anxiety over virginity from the male to the female. Mr. B. is, from the outset, less interested in Pamela's virginity than she is, characterizing her belief that "her virtue is all her pride" as "perverse and foolish" (280). Mr. B. desires Pamela's virgin body, but he does not concern himself with wondering whether or not it is actually virginal.[8] It is Pamela herself who must wonder about her virginity. Much has been made of her fainting spells during the rape attempts of Mr. B. As a result of these fits, Pamela does not know what has happened to her. She does not know, that is, whether she is still a virgin. When Mr. B. attempts rape by hiding in Mrs. Jervis's closet, Pamela faints and must be told by Mrs. Jervis what occurred. Even given the reliability of this witness, whom Pamela undoubtedly trusts, Pamela reports to her parents that she "believes" Mrs. Jervis saved her from "worse" and that she "hope[s]" that she is "honest" (97, 93). Pamela's female body is so unavailable to visual or sensual investigation that, even with a sentient and reliable eyewitness (something anatomy could not confidently produce), it is impossible for Pamela *herself* to know whether she is still a virgin. Later, when the unreliable and notoriously cruel Mrs. Jewkes, who aligns herself with Mr. B.'s interests over Pamela's, takes over guardianship of Pamela, Pamela must actually rely on Mr. B.'s assurance that he did not rape her. In this case, the man possesses all the information about female virginity, and Pamela assumes the previously male position of having to rely on someone else's "word" about its status. (This situation will of course be reversed for Clarissa, who, though insensible during the rape, knows exactly what has happened: "I have my senses" she declares to Lovelace when confronted with his equivocation about the rape). Pamela's lack of certainty about whether she is still a virgin seems farfetched, but nonetheless it works effectively as a plot device because the pervasive male concern about the truth of female virginity, due to the inscrutability of the female body, has been transferred to her.[9] Whereas the incomprehensibility of the early modern female body meant that men typically had to rely on a woman's "word" regarding her sexual history, this situation is perversely reversed in *Pamela*.

In an incident that critics have generally ignored, Pamela's crisis over her own virginity occasions a generic disruption in the novel when, after one of Mr. B.'s rape attempts, the fictional editor makes a singular intrusion upon the epistolary form:

> Here it is necessary that the reader should know, that when Mr. B. found Pamela's virtue was not to be subdued, and he had in vain tried to conquer his passion for her, he ordered his Lincolnshire coachman to bring his traveling chariot from thence, in order to prosecute his base designs upon the innocent virgin . . . thus in every way was the poor virgin beset. (123)

Since Pamela cannot testify to her own virginity, the editor (functioning here as an omniscient narrator) steps in to assure the reader that she is inviolate. The editor, like Pamela and her parents, initially uses "virtue" as a synonym for virginity but then makes rare use of the word "virgin," something Pamela, with her euphemistic style and with her lack of authority to speak about her own body, never does.[10] It is striking how seldom the word "virginity" appears in this text that hinges both its plot and its moral on Pamela's virginity, and it is instructive that a fictional male editor must be imagined in order to make use of this term in such an authoritative way. In short, whereas Pamela and the reader (as well as any imaginable scientific professional) may have some doubt about Pamela's virginity, the fictional male editor can testify authoritatively to its existence. This disruption of the epistolary form signals, and calls attention to the reasons for, the major shift in the novel's structure. After reassuring the reader of the heroine's virginity by providing a male authority in the figure of the narrator, *Pamela* becomes a text that is increasingly about the "inner" Pamela, about her virtue more than her virginity. Just as the questions about Pamela's virginity occasion a generic disruption (the appearance of a narrator), the epistemological quandary over Pamela's virtue is marked by a generic shift, from letters to journal. In the journal, the pretense of an immediate addressee disappears and we are left alone with Pamela—or, more to the point, Pamela is left alone with herself. And from here on, it is her words and feelings, not her body, that must undergo scrutiny. The emergent ideal of female virtue depends on thoughts, feelings, and intentions, not merely on actions or physical signs. Pamela's virginity is a necessary condition of her virtue, but it is not sufficient testimony on its own. Pamela's journal renders Pamela's interiority—like the body on an ideal dissecting table—completely "open," making her virtue available to rigorous examination, with a plausible pretense to objectivity. Mr. B.'s obsessive interest in reading her letters and journal is evidence that he has shifted his interest from her body to her subjectivity and that he believes her words have the status of, or at least provide some access to, truth. In giving priority to virtue over virginity, the novel makes Pamela's inscrutable and private body less relevant than her thoughts, and it promises the reader unfettered access to those thoughts through the journal form.

In addition to being more available to objective analysis, Pamela's virtue can better withstand the mandates of such research, specifically the repeatability of experiments and the presence of multiple objective witnesses. Whereas the only well-known virginity test, blood at coition, could provide merely retrospective, inconclusive, and non-repeatable evidence, virtue should—and does in this case—withstand multiple trials. Mr. B.'s repeated and unsuccessful attempts to rape Pamela provide increasingly reliable evidence of her virtue. Furthermore, *Pamela* situates its eighteenth-century readers in a community of objective witnesses who could, and did, debate the validity of the epistolary evidence. This reading community is a variation of the Royal Society, in which "matters of fact" are established through examination of evidence and through debate among people who have a shared body of evidence.[11] Since virtue can be subjected to the scientific method—and thus to male authority—in ways that virginity could not, by shifting the object of investigation from virginity to virtue, *Pamela* asserts greater epistemological authority over female virtue, and thus over femininity, than contemporary scientific texts had. J. G. A. Pocock (1985) has pointed out two important things about virtue in the eighteenth century: it becomes feminized, and it has epistemological authority.[12] *Pamela*'s formal strategies for representing virtue and virginity imply that this historical redefinition of virtue may be, in part, a response to the female body's resistance to scientific methods. *Pamela* is emblematic of the way that the sentimental novel gains authority over femininity: it creates a discursive space that is less interested in bodily interiors than subjective ones and thus that has the authority to speak about women in ways that science failed. In establishing Mr. B. and the editor as authorities over Pamela's virginity, the novel pulls a sleight of hand that would not work in science and that could not sustain a novel. But in shifting the object of inquiry from virginity to virtue, and in making Pamela both the investigator and the object of knowledge, *Pamela* more effectively resolves the epistemological crisis around femininity by completely displacing responsibility, and thus anxiety, for proving her virtue onto Pamela herself.

One of the defining features of virtue is the lack of artifice; Pamela cannot be deliberately deceptive. Therefore, she must scrutinize her own feelings and own up to them, a task that takes up a good deal of Pamela's journal writing. Interestingly, as virtue comes to reside in her intangible interiority instead of her body, Pamela is increasingly subject to confusion and self-deception. For example, upon Mr. B.'s declaration of love for her, Pamela discovers that she has feelings for him that contradict his actions: "I know too well the reason why all his hard trials of me, and my black apprehensions, would not let me hate him," she writes, alarmed by her own contradictory feelings (252). "I know not myself," she admits to Mr. B., putting herself on equal footing with him in the process of investigating her interiority, and she determines thereafter to better manage her "contradictory, ungovernable heart" (253, 280). As a reader of her own letters and an examiner of her own interiority, Pamela again assumes the formerly male position with respect to the deceptive, in body and in feelings, female. Thus *Pamela*, rather than resolving the epistemological crisis of virginity, transfers that crisis onto women and virtue, making virtue—as virginity had been before the scientific revolution—an entity concerning which woman's word is inherently suspect. The epistemological dilemma in the letters involved Mr. B.'s actions and Pamela's body: did his actions encroach on her virginity? The journal, by contrast, finds Pamela confused about her own feelings. And in both cases—that is, regarding both virginity and virtue—the female's access to the truth is no greater than the male's.

I have been arguing that *Pamela* redirects epistemological interest from virginity to virtue. Virtue's association with social productivity provides the ideological justification for this shift. Under the emergent ideal of companionate marriage in a capitalist system, a woman's virtue is useful, both economically and morally, to her husband.[13] One of Mr. B.'s first concerns about Pamela reflects this new standard of utility. As he rants about everyone's insistence on the language of virtue in describing Pamela, Mr. B. challenges Mrs. Jervis, "I know that Pamela has your good word; but do you think her of any use in the family?" (59). In opposing "word" to "use," Mr. B. disputes the value of virginity and simultaneously invokes the anxiety of having to rely on a woman's "word" about her virginity. In contrast to virginity, which is material but has no material use and cannot be proven materially, the uses of virtue are materially visible and verifiable in the economic, educational, and affective advantages of a well-run household. Quite simply, virtue, unlike virginity, generates children and manages domestic affairs. Mr. B.'s conversion from libertine to responsible head of household is perhaps the most remarkable product of Pamela's virtue, but her virtue also produces direct material benefit beyond her family; for example, after her marriage, she distributes money to the servants and takes Sally Godfrey's child under her care.[14] In order to produce these social benefits, Pamela must not completely devote her energies to the protection of her virginity; that is, her virtue becomes socially useful only when she is married and thus only when she is no longer a virgin.

As I discussed in chapter 2, the hymen has rarely been attributed a function in medical texts. Since the hymen is not always present and since its destruction, under a model of normative heterosexuality, is considered inevitable, it has a physiological status much different from other body parts. Midwife manuals like that of "Aristotle" had ascribed semiotic and social—but not physiological—usefulness to the hymen. A primary goal of the new anatomy was explanation of the physiological purpose of organs, but these texts do not propose that the hymen is useful semiotically, socially, or physically. In fact, they more commonly describe the hymen as performing a pathological function than as having a salutary or a useful purpose. The utility of virtue, by contrast, reflects emergent Protestant standards both for spirituality and for femininity. Under ancient and Catholic models, virginity contributes to spirituality and on occasion even produces prophets. The Catholic story of the virgin martyr, a woman whose virginity is not highly enough valued in the material world, had been one of the few possibilities for a female heroine, but the Reformation made lifelong virginity, or dying for virginity, unacceptable except in extremely specific circumstances, like the "Bride's Burial" discussed in chapter 3. Though the martyrdom of a virgin may be noble in Catholicism, virtue in Richardson's work—and Protestantism—refuses that particular notion of exemplarity and demands that Pamela must choose marriage, and defloration, rather than death. In the Protestant reconfiguration of feminine ideals, marriage supersedes virginity.

This choice—between virginity or virtue, marriage or death, a Catholic narrative or a Protestant one—has implications for the structure of the novel. Pamela's virginity must be lost in the service of procreation and other good works, but it must not be lost prematurely. Both defloration narratives and virgin martyrdoms have a limited possibility for delay and thus for narrative length; the imminent and inevitable demise of virginity—or the heroine—sets the conflict in motion. And narratives that depend upon preservation of virginity also depend upon stasis. By contrast, since it depends on constancy and on the production of something valuable, virtue must be represented in a lengthened narrative. The time necessary to test virtue, during which virginity must (except in an extraordinary case like Clarissa's, an exception that proves the rule) remain intact, establishes the ideal virginity as a protracted one. As Pamela heroically declares, "were my life to be made ever so miserable by it, I should never forgive myself, if I were not to lengthen out to the longest minute the time of my innocency" (176). The emergent Protestant standard of virtue depends not merely upon virginity, but upon protracted and terminable virginity, inevitable, but not precipitous, defloration. It thus depends upon a transformation, from virginity to marriage, in the state of the heroine, something antithetical to the genre of the virgin martyr. Thus both the ideology of virtue in *Pamela* and the generic form of the novel are better suited than medical texts to a sexual politics based on later, but mandatory, marriage.[15] In subsuming a new ideal of virginity under the category of virtue, Richardson's novel offers a narrative in which one can heroically preserve one's honor or virtue even while losing one's virginity. (This makes possible, of course, *Clarissa*'s (1747–1748) monumentally long narrative in which virtue survives virginity, even outside of marriage.) In short, virtue in *Pamela* not only substitutes for virginity—it supersedes it in usefulness, material reality, and social benefit.

I have described a problem with representing virginity in the early eighteenth century and argued that it occasions an epistemological crisis of male authority, not merely a crisis involving femininity or female virtue. As a result of the epistemological imperatives of the new science, virginity loses its ability to signify something about a woman: her virtue, chastity, or essence. Hence, the discourse on female virginity in medical literature becomes a site of investigation into the male—that is, his authority—rather than into the female; it becomes a risky discourse for the male scientific community, one that confronts that establishment with the limits of its expertise and threatens it with satire.[16] I proposed that this is why science abdicates authority over virginity and demonstrated that the generic features of the nascent novel form proved much more effective in shoring up masculine authority over women than scientific discourses had been. I showed how *Pamela* mollifies the threat of the female body by prioritizing virtue over virginity, and I argued that, as a result of her interest in her own virginity and virtue, it is Pamela herself (rather than a satirized male dupe) who is subject to deception and forced to rely on inadequate evidence. I conclude by suggesting that this is why *Pamela* generated such controversy and why Pamela herself was subject to satire. By making Pamela the defender of her own virginity, more concerned with it and valuing it more highly than Mr. B. does, *Pamela* displaces the threat of satire from the male to the female. Moreover, in placing the burden of proving virtue on Pamela and specifically on her words, *Pamela* invites its eighteenth-century readers to be the authorities over the veracity of those words. Pamela is deeply obsessed with her own virginity/virtue, and, like her male predecessors who demonstrated interest in the virginity of a woman, she has her motivations questioned and is subjected to satirization. While the fictional editor testifies to the truth of Pamela's virginity and Mr. B. comes to believe in her virtue, outside the context of the novel, there remained doubt surrounding the heroine's sincerity. The resounding response of the reading and writing public to *Pamela* was to debate the reliability of Pamela's words and thereby the veracity of her virtue and even of her virginity.

The most famous of these satires, of course, is Henry Fielding's *Shamela*, which puts the linguistic evidence of Pamela's virginity in the same category as the female body of anatomy; that is, "Shamela's" words are inscrutable and deceptive. While she passes as a virgin with Booby, we find out, via her letters to her mother, that she has already had a child by Parson Williams. And while she would much rather be having sex with Parson Williams, she is willing, for the sake of her future material advancement, to talk at length about her "vartue"; indeed on one occasion she indulges this conversation about nothing for a "full hour and a half" and on another "till dinnertime" (321, 323).

Poor Mr. Booby is so disconcerted by her that he struggles with what to call her: "why how now saucy chops, boldface . . . you are a d—d, impudent, stinking, cursed, confounded jade," he declares, and a few minutes later continues, "hussy, slut, saucebox, boldface, come hither" (311–312). This confusion about what to call her occurs despite the fact that early on in his attempts on her, he is easily enough satisfied as to the "matter" of her anatomy (314). Henry Fielding has turned Mr. B. of *Pamela* into the lowest kind of satiric object: Booby suspects—and even has evidence—that his object of attraction is faking it, but he is duped anyway. This is because her "vartue" is nothing more than language and thus cannot be verified. Although immaterial, this virtue allows Shamela to circumvent the truth of the body. Upon their marriage, she encounters no difficulty with regard to convincing her husband of her virginity: she "acts her part" so well that "no bridegroom was ever better satisfied with his bride's virginity" (330). In *Shamela*, even physical virginity, that is the hymen, is sub-sumed under a performance of virtue.[17]

Not surprisingly, the issue of inheritance figures prominently in *Shamela*. Shamela's initial aspirations do not include marriage, but rather a "settled settlement, for me and all my heirs," the typical arrangement for a well-regarded concubine, and an especially fortu-nate arrangement for one from her class, not to mention her sexual his-tory (313). But once she realizes that it is her "vartue" and not her "person" that Booby will pay for, she figures she can make a "great for-tune" instead of a little one (325). In other words, if it were only her physical virginity or sexual attractiveness that was worth something, she would be content with a settlement. But once she realizes that she can market a faked virtue, Shamela increases her financial expectations. The letter from the naïve Parson Tickletext to the worldly Parson Oliver that prefaces Shamela's letters indicates that what is at stake in *Pamela/Shamela*, that is in representations of virtue, is the way that the immaterial idea of virtue impacts the materiality of posterity:

> This book [*Pamela*] will live to the age of the patriarchs, and like them will carry on the good work many hundreds of years hence, among our posterity, who will not HESITATE their esteem with restraint. If the Romans granted exemptions to men who begat a *few* children to the Republic, what distinction (if policy and we should ever be reconciled) should we find to reward this father of millions, which are to owe for-mation to the future effects of his influence. (305)

Meditating on the immense influence that the neo-patriarch Richardson will achieve with his virtuous heroine—a posterity much more vast than a material virginity could hope to pass on—makes Parson Tickletext so excited that he feels another "emotion." This code for sexual excitement suggests that male desire for posterity and thus for patriarchal power is the motivation for sexual excitement. It also suggests that posterity will now be gained by writing about abstractions like virtue, not by sexuality or materiality.

In another kind of response to *Pamela,* Eliza Haywood's *Anti-Pamela* (1741) recounts the exploits of Syrena Trickster, who is not so much a satiric antagonist of Pamela as her opposite. She, like Shamela, relies on the codes of behavior that Pamela establishes to trick people into believing in her virtue. A female libertine more than a cunning opportunist, Syrena is not able to pursue her own "interest"— that is, her financial future—consistently because of her licentious disposition. Syrena loses her virginity almost accidentally, by allowing herself to become drunk with a man to whom she is attracted, and her "Jewel, on which all of the Hopes of living great in the World depended" is quite rapidly dispatched less than a tenth of the way into the narrative (34). Her sensible display of the codes of female virtue, established so well by Pamela, are so well faked that she easily passes for a virgin, a performance that is emotional rather than physical but that is subject to the standards of empirical proof. Her performance is so convincing that even the "whole College of Physicians" would not be able to imagine her emotions as "otherwise than real" (3). It is not just Syrena's performance of virtue that deceives men but also her beauty and youth. Over and over again, she is able to trick men into believing what they wish to believe about her because of this combination of physical attributes and convincing performance. Like *Pamela, Anti-Pamela* suggests that letters will give away the truth. Syrena's first few attempts to secure a luxurious future for herself by trading on a counterfeit virtue are aborted just moments before consummation by the lucky (for the men) accident of a letter being mislaid. Throughout the book, her letters, mostly to her mother, reveal the true perfidy that her emotional body so successfully conceals. One of her dupes, Mr. D., fantasizes that he could make appearances agree with reality: "fly forever from my sight" he admonishes Syrena in a letter, "lest I stamp Deformity on every Limb, and make thy Body as hideous as thy Soul" (137). Another lover likes Syrena's performance of virtue during sex, but this libertine, who has learned from experience, finds it to be a ridiculous "romantic stile" after sex (148). The ability of Syrena, like Shamela and women like them, to "appear" as an ideal of female virtue creates, in this text and repeatedly in representations of the period, a philosophical crisis about the relationship between appearances and reality. If the dematerialization of virginity into "virtue" was a response to the failure of scientific methods to interrogate the reality of the female body, these anti-Pamelas suggest that virtue is, if possible, even more subject to deception. But they also suggest that it is words that will give women away. This is why representations of virgin heroines are so central to the early novel and to the development of our modern notions of what constitutes literary language. If the body (virginity) is tested empirically, words (and virtue) are interrogated by literary analysis.

As these responses to *Pamela* demonstrate, in tightly connecting female virginity with female virtue, and in placing the burden of investment in female virginity on the woman instead of the man, Richardson exposes his heroine to satire and disbelief. Since she is the one who cares the most about the status of both her virginal body and (even more so) her virtue, she is the one who becomes the object of satire, and her words, like virginal bodies, become potentially deceitful. This projection of deceptiveness onto Pamela herself may be exactly what makes *Pamela* such a success. *Pamela* does not resolve the question of how to prove a woman's virginity—or for that matter, her virtue; it merely shifts the crisis of knowledge onto the woman and into the literary sphere. Whereas Pamela may be unsure about her virginity and her virtue, her readers have a readily available, if extremely complex, object of investigation, one that, given their putative objectivity, they are more authorized to investigate than Pamela, Mr. B., or even Richardson himself. The *Pamela* satires that proliferated in the wake of the novel's publication thus repeat Mr. B.'s initial skepticism: they anxiously intimate that virtue, like virginity, can be faked. Richardson obviously wanted readers to believe his heroine, but my argument about the investigation of Pamela's interiority suggests that the *Pamela* satires are an appropriate response to the novel, insofar as they continue to insist that someone's authority surpasses Pamela's own and insofar as they suggest that when forced to rely on a woman's "word," it is preferable that the words themselves, rather than the female body, constitute the ultimate locus of truth.

Novel Virgins: Libertine and Literary Pleasures in *Memoirs of a Woman of Pleasure*

John Cleland's pornographic novel *Memoirs of a Woman of Pleasure* (1749) presents itself—or perhaps it masquerades—as an anti-*Pamela*: libertinism replaces chastity as the route to marital and financial happiness in this scandal-plagued account of the career of a fictional prostitute. The narrator and protagonist, Fanny, is not a prostitute with a heart of gold. That is, our heroine does not display an admirable dissonance between material circumstances and sentimental development. Rather, Fanny's career is marked by prodigious sexual pleasure and financial success, and it culminates in the ultimate emotional reward: marriage with her first love/r. Neither sentimental victim nor emotionally virtuous exemplar, Fanny thrives, at least to some extent, due to her uncanny propensity for physical regeneration: her ability, despite smallpox and multiple episodes of acrobatic and painful sex, to remain unmarked. Similarly, her sexual adventures are converted into a pleasurable text by her linguistic inventiveness: her flair for creating ever more extravagant euphemisms for body parts and sexual acts. In short, Fanny's narrative depends upon both experience and novelty, or upon repetition and its disavowal. As such, it is, like Samuel Richardson's *Pamela* (1740) a novelistic response to empiricist philosophy. And, just as in *Pamela*, the heuristic for thinking through empiricism is, not coincidentally, female virginity.

Throughout this book, I have been treating virginity as presenting challenges to empiricism: virginity resists empirical investigation due to its peculiar physical characteristics, its historical association with mystical sanctification, and its resistance to the imperative of experience. In this chapter, I address another kind of epistemological problem that virginity presented to eighteenth-century empiricism. One of the key sticking points for empiricist philosophers was the relationship between the particular and the general.[1] Empiricist methodology demands repetition and categorization even as empiricist philosophy is grounded upon an assumption of absolute difference, what Gilles Deleuze (1984) calls the "here and now" of the "inexhaustibly new" (xx). The eighteenth-century novel stages the problem of empiricism via the theme of virginity precisely because virginity offers, materially and conceptually, a fit object for contemplation of the relationship between novelty (virginity, individuality, and the "here and now") and repetition (sex, exemplarity, and concepts). This is one reason why virginity is the darling of eighteenth-century empiricism as well as its antagonist and why, at this time, virginity is such a thoroughgoing obsession.

In the last chapter, I argued that *Pamela* resolves some of the epistemological anxiety around virginity at this time via strategies of displacement and formal innovation. By transferring epistemological responsibility from the male observer of virginity to the female subject/object of virtue, *Pamela* manages to meet the epistemological standards of empiricism, repeatability in particular, while simultaneously producing a novelistic character of both originality and exemplarity and, as such, an object worthy of extended empirical inquiry. *Memoirs of a Woman of Pleasure* responds somewhat differently to the epistemological problems of female virginity. First, it substitutes sexual and literary pleasures for the satisfaction promised, but so rarely fulfilled, by epistemological pursuits. Second, it pits originality in language against originality in sex. Finally, just as *Pamela* turned virginity into a trope (for virtue), so too does *Memoirs of a Woman of Pleasure* depend on a transformation of its source material from literal to literary: defloration provides not only the catalyst for the action of the story but also the underlying standard by which all sexual *and* narrative acts are measured. It is due to this focus on defloration rather than virginity—a painfully obvious difference between sentimental and pornographic narratives but one worth lingering over—that *Memoirs of a Woman of Pleasure* stages, rather more explicitly than *Pamela*, the empirical and novelistic challenge of integrating novelty and repetition.

*   *   *

The pornographic *Memoirs of a Woman of Pleasure*, with its dizzying accretion of sexual episodes, would seem to be antithetical to an ideal of female virginity. And indeed, the text explicitly disavows interest in virginity. All of the female characters insist that their own virginity is worthless to them; Fanny, for example, calls her "maidenhead" a "trinket" and a "bauble" whose loss will be a gain for her (23, 32). Nor is deflorative sex presented as offering, in this text devoted to pleasure, any special physical pleasure for the male partner. The idealized man, Charles, does not seek virginity out, recognize it when he does encounter it, or put much value on it, while those men who do seek virgins are depicted negatively by Fanny. Despite all of this considerable disavowal, and even though pornography and prostitution depend, in theory, on the absence of virginity, *Memoirs of a Woman of Pleasure* is undeniably obsessed with virginity. Virginal sex makes up a good deal of the sex described in the novel. Most of the first letter, which constitutes the first half of the novel, recounts Fanny's virginal career and first intercourse. The second letter, which follows Fanny's ultimately successful effort to market a counterfeit maidenhead, is punctuated by Fanny's three coworker prostitutes entertaining each other—and the reader—with their defloration stories. Moreover, many of the non-virginal sex acts mimic defloration in that the man is physically too large for the woman and in that her pain leads to pleasure for them both. Indeed, all good sex, in Fanny's recounting, begins with female pain and leads, all in good time, to pleasure. Finally, the text's larger sentimental plot, which begins with Fanny's orphanization and ends with her happy marriage to her first lover, repeats this same narrative pattern on an emotional rather than physical level. Defloration as represented in *Memoirs of a Woman of Pleasure* thus has a metaphorical or typological relation to the sentimental marriage plot.

The narrative of defloration in *Memoirs of a Woman of Pleasure*, which provides the basis for all of the narrative structuring in the novel, depends on the notion that defloration is painful, but the medical manuals that I analyzed in the chapter 2 very rarely refer to pain associated with first intercourse.[2] In the mid-eighteenth century, sexual activity was a risky and painful endeavor for women, but it was childbirth, not defloration, that was the site of the pain incumbent on female sexuality. As Ruth Perry has argued, in an era where one woman died in childbirth for every six deliveries and where pregnancy was thus both painful and dangerous, the narrative of pleasure and pain around female sexuality usually began with a hypothetical pleasure (since female pleasure was assumed necessary for conception in a "one sex" model) and ended with undeniable pain and often death.[3] The life of the prostitute at mid-eighteenth century added the problems of alcoholism, venereal disease, and violence to the dangers already inherent in sexual activity. When defloration is associated with negative consequences during this era—besides in pornography—those consequences tend to involve not physical pain but rather the social stigma of premarital sex or of the nonconsensuality of the sex. For example, in stories about fallen women and even in female-authored amatory fiction, women often enjoy the physical aspect of sex and then endure painful emotional and social consequences.[4] Like the midwife manuals discussed in the first chapter, *Memoirs of a Woman of Pleasure* depicts sex as pleasurable for women. But this novel, like other texts in the emergent genre of narrative pornography, suggests that the pain involved in heterosexual intercourse is necessary for women to achieve physical pleasure. At the moment that, according to Thomas Laqueur, the "two seeds" theory—and thus the necessity of female pleasure to conception—is being discredited by almost all medical writers, *Memoirs of a Woman of Pleasure* sets up pleasure as a natural outcome, in fact the purpose, of sex. It reverses the chronology of pleasure (sex) leading to pain (childbirth) with that of the pain of the loss virginity leading to the pleasure of orgasm and, ultimately if less directly, to marriage.

The lack of adverse physical or social consequences to Fanny's sexual debauchery is a long-standing complaint of critics of the novel, almost as common a complaint as the fact that the novel ends in marriage.[5] Fanny and the other prostitutes experience pain only on initial intercourse, initial penetration, or when, as in the flagellation scene, the pain is deliberately and consensually inflicted. For women, that is, sex begins with pain and leads only to positive outcomes. Over and over again, the text describes the female experience of sex as one of pain leading to pleasure, and thus pain is a cause, or a beginning, not a consequence, or an ending. The female's pain is, moreover, attributed entirely to her own physiology and deemed necessary to her pleasure. For example, while still a virgin, Fanny discovers that masturbation is, due to her intact hymen, painful to an extent that the pleasure it provides is not commensurate: "the pain my fingers gave me in striving for admission, though they procured me a slight satisfaction for the present, started an apprehension" (64). Fanny describes the physical pain of her first intercourse with a man in the most graphic terms. Charles' "stiff horn-hard gristle battering against the tender part" hurts Fanny "extremely" (77). She complains that she "could not bear it" and only her "extreme love" fortifies her to withstand such "extreme pain" (77). Although Fanny is putatively a "woman of pleasure" it is Charles's pleasure, not her own, that convinces her to "submit joyfully," and her defloration is described as "intolerable pain," an "agony" that is completed finally by a "violent merciless lunge" (78). Fanny's first intercourse does not end in orgasmic pleasure for her, and in fact it takes a few more attempts before she manages to arrive at "an excess of pleasure through an excess of pain" (80).

The trajectory of pain and pleasure surrounding the loss of virginity is repeated for three more women: Emily, Harriet, and Louisa. Each tells a tale with the same progression: increasing self-awareness and sexual interest, pain on first intercourse, and pleasure following. Their pleasure, however, follows faster than Fanny's had; moreover, the progression of women heightens this pace, as each one successively arrives at pleasure faster. Emily, the first speaker, feels the most pain among the three: "at length an omnipotent thrust murdered at once my maidenhead and almost me: I now lay a bleeding witness of the necessity imposed on our sex, to gather the first honey off the thorns" (137). The pain experienced by Harriet, the next storyteller, is displaced somewhat onto her objectified "virginity":

> I had neither the power to cry out, nor the strength to disengage myself from his strenuous embraces, before, urging his point, he had forced his way into me and completely triumphed over my virginity, as he might now as well see by the streams of blood that followed his drawing out, as he had felt by the difficulties he had met with in consummating his penetration. (141)

By her own account, Harriet's virginity constitutes a stable object of knowledge: the blood and the difficulty in penetrating allow her partner to "see" and "feel" both the virginity and the defloration, even though Harriet herself appears to include the details about blood and about her partner's difficulty as signifiers not of her actual virginity, which is not at issue for the reader, but rather of her pain and of his belief in her virginity. For Harriet, the transition from pain to pleasure happens more quickly than it did for either Fanny or Emily: "But how quick is the shift of passions from one extreme to another!" she remarks (141). Louisa, the last chronicler of her own sexual initiation, completes the narrative even faster: at "scarce twelve years old" she actively pursues sex, and for her, the most painful part is waiting for a male to relieve her (144). Despite her age and inexperience, pleasure follows rapidly on pain once a man is present. "I thought nothing too dear to pay for this the richest treasure of the senses, so that, split up, torn, bleeding, mangled, I was still superiorly pleased and hugged the author of this delirious ruin" (148). Here the "treasure" is her sexual pleasure, not (as in common tropological use) her hymen, and this pleasure more than recompenses for the fact that she herself, not just her hymen, is "torn up." The female body in *Memoirs of a Woman of Pleasure* presents a physical barrier to pleasure, and thus the pain of penetration is necessary in order for women to reach sexual pleasure. This is why the lesbian sexual encounters between women in the text are pleasant and not painful, but they are not wholly satisfying either.[6] Without the male body to inflict pain on her, a woman's pleasure is limited.

The fixation on virginity in *Memoirs of a Woman of Pleasure* extends beyond its narrations of actual defloration. All of the sex that is "good," according to Fanny's physical and moral standards, mimics the qualities of defloration, in that the woman's size relative to the man's necessitates some female pain and even blood.[7] Male virility, figured as penis size, and female pain are thus the standards for sexual intercourse in the novel, and blood is a signifier of both of these things. That is, blood, the visible, coveted, and elusive sign of deflo-ration is re-signified here to mean sexual success, similar to how the anecdote from William Cowper (in chapter 3) re-signified it to mean scientific success. For example, when Fanny seduces the young employee of Mr. H., the youth's size causes Fanny both extreme pain and pleasure, and it produces "streaks of blood, the marks of the rav-age of that monstrous machine of his, which had now triumphed over a kind of second maidenhead" (112). By contrast, the absence or the displacement of pain and blood marks sex that is satirized. When Fanny views Mrs. Brown's encounter with her virile young lover, the grotesque proportions of Mrs. Brown's "greasy landscape" provide the comic aspects of the scene (62). Mrs. Brown's "wide mouth open gap" forces her lover, though prodigiously endowed, to resort to some "hearty smacks" in order to initiate the sexual excitement (62). No longer able to experience pain or to bleed, Mrs. Brown's grotesque body manages to have reasonably acceptable sex only because her position as a madam gives her access to this talented lover. This depiction of sex early on in the narrative warns of the conse-quences of too much sex, which include less satisfying sex and a comical narrative.

Fanny's reliance on stories of defloration and on defloration as a model for sexual intercourse means that repetition is a major concern of the narration. On the one hand, the repetition of the defloration narrative is part of what establishes sexual normativity. And as a genre, pornography demands multiple sexual encounters; that is, the repeti-tion of "sex." On the other hand, repetition potentially threatens pleasure, both that of reading novels and of sex, two activities that rely, to some extent, on novelty. Fanny makes the importance of novelty clear several times in her narration: "novelty ever makes the strongest impressions, and in pleasure especially," she asserts (113). Later, in describing Harriet's beauty as "so excessive" that it "could not but enjoy the privileges of eternal novelty," Fanny admits that maintaining novelty, and thus pleasure, over time and repetition proves to be extremely unusual (153). Virginity is of course inherently a novelty and antithetical to repetition. Fanny herself is aware of the tension between repetition and the pleasures of novelty, as she reveals at the beginning of her second letter:

> I imagine, indeed, that you would have been cloyed and tired with the uniformity of adventures and expression, inseparable from a subject of this sort, whose bottom or groundwork being, in the nature of things, eternally one and the same, whatever variety of forms and modes the situations are susceptible of, there is not escaping a repetition of near the same images, the same figures, the same expression . . . (129)

In short, in writing as well as in sex, Fanny knows the value of novelty. Fanny's desire to avoid repetition accounts, paradoxically enough, for our libertine heroine's tendency to make every sex act "virginal." It also accounts (partially at least) for the most distinctive feature of the novel's prose: its high-wire euphemistic style with regard to sexual organs. Here is the paradox of Fanny's narrative: the value of each sex act—and its representation—is measured against a standard model, defloration, whose claim to narrative interest is based in novelty. So, repetition is both central to Fanny's project, which is to establish a model of good sex and to recount a narrative of sexual episodes, and something that must be denied. As an accommodation, Fanny avoids repetition in the language but not in the narrative structure. In the repetition of the narrative structure of defloration, the importance of the original—and thus of virginity as a narrative and a physical standard if not necessarily a moral one—is inscribed.[8] At the same time, in the originality of language, a sense of novelty is preserved. It is tempting to parallel Fanny's sexuality and her writing style even further. At the beginning of the first letter we find that Fanny hates "all long unnecessary prefaces," an aversion that is as true for sex as it is for writing (39). The writing style of Fanny's memoir preserves, through its evaluative criteria for sex and through its standard of linguistic originality, the ideal of virginity as a singular experience, while the narrative structure allows for multiple repetitions of that experience.

The title of Cleland's later etymological tract *The Way to Things by Words, and to Words by Things* (1766) refers to an esoteric, but somewhat popular at the time, linguistic theory: the idea that all languages are formed by the same monosyllabic root words. Its adherents thus pursued a theory of the radical non-arbitrariness of language. The link between this title—and its thesis—and *Memoirs of a Woman of Pleasure* is rather obscure, because Fanny notoriously avoids using words that get most directly at the things she is describing. Penises are distinguished by such metaphoric euphemisms as a "spitfire machine," a "maypole," an "instrument of mischief," and a "bauble" (82, 109, 143, 199). Some of the more remarkable metaphors for female sexual anatomy include the following: a "furnace mouth," a "soft laboratory of love," and a "queen seat" with its own "maxims of state" (118, 154, 176). Fanny's linguistic acrobatics raise the question: how many sexual "things" are there to talk about? Michael Ragussis argues that Cleland's style works to increase the "catalogue of erotic acts" (193). In this reading, the text's episodes would not be repetitions of the same signified, "sex," but rather would be distinct acts. That is, Cleland multiplies words in order to multiply the sexual things. Fair enough. A libertine text that increases sex acts hardly seems surprising. But it is the sex organs that are treated with linguistic multiplication in this text while the sex acts, as I have been arguing, share a similar narrative. Carolyn Williams has argued that in the eighteenth century, much theory and practice was devoted to the linguistic segregation of "ladies and gentlemen" (267). What then are we to make of the multiple metaphors for both male and female sexual anatomy? Fanny's narrational problem, it seems, is to distinguish each sexual act she encounters, without completely destabilizing the sexual difference upon which heterosexual pornography depends. Her euphemistic style, commonly assumed to be an effort to avoid obscenity charges, ends up suggesting either absolute difference (every sex organ is different from every other one) or at the very least a lack of stable sexual differentiation, since the elaborate metaphors apply to both men and women. In some cases, for example "bauble," the metaphors can serve both genders. One quite apposite example of mixed-gender metaphor is when Fanny describes Charles's "snow white bosom" as a "rose about to blow," thereby associating Charles with one of the most clichéd tropes for female virginity (82). But more to the point, the fact that both sex acts and body parts are linguistically, if not narratively, multiplied is crucial for the novel's relationship to empiricism. As Deleuze, via David Hume, has argued, empiricism is always a theory of the relationship between "terms" and "relations."[9] In Cleland's case, this problem is filtered through the relationship between body parts and sexual acts, as well as between individuals and narratives.[10] The text's euphemistic style delegitimizes body parts, since they cannot be fully compared nor distinguished, in favor of narrative. According to Hume, whose *Treatise of Human Nature* precedes *Memoirs of a Woman of Pleasure*, it is in constructing narratives, or ideas, that all moral meaning happens. This is why it is important to recognize that *Memoirs of a Woman of Pleasure* is interested in defloration, a narrative, and not the hymen, a material object. *Memoirs of a Woman of Pleasure*'s ethical and epistemological authority rest on narrative rather than on objects. It is only in the narrative, not in the details or "matter" that meaning, and thus morality, emerge for Fanny.

This is why, despite the links between Fanny's prose style and her sexuality—her desire, in both cases, to stave off boredom—and despite her stated desire to avoid repetition, Fanny ultimately considers the pursuit of variety in sexual acts, unlike in writing, perversity. To the extent that they mimic defloration, new sexual acts can be acceptable to Fanny. The undertaking of a new sexual act is like loss of virginity because it is a first time, and thus a novel and unrepeatable, experience. This is why we see Fanny decked in white, "a victim lead to a sacrifice," when she has her appointment with Mr. Barville (182). Further, this encounter is like virginity because it proceeds, like defloration, from pain to pleasure. This perhaps explains Fanny's relative physical satisfaction with the experiment: as was the case in her "real" defloration, Fanny's extreme pain is rewarded with "infinitely predominant delight" (189). Significantly, although Fanny's experiment with flagellation ends in pleasure, Fanny does not desire to repeat the "experiment," perhaps since repetition would sacrifice some of the similarity of this act to virginity for her. Fanny explains her reluctance: "I was not, however, at any time re-enticed to renew with him, or resort again to the violent expedient of lashing nature into more haste than good speed" (189). That is, although this sex act follows the correct order, as least for the female, in that pain is followed by pleasure, the timing, Fanny argues, is perverted. This is evidenced by Fanny's frustration that, when she is finally ready for sexual pleasure after her brutally painful whipping, her hopes of "immediate ease" are thwarted by the need to once again lash her partner into sexual functioning (188). The strange combination of haste and delays caused by logistical difficulties bring this flagellation episode close to comic farce. The narrative is restored by the "inventive" efforts of the pair, which brings sexual satisfaction to Fanny but which does not erase her memory of having been "intolerably maddened" by the process (188–189). And thus, Fanny makes a case against flagellation based on its violations of narrative: its "haste" and intermittent delays. Fanny's sexual adventurousness, then, can be seen as part of her conservative upholding of the importance of the first sexual experience. Fanny implicitly relates all sex acts to defloration and evaluates them according to their approximation of that narrative. The further that sex acts deviate from the narrative of defloration (pain leading to pleasure), they are proportionately perverse. In Fanny's estimation, "unhappy persons," like Mr. Barville, are those who are under a "subjection" to "arbitrary tastes" that are "infinitely diversified" (181). Perversity for Fanny is essentially a violation of mimesis: reaching sexual stimulation by way of a whip is an inadequate imitation of the real or ideal experience of pain in defloration. It is not, in other words, a completely different experience or an "arbitrary" taste.[11]

Toward the end of her career, in an incident that has been the crux of critical debates over the novel's bourgeois politics, Fanny finally encounters sex that truly crosses the line of acceptability when she views two men engaging in sodomy.[12] As Fanny watches the men enter the inn where she is staying, she does not imagine that they are going to have sex, for their haste does not signal the standard sexual narrative that she has been developing: For example, they have their horse in "readiness" for a quick departure; they move "briskly"; and the elder one is in "too much hurry" (193). So again, as with the flagellation scene, this sex act has a problem with timing, but for some reason—its novelty perhaps?—Fanny is curious enough about the intentions of these men to perch herself atop a chair in order to watch their actions through a hole in the wall. To her horror and fascination, she finds that their narrative perversions actually go further than a mere problem with timing, as the trajectory of pleasure and pain itself is perverted. The younger man endures pain—he "writh[es]" and "complain[s]"—but, in Fanny's representation of the event, is not rewarded with pleasure (195). The older man, who does the penetrating, undertakes pleasure with a risk of pain rather than enduring pain for the sake of pleasure. In a tautological logic, Fanny grounds her case against the sodomites at least partially on the fact that, due to the social stigma attached to this act, sodomy has the potential to end so horribly; that is, it can have undesirable legal consequences. The men's "rashness," Fanny argues, means that their "preposterous pleasure" can lead to the "very worst of consequences," consequences that she herself endeavors to ensure by reporting the men's crime (194). From her perspective, both the timing and the order of the defloration narrative are perverted by the sodomites, and thus their crime is against narrative as much as it is against natural sex, or at least this is the way that "Fanny" implicitly makes her case against them. For Fanny, undertaking pleasure at the risk of pain is the ultimate perversity.

Unlike the hasty sodomites, Fanny has "patience" enough to gather evidence about them. Her watching of this unpleasant episode is a "painful" lesson for her, but it is one that she is willing to undergo. Like them, though, haste is her downfall, as an "unlucky impetuosity" causes her to slip, pass out, and thus miss the chance to bring the men to "justice" (195). Her own haste imposes a poor consequence, from Fanny's perspective, on the narrative, as it means that the men escape. But more importantly for my purposes here, her haste, and its link to their haste, also introduces an element of farce—or "slapstick" as Donald Mengay calls it—into the novel (196). The source of the farce, which as Soren Kierkegaard explains always depends on comic repetition for effect, is the defloration narrative, now unrecognizable to Fanny herself. Thus, the sodomite's perverse "imitation" of the defloration narrative threatens to turn the pornography into farce, and in her own "haste," Fanny herself becomes a comic figure. The sodomy scene reveals that repetition always threatens to become farce, mocking, at least to some extent, the legitimacy of its source, in this case the defloration narrative.

Similar concerns with virginity, repetition, and farce resurface two years after the publication of *Memoirs of a Woman of Pleasure*, when Cleland translates and edits an Italian pseudo-medical treatise, *The Case of Catherine Vizzani* (1751). Written by well-known Italian anatomist, Giovanni Bianchi, and originally published in Italy in 1744, the English version was almost certainly intended to be read for pleasure, probably both comic and erotic, rather than for anatomical instruction.[13] It is often classified as pornography, but the source of that pornography derives from the fantasy of a scientific gaze, not—at least directly—from the representation of sexual fulfillment. The text follows the exploits of a woman who disguises herself as a man for many years, but whose dissection, by the author, after death reveals her not only to be a woman, since she has breasts, but also, and much more importantly, a virgin. Its long title advertises "some curious and anatomical remarks on the Nature and Existence of the Hymen," and the author recounts his dissection of the woman and his preservation of the hymen as follows:

> I found, as has been before said, the Hymen to be entire, and of a circular Figure, like the Valves of the Intestines, or those Rings, called

Diaphragms, placed within Telescopes to reverberate the Rays of Light. This Hymen, with the Approximate Parts, I have reposited among those which I found in many Virgins of different Age at *Sienna*. As for those which I dissected at *Armino*, I left them behind; for that the Hymen is no Fancy, but actually found in all Virgin Females, is not controverted among experienced Anatomists; yet, as there are not wanting some at *Sienna*, who sneer at such a thing, let them only take a View of my Collection of these membranes; and, if they will not stand out against ocular Evidence, they must own the Reality thereof. (42–43).

The hymen of this text proves quite different from the elusive hymen of England discussed in chapter 2. Here, the anatomist has been able to dissect many virgins and has been able to retain the visual evidence of his endeavors. The number of dissections allows him to generalize about women, and he has the ocular proof to stand by his claims. This hymen is far from fragile, and it does not function as an obstruction to understanding or to sex. In fact, the circular figure of the hymen helps to make the woman's vagina function like a "telescope" that actually aids sight and understanding.[14] The reader is seduced by the possibility of actually viewing the collection of hymens, a collection that demonstrates a female standard. The narrative, removed by claims of translation, physical distance, and uniqueness, can invoke a privileged position of knowledge with respect to virgin female anatomy that was no longer possible in the medical texts of England. It fantasizes access to a hymen without having to destroy the hymen in the process of uncovering its secrets and without subjecting the medical man to satiric derision. It is Catherine's female lovers, not scientists, who are deceived: the cross-dressing narrative thereby displaces male anxiety about the female body's ability to deceive onto the females, not males, who are duped by Catherine.

In a number of ways, however, the text undermines its own authority. The reader in England could not easily have gone to view this collection of hymens. Never having seen the physical example, he (let us assume a male reader) could not affirm it in any particular woman and certainly could not hope to have the opportunity to view such a dissection himself, and even if he could, such access is only available after death. Moreover, this discovery of the hymen is embedded in a narrative of female cross-dressing. As such, the ability of the female to deceive extends beyond her virginity to her gender, thereby infecting this narrative of scientific authority with the strong trace of male susceptibility to deception. *The Case of Catherine Vizzani* suggests the possibility of direct access to a collection of hymens and offers the possibility of general knowledge about women, but access to the evidence is reserved to a scientist in Italy. And ultimately that scientist disavows the value of physical evidence, when he criticizes the religious men who extol Catherine's preservation of her chastity: "These Reverend Gentlemen certainly took the Matter by a wrong Handle, a Woman's Sanctity not consisting only in preserving her Chastity inviolate, but in an uniform Purity of Manners" (41). This scientist, with his prized collection of notoriously elusive hymens, must, ironically, admit the irrelevance of anatomical evidence for establishing moral value in order to prevent the threatened popular canonization of Catherine.[15] Finally, the moment that the text switches from a narrative about a singular woman (the story of Catherine's life) to a scientific argument founded on repetition (the testament of the author's authority to speak about virginity in general) is a place of generic instability. This seemingly unique case of cross-dressing turns out to be just one of innumerable contributions to the author's unwieldy collection of hymens. In fact, he has so many that they cannot even be stored in one place and some are simply "left behind."[16] Although narrative has a place in medical discourse and although repetition is key to medical knowledge, the moment where narrative and repetition intersect shifts this medical narrative into farce. Instead of a very unusual case history, Catherine—and her hymen—are reduced to just another jar on a shelf. In short, repetition is central to medicine but antithetical to a narrative of an individual because it transmutes individuality into farce.

Thus *The Case of Catherine Vizzani*, like the medical, satiric, and comic texts discussed earlier, pits scientific knowledge against sexual pleasure and individuality against abstraction. These are the tensions, one could say, that always circulate in pornography and indeed that animate, but, I argue, do not dominate *Memoirs of a Woman of Pleasure*. The tension between individuality and abstraction speaks to the common confusion over the title of Cleland's novel. Unlike its Richardsonian counterparts which are eponymously named for their virgin heroines, *Cleland's* novel is not, at least in its original version, named after Fanny, but rather after "pleasure." But *Memoirs of a Woman of Pleasure* does not suggest, via satiric or didactic correction, that the libertine pleasures of sex should prevail over the elusive pleas-ures of knowledge or the imaginary pleasures of literature/unreality. On the contrary, the brilliance of Cleland's novel is that it promises the possibility of having it all, of not having to choose between sex, knowledge, morality, and the imaginary pleasures of literature. This is why virginity is so important to this pornography: more so than any other topic, virginity offers a site of interaction between the kinds of pleasures that have been so often set in opposition to each other in works discussed earlier. By way of developing this point, I want to look in some depth at Fanny's marketing of a false virginity.

I have been arguing that *Memoirs of a Woman of Pleasure* depends upon the notion that virginity provides, via its physical structure, pleasure to women. In some ways, this allows the text, like *Pamela* did, to disavow male interest in virginity. And, just as we have seen throughout this book, where men are interested in virginity, they become the object of satire. The most intense locus of this satire is of course Mr. Norbert. A rich and self-indulgent man who has been made decrepit and perverse by indulging his taste for virginity/novelty, Norbert is representative of the type of man, one that presumably existed, who actively pursued sex with virgins.[17] For these men, virginity obviously holds no value related to marriage and procreation, as their purpose is to sleep with as many virgins as possible. And it is not the physical pleasure of sex with a virgin that motivates Norbert, as he, like the other men who sleep with virgins in *Memoirs of a Woman of Pleasure*, receives no special physical pleasure from the act. Nor is his pursuit an epistemological or intellectual one. His laughably feeble attempt to confirm Fanny's virginity before his assault on it suggests otherwise. As does the remarkably easy method by which Fanny deceives him. Since Norbert is too excited to make a full inspection of Fanny, and too decrepit for his physical pleasure to have any impact on Fanny, one can only conclude that it is neither physical (mechanistic) pleasure nor the pursuit of knowledge that motivates Norbert. For men like Norbert, the hymen and the virgin female body have been fetishized as erotic stimulants. They are the deluded devotees of the hymen, which Brandford Mudge deems the "Holy Grail of sexual fetishes" at this time (207). Their pursuit of defloration is therefore motivated by a pleasure that is entirely imaginary, the product, perhaps, of a false consciousness that allows men to be deceived and exploited by women.

Indeed Norbert is quite the dupe, and the sex he pays for is quite inferior, from Fanny's perspective, compared to the other sex in the novel. Mutual consent and mutual pleasure, and thus the ability to interpret the signs of desire and pleasure, are important features of good, in both the moral and the physical sense, sex in *Memoirs of a Woman of Pleasure*. The enormous penises of men make their desires easily interpretable, and their desire tends, in most cases, to spark female desire, consent, and pleasure. Male desire thus often becomes the sign of female desire as well. By contrast, the desires of Fanny and Norbert are at cross-purposes: Fanny wants to sell a false maidenhead while Norbert wants to have sex with a virgin. Given that a reliable virginity test is not available and given the satiric, not to mention medical, threat of making mistakes, the pursuit of maidenheads requires a keen ability to interpret the signs of virginity. As Norbert has recourse to Mrs. Cole if he finds the bargain unsuitable, the stakes are perhaps not as high in maiden hunting as they are in marriage, but nonetheless a great deal is at stake in the efforts of Fanny and Norbert to interpret and manipulate signs. Norbert must determine Fanny's suitability for his purpose, sex with a virgin outside marriage, and must try to obtain his desire at a reasonable cost. Fanny must determine Norbert's suitability for her purpose; she must convince him of her suitability, which is a complicated performance, since she must appear vulnerable to seduction yet still a virgin; and she must get as much money as she can in the bargain.

On all counts, Fanny is the victor. She identifies Norbert as suitable to her purposes, convinces him of her virginity, and is paid well for her troubles. When Fanny sees Norbert, she almost immediately, and correctly, sizes up his desire, and Mrs. Cole easily and authoritatively confirms Fanny's evaluation of him. Norbert, on the other hand, spends a good deal of time and energy assessing Fanny's suitability, but his powers of discrimination are poor, while her powers of deception are adequate to the easy task he presents. By good chance Fanny is dressed simply when she meets him, and she and her female accomplices easily construct for Norbert all the signs he needs to believe that she is a virgin who can be seduced for a high price. Along with the obvious deceptions of clothing and expression, Fanny makes Norbert feel sure he is dealing with a virgin by seeming reluctant and unavailable. Mrs. Cole leads him through "all the gradations of difficulty and obstacles" necessary for him to believe that he is dealing with a virgin (168). That is, the difficulty of reaching his goal is one of the signs that Norbert needs in order to believe that Fanny's virginity is genuine and, presumably, one of the erotic pleasures of the "hunt" for sex with virgins. As I argued earlier, although women in *Memoirs of a Woman of Pleasure* desire sex and actively pursue it, their bodies, especially in their virgin ideality, provide physical resistance and experience pain. In order to deceive Norbert, Fanny and Mrs. Cole create a kind of social hymen: obstacles and emotional resistance create a personality and social structure for Fanny that mimics the physical properties of the hymen. She becomes like a virgin body: resistant, surrounded by obstacles, and subject to pain. Norbert, who is easily swindled by this performance, stands as a negative contrast to the healthy men, who do not trouble themselves much about virginity, and this is what qualifies him as an object that provides literary/satiric pleasure.

But upon closer inspection, Norbert cannot be so easily dismissed. Although he seems to be anomalous (he is one of only two committed deflowerers and the only one fooled), all men in this text are easily—and perhaps one could say, happily—deceived and thus can be linked to Norbert. Even the "good" men, like Charles, cannot identify virginity. As Fanny says, once men are "caught by the eye," it is easy to take advantage of them. Men's sexual arousal, which is via vision, clouds their ability to investigate. Charles does not know that Fanny is a virgin when they sleep together, and when he returns to make an inspection of her body, it is really the "havoc that he had made" that interests him. His inspection, moreover, is cut short by his sexual arousal (83). In other words, men cannot see women's bodies both because they are looking for their effect on the body, which turns out to be visible only in the abject shedding of blood, and because they become sexually aroused. By contrast, the visibility of the male's body is obvious in this text, with its myriad and gargantuan penises. No one could misunderstand the male body. Conversely, there is a gender difference in the ability to see female bodies. The women themselves are quite capable of interpreting the signs of other women's bodies. Mrs. Brown spots Fanny right away as "fit for her purpose" (44). Phoebe can "palpably satisfy herself" to Fanny's continued virginity; and after her first sexual experience, Fanny, unlike Charles, can make a reasoned physical examination of both herself and Charles. (59, 78–83). Unlike in the ballads discussed in chapter 3, where the deceptions run in both directions, no women are deceived in Cleland's novel. While critics like Leo Braudy see *Memoirs of a Woman of Pleasure* and pornography in general as coming out of a tradition of materialism and anatomy, my point is quite the opposite: *Memoirs of a Woman of Pleasure* is a radical critique of the male ability to make sense of physical evidence. It inscribes "virgin" sex as a fantasy of male power that resides in producing visible effects on the woman, but the male characters' insistence on the power of the visual as evidence is what allows them to be tricked.

But Cleland is also up to something more complex and subtle than simply revealing the hymen to be a false idol. For in this in this text, neither satirization nor deception is incompatible with pleasure: there is Norbert's imaginary pleasure, which distinguishes him from the hapless Fossile of *Three Hours After Marriage* (1717), as well as the reader's literary pleasure. As classically defined pornography, *Memoirs of a Woman of Pleasure* is narrated by a prostitute, and both narration and prostitution are important to the kinds of pleasure it provides. Prostitution depends on acknowledged performativity: both partners know that the money transacted buys the (usually) female's performance of what the male wants. Contemporary debates about pornography often focus on its blurring of the lines between representation and actual events, but this is a major difference between visual pornography, which may, like prostitution, involve real men and women, and written pornography. *Memoirs of a Woman of Pleasure*, like all written pornography, is a narrativized (or re-presented) representation of what is always already a performance. As literary pornography, it absolutely depends upon a visuality that is only present in the imagination.

Thus, while Norbert may be satirized for paying for a performance of virginity, the whole narrative is, after all, a performance of virginity: a fictionalized fantasy of multiple deflorations. Defloration provides, in this memoir about pleasure, even more narrative and imaginary pleasure than physical pleasure. Fanny performs virginity for Norbert, but everyone—even the exalted libertines who make up the women's best clients—enjoy defloration stories. Julia Epstein has called the group storytelling a "metavoyuerism that imitates the novel's narrative framing" (1989, 140). Female virginity and its voyeuristic narrative pleasures provide the content and the structure of the group storytelling, the Norbert incident, and the novel as a whole. Moreover, Cleland's novel is self-conscious of its status as representation, through, for example, Fanny's continual concern about her literary language. It is also self-conscious about the potential for female performativity in sex. In fact, overtly performative sex and sexual storytelling actually constitute much of the "pleasure" in the novel. Moreover, *Memoirs of a Woman of Pleasure* is obviously, unlike other early pornographies and memoirs, fictional. Although Cleland was not immediately identified as the author, the first advertisement for *Memoirs of a Woman of Pleasure* announced its fictionality by referring to the author as "a person of quality," and Cleland was in legal difficulty for writing it within months of its publication.[18] The text cannot be seen as strictly materialist/libertine because of its obvious investment in performative and imaginative pleasure.

The pleasure in these *Memoirs* is not merely sexual, whether real or imaged, but also intellectual, in that satire is a key component of its literary pleasure. The possibility that any sexual escapade might turn into satire—or comic farce—is part of what keeps the narrative pleasure going. Peter Wagner has claimed that the comedy in Cleland's novel is only a result of our retrospective standards; his argument takes a common view that pornography and comedy are incompatible (244–245). Most critics who do acknowledge the satire, if not the comic or farcical elements of the novel, suggest that its source is the tradition of anti-*Pamela* satires and its object is Pamela's implausible combination of innocence and efficacy. But *Memoirs of a Woman of Pleasure* is an anti-*Pamela* not just because of the heroine's sexual profligacy but also in her obvious fictionality. Whereas Pamela and *Pamela* aim for verisimilitude, Fanny and her *Memoirs* depend on fantasy, fictionality, and performativity. And whereas both *Pamela* and *Clarissa* detach virginity from the body in order to prioritize a subjective and spiritual ideal, the female masquerade in *Memoirs of a Woman of Pleasure* opens up the possibility that this disembodied ideal may become almost completely performative, and it investigates the erotic possibilities of that through its self consciously fictional and satiric narratives of defloration. A remarkable achievement of Cleland's work is its rare ability to successfully integrate sexual fantasy and satire. Masquerading as a woman, Cleland offers the male reader access to both knowledge about virginity and the repeated sexual satisfaction that virginity ostensibly precludes. But simultaneously, Fanny's perspective on men reveals them to be easily subject to deception and incapable of reconciling knowledge with sexual pleasure. In other words, the text both satirizes men and imaginatively ameliorates the satire of men through a literary sexual fantasy. This is accomplished through the assumption of the female voice and through the incorporation of the satire into narrative pleasure: although women know more than men and thus can make men the subject of satire, they use this knowledge, in Cleland's literary fantasy, in the service of male sexual pleasure.[19] Moreover, the satire of men is what sustains the narrative cycle of pain and pleasure and thus generates readerly pleasure. If one reads and engages in sexual activity for "pleasure," then Cleland's novel can be read as offering the virgin woman's body *and* story as a realistic locus of pleasure for the man. If, however, one's purpose is knowledge rather than pleasure, then *Memoirs of a Woman of Pleasure* turns out to be a fantastically sharp satire on men and their desire for knowledge of women. In short, the unique brilliance of Cleland's novel lies in its ability to negotiate a fine balance among satire, sexual fantasy, and literary satisfaction. The novel integrates the satiric with the pornographic, by way of fantasizing that, after all, men do not have to, and in fact cannot, choose between sexual pleasure and knowledge about women. In the end, *Memoirs of a Woman of Pleasure* can be read pornographically because the pleasure of the story of virginity, the imaginary pleasure of the male as deflowerer, compensates for the satiric threat to men, and it can be read for novelistic pleasure because the satire prevents brute repetition and thus boredom. This is part of the reason that the novel's sexual politics remain ambiguous.

Rather than disavowing, deflecting, or projecting the conditions for satire, Cleland revels in them as opportunities for literary pleasure.

I have been arguing for an inherent relationship among virginity, repetition, and fictional narration. The essential link between repetition and virginity is constituted by the fact that repetition is antithetical to defloration. This is perhaps why, as Louis Mackey has argued, Kierkegaard's famous meditation on repetition is centered on a virgin. J. Hillis Miller has argued that repetition is central to the novel: "Any novel is a complex tissue of repetitions and of repetitions within repetitions, or of repetitions linked in chain fashion to other repetitions" (2–3). Cleland's defenders often insist that his novel is not a "pornotopia"; that is, it does not rely on a kind of brute repetition. My argument is that the satire prevents such brute repetition. The narrative strategies of *Memoirs of a Woman of Pleasure*—repetition, literary masquerade, and linkage of the narrative of virginity loss to the narrative of a woman's life—offer literary pleasures as a substitution for the epistemological satisfaction that is usually elusive with respect to female virginity and for the sexual pleasure that offers the short-term gratification of novelty. *Memoirs of a Woman of Pleasure*, then, can be seen as an effort to get at the abstraction "pleasure" via the heuristic of virginity. Pleasure is a concept and all of the various ways of achieving it in this text, though they are linked by virginity, are not the same. And this is where my story ends, with virginity as a privileged narrative, one that brings various kinds of pleasure, including narrative and disembodied pleasure to the reader, regardless of gender. This chapter shows both how repetition is a link between virginity and the novel and how virginity is ultimately implicated in both fictionality and narrativity. I make these links in support of my larger argument about virginity's centrality to the development of the English novel in the eighteenth century. "The first enjoyment is decisive" declares Fanny, in an echo of Lovelace's libertine creed (98). What *Memoirs of a Woman of Pleasure* does is reconcile this libertine ideal of sex with the marriage plot by positing the importance of the "first time" as the maxim underlying the marriage plot as well as its seeming antagonists in satire and comedy.

Conclusion: Clarissa's Exceptional Infertility

And what would there have been in it of uncommon or rare, had I not been so long about it?

Richardson, *Clarissa*, 847

It is tempting to conclude this book by simply saying "Hence, *Clarissa*." After all, a 1,500-page book about the trials and tribulations of a virgin could only be produced at the height of an historically unprecedented obsession with virginity. But perhaps a more honest prediction of a reader's reaction would be this: But what about Clarissa? Surely she is the exception? And indeed, in important ways, Clarissa and *Clarissa* are exceptional. Although I claimed that my story was over in the last chapter, I offer here, in a short discussion of a very long novel, an ending historically coincident to Cleland's *Memoirs*. And in some ways, it is a more appropriate ending, since Clarissa is, quite literally, the end of her line. While Pamela bore children and *Pamela* spawned imitations, satires, and sequels, Samuel Richardson's second novel, *Clarissa* has produced much analysis—and very active participation from its readers—but neither the novel nor its heroine has anything that one could consider direct or worthy progeny. While Pamela has become the generic heroine, subject to imitation and satirization, Clarissa has become unique and inimitable, and the text of *Clarissa* has achieved a remarkable measure of sanctity, which may or may not be the kind of thing its eponymous heroine intended when she decreed that her body should not be dissected. Based on my argument about repetition and novelty in the last chapter, it would be easy to surmise that the exceptionality of Clarissa and *Clarissa*—as opposed to their exemplarity—must have something to do with narrative originality and to conclude that narrative originality demands some incomparable approach to virginity. To be sure, critics often credit the rape with *Clarissa's* critical difference from *Pamela*.

For example, Susan Staves accounts for the fact that Clarissa, unlike Pamela, cannot be satirized because she is raped, and rape cannot be comic (1994, 86). Tassie Gwilliam argues that an important difference between *Pamela* and *Clarissa* is the figure of Lovelace; "by locating disguise, duplicity, and transformation" in Lovelace, Gwilliam argues, "Richardson frees Clarissa from the accusations of hypocrisy and duplicity that dogged Pamela" (52). These arguments support my claim in chapter 5 that *Pamela's* multitudinous and hideous progeny are a function of the text's amenability to satire. But none of this accounts for *Clarissa's* originality, since Lovelace is a stock, if incredibly richly realized, character: a restoration rake whose duplicitous and predatory actions are a cliché by 1748 and who wanders in to a Richardson novel, unwilling, or unable, to be reformed. Moreover, virtue in distress can be just as clichéd—and, as we saw in chapter 3, just as available for comic and satiric treatment—as virtue triumphant.

No doubt the most strikingly exceptional thing about *Clarissa* is its length: often claimed to be the longest novel in English, it relates the events of just under a year in the lives of its characters (rather suggestively, the book skips the Christmas and New Year holidays, suggesting a lack of both New Testament Christian ideals and temporal progress). Reader's initial remarks about the book—and their assessment of its literary merits—often have to do with its length. For example, Hester Mulso said she would not quarrel with twice as many volumes, and at least two editors who tried to abridge it wound up declaring such an endeavor impossibly detrimental to the novel.[1] Richardson found himself having to defend the length of his novel, saying "long as the work is, there is not one Digression, not one Episode, not one Reflection, but what arises naturally from the Subject, and makes for it, and to carry it on."[2] His comments suggest that his novel's length must be justified in terms of its structure, a point not lost on its readers. The same readers who treated Pamela's virtue and virginity as matters of fact worth meditating about, replicating, or satirizing instead used the occasion of reading *Clarissa* as an opportunity to discuss the nature of literary merit. *Clarissa's* length engaged its first readers in a critical debate about storytelling, in particular about the proper subject matter for novels and about the relationship between, to use formalist terms, plot and story.[3] For example, in her *Remarks on Clarissa* (1749) Sarah Fielding recounts an amusing evening spent discussing *Clarissa*, where the claim by one conversant that he could "tell the whole story contained in the first two volumes in a few minutes" leads to another man telling the story of the history of Rome in as little time and thence to a general discussion of the appropriate topics for fiction (3–8). In much the same way that Clarissa makes her virginity irrelevant to her character, defenders of the book make the plot (if not the length) irrelevant to their evaluation of the novel. As its first readers recognized, the length and the originality of *Clarissa* do not arise naturally from the story of the rape of her virginity, which is manifestly mundane. Nor does any particular plot structure define the novel. *Clarissa* is not a novel of triumphant or defeated female virtue; nor is it a hagiography of a saint, who is martyred for her virginity. It is not a rape plot, nor a novel about a female—or a male—libertine or a feminist heroine. It is a novel about the conflict of these narratives, a novel whose originality derives from its unique historical access to all of these plots. What is more, the interaction of these plots makes *Clarissa* anachronistic to the eighteenth century on two levels. On one hand, *Clarissa* looks far backward, to a patriarchy based in authority and obedience and to a religious model of virginity based in transcendence. On the other hand, it looks forward to feminist critiques of eighteenth-century ideas about female sexuality and its importance to property and inheritance. As such, *Clarissa* is a novel whose originality and length—not merely its plot about a girl's virginity—are a function of a narrative conflict that could only be produced in the middle of the eighteenth century.

Paradoxically, in this monumentously long novel, the chief complaint of the main characters consists in being unnaturally rushed, and the principle action of the story abnormally shortens Clarissa's period of virginity and her life. As such, though a short summary of the plot might revolve around seduction and tragically early death, the real action of the narrative revolves around anxiety about time and delay. As we have seen throughout this book, virginity is a particularly vexed arena for questions about delay: greensickness and Protestant rhetoric testify to the danger of delay, pornography to its limited pleasures, and *Pamela* to its potential rewards. In *Clarissa*, persistent interruptions and suspensions of the narrative action force the characters, and their readers, to actively think about their relationship to various plot possibilities, including marriage, lifelong virginity, rape, and death. As a consequence, *Clarissa* is, like *Memoirs of a Woman of Pleasure*, about timing and narration as much as it is about seduction, virginity, patriarchy, or feminism. Or perhaps I should say, like *Memoirs of a Woman of Pleasure*, *Clarissa* leverages literary conventions about timing and narrative to interrogate social conventions about sexuality and marriage.

At the beginning of the action of the novel, Clarissa Harlowe is nineteen years old, on the young side of being marriageable.[4] Her literary sister Pamela and her step sister Fanny Hill have set a standard of trials and delay as the way to prove and develop both character and narrative interest. As we have seen throughout this book, permanent virginity as a means to virtue or as source of sexual or narrative pleasure is not available in England in the eighteenth century; there is no way, in 1748, to plot, or pursue, long-term virginity alongside virtue or pleasure. But perversely and regularly, Clarissa insists that her preference would be for a single life. Clarissa's professed desire for spinsterhood is seriously entertained by none of her family or friends, who interpret, strategically perhaps, her resistance to marriage as a conventionally virtuous commitment to ultimately marry. Clarissa's one mode of power in the marriage negotiations is delay, and as she strives to avoid marriage, delay becomes Clarissa's main mode of acting. For example, she implores, "Let me this once be heard with patience, and have my petition granted. It is only that I may not be hurried away so soon as next Thursday" (266). She comes to rely on unpredictable circumstances ("twenty things might happen to afford me a suspension at least"), active machinations on her part ("I have several ways to gain time"), and unsubstantiated hope ("I have still more hopes that I shall prevail for some delay") to afford delay (342, 375, 365). The friends and relations of both Clarissa and Lovelace are united in their determination to move things toward closure in the form of marriage. As Clarissa begs and negotiates for more time early in the novel, her family presses her to demonstrate her filial devotion by speedily marrying Solmes. And although Anna Howe posits herself as the anti-Harlowe, she assumes the role, after Clarissa has left her family's house, of insisting that there is no time to delay. "If any delay happen," she warns Clarissa, Lovelace is not to be trusted. "All punctilio is at an end" she claims, as she urges Clarissa to marry Lovelace as soon as possible; "be sure to delay not the ceremony," she vehemently advises (371). But delays continue, and these delays, in their very lack of teleology, constitute a profound challenge to the marriage plot that Clarissa's parents want to impose, and indeed to the nascent novel form more generally, which depends on development.

At first, Clarissa and Lovelace are drawn together by their shared resistance to the marriage plot and their corollary commitment to delay. Lord M. warns Lovelace that "*delays are dangerous*" but Lovelace prefers another of Lord M.'s clichés "patience is a virtue" (607). He insists that he must wait for the right time for his plots to "ripen into execution" (416). Lovelace often uses this trope of "ripening," a familiar trope for virginity, to emphasize the importance of timing, patience, and delay to his seductions and thus to his identity:

> Such a one as *I*, Jack, needed only, till now, to shake the stateliest tree, and the mellowed fruit dropped into my mouth . . . more truly delight-ful to me the seduction progress than the crowning act—for that's a vapour, a bubble! (616)

Unlike Clarissa's family, Lovelace understands the value of patience and, via his metaphors of ripening, even metaphorically insists upon its links to nature. He relegates the affairs of family and property to cul-ture and suggests that good plots, and the most exquisite pleasures, take their structure and their timing from nature. Although Lovelace is famously theatrical and a dedicated plotter, he claims that this is all in the service of natural narrative timing. In another example of the ripen-ing metaphor, he explains his reluctance to commit rape or marriage:

> Tis plain she would have given me up for ever; nor should I have been able to prevent her abandoning of me, unless I had torn up the tree by the roots to come at the fruit; which I hope still to bring down by a gentle shake or two, if I can but have patience to stay the ripening season. (601)

Lovelace's desire to see himself as one who waits for "ripening" con-flicts with his use of rape as a way to avoid marriage, causing him to construct a botanically untenable metaphor: the tree that has been torn up by the roots is unlikely to ripen its fruits. This is as true for Clarissa and *Clarissa* as it is for fruit trees, and Lovelace finds himself, midway through the novel, having to admit, however indirectly, that something unnatural is going on.

Clarissa and Lovelace also share status as the anxious objects of complicated paternal legacies. The original conflict that instigates the novel is Clarissa's grandfather's unusual bequest to her, which dis-rupts the line of inheritance in the Harlowe family. The grandfather legitimizes his deviance from primogeniture by proclaiming Clarissa to be his "own peculiar child" and insisting that she has prolonged his life (53). Clarissa's nonphysical traits—her virtue and not her virginity or her ability to transmit literal paternity—constitute her "value" and thus that catalyze her grandfather's transgression of inheritance pro-tocol. "Our two daughters are equally dear and valuable to us," Clarissa's mother asserts, disingenuously, we may assume, as all char-acters acknowledge Clarissa's superior value (189). The grandfather's legacy, and Clarissa's response to it, cause her familial relationships to be challenged. For example, Anna Howe asserts, "You are your mamma's girl," while the paternity of Clarissa's siblings, who clearly take after her father suffer no such doubt. "Do they not" Anna teases, "bear his stamp and image more that you do?" (67). While Clarissa's virginity is unquestioned and her virtue unparalleled, her own paternity and her ability to transmit paternal inheritance are fundamental problems in the novel. In a famous comment early in the novel, Clarissa asserts "in my opinion, the world is but one great family," a telling indication of Clarissa's anachronistic—or utopian—ideas about familial bonds (62). I am not suggesting that Mr. Harlowe's literal paternity of Clarissa is in doubt, but rather that the grandfather's bequest—a result of her unparalleled virtue as measured by new eighteenth-century standards—makes Clarissa's relation to the fallible Harlowe's questionable. For his part, Lovelace is the only male heir of his family. Lord M. pins his prospect of descendants on Lovelace, hoping that a marriage between the pair would produce an heir. He writes to Lovelace, "May this marriage be crowned with a great many fine boy (I desire no girls) to build up again a family so antient! The first boy shall take my surname by Act of Parliament. That is in my will" (787). Like Clarissa's grandfather, Lord M. has a will that will reach toward the past instead of the future and that will claim paternity for a child not his own. The potential marriage of Clarissa and Lovelace will determine the fate of two families whose succession rests on only one male heir, and it is their continued "perversity" that their actions and inactions disrupt the plans that others have for furthering their own schemes of family formation.

Because of their shared commitment to delay and their resistance to the marriage plot, Clarissa and Lovelace are both anachronistic characters: a libertine and a celibate caught in a modern world, that is, in a novel. Not surprisingly, both of them blame timing for their predicaments. Clarissa offers her youth and its accompanying "rashness" (as well as her family's impatience) as mitigating factors for her tragedy. For his part, Lovelace claims that their ages have made them ill timed as partners, since he encounters Clarissa "a little to late for my *setting out*, and a little too early in my *progress*" (870). In significant ways, then, the length of Clarissa's story is a function of the varying desires of the characters to lengthen or shorten different narratives, desires that are ultimately motivated by their ideas about what constitutes natural relationships among virginity, paternity, and posthumous legacy. In their efforts to convince Lovelace to marry Clarissa, Belford and Lord M. try to challenge Lovelace's idea of the narrative of the libertine by pointing out its downfalls and by positioning him in

another, more positive (from their perspective), kind of narrative—
that of paternal descent. Lovelace's friends and relations try to convince him that he is the beneficiary of the system of patrilinear
inheritance based on legitimacy, and that he therefore has an obliga-
tion to perpetuate it. Belford argues that those "in possession of
estates by *legal descent*" would have been "naked destitute varlots" if
their fathers had not had concern for their "posterity," and he argues
that Lovelace owes it to his own posterity to follow his father's
example (612). To bolster his case, Belford graphically describes the
demise of their libertine friend Belton. Belford blames Belton's
predicament on timing, saying, "Alas . . . I fear, I fear, he came *too
soon* into his uncle's estate" (1242). As a result of his "too soon" independence, Belton's life is shortened, and he no longer has the possibility
for immortality—or at least lasting memory—in the form of progeny,
since the children of Belton's long-term relationship with a mistress
are probably not his own. Belford deduces that "the strong health of
the chubby-faced, muscular whelps confirms the too great probability"
(616). The idea that men, like women, have a proper season for procreation and that the career of the libertine, which usually involves a
late marriage after much carousing, is problematic for paternity,
health, and longevity is seconded by Lord M. "The children of very
young and very old men last not long" Lord M. ruminates, as he
encourages Lovelace to forbear delay (607).

To counter Lovelace's narrative of libertinism (and his stalling for
time), Belford and Lord M. argue that chaste marriage—based on
premarital virginity and paternal legitimacy—is the natural foundation
of society. This narrative makes claims both on the past (ancestors)
and the future (descendants); it is both regressive and progressive. It
is the same argument that Samuel Johnson will later (in historical
time) articulate and the one with which I began this book. Belford's
admonitions to Lovelace on this account assume a religious fervor, as
he describes the late paternity of libertinism in a way that suggests
original sin:

If thou are not so narrow-minded an elf as to prefer thy own *single* satisfaction to *posterity* thou, who shouldst wish to beget children for duration,
wilt not postpone till the rake's usual time; that is to say, till diseases or
years, or both, lay hold of thee; since in that case thou wouldst entitle thy-
self to the curses of thy legitimate progeny for giving them a being altogether miserable; a being which thou callest the *worst*; to wit, upon the
doctor's courtesy, thy descendants also propagating (if they shall live and be
able to propagate) a wretched race that shall entail the curse. (502)

Through the use of biblical and anachronistic language as well as repeated references to time, Belford makes this argument sound traditional, even old testament, and linked to, in Paul Riceour's words, phenomenological time. This kind of time—and argumentation—is opposed to the "writing to the moment" of Richardson's style. Talk about legacies, legitimation, and progeny are ways to imagine oneself as existing within historical, narrative, and social time. As such, they are strategies of temporal compression that seek to project the individual into the past and future, and thereby deny death. By contrast, Richardson's famously sprawling and prolix writing style—of which Clarissa and Lovelace are the most dedicated practitioners—appears to make time expand, since writing always moves more slowly than experience. This style emphasizes the importance of the present and of the living individual, whose body and virginity are her own, over phenomenological time and the histories of the species or the family. In other words, that is in Paul Riceour's words, I have been describing a conflict over the meaning of time that leaves Clarissa and Lovelace, despite being the most obsessive scribblers in the book, unable or unwilling to "inscript" themselves into their society, left only with resistance and delay as strategies.[5]

The argument that heterosexuality and monogamy are the customary moral basis of society is, I have been arguing throughout this book, not traditional but in fact is produced in the seventeenth and eighteenth centuries.[6] Relations based in blood and property form the foundation of a new Protestant society in England, while both lifelong virginity and bastardy (the hallmarks of mariolatry and thus Catholicism) become the transgressors, the anachronisims, and, in the view of Clarissa and Lovelace's friends and relations, the site of the unnatural. Clarissa and Lovelace embrace these archaic models of sexuality—and to some extent, obedience—,which allows them to function simultaneously as anachronistic and prophetically transgressive figures to the naturalized model of sexuality and society that the other characters articulate.

But famously and irrevocably, and just when it seems that no one can stand it any longer, Lovelace relents before Clarissa does. Not only by raping her, but also by becoming subsequently obsessed with the possibility that she is carrying his child. He proclaims, for example, "Let me perish, Belford, if I would not forgo the brightest diadem in the world for the pleasure of seeing a twin Lovelace at each charming breast" (706). Like Lord M., Lovelace wants only boys, which, in his fantasy, would be little versions of himself and which would situate Clarissa as a more fertile version of the maternal Virgin Mary. He fantasizes that having children would lead to Clarissa's begging him to "deign" to marry her (706). In Lovelace's fantasy, he is beyond questions of legal or cultural sanction because he is "the father" in the sense that he has usurped God's role: he is the one who confers legitimation rather than hoping for it. The vehemence of his desire for this role and the esteem with which he holds it make his declarations rival Clarissa's own religiosity. For example, he is willing to foreswear all earthly power for a shot at this immortal power. He declares to Belford, "Oh Jack! Had I an imperial diadem, I swear to thee that I would give it up, even to my *enemy*, to have one charming boy by this lady" (916). Lovelace's paternal fantasies are technically anachronistic, in that they rely upon absolute authority, and yet they also help to reconcile him with Lord M., in terms of fulfilling Lord M.'s desire for earthly progeny. For both of them, virtuous virgins figure prominently in their desire for progeny as a way to cheat time. As such, Lovelace's fantasies reveal patriarchy's flexibility, not its complete transformation.

Clarissa thus not only exposes the persistence of patriarchy, but it also reveals its anxieties and thus the ways that it produces the conditions for a feminist critique. As Lovelace's access to Clarissa becomes even more imperiled, he ruminates on her possible pregnancy, which would have been conceived in virginity (or defloration) and out of wedlock. Clarissa's unparalleled virtue—of which her virginity at the time of sexual relations is only one manifestation—intensifies his unease about paternity, even as it makes his fantasies about the significance of his imagined paternity more grandiose.[7] His fantasies become more extravagant, until he has given birth to an unwieldy number of celestial creatures:

> If this should be the case, how I should laugh at *thee*! And (when I am sure of her) at the dear novice *herself*, that all her grievous distresses shall end in a man-child; which I shall love better than all the Cherubims and Seraphims that may come after; though there were to be as many of them as I beheld in my dream; in which a vast expanse of ceiling was stuck as full of them as it could hold. (1239)

In this quote, Lovelace's dreams of progeny with Clarissa, grand as they are, are fundamentally limited and anxious. The Cherubims and Seraphims are on the ceiling, suggesting a painting of heaven rather than the real thing, and they are so numerous that their repetition shifts the register of this excerpt into farce. Earlier, Lovelace admitted that he cannot even be sure that he remembers what his dreams were: he merely "thinks" he remembers what he saw (706). As we saw in chapter 6, discourses of virginity often verge on farce; this is because of virginity's complex relationship to novelty (or exceptionality) and repeatability (or exemplarity).

We have also seen throughout this book that anxieties about epistemological certainty emerge whenever patriarchy depends on the female body, and this is also true in *Clarissa*. Even though Clarissa's virginity is not at stake, in the sense that no one suspects her of lying about it, epistemological and generic instabilities surface around her body and her sexuality. Letters transmit the fact of the rape but, as Judith Wilt and others have shown, no truth about Clarissa's body is brought to light by the letters. Interest in female virginity has a perverse relationship to privacy: the virgin anatomy testifies to a physical privacy but must be proven through public examination. Without access to her body, Lovelace and her relatives, as well as readers for many centuries, can speculate about the possibility that Clarissa is pregnant, but they have no way of verifying it. Her family implores Clarissa's own "word" on the subject, while Lovelace depends on "time" to reveal the truth.[8] But after the rape, Clarissa insists that no men should come near her body and that her body should be sealed up after death. Despite this injunction, and not surprisingly but rather uncannily, Lovelace wishes to preserve Clarissa's heart in a glass jar.[9] Lovelace's desire for her physical heart is reminiscent of both the collection of hymens in *The Case of Catherine Vizzani* and the obsession with Belinda's hair in *The Rape of the Lock*, because it depends upon a conflation of material and metaphorical referents of virtue. Even though her "virtue" does not reside in her virginity, Clarissa's body becomes subject to the same kinds of investigative and imaginative desires as virginity produces. Clarissa is able to reserve her body from such investigative desires because she does not participate in any of the narratives that others try to impose. She is invested neither in the old-fashioned obsession with literal virginity nor in fixation on blood and property relations. The rape does not make her less virtuous; she leaves her legacy to no particular family; and her paternity goes back far past her grandfather, to God. When she writes to Lovelace that she will write him from her *"father's house"* she is not necessarily being metaphorical, for Mr. Harlowe has been the substitute (merely metaphorical) father all along. Lovelace's fantasy of divine paternity has obscured what he earlier suspected about Clarissa:

> If such a lady as Miss Harlowe chose to enter into the matrimonial state . . . and, according to the old patriarchal system, to go on contributing to get sons and daughters with no other view than to bring them up piously, and to be good and useful members of the commonwealth,

what a devil had she to do to let her fancy run a gadding after a rake?
One whom she *knew* to be a rake? (970)

Lovelace understands Clarissa's reluctance to participate cooperatively
in the worldly system of paternal descent. Clarissa is not trying to be
an anachronistic saintly recluse—after all she serves the "commonwealth" through her "poor"—but she reserves her body, and especially her virginity, from this worldly system. Once her virginity, her
privacy, and her free will have been martyred to mortal narratives,
Clarissa welcomes death. Clarissa's development thus involves the
acceptance of her loss of virginity and it explicitly links that loss with
death. The most common explanation for virginity's importance—
patrilinear legitimacy—is a means of denying and delaying death; it is
a secular substitute for a belief in the hereafter. Whereas a fantasy of
patriarchal descent is a denial of death—or an attempt to circumvent
its most identity-denying implications—for Clarissa, virginity and virginity loss function as heuristic devices that ultimately prepare her for
death. Belford proves his understanding of this point when, in presenting Lovelace with the negative example of Belford, he declares
that things might have been different "if a man were to live always"
(1242). That is, if a man were to live always, he need not concern
himself with paternity, with death and, specifically in this case, with
Clarissa's virginity, or, for that matter, with her corpse.

The belief that patrilinear legitimacy is the root of obsession with
virginity always locates this belief, and the conflict that instantiates it
at any given time, in the past, even as it stakes a claim on the future.
This is why, very soon after *Clarissa*, we see the development of the
gothic novel, in which plots of familial tyranny over a girl's virginity
are set in the medieval past or in Roman Catholic countries. These
gothic novels are *Clarissa's* most direct descendants because they
embed regressive social practices in the new form of the novel and
because they receive their narrative movement (both forward, backward, and delayed) from the tension between older and newer modes
of thinking about the relationship between the virgin and the patriarch. Earlier, I described the way that delays in *Clarissa* (both for
characters in the novel and for its readers) become the occasion for a
discussion of narrative pleasure and social correctness. We will see this
same self-consciousness about storytelling and timing in the gothic
novels later in the century.[10] Critical debate about *Clarissa* frequently
focus on its feminist credentials and its plot tensions. My argument in
this conclusion, indeed in this whole book, has been to show how
these two issues relate, and how they were simultaneously produced

by England's slow transition to Protestant and parliamentary rule. The long eighteenth century is both conservative and progressive in that it produces both modern mythologies about virginity and their feminist critiques. This is why *Clarissa* does and does not belong to the eighteenth century, why she is both the exception to and the exemplar of the eighteenth-century preoccupation with virginity.

Notes

Introduction: Virginity and Patrilinear Legitimacy

1. Boswell, volume III, 406.
2. Pregnancy makes sex more verifiable than celibacy but it does not necessarily reveal paternity.
3. Bruce Boehrer has an important essay on this topic, in which he argues that an ideal "wedded chastity" emerges as a strategy for promoting marriage and procreation in a society that has traditionally idealized celibacy and virginity; "indeed," he continues, "at heart the concept of wedded chastity is little more than the willful destabilizing of an inconvenient signifier, calculated to serve the procreative demands of an emergent political economy" (557).
4. For an important discussion of divine right of kings, see Figgis, 137–177, and for an analysis of the different strands of patriarchalist thought, see Schochet, 1–18.
5. See Boehrer for a discussion of Elizabeth's legitimacy issues, which he uses as a context for reading Spencer. He argues that a "Legend of Chastity" functions as a displacement of the anxiety of legitimacy (566). On Elizabeth's virginity, see also Hackett; and John King. On early modern virginity generally, see Jankowski; Kathleen Coyne Kelly; Loughlin; Scholz; and Schwarz.
6. Marie Loughlin argues for the relationship between Stuart political projects and virginity. James I had a habit of visiting married couples after the wedding night because, according to Loughlin, in the moment when the virgin daughter becomes the chaste bride "James's configuration of the patriarchal state and his various political projects are materialized" (1996), 847.
7. For more on this, see McKeon (1987), 209.
8. Since the determination of firstborn son was not clear, firstborn illegitimate children often held some stake to the birth-right of the heir. Locke is interesting regarding these "Questions of Legitimation," asking rhetorically: "and what in Nature is the difference betwixt a Wife and a Concubine?" (1967), 231.
9. To the extent that "birth" can confer virtue, it is through the matrilineal inheritance. The mother's virtue (exemplified by her protracted virginity and her steadfast chastity) confers on the child an inheritance of virtue.

Virginity, then, is more a sign than a material reality, and the Protestant virgin, at least in theory, much less embodied than her Catholic ancestor.

10. Thomas Sprat argues that the Royal Society and the Anglican Church "both may lay equal claim to the word Reformation" (part 3, section 23, page 371). Elizabeth Eisenstein argues for the relationship between the Reformation and the new science via exploitation of printing (697, 701); Ernst Cassirer examines the process whereby the "truth of nature" became much more reliable than the "word of God" (43). On this topic, see also Keith Thomas; and Shapin and Schaffer.

11. On the epistemology of the novel and its relation to science, see, most famously, Watt; and McKeon (1987), both of whom consider the topic of virginity and the epistemological strategies of science crucial to the novel, but they do not link these topics. John Bender analyzes the opposition between fiction and science. Ann Van Sant's discussion of the empirical "testing" of Clarissa by Lovelace links the epistemology of the novel and science in the manner I am suggesting, but she does not explore the implications of the fact that what are being tested are virginity and virtue. April Alliston does link virginity to the epistemological strategies of the novel, saying "the truth about female sexual conduct . . . remains the ultimate truth for fiction in France and England" (19).

CHAPTER 1   BLESSED VIRGINS: ANTI-CATHOLIC PROPAGANDA AND CONVENT FANTASIES

1. First published as *Five Love-Letters from a Nun to a Cavalier* (1678) by Gabriel Joseph de Lavergne Guilleragues. Authorship is still a matter of debate.

2. See, in particular, his discussion of truth and virtue (1987), 265–272.

3. The English Short Title Catalogue (ESTC) lists over twenty versions between 1678 and 1777.

4. 1 Corinthians 7:34.

5. Calvin exhorted that priestly celibacy is the product of an "impious tyranny not only against God's word but against all equity" (1250) IV.12.23.

6. Freeman, 25.

7. Hobbes, part 4, chapter 44, 337. See Thomas for more on the Reformation, Catholicism, and magic.

8. Council of Trent, session XXIV, canto 10.

9. H. C. Lea and Eric Josef Carlson argue that clerical marriage in England was far more contested than in other countries that adopted Reformation ideals, though Helen Parish finds less ambivalence about celibacy in England than they do.

10. Lawrence Stone's argument has been criticized by Patrick Collinson and Susan Dwyer Amussen, but recently defended by Anthony

Fletcher. I do not dispute the emergence of a new companionate (Protestant) view of marriage, but I question whether it gave women more options: they might marry whomever they chose, but marry they must, if social prestige and spiritual development were desired.

11. Rogers, "The Enclosure of Virginity," shows how the doctrine of passive resistance demonstrates nostalgia for the possibility of retirement as fertile and argues that it was imagined to be a way (for men) around active (military) engagement, but I think that such a passive, ascetic route to religiosity is usually gendered female under Catholicism, since women's *only* religious role is passive.

12. For other examples of beliefs in special powers of virginity, see Keith Thomas, 215, 268–269.

13. Shuger (1997) argues, against the traditional reading, that the Lady is immobilized due to her sexuality, not empowered due to her chastity. In any case, she rather miraculously escapes rape.

14. Dolan makes a similar point but locates the origin slightly earlier, arguing, "by 1680, it was almost impossible to defend a Catholic woman publicly and credibly" (13).

15. There was a heated debate amongst Protestants over whether monasteries were a part of the ancient church or were a corruption to be reformed. English defenders of (ancient) monasteries often emphasized them as centers of learning and of valuable property. Tanner, e.g., documented the history of English monasteries because they were a part of "the glory of our English Nation" (2).

16. Cavendish's text does not explicitly assign religion to either side, but it does counterpose a convent with male political interests, and one male character deems Lady Happy's plan as "heretic."

17. Cited in *The Catholic Encyclopedia*, volume XV, 459.

18. The author is listed as L. Sherling but both OCLC/World Cat and the Huntington Library identify L. Sherling as a pseudonym for Daniel Pratt.

19. This is not to ignore the sexualized Catholic representation of the nun as "bride of Christ," nor the spiritual aspects of chaste sexuality, but rather to argue that the connection between sex and religion is in this case deployed to de-spiritualize the nun.

20. See Wharton.

21. I do not mean to suggest that Catholicism coincides with better treatment for women, or that Protestantism disallowed insubordination more than Catholicism. Throughout this chapter, I analyze and interrogate the Protestant perspective on Catholicism, but I certainly do not mean to take sides.

22. The text is infamous due to its censorship and role in obscenity legislation. See Foxon; and Pettit. The 1683 edition, to which I refer, consists of three dialogues. Later versions expanded to six dialogues.

23. See also Turner, who argues, like Pettit, that the anti-Catholic satire is a pretext for pornography. Turner does argue that the Reformation rhetoric becomes increasingly crucial in later versions: "Venus' erotic

naturalism always had an evangelistic tinge, establishing the equivalence of sexual awakening, 'primitive' innocence, direct access to Scripture, and Cartesian understanding of physical nature. But now the sexual tenor becomes the vehicle, the pretext for Protestant discipline and holy matrimony" (2003, 353). But I am working with the first edition of *Venus* and argue that even here the pornography is not separable from the Protestant agenda. Wagner has asserted that pornography is often a "vehicle for revolutionary thought" (17).

24. One very simple support for my point is the fact that most anti-Catholic propaganda is not pornographic, but most pornography is anti-Catholic. Lynn Hunt argues that early pornography is "almost always an adjunct to something else" (10).

25. Kate Chedgzoy argues that in a number of seventeenth-century texts, a woman's desire for the life of a female community is seen as a withdrawal from the circuit of exchange and reproduction that guarantees the future of the patriarchal family (58).

26. See Bowden.

27. Cited in Dolan, 34.

28. See, e.g., George Duckett, who argues that the Pretender will return the wealth of the monasteries to the papacy. His concerns were not without foundation. William Dugdale (a well-known royalist) and Roger Dodsworth and his (William Dugdale's) successors had been, since the 1640s, documenting the history and wealth of monasteries for the royalist/Catholic cause.

29. Boccaccio's *Decameron*, e.g., has stories of lascivious priests. The early Reformation in England also had its examples in John Foxe and John Bale, and later John Donne would invoke this trope.

30. This text is attributed, like *Venus in the Cloister*, to Barrin (1678), 24.

31. The *Dictionary if National Biography* (DNB) relies on Gavin's own self-representation, which I find specious.

32. This story appears in volume three. All page references are to that volume.

33. *Venus in the Cloister* similarly suggests that Catholic religious houses have "remedies" against pregnancy by the priests, Barrin (1683), 83.

34. Barrin (1678), 93.

35. Infallibility is interesting here: it seems to be a sarcastic reference to the pope's infallibility, but ironically the remedy, in this case, does prove miraculously efficacious.

36. Sedgwick famously argues that in much literature, the relations between men are mediated by the exchange of women and that women are frequently an alibi for a circuit of desire between men.

37. Quotes are from the "Epistle to the Reader" in *Romes Glory* by Burnet (1673), A1.

38. See, e.g., Broughton; also see Stephens.

39. The first comprehensive discussion of this Protestant point of view was in 1588. For more on the history of this argument, see Elm.

40. Joseph Mede similarly claims a metaphorical virginity for Protestantism.
41. For a contemporary account of the importance of the will to the monastic, see Stephens.
42. Behn's relationship to libertinism is complicated. While feminists (e.g., Laurie Finke) tend to argue that Behn's feminism is incompatible with libertinism, some critics (e.g., Stapleton) see her as a relatively self satisfied libertine. Todd argues simultaneously that "the Restoration accepted that the sexual act ended a woman's power over a libertine" and that libertinism is defined at least as much by class as by gender (341). She suggests that Behn had female libertine inclinations that were perhaps thwarted by her class.
43. Evidence for Behn's Catholicism is discussed by Gerald Duchovnay.
44. Such allegorical readings are produced by an effort to split off sex from politics. Ballaster's reading of Behn is that woman is always a metaphor for man. Similarly, Toni Bowers accounts for the gender politics of Tory seduction narratives by locating the representation of ambiguous sexual agency in the floundering of the Tory cause. Catherine Gallagher makes the opposite move: taking feminism as a motivational force, she argues that models of monarchy provide the basis for imagining (both in amatory fiction and in political philosophy) an autonomous subjectivity for women. In this way, politics is merely the imaginative vehicle for feminism. All of these readings privilege either sex or politics at the expense (via metaphorization) of the other. Weil makes a compelling case for the Tory feminism of Astell (142–161).
45. The case for Burnet's intervention rests on a report by George Ballard over 50 years later. For this reason, I hesitate to take it at face value.
46. Cited in Wojciehowski, 91. See this text also for discussion of the humanist "unbounded" will.
47. See Rivers for a thorough treatment of the history of these debates.
48. For interesting analyses of the historical relationship between the physical heart, whose circulatory functions were just being accepted, and the emotional heart, an important locus for the cult of sensibility, see Robert Erickson (1997); and Scott Manning Stevens.
49. Nicolas Malebranche is an important influence on this theory.
50. Astell's argument in the second part is not wholly new, for she talks about the love of God in the first part also. It is rather a matter of emphasis: in the first she emphasizes reason and in the second the love of God.

CHAPTER 2   THE HYMEN AND ITS DISCONTENTS: MEDICAL DISCOURSES ON VIRGINITY

1. See the Hippocratic text *The Diseases of Young Girls* for an early instance. As this treatise does not appear in the Loeb edition of

Hippocrates, I recommend Emile Littré's French edition. See Helen King (1998) for information about this text.

2. See Schiebinger (1993), 93–94 for a fascinating discussion of the hymen's role in determining the relationships between plants, animals, and humans.

3. The decreased cost of printing clearly influenced this phenomenon. But the seventeenth century also experienced a need for information about sexual difference in particular, since medical and scientific advances were questioning the old ways of thinking about the relationship between the sexes.

   Throughout this chapter, I refer to the dates of first (English) editions, in order to give the reader a sense of print history, though I sometimes cite later editions, as referenced in the bibliography.

4. For a publication history of this text, see Porter (1985). Porter estimates at least 43 editions of *Aristotle's Master-Piece* between 1684 and 1800. Also see Eccles, 12.

5. Aristotle's description is far from original, as originality of neither ideas nor language was a standard. For example, the "rose-bud half blown" simile appears earlier in Helkiah Crooke's text. Much earlier still, Albert the Great (Albertus Magnus) invoked much of the same language as Aristotle—of the "proven signs" of virginity. And many of the metaphors and language usages of Aristotle recur in later texts. In a strange example, the English translation of the French medical writer, Mauriceau, uses virtually identical descriptions of the female reproductive anatomy. I am not sure if the translator or Mauriceau is the "plagiarist" here.

6. Venette is part of what Lesley Hall and Roy Porter call the "second wave" of midwife manuals in England, which came mostly via French translations and which evidenced influence from the new science. For more on the publication history, see Hall and Porter (81–90); and Blackman.

7. Both William Harvey (1963); and Robert Burton, two of the most important medical writers of the early seventeenth century warn of the dangers of greensickness. Harvey recounts a case in which a girl is "cured" of greensickness by being sent to a brothel. For more see Burton, 250–253.

8. A translation from German of Michael Ettmüller's *Practice of Physic*.

9. For more about Jane Sharp see Hobby (1999 and 2001); and Fife.

10. See Amy Erickson, 48.

11. For general histories of greensickness, see Helen King; and Loudon (1984).

12. Greensickness was still a common disease, but it no longer signaled a pathological virginity and in some cases was no longer exclusively associated with virginity.

13. While modern medicine has developed more "accurate" ways to look at the hymen (see, e.g., the studies by P. A. Pugno and A. B. Berenson et al.,

which deal mainly with the hymen as evidence for sexual abuse), some of the same cultural questions about medicine's legitimacy with regard to the hymen persist. See, e.g., the article by F. A. Goodyear-Smith and T. M. Laidlaw. For the status of the hymen in ancient Greece, see Sissa. For a discussion of these issues in medieval writers, see Schulenburg; and Jacquart and Thomasset.

14. Literary examples occur in Middleton's and Rowley's *The Changeling* (1958) and in Gay's and Smith's *Three Hours After Marriage* (1717) (discussed in chapter 5). For examples of patristic and medieval texts that discuss virginity tests, see Kathleen Coyne Kelly. Modern debates on the hymen should possibly be excepted here. Though the procedures are extremely controversial, there are currently protocols for measuring the hymen and determining whether penetration has happened. Today, the knowledge is used primarily in cases of rape. There are still such secretive "virginity tests" performed on prospective brides, such as the much rumored physical exam of Princess Diana before her marriage, but the medical literature does not share the basis for such tests.

15. The propriety of conducting such procedures has long been debated. Etmüllerus simply states how to do it. Other texts seem to suggest that it should not or cannot be done successfully. Today, the debate is still quite controversial and perhaps more prevalent than one might think. Samuel Janus and Cynthia Janus claim that in the United States there was a revival of such surgery, wherein a "lover's knot" is constructed by stitching the labia together, from the 1920s to the 1950s. In a 1998 edition of the *British Medical Journal*, doctors debated the ethics of performing such surgeries, the requests for which are apparently increasing among female immigrants, including ones who are still virgins. The medical profession is thus still mediating sexual and marital relations through its knowledge of the hymen.

16. I am grateful to Ann Jessie Van Sant for noticing this text. The author is not explicitly referring to the hymen, but its implication is obvious. Jerome's words read something more explicitly like "He cannot raise up a virgin after she has fallen." This elision between "virginity" and "chastity" in this text has serious implications for notions of physicality and the importance of virginity. Since virginity becomes a predictor of married chastity, the physical implications of virginity must be ignored (except for the notion that prolonged physical virginity is harmful). My point is that this author's translation of Jerome's direct reference to virginity into a reference to chastity is signaling some very important changes, both in thinking about virginity and in thinking about bodily determinism.

17. The provenance of these texts is unclear. The first version was probably (according to Hall and Porter) written in 1684. Some of the editions have introductions by the editors, who were also anonymous, that claim they are translations from Aristotle. As Hall and Porter have

shown, it is clear that the editors and publishers made major revisions on some versions. In *The Facts of Life* they separate these versions into three major categories. The versions I am using correspond to the earliest and latest of the categories.

18. See Hobby for an analysis of Sharp's tone and purpose with regard to gender and authority in the field of midwifery (1999), 185–187.

19. Sharp's text testifies to the oversimplicity of the dichotomy of "ancient" versus "modern" authority. This is, after all, the emergence of the "neoclassical age." Ancient authors were far from discarded, but the reader's ability to select and appropriately contextualize ancient sources became key. Thus, it is the discrimination of the reader of the sources that helps to authorize them.

20. T. Hugh Crawford explains the importance of objectivity and the "exposure of physical detail" to anatomy (66–79, 67). See also Shapin and Schaffer. Dorothy Kelly argues that the male scientist's desire for objectivity is motivated by a desire to master femininity/maternity (231–246).

21. This trend in anatomy is reflected in the "second wave" of midwife manuals that arrive from France. For example, Venette constitutes his authority by citing his academic and professional credentials, not his familiarity with ancient authority. He laments the fact that ancient authorities have not been preserved, but concedes "tho' we are destitute of such Tracts, yet methinks our Experience, in Conjunction with that of our Friends, may furnish us a sufficient share of knowledge" (A2). But he also explains that Nature "is nothing but God himself," suggesting that by studying nature one can discern God's plan (rather than invoking scripture to explain nature) (A2).

22. Luke Wilson also explains the importance of the "visible" to anatomy.

23. On the politics of dissection, see Ruth Richardson.

24. Thomas Sprat's famous statements on this include the following: "[the Royal Society has] been most rigorous in putting in execution, the only Remedy, that can be found for this *extravagance*: and that has been, a constant Resolution, to reject all the amplifications, digressions, and swellings of style; to return back to the primitive purity, and shortness, when men deliver'd so many *things*, almost in an equal number of words" (113).

25. Ernelle Fife argues that women writers on midwifery used a more metaphorical style than male writers. She links professionalization, male midwifery, and "linear discourse" (185).

26. Bernard de Mandeville argues, rather like Venette, that some women are more chaste than others, based perhaps on the "formation of nerves" or "velocity of blood." Mandeville uses this view of differential corporeal-based virtue to support his argument for prostitution (41–42).

27. Venette claims that the "caruncles, joyn'd together by small membranes" are frequently taken to be a hymen, but he disagrees with this (14).

28. Of course this split does continue, as most midwives continue to be women. But those who write about midwifery (mainly men) now have also to practice it.

29. Sarah Stone claims to have learned midwifery by assisting her mother, the typical way that practicing female midwives would have gained authority, according to Doreen Evendon. So in a way, the "new standards" are really just the old ones applied to writing as well as to practice. The English text by John Maubray is an exception to this trend. As Eccles points out, though, the text is heavily indebted to Hendrik van Deventer's text, written in Latin, of 1701 (16).

30. Robert Erickson (1982); Jean Donnison; and Adrian Wilson have all suggested that around the 1720s–1730s, male midwives made great inroads into medical care for women. For general histories of the change to male midwifery, see Cody; Cressy; Donegan; Donnison; Smith; and Spencer.

31. Patricia Crawford cites evidence that midwives masturbated patients to remove seed. See also Paré, 942; and Eccles, 82–83.

32. Jackson counters the assumption that midwives were mistrusted and generally argues for their influence and respectability, but he nonetheless concludes that their influence in legal cases diminished during the eighteenth century due to the "expanding role of male medical practitioners" (71). Rebecca J. Tannenbaum makes a similar case for the American context.

33. See *The Cases of Impotency and Virginity Fully Discusse'd* by Catherine Elizabeth Weld.

34. See also Venette who argues, "Matrons, by custom, render'd Arbiters of Virgins Maidenheads, and Women's Chastity have but weak insight into those Matters, to be the only Persons to trust to a Decision. One ought to be better instructed in Anatomy, than they are, to make just and true Reports" (50).

35. As noted earlier, by the middle of the eighteenth century, midwife manuals focused almost exclusively on procreation, while anatomy texts paid only minimal attention to the hymen and virginity. Neither generalized about female nature or gave marital advice, as earlier midwife manuals had. General medical texts (like James's *Medicinal Dictionary*), still discussed virginity and virgin's disease, but in non-controversial and nonanatomical ways.

36. See the *Dictionary of National Biography*, volume V, 388–389.

37. Cowper's introduction evidences his interest in the "usefulness" of anatomy, a point crucial to my argument: "Without a due Knowledge of the Animal Mechanism, I doubt all our Attempts to Explain the Multiform Appearance of Animal Bodies, will be Vain and Ineffectual, and our Ideas of the Causes of Diseases and their Symptoms, as Extravagant as Absurd as those of the *Chinese* and *Indians*; nay I am afraid the whole Art of Physick will be little better than Empirical." The hymen presents both empirical (anatomical, in our modern

sense) and conceptual (physiological, or associated with functioning) problems.

38. Cowper, fifty-first table, figure 3.

39. Cowper, fifty-first table, figure 3.

40. Luke Wilson explains the function of anatomy drawings as being to represent an ideal: "This visualization of all aspects of anatomy upset the traditional relation between body and text by inserting between the corporeal and particular and the disembodied and ideal a mode of access to the body capable of fleshing out the universal in its particular instances" (69). My point is that the hymen resists such positivist generalizations. T. Hugh Crawford discusses the standard of "reproducible representations"—i.e., the text (including words and images) must accurately reproduce the experiment (70). All of these standards are missing in this situation.

41. Cowper, fifty-first table, figure 3.

42. The Chamberlens were a famous French midwife dynasty, who discovered the forceps and kept the secret within the family for generations. For discussions of the Chamberlen family, see Adrian Wilson; Donegan; and Eccles.

43. Shapin and Schaffer talk about disinterestedness (69). See also T. Hugh Crawford, who discusses the implications of objectivity for anatomy.

44. Narratives do not completely disappear from medical texts, but they become contained as "case studies" and do not serve as evidence. For an interesting account of the complex relationship between medicine and narrative, see Epstein (1995). John Bender shows that eighteenth-century science had a fraught relationship with narrative because, he claims, "narration bears with it the infection of fictionality" (12).

45. The ability to repeat an experiment and achieve the same result is a foundation of modern science. Shapin argues that at least the plausibility of repeatability (based on trust in the experimental situation) must exist and that plausibility comes from the authority of the social space (20–79).

46. The truth status of the unusual or marvelous is complicated. The Royal Society discredited "monstrous" stories by aligning them with the ancients (see Sprat, 90–91). But according to both Shapin and McKeon, such stories could also attain truth status in the new science (Shapin, 193–242; McKeon [1987], 45–47). For an extended treatment of stories of "wonder," see Daston and Park who argue that access to and possession of wonders ceased to have cultural capital during the eighteenth century. In this case the "strange but true" narrative works to establish a fragile kind of evidence, but one that is superior to that available in the standard description. Because the "experiment" cannot be repeated under controlled circumstances, the anatomist's claims cannot be corroborated by other scientists, but neither can they be challenged. Given the standards of scientific method, this "strange but true" case offers only fragile, indirect evidence of standard virgin anatomy.

47. This is Ivan Bloch's term.

48. Alliston also links virginity to the epistemological strategies of the novel, saying "the truth about female sexual conduct . . . remains the ultimate truth for fiction in France and England" (19).

49. I am thinking of Richard Kroll's important argument that post-Restoration intellectual inquiry was premised on skeptical empiricism and on a commitment to notions of contingency and the inescapability of linguistic mediation (10–16).

CHAPTER 3   HYMEN HUMOR: BALLADS
AND THE MATTER OF VIRGINITY

1. Although most ballads were anonymous, scholars surmise that the majority were written by men. Natascha Würzbach, e.g., seems to assume a male writer, and reports that in the few cases where authorship is known, those authors are men (21–22). Würzbach also makes the case that the ballad writers experienced very different work conditions from other kinds of literary writers because they were outside the patronage system. Holloway and Black make the case for female singers. Eric Josef Carlson argues that women made up a substantial portion of the audience for ballads. Deborah Symonds argues that oral culture was more dominated by women than written ballads, though Sandra Clark is not so sure that this assumption can be made, even though she admits that there is no evidence that any women wrote ballads (224–226, 103–104). Given their content, I would be not surprised if scholars eventually find much more female involvement than is currently assumed or authenticated.

2. Würzbach identifies the years 1550–1650 as the time of the rise of street ballads. The mid-eighteenth century begins the "ballad revival," a time when people had a keen interest in looking at ballads from the past. Würzbach would thus see the time period of this study as one of decline, though other critics would disagree. In their introduction to *The Common Muse*, Vivian de Sola Pinto and Allan Edwin Rodway argue that the reign of Queen Anne was a great age of balladry, though this claim is based primarily on the fact that the greatest writers and wits of the age also wrote ballads, 24. Hyder Edward Rollins (1929), in the preface to *The Pepys Ballads*, volume VII (covering 1693–1702) says, "Thanks largely to the newspapers, at the close of the seventeenth century the importance of the ballad practically comes to an end; but it would be a grave mistake to believe that balladry actually died out at this time." He explains that while there were many fewer historical and political ballads, there were many more about love and love problems. This would support my observation that they are an important source of discourse on sex and that they are dominated by sexual topics in the late seventeenth century.

3. Technically broadside indicates one sheet of paper printed on one side, while broadsheet refers to a single sheet printed on two sides. I do not distinguish these two, and throughout refer to both kinds as "broadsides," something that other critics also do. Broadsides are distinguished both from folk, or oral, ballads, and the literary ballads that would become popular in the later eighteenth century.

4. This argument is speculative and rests, to some extent on the study by Pamela Brown, which focuses on marital strife as key to a culture of female jesting.

5. The notable exception to this diversity is the lack of single women in ballads, unless their commitment to that state is being challenged.

6. I have not been able to date this ballad, taken from *The Common Muse*, no. CXC (ballad number), pp. 365–368. Because ballads were designed as an almost disposable form, most have not survived. In this chapter, I am trying to look only at ballads that were printed and sung on the streets of London during 1685–1750, though dating them exactly is difficult. Printed ballads generally did not have the dates on them, though they did usually have the publisher, and occasionally the licenser. Where possible, I have used original sources (like Cyprian Blagden, James Lydovic Lindsay Crawford, and Holloway and Black) about when publishers and licensers worked in order to date the ballads myself. For example, according to John Holloway (in his introduction to the *Euing Collection*) Richard Pococke succeeded Sir Roger L'Estrange in 1685 as Licenser of the Press. In 1688, he was replaced by J. Fraser. If they were properly licensed (and the penalty for not doing so was quite high), the woodcuts usually have the inscription "This may be printed" followed by the initials of the licenser, so the date may be narrowed down in this way. Some work has also been done on tracking down when certain printers were in business. The printers' names almost invariably appear on the woodcuts and thus can be used to date the ballads. Blagden's article is quite helpful in identifying when certain printers and printing partnerships were in business. Most of the nineteenth-century editors tried to date their ballads and, where necessary, I relied on these dates. If no date is indicated, I could not limit the date.

7. The earliest *OED* citation for greensickness is 1593. The earliest ballad that I found dealing with this pattern, though it does not mention greensickness specifically, is "The Maid's Comfort" (ROX, volume II (supplementary volume), 1–5 [1620–1642]), in which the maid laments, "Why was I borne to live and die a Maid?" and her suitor replies, "A medicine for thy griefe I can procure." The earliest specific mention of greensickness that I found in a ballad is "The Green-sickness grief" (Euing No. 125), which Rollins (1929) dates as 1629, though Blagden's analysis of printers would put this at 1663–1674. By the mid-eighteenth century, there are very few greensickness ballads, and the ones that do survive are much changed. A poem from 1735 (in *The Bath, Bristol, and Epsom Miscellanies* and analyzed by Barbara Benedict) is driven by the thesis that it is London (rather than a condition inherent to protracted virginity)

that perverts the virgin's desires. Lending further support for this chronology, an *OED* citation from 1746 seems to suggest that symptoms of greensickness (eating chalk) are instead the cause of the ailment; as such it is no longer virginity itself that is pathological.

8. This version is from Farmer, volume II, 108–111 (1685–1688). There is also a copy in the *Roxburghe Ballads* (ROX, part XI: [volume IV, part 2], 418).

9. This is true even though "thing" could have sexual connotations, as Carolyn Williams argues.

10. There are economic metaphors (like spending seed) for male sexuality, but they do not appear in the ballads and they do not treat the penis itself as a commodity.

11. Bagford, division I, 75 (1702).

12. Claude Lévi-Strauss famously argues that "the woman figures only as one of the objects of exchange, not as one of the partners" (115). This claim has been further interrogated by many feminist scholars, most famously Gayle Rubin and Eve Kosofsky Sedgwick.

13. Farmer, volume I, 194 (from *Pills to Purge Melancholy*, 1707).

14. A woman's genitals were frequently euphemized as "nothing" (in comparison to the man's "thing"). Thus, this woman's insistence on her possession of her "thing" suggests appropriation of a masculine form of value. I thank Susan Lamb for pointing this out to me.

15. This is not to say that there is not satire in these ballads, but rather that virginity acts as a vehicle for the satire, rather than as an object of satire.

16. ROX, part VIII: [volume VII, part 1], 42 (1636).

17. ROX, part XVII: [volume VI, part 2], 253 (several versions at least one after 1694); Euing No. 196 (1658–1664); and ROX (1674–1679).

18. Euing No. 70 (1672).

19. See, e.g., "The Deceiver deceived or the virgin's revenge." ROX, part X: [volume IV, part 1], 34 and Pepys, III.83.

20. Roger de V. Renwick's structural analysis of courtship ballads in his chapter "The Semiotics of Sexual Liasons" is quite interesting. He figures out a number of "rules" for courtship, and his "precept #6" is as follows: if a man "engages in a sexual liaison with a maid who has the masculine ability to be innovative [a strategic act or verbal dexterity], then you will have a tragic experience" (77). Renwick analyzes oral ballads of another time; the men in the broadside ballads I read may become an object of satire, but they are not victims in the sense that we are to feel sorry for them or even to learn from their mistakes. I also think that the success of a woman's wittiness is historically determined, a point I will also get to later. The evaluation of the verbal dexterity and wit of potential mates has a long history in popular literature. Francis James Child categorized a whole genre of (oral) ballads that he calls "Riddles Wisely Expounded," in which both men and women pose complicated riddles to each other in order to determine whether they are appropriate marriage partners. While Child lists several versions from the period that I am studying, much more common in the street literature are the

ballads where the verbal dexterity has material consequences more immediate than marriage: pregnancy, impoverishment, imprisonment, and so on. These consequences, of course, are not the same for both genders. In the "Riddles" ballads, the tricky words are like an objective third party to the courtship, and they are remarkable for their equality of treatment between the males and females, who seem equally to pose the riddles and to successfully answer them. When sex is introduced to the equation, however, the terms of comparison and the range of potential outcomes become more complicated, and the competition becomes more of one between the sexes at large, rather than a test of an individual man or woman. It is these ballads that I discuss here because they are much more common in the street literature of Augustan England.

21. Farmer, volume II, 210–211.
22. ROX, part XXI: [voume VII, part 2], 475 (1690–1694).
23. Euing No. 215.
24. ROX, part VII: [volume III, part 1], 47 (1631).
25. Euing No. 179 "The Loving Chamber-Maid."
26. For a rare exception to this anonymity, see "The Buxome Virgin" and its "Answer." ROX, part VIII: [volume III, part 2], 364–368 (1672–1695).
27. Farmer, volume III, 144–150.
28. Discussed in Bagford, division I, 462–468 (1680–1690).
29. Rollins's "Index" lists several: 1603, 1624, and 1675. James Crawford lists a version from 1790 to 1800. Chapell claims that it was probably published well into the nineteenth century. I looked at three versions, one from 1624 (ROX, part I: [volume I, part 1], 185–189), one from 1663–1674 (Euing No. 21), one that is probably (according to Blagden) from 1694 to 1706 (Euing No. 22). Except for spelling and minor corruptions, the versions do not change.
30. Other ballads also invoke the phrase "a maiden and a wife," and are structured around the possibility of a married woman dying before consummation of the marriage. See, e.g., Euing No. 271 (1663–1674) in which two men fight over a woman, her husband is killed, and she dies "a maiden and a wife."
31. This was a very popular ballad with many versions. A virgin is seduced before the wedding and then abandoned. She dies in childbed. The admonition is for women to beware of flattering words.
32. In ballad culture more broadly, as Child has shown, blood is frequently used as evidence of a crime, but blood is, of course, an especially salient symbol of virginity loss.
33. From Hales and Furnivall, volume IV: "Loose and Humorous Songs," 96. The date appears to be about 1650.
34. See Conran.
35. The first reference that I found is in Rollins, which lists a broadside title from 1638. Child includes a nineteenth-century Scottish version (volume II, 372–375). For more on this ballad, especially the problem of infanticide, see Symonds.

36. I have been reading these "life and death" texts as vestiges of a Catholic ideal of virginity, but there are also very real "life and death" consequences to sex for women and children. The incidence of childbirth death and infant mortality was quite high, and the rate of infanticide was probably rising during this time period. "The Cruel Mother" may have emerged as a result of rising infant mortality rates, though those rising rates may also have been an effect of changing attitudes toward sex and virginity to which the ballad testifies.

37. This ballad is also discussed by Child. This version is from a late seventeenth-century broadside (entitled "Fair Margaret's misfortune" [1685]) and printed in Percy (1869), volume 3, book 2, 124. In another version, from 1775, it is the bride who sees the bloody vision. This also happens in "Fair Annie," a ballad written down by Child from oral performance in the early nineteenth century, in which the new bride discovers the treachery in time. These ballads also have similarities with the Bluebeard fairytale, and the general narrative pattern seems to have been very popular in the nineteenth century (the example of *Jane Eyre* comes to mind).

38. Even in cases where no sex has happened, the pattern of a bloody woman accusing a man appears. Betrayal of vows can lead to consequences as bad as seduction. See ROX, part VIII: [volume III, part 2], 459 (1684–1686). See also "Margaret's Ghost," a 1724 adaptation of the "Fair Margaret" in Percy, volume 3, book 3, no. 16.

39. There are a number of ballads that invoke the image of a bleeding woman or the ghost of a dead woman. The typical scenario is one in which a woman has been seduced and abandoned. She dies or (frequently) kills herself, and her ghost then goes on to haunt her seducer, who is often penitent and frequently dies himself. One of the most striking things about these ballads is their often vivid description of the woman's maimed and bloody body.

Chapter 4 Virgin Idols and Verbal Devices: Pope's Belinda and the Virgin Mary

Epigraph. Young criticizes Pope for idolatrously worshipping writers saying, "His taste partook the error of his Religion" (67). I will argue, conversely, that *The Rape of the Lock* is anti-idolatrous.

1. See, e.g., Pollak and Wasserman.

2. Crehan argues that critics misread the poem when they assume an idea of virginity that was not yet current. Part of my point in this chapter is

194 ◈ NOTES

to situate a discourse on virginity in the historically specific context of Catholic-Protestant debates over idolatry.

3. *Oxford English Dictionary* (OED) shows that both meanings would have been in use at this time.

4. Quote is from the anonymous *Amours of Messalina, Late Queen of Albion*, an anti-Catholic allegory of the incident (59).

5. For background and astute analysis of the warming pan scandal see Weil, 86–104.

6. Pope to Atterbury, November 20, 1717, quoted in Mack, 826, note 31.

7. For a discussion of the Baron as fetishist, see Myers, 71–76.

8. Ronald Paulson points out Belinda's dual role as idol and idolater, and he sees Pope as part of a Georgian "remaking" that follow the more iconoclastic poetry of Jonathan Swift, but I am arguing that Pope is more radically iconoclastic even than Swift.

9. Carnall suggests that she may actually use the pages of the Bible to make the curl, since curls were made with paper, 130–138.

10. For a discussion of this aspect of marionism, see Freeman, 8–9.

11. Augustine says that "it is servile to follow the letter and take signs for the things they signify" (87).

12. 1 Corinthians:7.

13. In an interesting twist, though, both Mary and Belinda's bodies lie in ways exactly opposite to one that men worry about. Theresa Colletti argues that the representational and epistemological crisis around Mary derives from the fact that, though quintessentially virginal, her pregnancy makes her "appear" to no longer be a virgin. In Mary's case, visual "evidence" does not reliably point to the truth: a pregnant virgin, but the fallout from that deception will be borne by the woman, rather than by a man who may be deceived by her. There is no suggestion that Belinda's locks are a deceptive representation of her virginity, but once they are cut, she, like Mary, comes to have a body that signals lack of virginity despite the "truth." Thus the virginal bodies of both Belinda and Mary do seem to lie about the status of their virginity, though in ways that disavow the male anxiety that this possibility presents.

14. For examples of the treatment of Mary's body, see Lewis; Hickes; and Master.

15. The connections between the heart (as physical and emotional) and virginity (as physical and moral) are interesting. Both are parts of the body undergoing radical rethinking and both are strongly implicated in the emergent standard of sensibility. For more, see Robert Erickson (1997); and Stevens.

16. Tracy finds these symbolic synecdoches quite evocative, suggesting that "we know all we need to know" about Sir Plume through his objects (xxiv). I agree in principle but disagree over what it is that we actually know. I do not find the objects as significant as the fact that

Plume is investing them with symbolic power. To the extent that Tracy and other critics also invest these objects with symbolic power, I argue that they miss the point of the poem's skepticism about the possibility of interpretation.

17. See also Crehan.

18. For more on the logic of Pope's rhymes, see Kenner.

19. Moshe Halbertal and Avishai Margalit explain that the historical reason that images and not language are potentially idolatrous is that "with pictorial representations there is always the fear that the representing object will at some stage be transformed into the permanent dwelling place of God . . . whereas language does not create an object that can undergo such a transformation" (52). My point is that Pope's poem, though an object that can undergo transformation, resists idolatry by resisting meaning.

20. While the resistance to stable meaning opposes idolatry, the beauty and technical perfection of Pope's poem, which are so often remarked upon, threaten to turn his secular poem into an idolatrous object (in Augustine's terms, something not useful but merely enjoyable).

21. Pope parodies the Protestant notion that the Bible could be used as an interpretive key to all human events.

22. On this topic, see Wallace; and Crehan.

23. Both sides are thus trying to align themselves on the side of spirituality and faith, against a more objective, scientific approach to knowledge, and both are trying to claim jurisdiction over knowledge that must be interpreted. Thus, while they argue with each other, both sets of religious writers are also clearly staking out a critique of the eighteenth-century scientific revolution.

24. Ruth Vanita argues that when the literal becomes symbolic or suggestive, its radical potential surfaces.

25. For an example of this common rhetorical usage, see the Catholic Church's *Primer*, 79.

CHAPTER 5   FAKING IT: VIRTUE, SATIRE, AND PAMELA'S VIRGINITY

1. From *Three Hours After Marriage*, commonly attributed to Gay and Smith (31–32). The play was written with the help of fellow Scriblerians Pope and Arbuthnot. Peter Lewis and Nigel Wood describe this play as the only "genuinely Scriblerian" theatrical work, but they credit Gay as the "prime mover and principal contributor" (127).

2. The blush usually signifies virginity but in this case the test produces a blush on the unchaste woman. For more on the blush as a complicated sign, see Yeazell.

3. Fossile misses the jokes and double entendre, and his diagnostic and therapeutic efficacy as a doctor is manifestly ludicrous: all his patients

get the same treatment, even one who seems to be clearly manifesting the signs of greensickness, or virgin's disease.

4. As Brandford Mudge argues, Mr. B. is converted from a belief in one kind of femininity to another (188–193).

5. For more on the epistemological issues in *Pamela*, see Stevenson; Pierce; Armstrong (108–134); and McKeon (1987), 357–380. For these issues in novels more generally, see Van Sant; and Alliston.

6. Ian Watt; McKeon (1987); and Bender analyze the relationship between fiction and science.

7. For a description of "the *Pamela* vogue" see Eaves and Kimpel (1971), 119–153. For reprints and contextualization of many of the responses to *Pamela*, see Keymer and Sabor. More recent scholarship on the Pamela craze is summarized in Turner (1994).

8. His lack of interest in her physical virginity is probably linked to her class status and his related assumption that he will not marry her.

9. Patricia Meyer Spacks, in discussing the novels of Richardson and Henry Fielding, argues that trickery is the source of female power, thus offering an explanation for the motivation to avoid or disguise one's investment in female virginity (1990), 55–57.

10. Mr. B. is the only character who uses the word "virgin." In fact, even when it is clearly Pamela's physical virginity is at stake, "virginity" is rarely used. For instance, in the first edition (searchable as an e-text through LION) "virtue" appears over 130 times, while "virginity" makes only about a dozen appearances. The causal connections between Pamela's euphemistic style and her lack of authority to speak about her body are, of course, more complicated than I can explore here.

11. For the procedures of the Royal Society, see Sprat.

12. See Pocock (1985), 253 for a discussion on the feminization of virtue. He also discusses "the cognition of things as they really are," see Pocock, 457.

13. Nancy Armstrong makes this point. For a discussion of the importance of benevolence to emergent ideas of virtue, see also Morse, 1–23.

14. Clarissa's will accomplishes a similar thing. It allows her virtue to transcend death, as Pamela's transcends marriage. In this way, marriage and death are not the "end" of these stories at all.

15. According to Lawrence Stone, early modern England had a long-standing pattern of delaying marriage for quite a while after sexual maturity, but the amount of time increases significantly in the late seventeenth and early eighteenth centuries. In the mid-sixteenth century, the average age of marriage for girls was 20. By the late eighteenth century, it had, according to Stone, risen to 23 (46–54). E. A. Wrigley and R. S. Schoefield argue something different; they say that average age of marriage peaks in 1650–1699, and it begins to fall in the second half of the eighteenth century (257–263).

16. Interest in female virginity routinely indicates a crisis of male authority. My point is that this crisis took a particular form in the early eighteenth century.

17. Margaret Anne Doody argues that it is significant that Henry Fielding's protagonist is not a virgin because this allows *Shamela* to maintain the link between virginity and "real" virtue, since it is not as if a real virgin is falsely claiming virtue (72).

CHAPTER 6   NOVEL VIRGINS:
LIBERTINE AND LITERARY PLEASURES
IN *MEMOIRS OF A WOMAN OF PLEASURE*

1. This was a point of contention among philosophers. John Locke (1975) argued that humans have the capacity for abstract ideas, a point that was challenged/revised by Berkeley's theory of the association of ideas and Hume's development of this in his theory of abstract ideas.

2. Sigmund Freud's whole argument about virginity is that women never forgive the men for inflicting pain on defloration (1957a). But the emphasis on female pain at defloration is far from a dominant idea in this period. Venette, though he does describe defloration as painful, claims that women are so indebted to their first lover that "if by some great consideration, they are oblig'd to be ally'd to others, they still preserve some Tenderness in their Heart for him that had the Flower of their Virginity" (161). Maubray calls the pain of defloration "trifling" (193). *Aristotle's Midwife* (1711) explains that the caruncles (which are held together by the hymen) will be "pressed and bruised" by intercourse but also that one of their main purposes is to "increase the mutual pleasure of intercourse" (10–11). In his *Master-Piece* (1741), the hymen is "fractured and dissipated by violence" (88). In these cases, there is violence, but not pain, and it is the hymen itself—not the woman—that experiences it. Jane Sharp, the dissenting midwife in several respects, does discuss pain on defloration but focuses on it as a sign, for the male, rather than something that the female must suffer: "some maids suffer not so much pain to lose the Maidenhead as others do," she avers, by way of accounting for female difference, not female pain (49). In short, the most distinguishing feature of the sex and the narrative structure in *Memoirs of a Woman of Pleasure*—the trajectory of female pain and pleasure—is founded on the notion that defloration is painful to women, a belief that we take for granted nowadays but that was not commonly represented in the early eighteenth century and that *Memoirs of a Woman of Pleasure* may, in fact, have had a role in popularizing pain.

3. Perry points out that many women writers, including Mary Astell, connect sexuality to danger (143–144). Randolph Trumbach (1988) criticizes *Memoirs of a Women of Pleasure* for its lack of realism in portraying prostitution, although Lena Olsson disagrees.

4. Amatory fiction, even where the ending is happy, typically presents the trajectory of pleasure and pain as opposite or cyclical; usually

beginning with pleasure, a vacillation between pleasure and pain is inevitable. For example, as Melliora says to her seducer in Eliza Haywood's *Love in Excess* "think what 'tis that you would do, nor for a moment's joy, hazard your peace forever" (1994), 128; and Monsieur Frankville's story typically finds that a "scene of happiness changed to the blackest despair" (due, interestingly, to a misunderstanding about virginity) (1994), 220. Where pain is invoked, its source is emotional. So Melliora's "painful pleasure" is occasioned by her knowledge that adultery is wrong. The narrator sums up this different attitude toward the relationship of pleasure and pain in love: "That passion which chiefly aims at enjoyment in enjoyment ends, the fleeting pleasure is no more remembered [*sic*], but all the stings of guilt and shame remain" (1994), 250.

5. Patricia Meyers Spacks calls the lack of consequences "conventional pornographic sentimentality" (1987), 274. Rosemary Graham says "that *Fanny Hill* ends in marriage is another of its absurdities" (582). See also Shinagel; and Simmons.

6. John Benyon and Lisa Moore (49–74) argue against this reading.

7. Antje Schaum Anderson has argued both that female sexuality is unique in its linking of pleasure and pain and that, in *Memoirs*, all sexual acts are measured against defloration in terms of "novelty and pain" (117). See also Flynn.

8. J. Hillis Miller would call this idea of repetition "Platonic," or "grounded in a solid archetypical model which is untouched by the effects of repetition" (6). My point about the relationship between the repetition of the defloration narrative and the way that the defloration plot repeats the marriage plot concurs with Miller's argument about the relationship between Platonic and Neitzschean (the "opaque similarity" of things) repetition: i.e., both types of repetition are always present (8).

9. See Deleuze (1991).

10. Ragussis describes this problem as a conflict between novelistic narrative and erotic classification (190–198).

11. Here I disagree somewhat with Jody Greene, whose essay on taste argues that the episodes with Norbert, Barville, and the sodomites are different in kind from the rest of the sex.

12. Wagner, e.g., argues that *Memoirs of a Woman of Pleasure* is a novel thoroughly dominated by eighteenth-century bourgeois thought (243). Bernard Ruth Yeazell and Randolph Trumbach (1988) follow a similar line. Braudy sees the novel as a polemical attack against Richardsonian ideals of moral and sexual nature. More recently, critics see the sexual politics as complicated. Mengay, e.g., says "*Fanny Hill* is not the straightforward celebration of the code of bourgeois heterosexuality that most critics claim it to be" (197).

13. Peter Sabor puts the "edited" in quotes, since the English version amends some "certain needful remarks by the English Editor." See his

chronology in his edition of *Memoirs of a Woman of Pleasure*. But both Hans Galfelder and Clorinda Donato have said (in private conversations) that the English version is a pretty strict translation of the Italian. One key difference, for my purposes, is that the long title of the Italian emphasizes the cross-dressing aspect of the story whereas the English title puts much more emphasis on the hymen. My implication is that the English version produced by Cleland is, in fact, an English text and belies the peculiarly English obsession with virginity. My project focuses, however, only on England, and I have throughout this book been making claims about England's unique political and religious situation. My assumption is that virginity would be viewed differently in other countries (e.g., in Catholic Italy), but it is far beyond the scope of this project to suggest what those differences might be.

14. The idea of the hymen as a telescope also suggests that the hymen points to something beyond itself, allowing the viewer to "see" something else that is presumably more important than the hymen. The telescope did have its critics. See McKeon (1987), 71– 72.

15. The anti-Catholicism would have obvious appeal to an English audience.

16. The idea of a "collection" of hymens indicates both that hymens are unique in some ways and that there is some "essence" to the hymen that can be understood only by looking at a number of them. So the author's contention that he can leave some behind is evidence of repetition significant enough to establish his authority.

17. Ivan Bloch calls this fad, which he identifies as a peculiarly English obsession, "defloration mania." He identifies the causes as English desire to have "only the best" and to sadism (635).

18. See Wagner's "Introduction," 12.

19. I do not disagree with critics, such as Nancy K. Miller, Carmen McFarlane, and Simmons, who find the female masquerade a way of interpolating female desire into male desire. Miller says the text is "a self-congratulatory and self-addressed performance destined to be celebrated by other men" (150). But in locating a subversive element to Cleland's masquerade and in suggesting that it is male sexuality and subjectivity that are being scrutinized and satirized, I am trying to complicate the view of the male desire that is authorized by the text.

Conclusion: Clarissa's Exceptional Infertility

1. See Eaves and Kimpel (1971), 205–212 and 236–238.

2. Quoted from his "Hints of Prefaces" in Eaves and Kimpel (1971), 236.

3. In a letter to Elizabeth Carter. Quoted in Eaves and Kimbel (1971), 236, 30.

4. See Lawrence Stone for demographics on marriage age, 46–54.

5. This is Paul Ricoeur's term, From *Time and Narrative*, volume 3.

6. Rachel Weil has convincingly shown that an older model of patriarchy, in which virtue is determined by obedience to authority, does not depend as heavily on familial bonds as the patriarchal form emergent in the seventeenth and eighteenth centuries, when standards of patrilinear legitimacy, individuality, and moral heterosexuality begin to predominate over notions of passive obedience to authority (230–235). Weil locates the emergence of this "Whig" view of sexuality and virtue in the period prior to 1688. I have been showing that between 1688 and 1750, this position becomes so solidified that it can be claimed, in *Clarissa*, as traditional.

7. Margaret Doody argues that Lovelace sees Clarissa as an otherwordly being but nonetheless wants her as a mother—he wants to be perpetually loved and forgiven by her. This figures Clarissa as a divine parent, which concurs with my reading of the attractions of virginity.

8. See also McCrea for more on the pregnancy and speculations about it, as well as for an important reading of familial relations in *Clarissa*. McCrea argues that because the patriarchy is weak, "fictive" relationships take over. I am revising this argument by questioning the cause.

9. See Robert Erickson (1997) for more on the significance of Clarissa's heart.

10. For example, see Ann Radcliffe's *The Italian* and Matthew Gregory Lewis's *The Monk*, among other gothic novels.

WORKS CITED

A list of the monasterys, nunnerys, and colleges, belonging to the English papists in several popish countrys beyond sea published to inform the people of England of the measures taken by the popish party for the reestablishing of popery in these nations: in a letter to a member of Parliament. London: Printed for A. Baldwin, 1700.

Alliston, April. "Female Sexuality and the Referent of *Enlightenment Realisms.*" In *Spectacles of Realism: Body, Gender, Genre,* ed. Margaret Cohen and Christopher Prendergast. Minneapolis and London: University of Minnesota Press, 1995, 11–27.

The Amours of Messalina, late queen of Albion. In which are briefly couch'd, secrets of the imposture of the Cambrion prince, the Gothick league and other court intrigues of the four last years reign, not yet made publick. By a woman of quality, a late confident of Q. Messalina. London: Printed for J. Lyford, 1689.

Amussen, Susan Dwyer. *An Ordered Society: Gender and Class in Early Modern England.* Oxford: Basil Blackwell, 1988.

Anderson, Antje Schaum. "Gendered Pleasure, Gendered Plot: Defloration as Climax in *Clarissa* and *Memoirs of a Woman of Pleasure.*" *The Journal of Narrative Technique* 25.2(1995):108–138.

Anderton, Lawrence. *The English nvnne being a treatise wherein (by way of dialogue) the author endeauoureth to draw yong & vnmarried Catholike gentlewomen to imbrace a votary and religious life.* London: St. Omers English College Press, 1642.

Aristotle's compleat master-piece: in three parts: displaying the secrets of nature in the generation of man, regularly digested into chapters and sections . . . to which is added A treasure of health, or The family physician . . . London, 1741.

———. *Aristotle's compleat and experienc'd midwife; in two parts. I. A guide for child-bearing women . . . II. Proper and safe remedies for the curing all those distempers that are incident to the female sex.* London, 1711.

———. *Aristotle's Master-Piece: or, The Secrets of Generation Display'd in all the Parts therof.* London, 1695

Armstrong, Nancy. *Desire and Domestic Fiction: A Political History of the Novel.* Oxford and New York: Oxford University Press, 1987.

Astell, Mary. *Letters Concerning the Love of God, between the Author of the Proposal to the Ladies and Mr. John Norris.* London, 1695.

Astell, Mary. *Some reflections upon marriage occasion'd by the Duke & Dutchess of Mazarine's case, which is also considered.* London: Printed for John Nutt, 1700.

Augustine, Saint. *On Christian Doctrine,* trans. D. W. Robertson. Indianapolis: Bobbs-Merrill, 1958.

Bagford Ballads, ed. Joseph Woodfall Ebsworth. 2 vols. Hertford: Printed for the Ballad Society by Stephen Austin and Sons, 1878.

Bahktin, Mikhail. *Rabelais and His World,* trans. Helen Iswolsy. Bloomington: Indiana University Press, 1968.

Bale, John, Bishop of Ossory. *The actes of Englysh votaryes.* Photo reprint of the 1560 ed. Amsterdam: Theatrum Orbis Terrarum; Norwood, NJ: W. J. Johnson, 1979.

Ballard, George. *Memoirs of several ladies of Great Britain: who have been celebrated for their writings or skill in the learned languages, arts, and sciences.* Oxford: W. Jackson, 1752.

Ballaster, Rosalind. *Seductive Forms: Women's Amatory Fiction from 1684–1740.* Oxford: Clarendon, 1992.

[Barrin, Jean]. *The monk unvail'd: or, A facetious dialogue, discovering the several intrigues, and subtil practises, together with the lewd and scandalous lives of monks, fryers, and other pretended religious votaries of the Church of Rome,* trans. C. V. Gent. London, 1678.

———. *Some Reflections Upon Marriage.* London, 1700.

———. *Venus in the cloister, Or The nun in her smock. In curious dialogues, addressed to the Lady Abbess of Loves Paradice.* London, 1683.

The Bath, Bristol, Tunbridge and Epsom miscellany. Containing, poems, tales, songs, epigrams, lampoons . . . London, 1735.

Behn, Aphra. *The Fair Jilt.* In *Oroonoko and Other Stories,* ed. Maureen Duffy. By Aphra Behn. London: Methuen, 1986.

———. *The Feign'd Curtizans, or A Nights Intrigue.* London: Printed for Jacob Tonson, 1679.

———. *The History of the Nun.* In *Oroonoko and Other Stories,* ed. Maureen Duffy. By Aphra Behn. London: Methuen, 1986.

———. *Love Letters between a Nobleman and his Sister.* London: Virago, 1987.

———. *The Rover.* Oxford: Oxford University Press, 1995.

———. *The Town-Fopp; Or Sir Timothy Tawdrey.* London, 1677.

Bender, John. "Enlightenment Fiction and the Scientific Hypothesis." *Representations* 61(1998):6–28.

Benedict, Barbara. "Consumptive Communities: Commodifying Nature in Spa Society." *The Eighteenth Century: Theory and Interpretation* 36.3(1995):203–219.

Benyon, John. " 'Traffic in More Precious Commodities': Sapphic Erotics and Economics in *Memoirs of a Woman of Pleasure.*" In *Launching Fanny Hill,* ed. Patsy S. Fowler and Alan Jackson. New York: AMS, 2003, 3–26.

Berenson, A. B. et al. "A Case-Control Study of Anatomic Changes Resulting from Sexual Abuse." *American Journal of Obstetrics and Gynecology* 182.4(2000):820–831.

Bernini, Gianlorenzo. *Ecstasy of St. Teresa*. Santa Maria della Vittoria, Rome, Italy.

Bianchi, Giovanni. *Historical and Physical Dissertation on The Case of Catherine Vizzani, containing the adventures of a young woman, born at Rome, who for eight years passed in the habit of a man*. London, 1751.

Blackman, Janet. "Popular Theories of Generation: The Evolution of Aristotle's Works. The Study of an Anachronism." In *Health Care and Popular Medicine in Nineteenth Century England*, ed. J. Woodward and D. Richards. New York: Holmes and Meier, 1977, 56–88.

Blagden, Cyprian. "Notes on the Ballad Market in the Second Half of the Seventeenth Century." *Studies in Bibliography*. Volume 6, ed. Fredson Bowers. Charlottesville: Bibliographical Society of the University of Virginia, 1953.

Bloch, Ivan. *The Sexual Life of our Time in its Relation to Modern Civilization*. New York: Rebman, 1923.

Boehrer, Bruce. " 'Carelesse modestee' Chastity as Politics in Book 3 of the Fairie Queene." *ELH* 55.3(1988):555–573.

Bossuet, Jacques Benigne, Bishop of Meaux. *A pastoral letter from the Lord Bishop of Meaux to the new Catholicks of his dioceses exhorting them to keep their Easter, and giving them necessary advertisements against the false pastoral letters of their ministers: with reflections upon the pretended persecution*. London, 1686.

Boswell, James. *Boswell's Life of Johnson*, ed. George Birbeck Hill and L. F. Powell. Oxford: Clarendon, 1934.

Bourdieu, Pierre. *The Logic of Practice*, trans. Richard Nice. Stanford: Stanford University Press, 1990.

Bowden, Caroline. "The Abbess and Mrs. Brown: Lady Mary Knatchbull and Royalist Politics in Flanders in the Late 1650's." *Recusant History* 24.3(1999):288–308.

Bowers, Toni. "Seduction Narratives and Tory Experience in Augustan England." *ECTI* 40.2(1999):128–154.

Braudy, Leo. "*Fanny Hill* and Materialism." *Eighteenth-Century Studies* 4.1(1970):21–40.

Bronfen, Elizabeth. *Over Her Dead Body: Death, Femininity and the Aesthetic*. New York: Routledge, 1992.

Brontë, Charlotte. *Jane Eyre*. London: Virago, 1990.

Broughton, Richard. *Monastichon Britanicum: or, A historicall narration of the first founding and flourishing state of the antient monasteries, religious rules and orders of Great Brittaine, inthe tymes of the Brittaines and primitive church of the Saxons*. London, 1655.

Brown, Laura. The Ideology of Neo-Classical Aesthetics: Epistles to Several Persons. In *Pope*, ed. Brean Hammond. London: Longman, 1996.

Brown, Pamela. *Better a Shrew Than a Sheep: Women, Drama, and the Culture of Jest in Early Modern England*. Ithaca: Cornell University Press, 2003.

Brown, Peter. *The Body and Society: Men, Women, and Sexual Renunciation in Early Christianity*. New York: Columbia University Press, 1988.

Burnet, Gilbert. *The First Part of the History of the Reformation of the Church of England*. London, 1681.

[———]. *Romes Glory: or, A Collection of divers Miracles Wrought by Popish Saints, Both during their Lives, and after their Deaths*. London, 1673.

Burton, Robert. *Anatomy of Melancholy, what it is*. Oxford: Printed by John Litchfield and James Short for Henry Cripps, 1621.

Bynum, Caroline Walker. "The Body of Christ in the Later Middle Ages." *Renaissance Quarterly* 39(1986):399–439.

Calvin, John. *Calvin: Institutes of the Christian Religion*, trans. Ford Lewis Battles. ed. John T. McNeill. Volume II. London: S. C. M. Press, 1960.

Carlson, Eric Josef. *Marriage and the English Reformation*. Oxford: Blackwell, 1994.

Carnall, Geoffrey. *Belinda's Bibles*. In *Alexander Pope: Essays for the Tercentenary*, ed. Colin Nicholson. Aberdeen: Aberdeen University Press, 1988.

Cassirer, Ernst. *The Philosophy of Enlightenment*, trans. Fritz Koelln and James Petterove. Boston: Beacon, 1951.

Catholic Church. *The primer or, Office of the Blessed Virgin Mary in English: exactly revised, and the new hymns and prayers added, according to the Reformation of Pope Urban. 8*. London, 1672.

The Catholic Encyclopedia, ed. Haberman et al. New York: Appleton, 1912.

Cavendish, Margaret. *The Convent of Pleasure*. In *Plays, never before printed*. London: Printed by A. Maxwell, 1668.

Chaber, Lois A. " 'This Affecting Subject' ": An 'Interested' Reading of Childbearing in Two Novels by Samuel Richardson." *Eighteenth-Century Fiction* January 8(2) (1996):193–250.

———. "Childbearing in Two Novels by Samuel Richardson." *Eighteenth-Century Fiction* 8.2(1996):193–250.

Chapman, Edmund. *An essay on the improvement of midwifery: chiefly with regard to the operation; to which are added fifty cases, selected from upwards of twenty-five year practice*. London, 1733.

Chappel, W. Introduction. *Roxburghe Ballads*. Reprint from the 1869 first issue. Hertford: Printed for the Ballad society by S. Austin and Sons, 1877.

Chedgzoy, Kate. " 'For Virgin Buildings Oft Brought Forth': Fantasies of Convent Sexuality." In *Female Communities 1600–1800*, ed. Rebecca D'Monté and Nicole Pohl. Houndsmill: MacMillan, 2000, 53–75.

Cheselden, William. *The anatomy of the humane body: illustrated with twenty-three copperbplates of the most considerable parts; all done after the life*. London, 1713.

Child, Francis James. *English and Scottish Ballads*. Boston: Little, Brown, 1890.

Clagett, William. *A discourse concerning the worship of the Blessed Virgin and the saints with an account of the beginnings and rise of it amongst Christians, in answer to M. de Meaux's appeal to the fourth age, in his Exposition and pastoral letter. A Discourse Concerning the Worship of the Blessed Virgin and the Saints*. London, 1686.

Clark, Sandra. "The Broadside Ballad and the Woman's Voice." In *Debating Gender in Early Modern England, 1500–1700*, ed. Cristina Malcolmson and Mihoko Suzuki. New York: Palgrave MacMillan, 2002, 103–120.

Cleland, John. *Memoirs of a Woman of Pleasure*, ed. and intro. Peter Wagner. London: Penguin, 1985.

——. *The way to things by words, and to words by things; being a sketch of an attempt at the retrieval of the antient Celtic, or, primitive language of Europe. To which is added, a succinct account of the Sanscort, or learned language of the Bramins. Also two essays, the one on the origin of the musical waits at Christmas. The other on the real secret of the Free Masons.* London: Printed for L. Davis and C. Reymers, 1766.

Cody, Lisa. " 'The Politics of Reproduction: From Midwives' Alternative Public Sphere to the Public Spectacle of Man-Midwifery." *Eighteenth-Century Studies* 32.4S(1999):477–495.

Colletti, Theresa. "Purity and Danger: The Paradox of Mary's Body and the En-gendering of the Infancy Narrative in the English Mystery Cycles." In *Feminist Approaches to the Body in Medieval Literature*, ed. Linda Lomperis and Sarah Stansburg. Philadelphia: University of Pennsylvania Press, 1993.

Colley, Linda. *Britons: Forging the Nation, 1707–1837.* New Haven: Yale University Press, 1992.

Collinson Patrick. *The Birthpangs of Protestant England.* New York: St. Martin's, 1988.

Connon, Derek. " 'Mystification': Subversion and Seduction." *British Journal for Eighteenth-Century Studies* 13.1(1990):33–45.

Conran, Tony "The Maid and the Palmer." In *Ballads into Books: The Legacies of Francis James Child*, ed. Tom Cheesman and Sigrid Rieuwerts. Bern: Peter Lang, 1997.

Coterill, Anne. "Marvell's Watery Maze: Digression and Discovery at Nun Appleton House." *ELH* 69.1(2002):103–132.

Council of Trent, *Session XXIV*, canto 10.

Cowper, William. *The anatomy of humane bodies: with figures drawn after the life by some of the best masters in Europe and curiously engraven in one hundred and fourteen copper plates: illustrated with large explications containing many new anatomical discoveries and chirurgical observations: to which is added an introduction explaining the animal oeconomy: with a copious index.* London: Printed at the Theater for Sam. Smith and Benj. Walford, 1698.

Crawford, James Ludovic Lindsay, Earl of. *Bibliotheca Lindesiana: Catalogue of a Collection of English Ballads of the XVIIth and XVIIIth Centuries.* Aberdeen: Privately printed through Aberdeen University Press, 1890.

Crawford, Patricia. "Attitudes To Menstruation in Seventeenth Century England." *Past and Present* 91(1981):47–73.

Crawford, T. Hugh. "Imaging the Human Body: Quasi Objects, Quasi Texts, and the Theater of Proof." *PMLA* 111.1(1996):66–79.

Crehan, Stewart. "*The Rape of the Lock* and the Economy of 'Trivial Things.' " *ECS* 31.1(1997):45–68.

Cressy, David. "The Cultural Performance of Childbirth in Early Modern England." Lecture at *Childbirth in Early Modern Europe*. UCLA Center for Medieval and Renaissance Studies. February 9, 1996.

Crooke, Helkiah. *Mikrokosmographia: a description of the body of man: together with the controversies and figures thereto belonging*. London, 1631.

Culpeper, Nicholas. *A Directory for Midwives: Or, A Guide for Women in Their Conception, Bearing, and Suckling of Their Children*. London, 1651.

The British Medical Journal. Forum and Commentary: "Ethical Dilemma: Should Doctors Reconstruct the Vaginal Introitus of Adolescent Girls to Mimic the Virginal State? (Who Wants the Procedure and Why)." 1998, 316:459–468.

Daston, Lorraine and Katharine Park. *Wonders on the Order of Nature 1150–1750*. New York: Zone, 1998.

Defoe, Daniel. *An Essay Upon Projects*. London: Printed by R. R. for T. Cockerill, 1697.

———. *Reasons humbly offer'd for a law to enact the castration of popish ecclesiastics, as the best way to prevent the growth of popery in England*. London, 1700.

Deleuze, Gilles. *Difference and Repetition*, trans. P. Patton. London: Althone Press, 1984.

———. *Empiricism and Subjectivity: An Essay on Hume's Theory of Human Nature,*. translated and with an introduction by Constantin V. Boundas. New York: Columbia University Press, 1991.

Deutsch, Helen. *Resemblance and Disgrace: Alexander Pope and the Deformation of Culture*. Cambridge, MA: Harvard University Press, 1996.

Deventer, Hendrik van. *The art of midwifery improv'd: fully and plainly laying down whatever instructions are requisite to make a compleat midwife: and the many errors in all books hitherto written upon this subject clearly refuted . . . also a new method, demonstrating, how infants ill situated in the womb . . . may, by the hand only . . . be turned into their right position*. 3rd ed., corrected. London, 1728.

Dictionary of National Biography. London: Smith and Elder, 1887.

Dionis, Pierre, Mr. *The Anatomy of Humane Bodies improv'd, according to the circulation of the blood and all the modern discoveries*. 2nd ed. London, 1716.

Dolan, Frances. *Whores of Babylon: Catholicism, Gender and Seventeenth-Century Print Culture*. Ithaca: Cornell University Press, 1999.

Donegan, Jane. *Women and Men Midwives: Medicine, Morality and Misogyny in Early America*. London: Greenwood, 1978.

Donne, John. *Ignatius His Conclave*, ed. T. S. Healy. Oxford: Clarendon, 1969.

Donnison, Jean. *Midwives and Medical Men: A History of Inter-Professional Rivalries and Women's Rights*. London: Heinemann Educational, 1977.

Doody, Margaret Anne. *A Natural Passion: A Study of the Novels of Samuel Richardson*. Oxford: Clarendon, 1974.

Dryden, John. *Absalom and Achitophel: A Poem*. London: Printed for T. J., 1681.

Duchovnay, Gerald. "Aphra Behn's Religion." *Notes and Queries* 221(1976): 235–237.

Duckett, George. *A summary of all the religious houses in England and Wales with their titles and valuations at the time of their dissolution. And a calculation of what they might be worth at this day. Together with an appendix concerning the several religious orders that prevail'd in this kingdom* . . . London: Printed for James Knapton and Timothy Childe, 1717.

Duffy, Maureen, ed. *Oroonoko and Other Stories.* By Aphra Behn. London: Methuen, 1986.

Dugdale, William, and Roger Dodsworth. *Monasticon anglicanum, sive, Pandectæ coenobiorum.* London, 1655.

Eaves, T. C. and Ben D. Kimpel. "Richardson's Revisions of *Pamela*." *Studies in Bibliography* 20(1967):61–88.

———. *Samuel Richardson, A Biography.* Oxford: Clarendon, 1971.

Ebsworth, Joseph Woodfall, ed. Introduction. *Bagford Ballads.* Hertford: Printed for the Ballad Society by Stephen Austin and Sons, 1878.

Eccles, Audrey. *Obstetrics and Gynecology in Tudor and Stuart England.* Kent: Kent State University Press, 1982.

Eco, Umberto. *Semiotics and the Philosophy of Language.* Bloomington: Indiana University Press, 1986.

Eisenstein, Elizabeth. *The Printing Press as an Agent of Change: Communications and Cultural Transformation in Early Modern Europe.* Cambridge: Cambridge University Press, 1979.

Elm, Susanna. *Virgins of God: The Making of Asceticism in Late Antiquity.* Oxford: Clarendon, 1994.

Engels, Frederick. *The Origin of the Family, Private Property and the State.* New York: Pathfinder, 1972.

Epstein, Julia. *Altered Conditions: Disease, Medicine, and Storytelling.* New York: Routledge, 1995.

———. "Fanny's Fanny: Epistolarity, Eroticism, and the Transsexual Text." In *Writing the Female Voice: Essays on Epistolary Literature*, ed. Elizabeth Goldsmith. Boston: Northeastern University Press, 1989, 135–153.

Erickson, Amy. *Women and Property in Early Modern England.* New York: Routledge, 1993.

Erickson, Robert. " 'The Books of Generation': Some Observations on the Style of the British Midwife Books, 1671–1764." In *Sexuality in Eighteenth-Century Britain*, ed. Paul-Gabriel Bouce. Manchester: Manchester University Press, 1982.

———. *The Language of the Heart, 1650–1750.* Philadelphia: University of Pennsylvania Press, 1997.

Etmullerus abridg'd, or, a compleat system of the theory and practice of physic: being a description of all diseases incident to men, women and children: With an account of their causes, symptoms, and most approved methods of cure, physical and chirurgical. To which is prefix'd a short view of the animal and vital functions; and the several vertues and classes of med'cines, translated from the last edition of the works of Michael Etmullerus. London: Printed for E. Harris and A. Bell, 1699.

Evendon, Doreen. *The Midwives of Seventeenth-Century London.* Cambridge: Cambridge University Press, 2000.

Farmer, John. *Merry Songs and Ballads, Prior to the Year 1800.* Privately printed 1897.

Ferguson, Margaret. Foreword. *Menacing Virgins: Representing Virginity in the Middle Ages and Renaissance,* ed. Kathleen Coyne Kelly and Marina Leslie. Newark: University of Delaware Press, 1999, 1–14.

Fielding, Henry. *Joseph Andrews/Shamela,* ed. Martin Battinson. Boston: Houghton Mifflin, 1961.

Fielding, Sarah. *Remarks on Clarissa.* Los Angeles: Augustan Reprint Society, 1985.

Fife, Ernelle. "Gender and Professionalism in Eighteenth-Century Midwifery." *Women's Writing* 11.2(2004):185–2000.

Figgis, Neville. *The Divine Right of Kings.* New York: Harper and Row, 1965.

Filmer, Robert. *Patriarcha and Other Writings.* Cambridge: Cambridge University Press, 1991.

Finke, Laurie. "Aphra Ben and the Ideological Construction of Restoration Literary Theory." In *Rereading Aphra Behn: History, Theory, and Criticism,* ed. Heidi Hutner. Charlotteville: University Press of Virginia, 1993, 17–43.

Five Love-Letters Written by a Cavalier: In Answer to the Five Love-Letters Written to Him by a Nun. London, 1694.

Fletcher, Anthony. *Gender, Sex and Subordination in England, 1500–1800.* New Haven: Yale University Press, 1995.

Flynn, Carol Houlihan. "What Fanny Felt: The Pains of Compliance in *Memoirs of a Woman of Pleasure.*" *Studies in the Novel* 19.3(1987): 284–295.

Foxe, John. *Acts and Monuments.* Philadelphia: John C. Winston, 1926.

Foxon, David F. *Libertine Literature in England, 1660–1745, with an appendix on the Publication of John Cleland's Memoirs of a Woman of Pleasure, commonly called Fanny Hill.* Reprint with revisions. London: Book Collector, 1964.

Freeman, Samuel. *A Discourse Concerning Invocation of Saints.* London: Printed for Ben. Tooke, and F. Gardiner, 1684.

Freud, Sigmund. "Jokes and Their Relation to the Unconscious." In *The Standard Ed. of the Complete Works of Sigmund Freud,* trans. and ed. J. Strachey. Volume VIII. London: Hogarth Press, 1957a (1953–1974), 3–236.

———. "The Taboo of Virginity." In *The Standard Ed. of the Complete Psychological Works of Sigmund Freud,* trans. and ed. J. Strachey. Volume XI. London: Hogarth Press, 1957b (1953–1974), 192–208.

Gallagher, Catherine. *Nobody's Story: The Vanishing of Women Writers in the Marketplace, 1670–1820.* Berkeley: University of California Press, 1994.

[Gavin, Antonio]. *The frauds of Romish monks and priests set forth in eight letters, and publish'd for the benefit of the publick.* 2nd ed. London: Printed by Samuel Roycroft for Robert Clavell, 1691.

———. *Master-Key to popery in five parts.* London, 1724.

———. *Observations on a journey to Naples: Wherein the frauds of Romish monks and priests are farther discover'd.* London, 1725.

———. *A short history of monastical orders in which the primitive institution of monks, their tempers, habits, rules, and the condition they are in at present, are treated of.* London, 1693.

Gay, John, and John Harrington Smith. *Three Hours After Marriage.* London, 1717.

Gibson, Thomas. *The anatomy of humane bodies epitomized wherein all parts of man's body, with their actions and uses, are succinctly described, according to the newest doctrine of the most accurate and learned modern anatomists.* London, 1682.

Giffard, William. *Cases in Midwifry.* London, 1734.

Glanvill, Joseph. *Essays on Several Important Subjects in Philosophy and Religion.* In *Collected Works.* Volume VI. Facsimile ed. 1676. Hildesheim: George Olms Verlag, 1979.

Goodyear-Smith, F. A., and T. M. Laidlaw. "What Is an 'Intact' Hymen? A Critique of the Literature." *Medicine, Science and the Law* 38.4(1998): 289–300.

Gother, John. *A papist misrepresented and represented, or, A twofold character of popery: the one containing a sum of the superstitions, idolatries, cruelties, treacheries, and wicked principles laid to their charge: the other laying open that religion which those termed Papists own and profess, the chief articles of their faith, and the principal grounds and reasons which attach them to it.* London, 1685.

Graham, Rosemary. "The Prostitute in the Garden: Walt Whitman, Fanny Hill, and the Fantasy of Female Pleasure." *ELH* 64.2(1997):569–597.

Greene, Jody. "Arbitrary Tastes and Commonsense Pleasures: Accounting for Taste in Cleland, Hume, and Burke." In *Launching Fanny Hill*, ed. Patsy S. Fowler and Alan Jackson. New York: AMS, 2003, 221–266.

Gregory of Nyssa. "On Virginity." In *Saint Gregory of Nyssa: Ascetical Works*, trans. Virginia Woods Callahan. Washington, DC: Catholic University Press of America, 1967.

Gross, Kenneth. *Spencerian Poetics: Idolatry, Iconoclasm and Magic.* Ithaca: Cornell University Press, 1985.

Guilhamet, Leon. *Satire and the Transformation of Genre.* Philadelphia: University of Pennsylvania Press, 1987.

[Guilleragues, Gabriel Joseph de Lavergne]. *Five love-letters written by a cavalier: in answer to the Five love-letters written to him by a nun.* London: Printed for R. Bentley, at the Post-house in Russel Street in Convent-Garden., 1694.

Gwilliam, Tassie. *Samuel Richardson's Fictions of Gender.* Stanford: Stanford University Press, 1993.

Hackett, Helen. *Virgin Mother, Maiden Queen: Elizabeth I and the Cult of the Virgin Mary.* New York: St. Martin's Press, 1995.

Halbertal, Moshe and Avishai Margalit *Idolatry.* Cambridge, MA: Harvard University Press, 1992.

Hales, John, and Frederick Furnivall, eds. *Bishop Percy's Folio Manuscript.* London: N. Trubner, 1867–1868.

Hall, Lesley and Roy Porter. *The Facts of Life: The Creation of Sexual Knowledge in Britain,1650–1950.* New Haven: Yale University Press, 1995.

Halliwell-Phillipps, James Orchard. *Euing Collection of English Broadside Ballads,* ed. John Holloway. Glasgow: University of Glasgow, 1971.

Harol, Corrinne. "Faking It: Female Virginity and Pamela's Virtue." *Eighteenth-Century Fiction* 16.2(2004):197–216.

———. "Virgin Idols and Verbal Devices: Pope's Belinda and the Virgin Mary." *Eighteenth Century: Theory and Interpretation* 45.1(2004):41–59.

Harvey, William. "The Second Anatomical Essay to Jean Riolan." In *The Circulation of the Blood: Two Anatomical Essays by William Harvey,* trans. and ed. Kenneth Franklin. Oxford: Blackwell Scientific Publications, 1958.

Harvey, William. Excerpt on "Hysteria and Pseudocysesis." In *Three Hundred Years of Psychiatry: 1535–1860,* ed. Richard Hunter and Ida Macalpine. London: Oxford University Press, 1963.

[Hascard, Gregory]. *A discourse about the charge of novelty upon the reformed Church of England made by the papists asking of us the question, Where was our religion before Luther?* London, 1683.

Haywood, Eliza. *Love in Excess, or The fatal enquiry,* ed. David Oakleaf. Peterborough, ON; Orchard Park, NY: Broadview Press, 1994.

[———]. *Anti-Pamela, or, Feign'd innocence detected: in a series of Syrena's adventures: a narrative which has really its foundation in truth and nature . . .* London, 1741.

Heister, Lorenz A. *A compendium of anatomy. Containing a short but perfect view of all the parts of humane bodies. Wherein are inserted, the modern discoveries: together with a varietyof curious observations never before made publick. Compendium of Anatomy.* London, 1721.

Hickes, Georges. *Speculum Beatae Virginis: A Discourse of the Due Praise and Honour of the Virgin Mary.* London, 1686.

Hill, Bridget. "A Refuge from Men: The Idea of the Protestant Nunnery." *Past and Present* 117(1987):107–130.

Hippocrates. "Les Maladies des Femmes." In *Oeuvres Complètes d'Hippocrate,* trans. Emile Littré. Volume 8. Amsterdam: Hakkert, 1961–1962. Translation of *Peri parthenôn.*

Hobbes, Thomas. *Leviathan, or, The matter, form, and power of a commonwealth ecclesiastical and civil.* London: Printed for Andrew Crooke, 1651.

Hobby, Elaine, ed. *Midwives book, or the whole art of midwifery discovered.* By Jane Sharp. New York: Oxford University Press, 1999.

———. " 'Secrets of the Female Sex': Jane Sharp, the Reproductive Female Body, and Early Modern Midwifery Manuals." *Women's Writing* 8.2(2001):201–212.

———. *Virtue of Necessity: English Women's Writing 1649–1688.* Ann Arbor: University of Michigan Press, 1989.

Holloway, John, eds. *Euing Collection of English Broadside Ballads.* Glasgow: University of Glasgow Press, 1971.

Holloway, John, and Joan Black. *Later English Broadside Ballads.* Lincoln: University of Nebraska Press, 1975.

Hume, David. *A Treatise of Human Nature,* ed. L. A. Selby-Bigge and P. H. Nidditch. Oxford: Clarendon, 1978.

Hunt, Lynn A. Introduction. In *The Invention of Pornography: Obscenity and the Origins of Modernity, 1500–1800.* Ed. Hunt. New York: Zone Books, 1993, 9–48.

Jackson, Mark. *New-Born Child Murder: Women, Illegitimacy and the Courts in Eighteenth-Century England.* Manchester: Manchester University Press, 1996.

Jacquart, Danielle, and Claude Thomasset. *Sexuality and Medicine in the Middle Ages,* trans. Matthew Adamson. Cambridge: Polity Press, 1985.

James, Robert. *A Medicinal Dictionary.* London, 1743–1745.

Jankowski, Theodora. *Pure Resistance: Queer Virginity in Early Modern English Drama.* Philadelphia: University of Pennsylvania Press, 2000.

Janus, Samuel, and Cynthia Janus. *The Janus Report on Sexual Behavior.* New York: John Wiley and Sons, 1993.

Jerome, Saint. "On Marriage and Virginity. From *Letter XXII to Eustochium.*" In *St. Jerome: Letters and Select Works,* trans. W. H. Fremantle. *Select Library of Nicene and Post-Nicene Fathers.* Series 2, volume VI. Edinburgh, 1892.

Jordanova, Ludmilla J. Introduction. *The Quick and the Dead: Artists and Anatomy,* ed. Deanna Petherbridge and Ludmilla Jordanova. Berkeley: University of California Press, 1997.

Keill, James. *Anatomy of the Humane Body Abridg'd; Or, A Short and full View of all the Parts of the Body together with their several uses drawn from their compositions and structures.* 6th ed. London, 1718.

Kelly, Dorothy. "Experimenting on Women: Zola's Theory and Practice of the Experimental Novel." In *Spectacles of Realism: Body, Gender, Genre,* ed. Margaret Cohen and and Christopher Prendergast. Minneapolis and London: University of Minnesota Press, 1995, 231–246.

Kelly, Kathleen Coyne. *Performing Virginity and Testing Chastity.* New York: Routledge, 2000.

Kelly, Kathleen Coyne, and Marina Leslie, eds. *Menacing Virgins: Representing Virginity in the Middle Ages and Renaissance.* Newark: University of Delaware Press, 1999, 1–14.

Kenner, Hugh. "Pope's Reasonable Rhymes." In *Pope: Recent Essays by Several Hands,* ed. Maynard Mack and James Winn. Hamden: Archon Books, 1980, 63–79.

Keymer, Thomas, and Peter Sabor. *The Pamela Controversy.* London: Pickering and Chatto, 2001.

Kierkegaard, Soren. *Fear and Trembling/Repetition,* trans. and ed. Howard Hong and Edna Hong. Princeton: Princeton University Press, 1983.

King, Helen. *The Disease of Virgins: Green Sickness, Chlorosis, and the Problems of Puberty*. London, New York Taylor and Francis, 2004.

———. "Hippocrates, Galen, and the Origins of the 'Disease of Virgins.' " *International Journal of the Classical Tradition* 2.3(1996):372–387.

King, John. "Queen Elizabeth I: Representations of the Virgin Queen." *Renaissance Quarterly* 43.1(1990):30–74.

Koestler, Arthur. *The Act of Creation*. London: Hutchinson, 1964.

Kramnick, Jonathan Brody. "Locke's Desire." *YJC* 12.2(1999):189–208.

Kreiger, Murray. "The 'Frail China Jar' and the Rude Hand of Chaos." In *Pope: The Rape of the Lock: A Casebook*, ed. John Dixon Hunt. London: Palgrave Macmillan, 1968, 201–219.

Kroll, Richard. *The Material Word: Literate Culture in the Restoration and Early Eighteenth Century*. Baltimore: Johns Hopkins University Press, 1991.

Laqueur, Thomas. *Making Sex: Body and Gender from the Greeks to Freud*. Cambridge, MA: Harvard University Press, 1990.

Lea, Henry C. *The History of Sacerdotal Celibacy in the Christian Church*. 3rd ed. London: Kessinga, 1907.

Lerner, Gerda. *The Creation of Patriarchy*. New York: Oxford University Press, 1986.

Lévi-Strauss, Claude. *Elementary Structures of Kinship*, trans. James Harle Bell, ed. Richard Sturmer and Rodney Needham. Boston: Beacon, 1969.

Lewalski, Barbara. *Protestant Poetics and the Seventeenth-Century Religious Lyric*. Princeton: Princeton University Press, 1979.

Lewis, Matthew Gregory. *The Monk*. Oxford: Oxford University Press, 1995.

Lewis, Peter, and Nigel Wood, eds. *John Gay and the Scriblerians*. London: Vision Press, 1988.

Lewis, Thomas. *An Inquiry into the shape, the beauty, and stature of the person of Christ, and of the Virgin Mary. Offered to the consideration of late converts to popery*. London, 1735.

Literature Online. Cambridge: Chadwyck-Healey. April 19, 2006. http://lion.chadwyck.com/.

Locke, John. *An Essay Concerning Human Understanding*, ed. Peter Nidditch. Oxford: Clarendon, 1975.

———. *Two Treatises on Government*, ed. Peter Laslett. 2nd ed. Cambridge: Cambridge University Press, 1967.

Loudon, I. "Chlorosis, Anaemia, and Anorexia Nervosa." *British Medical Journal* cclxxxi(1980):1–19.

———. "The Disease Called Chlorosis." *Psychological Medicine* XIV(1984):27–36.

Loughlin, Marie. *Hymeneutics: Interpreting Virginity on the Early Modern Stage*. Lewisburg, PA: Bucknell University Press, 1997.

———. " 'Love's Friend and Stranger to Virginitie': The Politics of the Virginal Body in Ben Jonson's *Hymenaei* and Thomas Campion's *The Lord Hay's Masque*." *ELH* 63.4(1996):833–849.

Lowe, Soloman. *The Protestant family-piece, or, a picture of popery: drawn from their own principles, exprest in the words of their popes, councils, canons, and celebrated writers, faithfully collected and translated* . . . London, 1716.

Luther, Martin. *Luther's Works*, ed. J. Pelikan and H. C. Oswald. American ed. Volume. I. St. Louis: Concordia, 1955–1976.

Mack, Maynard. *Alexander Pope: A Life*. New York: Norton, 1985.

Mack, Maynard, and James Winn, eds. *Pope: Recent Essays by Several Hands*. Hamden: Archon Books, 1980.

Mackey, Louis. "Once More with Feeling: Kierkegaard's Repetition." In *Kierkegaard and Literature: Irony, Repetition, and Criticism*, ed. Ronald Schleifer and Robert Markley. Norman: University of Oklahoma Press, 1984.

Malebranche, Nicolas. *Malebranche's search after truth: or a treatise of the nature of the humane mind*. London, 1695.

[Mandeville, Bernard de]. *A Modest Defence of Publick Stews; or, An Essay upon Whoring, as it is now practis'd in these Kingdoms. Written by a layman*. London, 1724.

Markley, Robert. *"Two-edg'd weapons": Style and Ideology in the Comedies of Etherege, Wycherley, and Congreve*. Oxford: Clarendon, 1988.

Markley, Robert, and Molly Rothenberg. "Contestations of Nature: Aphra Behn's 'The Golden Age' and Sexualizing of Politics." In *Rereading Aphra Behn: History, Theory and Criticism*, ed. Heidi Hutner. Charlottesville: University Press of Virginia, 1993, 301–321.

Marvell, Andrew. "To His Coy Mistress." from *Miscellaneous Poems*. 1681.

———. "A Marvelous Medicine to Cure a Great Pain, if a Maiden-Head be Lost to Get it Again." London, 1657.

———. "Upon Appleton House." In *Complete Poems*, ed. Elizabeth Story Dunno. New York: St. Martin's Press, 1972.

Marvell, Andrew. "To His Coy Mistress." In *Complete Poems*, ed. Elizabeth Story Dunno. New York: St. Martin's Press, 1972.

Marx, Karl. *Capital: A Critique of Political Economy*. New York: Modern Library, 1936.

Masham, Damaris. *Discourse Concerning the Love of God*. London, 1696.

Massinger, Philip and Thomas Dekker. *The Virgin Martyr: a tragedie*. London, 1651.

Master, Thomas. *The Virgin Mary. A sermon preach'd in Saint Mary's College, (Vulgo New -College) Oxon, March the 25th, 1641*. London, 1710.

Maubray, John. *The female physician, containing all the diseases incident to that sex, in virgins, wives, and widows: together with their causes and symptoms, their degrees of danger, and respective methods of prevention and cure: to which is added, the whole art of new improv'd midwifery, comprehending the necessary qualifications of a midwife, and particular directions for laying women, in all cases of difficult and preternatural births, together with the diet and regimen of both the mother and child*. London: James Holland, 1724.

Mauriceau, Francois. *The diseases of women with child and in child-bed as also the best means of helping them in natural and unnatural labors: with fit remedies for the several indispositions of new-born babes: illustrated with divers fair figures newly and very correctly engraven in copper: a work much more perfect than any yet extant in English, very necessary for chirurgeons and midwives practicing this art The Disease of Women with Child and Childbed*. 2nd Ed. London: John Darby, 1683.

McKeon, Michael. "Historicizing Patriarchy." *Eighteenth-Century Studies* 28.3(1995):295–322.

———. *The Origins of the English Novel, 1600–1700*. Baltimore: Johns Hopkins University Press, 1987.

McFarlane, Carmen. *The Sodomite in Fiction and Satire*. Columbia: Columbia University Press, 1997.

Mede, Joseph. *The apostasy of the latter times in which (according to divine prediction) the world should wonder after the beast, the mystery of iniquity should so farre prevaile over the mystery of godlinesse, whorish Babylon over the virgin-church of Christ, as that the visible glory of the true church should be much clouded, the true unstained Christian faith corrupted, the purity of true worship polluted: or, the gentiles theology of dæmons, i.e. inferious divine powers, supposed to be mediatours between God and man: revived in the latter times amongst Christians, in worshipping of angels, deifying and invocating of saints, adoring and templing of reliques, bowing downe to images, worshipping of crosses, &c.: all which, together with a true discovery of the nature, originall, progresse of the great, fatall, and solemn apostasy are cleared*. London, 1641.

Mengay, Donald. "The Sodomitical Muse: *Fanny Hill* and the Rhetoric of Crossdressing." In *Homosexuality in Renaissance and Enlightenment England: Literary Representations in Historical Context*, ed. Claude Summers. New York: Haworth Press, 1992, 185–198.

Methodius, Saint. *The Symposium: A Treatise on Chastity*, trans. Herbert Musurillo. Westminister, MD: Newman Press; London: Longman, Green, 1958.

Middleton, Thomas, and William Rowley. *The Changeling*. London, 1653.

Miller, J. Hillis. *Fiction and Repetition: Seven English Novels*. Cambridge, MA: Harvard University Press, 1982.

Miller, Nancy K. *Heroine's Text: Readings in the French and English Novel, 1722–1782*. New York: Columbia University Press, 1980.

Milton, John. *A maske presented at Ludlow Castle, 1634 on Michaelmasse night, before the Right Honorable, Iohn Earle of Bridgewater, Vicount Brackly, Lord Praesident of Wales, and one of His Maiesties most honorable Privie Counsell.*, London: Printed (by Augustine Mathewes) for Humphrey Robinson, at the signe of the Three Pidgeons in Pauls Church-Yard, 1637.

Moore, Lisa. *Dangerous Intimacies: Toward a Sapphic History of the British Novel*. Durham: Duke University Press, 1997.

More, Henry. *Enthusiasmus triumphatus, or, A discourse of the nature, causes, kinds, and cure, of enthusiasme*. London, 1656.

Morse, David. *The Age of Virtue: British Culture from the Restoration to Romanticism*. Houndsmill, Basingstoke, Hampshire: MacMillan Press, 2000; New York: St. Martin's Press.

Mudge, Brandford. *The Whore's Story: Women Pornography, and the British Novel, 1684–1830*. Oxford: Oxford University Press, 2000.

The musical miscellany; being a collection of choice songs, set to the violin and flute, by the most eminent masters. London, 9–31.

Myers, Jeffrey. "The Personality of Belinda's Baron: Pope's 'The Rape of the Lock.' " *American Imago* 26(1969):71–77.

Norris, John. *The theory and regulation of love. A moral essay, in two parts: to which are added letters philosophical and moral between the author and Dr. Henry More*. London, 1688.

Olsson, Lena. "Idealized and Realistic Portrayals of Prostitution in John Cleland's *Memoirs of a Woman of Pleasure*." In *Launching Fanny Hill: Essays on the Novel and Its Influences*, ed. Patsy Fowler and Alan Jackson. New York: AMS, 2003. 81–101.

Ortner, Sherry. "The Virgin and the State." *Feminist Studies* 4.3(1978): 19–35.

Paré, Ambroise. *The workes of that famous chirurgion Ambrose Parey*, trans. Thomas Johnson. London, 1634.

Paster, Gail Kern " 'In the Spirit of Men there Is no Blood': Blood as a Trope of Gender in *Julius Caesar*." *Shakespeare Quarterly* 40.3(Fall 1989):284–298.

Pateman, Carole. *The Sexual Contract*. Stanford: Stanford University Press, 1988.

Paulson, Ronald. *Breaking and Remaking*. New Brunswick: Rutgers, 1989.

Percy, Thomas. *Reliques of ancient English poetry, consisting of old heroic ballads, songs, and other pieces of our earlier poets, together with some few of later date. Reliques of Ancient English Poetry*. Edinburgh: William Nimmo, 1869.

Perry, Ruth. *The Celebrated Mary Astell: And Early English Feminist*. Chicago: University of Chicago Press, 1986.

Pettit, Alexander. "Rex v. Curll: Pornography and Punishment in Court and on the Page." *Studies in the Literary Imagination* 34.1(2001):63–78.

Pierce, John. "*Pamela's* Textual Authority" *Eighteenth-Century Fiction* 7(1995):131–146.

Pinto, Vivian de Sola, and Allan Edwin Rodway. *The Common Muse: An Anthology of Popular British Ballad Poetry, XVth–XXth Century*. New York: Philosophical Library, 1957.

Pocock, J. G. A. *The Machiavellian Moment: Florentine Political Thought and the Atlantic Republican Tradition*. Princeton: Princeton University Press, 1975.

Pocock, J. G. A. *Virtue, Commerce and History: Essays on Political Thought and History, Chiefly in the Eighteenth Century.* Cambridge: Cambridge University Press, 1985.

Pollak, Ellen. *The Poetics of Sexual Myth: Gender and Ideology in the Verse of Swift and Pope.* Chicago: University of Chicago Press, 1985.

Pope, Alexander. *An Essay on Man. Address'd to a friend . . .* London, 1733.

———. [Barnivelt, Esdras, apoth.]. *A key to the lock; or, A treatise proving, beyond all contradiction, the dangerous tendency of a late poem, entituled, The rape of the lock, to government and religion.* London: J. Roberts, 1715.

———. *The Rape of the Lock. The Twickenham Ed. of the Poems of Alexander Pope,* 11 vols. Volume II, ed. John Butt et al. London: Metheun, 1939–1969.

Porter, Roy. *The Popularization of Medicine 1650–1850.* London: Routledge, 1992.

———, ed. "The Secrets of Generation Diplay'd: Aristotle's Master-Piece in Eighteenth-Century England." *Eighteenth-Century Life* 9.3(1985):1–16.

[Pratt, Daniel]. The *Life of the Blessed St. Agnes, Virgin and Martyr.* London, 1677.

Prendergast, John S. "Pierre Du Moulin on the Eucharist: Protestant Sign Theory and the Grammar of Embodiment." *ELH* 65(1998):47–68.

Pugno, P. A. "Genital Findings in Prepubertal Girls Evaluated for Sexual Abuse: A Different Perspective on the Hymen." *Archives of Family Medicine* 8.5(1999):403–406.

Radcliffe, Ann. *The Italian, or, the confessional of the Black Penitents: A Romance.* Oxford: Oxford University Press, 1998.

Ragussis, Michael. *Acts of Naming: The Family Plot in Fiction.* Oxford: Oxford University Press, 1986.

Renwick, Roger de V. *English Folk Poetry: Structure and Meaning.* University of Pennsylvania Press, 1980.

Richardson, Ruth. *Death, Dissection and the Destitute.* London: Routledge, 1987.

Richardson, Samuel. *Clarissa, or the history of a young lady.* London: Penguin, 1985.

———. *Pamela; or, Virtue Rewarded,* ed. Peter Sabor. London: Penguin, 1980.

Richetti, John. "*Love Letters Between a Nobleman and His Sister:* Aphra Behn and Amatory Fiction." In *Augustan Subjects: Essays in Honor of Martin C. Battestin,* ed. Albert J. Rivero. Newark, DE and London, England: University of Delaware Press; Cranbury, NJ: Associated University Press, 1997, 13–28.

Ricoeur, Paul. *Time and Narrative,* trans. Kathleen McLaughlin and David Pellauer. Chicago: University of Chicago Press, 1994.

Rivers, Isabel. *Reason Grace and Sentiment.* Cambridge: Cambridge University Press, 1991.

Rogers, John. "The Enclosure of Virginity: The Poetics of Sexual Abstinence in the English Revolution." In *Enclosure Acts: Sexuality, Property and*

Culture in Early Modern England. Cornell: Cornell University Press, 1994, 229–250.

———. *The Matter of Revolution: Science, Poetry, and Politics in the Age of Milton*. Ithaca: Cornell University Press, 1996.

Rollins, Hyder Edward. "An Analytical Index to the Ballad-Entries in the Registers of the Company of Stationers of London." *Studies in Philology* 31.1(1924):1–324.

———. *The Pepys Ballads*. 8 volumes. Volumes III and VII. Cambridge, MA: Harvard University Press, 1929.

Ross, Malcolm. *Poetry & Dogma: The Transfiguration of Eucharistic Symbols in Seventeenth-Century English Poetry*. New Brunswick, NJ: Rutgers University Press, 1954.

Roxburghe Ballads. With Short notes by W. Chappel. Hertford, 1874–1875.

Rubin, Gayle. "The Traffic in Women: Notes on the 'Political Economy' of Sex." In *Toward an Anthropology of Women*, ed. Rayna Reiter. New York: Monthly Review Press, 1975, 157–210.

Sabor, Peter. "The Censor Censured: Expurgating *Memoirs of a Woman of Pleasure*." In *'Tis Nature's Fault: Unauthorized Sexuality During the Enlightenment*, ed. Robert Maccubin. Cambridge: Cambridge University Press, 1987, 192–201.

Sabran, Lewis. *A letter to a peer of the Church of England clearing a point touched in a sermon preached at Chester, before His Most Sacred Majesty, on the 28th of August, in answer to a post-script joyned unto the answer to Nubes testium*. London, 1687.

Salmon, Thomas. *A critical essay concerning marriage; to which is added, an historical account of the marriage rites and ceremonies of the Greeks and Romans, and our Saxon ancestors, and of most nations of the world at this day*. London: C. Rivington, 1724.

Schiebinger, Londa. *The Mind Has No Sex? Women in the Origins of Modern Science*. Cambridge, MA: Harvard University Press, 1989.

———. *Nature's Body: Gender in the Making of Modern Science*. Boston: Beacon Press, 1993.

Schochet, Gordon. *Patriarchalism in Political Thought*. New York: Basic Books, 1975.

Scholtz, Susanne. *Body Narratives: Writing the Nation and Fashioning the Subject in Early Modern England*. New York: St. Martin's Press, 2000.

Schulenburg, Jane Tibbets. "The Heroics of Virginity." In *Women in the Middle Ages and the Renaissance: literary and historical perspectives*, ed. Mary Beth Rose. Syracuse: Syracuse University Press, 1986.

Schwarz, Kathryn. "The Wrong Question: Thinking Through Virginity." *Differences: A Journal of Feminist Cultural Studies* 13.2(2002):1–34.

Scott, Sarah. *A Description Of Millenium Hall, And The Country Adjacent*. London: J. Newbery, 1762.

Sedgwick, Eve Kosofsy. *Between Men: English Literature and Male Homosocial Desire*. New York: Columbia University Press, 1985.

Sermon, William. *The ladies companion, or, The English midwife wherein is demonstrated the manner and order how women ought to govern themselves during the whole time of their breeding children and of their difficult labour, hard travail and lying-in, etc.: together with the diseases they are subject to (especially in such times) and the several wayes and means to help them: also the various forms of the childs proceeding forth of the womb, in 17 copper cuts, with a discourse of the parts principally serving for generation The Labours Companion, or The English Midwife.* London, 1671.

Shaftesbury, Anthony Ashley Cooper, third Earl of. *Characteristics of Men, Manners, Opinions, Times.* London, 1711.

Shapin, Steven. *A Social History of Truth: civility and science in seventeenth-century England.* Chicago: University of Chicago Press, 1994.

Shapin, Steven, and Simon Schaffer. *Leviathan and the Air-Pump: Hobbes, Boyle and the Experimental Life.* Princeton: Princeton University Press, 1985.

Sharp, Jane. *The midwives book. Or the whole art of midwifery discovered: Directing childbearing women how to behave themselves.* London: S. Miller, 1671.

Sherlock, William. *A preservative against popery. The first part being some plain directions to vnlearned Protestants, how to dispute with Romish priests.* London: William Rogers, 1688.

Shinagel, Michael. "*Memoirs of a Woman of Pleasure*: Pornography and the Mid-Eighteenth Century Novel." In *Studies in Change and Revolution: Aspects of English Intellectual History, 1640–1800*, ed. Paul J. Korshin. Menston, Yorkshire: Scolar Press, 1972.

Shuger, Debora Kuller. " 'Gums of Glutinous Heat' and the Stream of Consciousness: The Theology of Milton's Maske." *Representations* 60(1997):1–21.

———. *The Renaissance Bible: Scholarship, Sacrifice and Subjectivity.* Berkeley: University of California Press, 1994.

Simmons, Philip E. "John Cleland's *Memoirs of a Woman of Pleasure*: Literary Voyeurism and the Techniques of Novelistic Transgression." *ECF* 3.1(1990):43–63.

Sissa, Giulia. *Greek Virginity*, trans. Arthur Goldhammer. Cambridge: Harvard University Press, 1990.

Sitter, John. *Arguments of Augustan Wit.* Cambridge, England; New York: Cambridge University Press, 1991.

Smellie, William. *A Set of Anatomical Tables, With Explanations, and an Abridgement of the Practice of Midwifery, with a View to Illustrate a Treatise on that Subject, and Collection of Cases.* London, 1754.

Smith, Hilda. "Gynecology and Ideology in Seventeenth Century England." In *Liberating Women's History: Theoretical and Critical Essays*, ed. Berenice Carroll. Urbana: University of Illinois Press, 1976.

Spacks, Patricia Meyer. *Desire and Truth Functions of Plot in Eighteenth-Century English Novels.* Chicago: University of Chicago Press, 1990.

———. "Female Changelessness: Or, What Do Women Want?" *Studies in the Novel* 19.3(1987):273–283.

Spencer, Herbert. *The History of British Midwifery from 1650 to 1800.* London: Bales and Son, 1927.

Sprat, Thomas. *The History of the Royal-Society of London for the Improving of Natural Knowledge.* London, 1667.

Springborg, Patricia. Introduction. In *A Serious Proposal to the Ladies.* Toronto: Broadview, 2002.

Stallybrass, Peter. "Patriarchal Territories: The Body Enclosed." In *Rewriting the Renaissance: The Discourses of Sexual Difference in Early Modern Europe,* ed. Margaret Ferguson, Maureen Quilligan, and Nancy Vickers. Chicago: University of Chicago Press, 1986, 123–142.

Stanton, Donna. "Sexual Pleasure and Sacred Law: Transgression and Complicity in *Vénus dans le cloître.*" *L'Esprit Créateur* 35.2(1995):67–83.

Stapleto, M. L. "Aphra Behn, Libertine." *Restoration: Studies in English Literary Culture* 24.2(2000):75–97.

Staves, Susan. "Fielding and the Comedy of Attempted Rape." In *History, Gender and Eighteenth-Century Literature,* ed. Beth Fowkes Tobin. Athens: University of Georgia Press, 1994, 86–112.

———. *Player's Scepters: Fictions of Authority in the Restoration.* Lincoln: University of Nebraska Press, 1979.

Stephens, Edward. *Asceticks, or, The heroick piety & virtue of the ancient Christian anchorets and coenobites.* London, 1696.

Stevens, Scott Manning. "Sacred Heart and Secular Brain." In *The Body in Parts: Fantasies of Corporeality in Early Modern Europe,* ed. David Hillman and Carla Mazzio. New York: Routledge, 1997.

Stevenson, John. " 'Never in a Vile House': Knowledge and Experience in Richardson." *Literature and Psychology* 34(1988):4–16.

Stone, Lawrence. *The Family, Sex and Marriage in England, 1500–1800.* London: Weidenfeld and Nicolson, 1977.

Stone, Sarah. *A complete practice of midwifery: consisting of upwards of forty cases or observations in that valuable art, selected from many others, in the course of a very extensive practice: and interspersed with many necessary cautions and useful instructions, proper to be observed in the most dangerous and critical exigencies, as well when the delivery is difficult in its own nature, as when it becomes so by the rashness or ignorance of unexperienc'd pretenders: recommended to all female practitioners in an art so important to the lives and well-being of the sex.* London, 1737.

Symonds, Deborah. *Weep not for Me: Women, Ballads and Infanticide in Early Modern Scotland.* University Park, PA: Penn State University Press, 1997.

Tannenbaum, Rebecca J. *The Healer's Calling: Women and Medicine in Early New England.* Ithaca: Cornell University Press, 2002.

Tanner, Thomas. *Notitia monastica, or, A short history of the religious houses in England and Wales.* London, 1695.

Teresa, Saint. *The Flaming Hart.* Antwerpe, 1642.

Teresa, Saint. *The works of the holy mother St. Teresa of Jesus foundress of the reformation of the discalced Carmelites: divided into two parts.* London, 1675.

Thomas, Keith. *Religion and the Decline of Magic: Studies in Popular Beliefs in Sixteenth- and Seventeenth-Century England.* New York: Oxford University Press, 1997.

Thompson, Roger. *Unfit for Modest Ears: A Study of Pornographic, Obscene and Bawdy Works Written or Published in England in the Second Half of the Seventeenth Century.* London: MacMillan, 1979.

Todd, Janet. *The Secret Life of Aphra Behn.* New Brunswick: Rutgers University Press, 1997.

Tracy, Clarence. *The rape observ'd: an edition of Alexander Pope's poem The rape of the lock, illustrated by means of numerous pictures, from contemporary sources, of the people, places, and things mentioned, with an introduction and notes.* Toronto: University of Toronto Press, 1974.

A Treatise Concerning Adultery and Divorce. London: R. Roberts, 1700.

Trumbach, Randolph. "Erotic Fantasy and Male Libertinism in Enlightenment England." In *The Invention of Pornography: Obscenity and the Origins of Modernity, 1500–1800,* ed. Lynn Avery Hunt. New York: Zone Books, 1993, 253–282.

———. "Modern Prostitution and Gender in *Fanny Hill*: Libertine and Domesticated Fantasy." In *Sexual Underworlds of the Enlightenment,* ed. G. S. Rousseau and Roy Porter. Chapel Hill: University of North Carolina Press, 1988, 69–85.

Turner, James Grantham. " 'Novel Panic': Picture and Performance in the Reception of Samuel Richardson's *Pamela*." *Representations* 48(1994): 70–96.

———. *Schooling Sex: Libertine Literature and Erotic Education in Italy, France, and England, 1534–1685.* Oxford, NY: Oxford University Press, 2003.

Van Sant, Ann. *Eighteenth-Century Sensibility and the Novel: The Senses in Social Context.* Cambridge: Cambridge University Press, 1993.

Vanita, Ruth. *Sappho and the Virgin Mary: Same-Sex Love and the English literary Imagination.* New York: Columbia University Press, 1996.

Venette, Nicolas. *Mysteries of Conjugal Love Reveal'd.* London, 1712.

Wagner, Peter. *Eros Revived: Erotica of the Enlightenment in England and America.* London: Secker and Warburg, 1988.

———. Introduction. In *Memoirs of a Woman of Pleasure.* By John Cleland. Ed. Wagner. London: Penguin, 1985.

Wallace, John. "Examples are Best Precepts: Readers and Meaning in Seventeenth Century Poetry." *Critical Inquiry* 1.1(1974):273–290.

Wasserman, Earl. "The Limits of Allusion in *The Rape of the Lock*." In *Pope: Recent Essays by Several Hands,* ed. Maynard Mack and James Winn. Hamden: Archon Press, 1980, 224–246.

Watt, Ian. *The Rise of the Novel; Studies in Defoe, Richardson, and Fielding.* Berkeley: University of California Press, 1957.

Weber Samuel. *The Legend of Freud.* Minneapolis: University Minnesota Press, 1982.

Weil, Rachel. *Political Passions: Gender, the Family, and Political Argument in England, 1680–1714.* Manchester: Manchester University Press, 1999.

Weld, Catherine Elizabeth. *The cases of impotency and virginity fully discuss'd. Being, the genuine proceedings, in the Arches-Court of Canterbury, between . . . Catherine Elizabeth Weld, alias Aston, and her husband Edward Weld.* Published by John Crawfurd, L. L. D. London: Printed for Thomas Gammon and sold by W. Mears, 1732.

Wharton, Henry. *The enthusiasm of the church of Rome demonstrated in some observations upon the life of Ignatius Loyola.* London, 1688.

Wheler, George. *The Protestant monastery: or, Christian oeconomicks. Containing directions for the religious conduct of a family . . .* London, 1698.

Wilkins, John. *Of the Principles and Duties of Natural Religion.* London, 1699.

Williams, Carolyn. "*The Way to Things by Words*: John Cleland, the Name of the Father, and Speculative Etymology." *YES* 28(1998):250–275.

Wilson, Adrian. *The Making of Man-Midwifery: Childbirth in England, 1660–1770.* Cambridge, MA: Harvard University Press, 1995.

Wilson, Luke. "William Harvey's *Prelectiones*: The Performance of the Body in the Renaissance Theater of Anatomy." *Representations* 17(1987): 62–95.

Wilt, Judith. "He Could Go No Farther: A Modest Proposal about Lovelace and *Clarissa*." *PMLA: Publications of the Modern Language Association of America* 92.1(January 1977):19–32.

Wimsatt, W. K. *The Verbal Icon: Studies in the Meaning of Poetry.* Lexington: University Press of Kentucky, 1954.

Wojciehowski, Dolora. *Old Masters, New Subjects: Early Modern and Poststructuralist Theories of Will.* Stanford: Stanford University Press, 1995.

Wollstonecraft, Mary. *A vindication of the rights of woman with strictures on political and moral subjects.* London: J. Johnson, 1792.

Woodman, Thomas. "Pope: The Papist and the Poet." *Essays in Criticism* 46.3(1996):219–233.

Wrigley, E. A. and R. S. Schoefield. *The Population History of England 1541–1871: A Reconstruction.* Cambridge: Cambridge University Press, 1989.

Würzbach, Natascha. *The Rise of the English Street Ballad.* Cambridge: Cambridge University Press, 1990.

Wycherley, William. *The country-wife a comedy acted at the Theatre Royal.* London: Printed for Thomas Dring, 1675.

Yeazell, Ruth Bernard. *Fictions of Modesty: Women and Courtship in the English Novel.* Chicago: Chicago University Press, 1991.

Young, Edward. *Conjectures on original composition. In a letter to the author of Sir Charles Grandison.* London, 1759.

Index

pleasure—*continued*
  see defloration
  see desire
  epistemological versus sexual,
    131–4, 148, 159
  and false consciousness, 160–3
  see Libertinism
  moderate, 30–1, 49
  narrative, 98, 159–65, 167–71
  and novelty, 152–6, 167–9
  obstacles to, 150, 152, 161
  and pain, 14, 149–52, 155–7
  sacrificed, 24–7, 32, 52, 54
  in satire, 163–5
  spiritual versus sexual, 28–30, 43–4
  see timing
Pocock, J.G.A., 139
politics
  and female sexuality, 1, 4,
    7–8, 11, 30, 33–4, 61, 65,
    68, 107
  Liberalism, 6–8, 11, 42, 56, 178
  see monarchy
  parliament and monarchy, 5, 6, 11
  philosophy, 6–7
  and property, 1, 5–8
  and religion, 5, 6
Pollack, Ellen, 124–5
Pope, Alexander, 44, 111–29
  as Catholic, 115
  critique of consumerism, 124
  critique of symbolic practices,
    111–16, 121, 126–7
  An Essay on Man, 128
  fetishization, 111, 117–18,
    123–4, 126
  formal devices, 117–18, 124–5, 128
  iconoclasm, 116, 121, 124–27
  idolatry and words, 119–20
  A Key to the Lock, 127
  and the mock-epic, 111, 121, 127
  The Rape of the Lock, 13–14,
    111–12, 115–21; 123–9
  Reading *The Rape of the Lock*,
    127–8
  subjectivity versus objectivity, 123

Popular culture, 13, 85, 93, 96,
  97, 112
Porter, Roy, 184 n. 4, 6
The Portuguese Letters, 17–18, 24,
  28–30, 32, 44
  reception of, 17, 28
pornography
  anti-Catholic, 12, 18, 23–4,
    30–2, 34, 44
  Barrin, Jean, *Venus in the Cloister*,
    24, 30–2
  see also Cleland, John, *Memoirs
    of a Woman of Pleasure;
    The Case of Catherine
    Vizzani*
  conventions of, 2, 18, 24,
    30–2, 68, 73, 150, 152,
    162–3, 169
  and gender, 154
  history, 5, 34, 162
  obsession with defloration, 2, 83,
    148–9
  and performance, 163–4
  see also novel, pornographic
  and repetition, 98, 148–57,
    164–5
  and prostitution, 27, 147,
    149–50, 162
  and satire, 14, 157, 160–5
  see sexuality
  tensions within, 159
  visual versus literary, 163
posterity, *see* inheritance; timing
Pratt, Daniel, 27–8
  *The Life of the Blessed St. Agnes,
    Virgin and Martyr*, 27–8, 32
Prendergrast, John S., 128
property
  see inheritance
  of monasteries in England, 33
  private, 1–13, 42, 93, 169,
    171–7
Prostitution, *see* pornography
Protestantism
  anti-Catholic propaganda, 12–13,
    18, 22–3, 32–9, 111–16

Printed and bound by CPI Group (UK) Ltd, Croydon, CR0 4YY